AUTUMN

A LOVE STORY

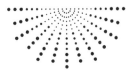

NORIAN LOVE

ISBN-13: 978-1-7366707-1-2

ISBN-10: 1-7366707-1-9

Cover art by Nieko Keener

IG: @_nieko

www.norianlove.com

To love — in all its wonderful forms.
Norian

FOREWORD

~

Before we begin the book, I want to make sure you have Autumn: A
Love Story, The Soundtrack. My gift to you for taking your time to
read this novel. While every song was written by me, many talented
people worked hard on this, and I don't want to leave out their efforts
and talent; I was fortunate to be able to work with everyone who
contributed. Please give it a listen for their sake. The soundtrack is
free and only meant to enhance the experience of reading the book.

Again, I thank everyone for their collective efforts in helping to
produce what I believe to be quality love songs. The soundtrack is
available on all streaming services. There is also a Spotify playlist to
accompany the novel. For those of you interested in books with
Easter eggs, you're in for a treat. I'll leave you to find the correlation.
You can go to my website (www.norianlove.com) to find out more
about both.

There are so many people I need to thank for helping this one come
to life. And while I can't thank them all, I hope they know how much
their love, patience, and support have meant to me. At the top of the

list is my family always for their undying love and support. The visionary artist for the cover, my editor for his time, the greatest assistant in the world for keeping a foot on my neck (and making an unspecified amount of death threats) until this was in your hands. My confidants, for keeping me focused and allowing me to flesh out much of what you will read. The beautiful people, places, and things I drew inspiration from and everyone who worked on the soundtrack, again, thank you.

To the reader: This book, in some cases, is one long love letter; in others, it's a journey through an open wound. Try not to judge too harshly. I can't remember any pleasant feelings about the process of birthing this book, but there were pleasant feelings, even beautiful ones, moments higher than any I've ever felt. There were times I wanted to abandon it. There were times I wanted to change it. There were times I did change it. And it's my hope that it's been for the better. Like birth itself though, throughout all the pain, in my opinion, came something uniquely beautiful.

I hope this story settles in your heart. If you are reading this, know there are no goodbyes, just transitions. Live every day as if it were Autumn.

-Norian

PREFACE

~

To truly understand love you must first understand the weather.

Once you realize it's impossible to predict or control, only then will you understand love.

-Norian

CAN YOU STAND THE RAIN?

"*There* are some moments in life that when they happen, you know you'll never be the same. You meet someone special, or something happens, and you know in an instant that this one moment is different." Tatum "Reverend" Clarke said, his deep dark brown hue - shimmered against the sun beaming through the sunroof of his best friend's GS350 Lexus. Bristles from his jet-black hair fell against his black t-shirt as the wind blew slightly in from the open roof. "I've only had a handful of those moments—the day I met you being one of them. But this trumps them all. It was probably the most special moment of my life. I knew my life would never be the same; I would never be the same."

"So that's what it's like, huh?"

"Yeah, Stone, that's what being a father is like," Tatum responded to his best friend, Kenley Stoneridge.

"Rev, you are such a sentimental bitch," Stone said, laughing.

"Eat a dick, Stone. Why are you such a full-time hater?"

"Dog, you've been a father all of three weeks, and now you're talking some circle-of-life, Mufasa-is-my-son-kinda shit?"

"It's been a month, and technically, Mufasa is the dad. You meant to say Simba."

"I meant to say these nuts. Technically, of course."

"And I meant to say eat two dicks. I'm just saying if you're going to use an analogy, use the right one."

"Man, I ain't trying to hear all that, Rev. You just probably got some pussy from Monique, so you're out here being Ghetto Confucius. You know how you be."

Stone said as he closed the sunroof to spare his sandy-tanned skin any more punishment from the sun. His jet-black Trinidadian hair rested shoulder-length against his white t-shirt and began to ruffle as the sunroof closed.

Tatum shook his head and looked at his friend. "First of all, she can't do nothing yet—she just had the baby, bro, and second, why can't I just love my so-"

"So wait—hold the fuck up," Stone said in agitation and excitement before taking a puff of the blunt he rolled up and handed to Tatum.

"So let me get this straight...y'all can't smash yet?"

Tatum put his hands over his face for a second. He instantly regretted this conversation, which wasn't going to end anytime soon if he knew his friend.

"Answer me, motherfucker—are you on a cheek diet or not?"

"She's my wife, not one of your expendables, Stone."

"This dude right here! I swear you be letting them off the hook, Rev."

"What you talking about?" Tatum asked defensively.

"She's your wife, right?"

"Yeah, so?"

"All the more reason you should be getting POD."

"And what the hell is POD?"

"Pussy on demand. You put a ring on that trim, and she gotta put out, period. That shit's in the vowels somewhere, on some postal service oath shit. You know—sunshine, rain, sleet, snow, a wife's gotta ho." Tatum laughed at his friend's logic and fought the urge to let his friend know he meant *vows* instead of vowels as he handed him back the blunt.

"What in the fuck is wrong with you?" Tatum responded, shaking his head.

"All I'm sayin' is you gave up the right to go satisfy your needs at any other restaurant, so the kitchen at home needs to be open."

"So now we're comparing pussy to restaurants?"

"It's a goddamn buffet if you're eating it right," Stone said, laughing as he stuck his tongue out to mimic going down on a woman."

Tatum turned his nose up in disgust. He waited until his friend was done clowning around to respond.

"She also just did the single most difficult thing in human history. Can she get some recovery time?"

"Alright, alright...I'm just fuckin' around, Rev. It's some beautiful shit," Stone said as they got on the highway. There was an awkward silence for a moment. Love him or hate him, Kenley Stoneridge was never one to mince words.

"I'm just saying no throat action? A handy? Nothing?"

"I'm not doing this with you."

"Come on, Reverend!"

"You do realize this whole conversation started with you asking what's it like to be a father?"

"Yeah, but then you went all dark-skinned Drake on me, and this is way more interesting."

Tatum rolled his eyes. "Well, let's change the subject."

"We absolutely will the fuck not," Stone rebutted. Tatum took a breath. He knew his friend was not the type to leave this issue alone.

"So, Tatum Clarke, the Black Male Delegation would like to know exactly how long you without...shall we say...moisture in your life?"

"See, this right here is why we call you Stone—'cause you dumb as a fucking rock!"

"I'm dumb? Motherfucker, you're the one working two jobs and going to night school all so you can hurry home and beat your meat!"

"Motherf—" Tatum said as he playfully lunged at Stone while driving.

"You better quit playing with me, Reverend. I'll drive this bitch off the highway, and we'll both have a life-defining moment!"

"You're such an asshole," Tatum said jokingly, to which his friend Stone nodded.

"Now that's a good point. So...no backdoor action?"

"Hoe, I'm not talking about this with you no more. Just drop me off, please. Anywhere."

The two friends continued their kidding the last few miles to Tatum's home. While it was all in jest, the conversation hit a sore spot. He was horny as hell, and Monique was in no way, shape, or form eligible to satisfy the urges he'd been repressing. He was trying to hurry home to beat his meat before he had to take off for class, and talking about sex at this point was as agitating as not having it. He desperately wanted to move past the subject and was thankful his friend took the hint and moved on.

"Hey, what time is your class?"

"You already know the answer to that."

"I know, I know, but I need to make a stop real quick."

"Damn it, Stone."

"Rev, I swear it ain't gonna take long."

Tatum rolled his eyes. *It ain't gonna take too long* was Stone's way of saying it's probably gonna take a while. But "I *swear* it ain't gonna take long" meant he had no idea how long it was going to take, nor did he have any intent on being done anytime soon. Fortunately for Tatum, he had some time before class and didn't have to pick up their baby boy, Solomon, today since Monique used the car to take him to the pediatrician for his one-month checkup. But it did mean he wouldn't have time to take care of his urges before class. Recognizing this, he accepted he was all but at the mercy of his best friend.

"Whatever, man, just get me back to the house."

"I got you. Don't worry."

The two exited 610 East heading toward the neighborhood where they both grew up: Sunny Side, an older subdivision in Houston, a ghetto abandoned by the city long ago. An abandonment they knew all too well, although Tatum now lived on the Third Ward's outskirts, or what was now being called Medical Center East post-gentrification. He always loved going to his old neighborhood because he considered it his home, but as much as he wanted to hang out, he didn't have time to shoot the shit today. But the farther they drove into the neighborhood, the more he realized this was more than a casual visit. In the back of his mind, he always knew getting a ride from Stone meant this would be no quick trip. As they continued on Scott Street, they moved into an area being developed. *Fuck,* Tatum thought to himself as they turned into a subdivision under construction and likely expensive. Several houses were more than halfway done, and several more had already been framed. His agitation and apprehension increased as they drove to one of the houses in the very back where a contractor was working with his crew. Tatum cut his eyes at Stone, who purposefully made no eye contact. He now knew why Stone was so eager to pick him up from work.

"Man, Tate, it's not gonna take long."

"Fuck you. Let's get this shit over with."

When they pulled up to the unfinished house, Kenley reversed the car and backed into the driveway. Tatum actively scanned the area. There was no movement to note—just construction workers carrying equipment in and out of the soon-to-be home. As Kenley backed into an unfinished garage, he parked the car, and the two men exited the vehicle. Tatum gritted his teeth as he continued to take inventory of his surroundings. Other than this construction crew, everything was very quiet, and that made him uneasy. As he narrowed his focus on the men working on the home, he recognized who they came to meet. Two Hispanic men waved them into the center of the open home. One—who appeared to be the head contractor—he'd never met before. He was a thin, clean-shaven man, which made him look relatively young, although Tatum guessed he was probably in his mid-forties due to his graying sideburns. He wore brown cowboy boots and a white and blue-striped button-up shirt tucked into his blue jeans. His belt matched his boots precisely, connected by a large gold buckle with the state of Texas on the emblem. The other was a slender man with a buzz cut in an oversized gray t-shirt, blue jeans, and black and white Nike Cortez tennis shoes with a pencil in his ear. This man he knew all too well.

"Oh shit, Tatum. What's up, man?" the gentleman said.

"Stavo," Tatum half-replied to Gustavo Gonzales, his former high-school classmate.

As the other gentleman walked up and shook Kenley's hand, he said, "¿Que pasa, Stone?"

"Ernesto, what's cracking?" Stone replied, shaking the man's hand. Tatum could smell the Joop cologne radiating from the gentleman the closer he got. It all but confirmed the man was definitely in his late forties or early fifties at that point. The only other person he knew to wear that scent was his father. As the pair shook hands, an older, black Silverado with a dent on the right side of the front grill underneath the headlight pulled up to the home. The truck also reversed into the driveway. As it shut off, a six-foot-one, muscular, bald, dark-skinned man emerged from the driver's side wearing blue overalls, a fitted black muscle shirt, and construction boots. This eased Tatum's growing apprehension since he knew this man almost as well as he knew Stone.

"Damn, I didn't expect to see you. What's good, Reverend?" the man said, also in on Tatum's high-school nickname. Tatum walked closer to greet Parish Tisdale, a childhood friend. Tatum could tell he was extremely surprised to see him here.

"P, what's good with ya, bruh?" Tatum responded as the two men embraced each other. While he had no issue with Parish, Tatum had little to no respect for Gustavo. Gustavo was a sleazy, low-life wannabe ever since they met in the fourth grade, as far as he was concerned. Parish agreed because he didn't acknowledge Gustavo's presence at all as he walked past his extended hand. Tatum scoffed, recognizing their mutual disdain for him.

As Stone talked to Ernesto. Parish, still startled by Tatum's presence, turned to him and whispered, "Hey, bro, I didn't know y—"

"Fucking Stone, man." Tatum cut off his friend, his tone saturated with disgust. Tatum realized Parish sensed this hostility and said nothing further as they watched Stone wrap up business with the gentleman. Once done, Stone turned and walked back to the two of them.

"Hey, can we load the truck up with the sheetrock and the bags in the other room there? We also need to get the cement bags—about six apiece. Yo, Rev, my friend over there has a bad cold. You think he can come by the job and pick up some medication, say, for a month?"

"I can't do a month."

"Okay...what about three weeks?"

"Yeah, that should be fine," he murmured reluctantly.

"Cool. He'll come by tomorrow night."

"A'ight," Tatum said. He was upset but knew now wasn't the time to show it. Still, he was losing the battle to break ranks.

"Cool. You want to help P load up the truck with the cement bags?"

"I'm good," Tatum responded. His cold gaze indicated he was not interested in his friend's request.

Sensing the awkwardness of the response, Ernesto interjected, "It's no worries, my friends. I'll have my men load the truck." He turned to his men and commanded, "¡Hombres, vamonos!"

Two of the workers stopped what they were doing to load the truck. Tatum could tell that Stone was slightly embarrassed by the entire exchange. He directed his next comment to Parish with more authority, trying to assert himself.

"Alright...cool. Parish, make sure everything is correct and be on that shit. Tate, you think you can grab those two bags of tools out the trunk and give them to Gustavo?"

This time he didn't buck. He just nodded and headed to the back of the car. *Motherfucker,* he thought to himself but said nothing as he walked past Gustavo, who followed him to the back of the sedan. As he stood at the back of the car waiting for Kenley to pop the trunk, he scanned the neighborhood again. It was quiet and empty. He turned back toward the trunk of the Silver Lexus, pulled out two duffel bags, and rested them on the edge of the open trunk. He unzipped them and waved Gustavo over.

"Come help me with these tools," he said halfheartedly. He loved Stone, but doing a drug deal in broad daylight was where he drew the line. He knew the moment they pulled into this neighborhood what was happening. The cement bags contained uncut cocaine, and the duffel bags contained what Tatum ascertain from the weight to be about thirty-five thousand dollars each. It was the perfect place to do business—a lot of equipment, reasons for large amounts of cash, and if properly packaged, white powder that looked like another white power ready to be transported. Even this part of the city was optimal because there wasn't a ton of foot traffic or any kind of activity, for that matter, let alone police activity. Still, Tatum wanted no parts of this. Stone had been dealing drugs since high school, and while Tatum loved him, he didn't like him risking his life. Parish worked for him since the early days and had become somewhat of an enforcer. Tatum was there to secure prescription drugs from his employer, Simmons Pharmaceuticals, something he did once in a while when he saw an opportunity. He told Stone he'd no longer do it since Solomon was born, which was why he was so upset now. He couldn't leave him hanging in this situation. He wanted to rip his head off.

"So, you're...um...rollin' now, eh?" Gustavo asked, rubbing his hands across his dark black buzz.

"No, I'm not. "

"Oh, I see. Just helping a friend?"

"Something like that," Tatum said as dry as possible.

"Yeah, man, me too. Ernesto is a friend. I guess you gotta pay those student loans, right?"

Tatum ignored him and examined the neighborhood one more time.

"For a second there, I thought you were picking up where your old man I—"

"I'm not."

"Oh, okay. Hey man, how's college? You graduate yet?"

"I did."

"But I thought I heard you were still in schoo—"

"The fuck, Stavo? Is this Twenty Questions? Or are we gonna do what we came to do?"

"Chill out, ése. I just want to catch up with an old friend."

"Well, let's finish what we came to do so you can go catch up with one," Tatum responded—a response that made the men within earshot laugh at Gustavo's expense.

"¿Está el dinero ahí?" Ernesto asked Gustavo. A reprieve Tatum welcomed as his prayers being answered.

"Si, jefe, it's all here," Gustavo said as he took the bags and cut his eyes back at Tatum, who was already closing the trunk and looking in the other direction. As Tatum was about to get in the car, he heard Gustavo's voice. "Say hi to Monique for me, man."

Tatum smirked. It was clear he was trying to provoke him since they were not friends and never would be. He wasn't going to let it slide.

"Stavo, you're too ugly to be trying to be cute right now."

"What did you say to me, homes?"

Tatum looked at him, unmoved by his theatrics.

"I said you're an ugly motherfucker...in the face."

As Gustavo put down the bags, Ernesto interrupted. "Stavo, put the goddamn tools inside the house...now!"

Gustavo froze in his tracks. He was beyond upset, but there was nothing he could do. The wannabe thug picked up the bags and walked inside the house. Tatum turned his cold gaze to his Kenley who, looked over at Parish and nodded as he inspected his truck's cargo and opened the door to get in the driver's seat.

"Thanks, Ernesto. Tate, let's roll." Stone was near the driver's door about to get in the car. Tatum followed suit, agitated by the entire ordeal. He got in the car as Gustavo glared at him through the window. He partly felt remorse that this situation only escalated because he was upset with his best friend. Now, he could redirect this frustration to the appropriate party. Stone knew his friend well enough and long enough to know that he was upset, but he was going to remain silent until they were out of here. One fight that might draw attention was bad enough. Two was uncalled for.

That didn't mean he wouldn't say something the moment they were back on the main road.

"Dog, I was gonna tell yo—"

"What the fuck, Stone? You got me out here in the middle of your bullshit?

"Reverend, chill."

"Man, it's one thing for you to be out here in the streets. Fine, take your penitentiary chance. It's another to involve me in this. I got a son I gotta look after. I knew it was some fuck shit the moment I saw P driving your truck."

"Tate, yo—"

"Just take me to the house, bruh. I ain't being an accessory to shit!" Tatum scoffed as Stone lit a marijuana cigar he'd been holding onto for the highway, inhaled the joint, and held his lungs for a dramatic pause. Finally, he exhaled as the smoke flew out of the car via the window.

"It's funny. The son of the legendary J.C. Money is talking about the game is bullshit."

"Fuck you, J.C. Money, and the game," Tatum responded adamantly. Stone took another hit off the blunt and passed it to Tatum, who took it and inhaled.

"You know Johnny Clarke was one of the biggest dope dealers on the south side of H-town. The man that taught me everything I know, the only reason I got this connect is because of J.C."

"What's your point?"

"My point is, put some respect on his name. And if you can't do that, then put some respect on the game, 'cause like it or not, it's in your DNA," Stone said as Tatum handed him the blunt. Tatum exhaled the smoke and responded to Stone.

"I don't hustle, Stone. You know that, and as far as Johnny goes, how did that shit work out for him?"

"Oh, but you do hustle, my brother, you do indeed. Unless you graduated pharmacy school in the last two hours, and I missed the invite."

"Bruh, I—"

"I tell you what, Reverend—you don't have to worry about the prescription drugs, but Stavo was right. Them student loans a motherfucker."

"You know that shit's different, Stone. You're moving weight that's just—"

"Motherfucker, they're both crimes! You think just because your junkies go to U of H and mine lay up in a row house for days; they're both not getting high? You think we get caught moving a pound of Promethazine they're just letting us go? They're throwing our black asses in jail and throwing away the key, fam. You're getting paid off of these scripts the same way I'm getting paid in the trap. Only difference is I wear Jordans, and you wear a lab coat."

Tatum knew he had a point but didn't want to concede just yet.

"Technically, I didn't *steal* anything. I just know the loopholes in our system, so it's all good."

"You're something else, Rev. Yeah, maybe I got it wrong. I wonder what would happen if you tell the judge that shit. I'm sure the case will be dismissed under the I-know-the-loopholes-so-it's-all-good clause. Yeah, that shit happen to black folk all the time."

"That's not the point."

"Reverend, that's the only point! This is me you're talking to. You can play dumb if you want to, but the bottom line is this: I'm a dealer, and you're a supplier. Just different parts of the same game."

The statement was doused in reality, one Tatum had not really accepted. He was indeed in the same game. Albeit he didn't make it a regular occurrence, there was no question that if he saw an opportunity, he took it. In that respect, this particular opportunity was no different. It fit the bill. Simmons Pharmaceuticals was one of the largest companies in the world and certainly in the city. Housing nearly fourteen thousand employees in three buildings downtown, the company was steeped in employee inefficiency. They kept terrible accounting and receiving records. He often used this to his advantage and spent a great deal of time in the office early. The firm had several locations worldwide and never seemed to pay attention to details when shipments of anything went missing. Eventually, he learned to take advantage of the system. When he moved into Dr. Peterson's department, he was able to take advantage of one part of the system: Percocet, something he knew Stone could move with ease. The money was quick, the risk was low, and his student loans were piling up. But after Solomon was born, he knew it was time to put this in the past. Stone reflected a light in the mirror, and on the other side was a hypocrite.

"Alright, Kenley, you got a point...but I'm done with that. I told Monique the other day the last time was the last time."

His friend took another puff of the cigar and exhaled quickly.

"Look, Reverend, I respect the fuck out of what you're trying to do. Be the next Uncle Phil, good husband and dad, that's some beautiful shit. I rides with Team Tatum all day, but don't act like you weren't covering your student loans, taking Monique to Spindle Top, and paying medical bills and all that other shit off. Just don't knock the next man's hustle on your climb up."

"My bad. It wasn't my intent."

"Yeah, but you sure did hop on your high horse and ride that motherfucker."

The pair chuckled as Tatum nodded in agreement. Stone always had a way to bring him down to earth, and he appreciated that. *Keep it 100* was his mantra. He lived by it, which is why he said it so often in situations like these. As the natural laughter died, Stone continued.

"Hey, speaking of climbing off your *high* horse...I saw your pops today."

"I don't want to hear shit about Johnny Clarke," Tatum said sharply, cutting off the conversation. Stone paused only briefly. The statement soured the truce the pair had just formed. Tatum again wanted no parts of the conversations, and again Stone persisted.

"Tatum, he's trying. Now you know I don't sell to him, but I can't keep him from scoring. So he's been going over there off of Reed Road to get his product. You know, in them row houses back there. Well, Big Booty Kim works at that Valero station on the corner, and every time I go in there, I hear, 'How's Tatum? Tell him I just seen his daddy,'" Stone said in a nasal voice, imitating Big Booty Kim perfectly. Tatum smirked at the gesture as his friend carried on. "Well, lately, she been saying, 'How's Tatum? You know, I don't see his daddy as much as I use to.' That's gotta count for something."

"Oh good, so he's a diet cokehead now."

"You back on that high horse, Reverend. I don't know how you got like this, bruh, but everything ain't black and white. The world is a whole lotta gray." Stone handed the marijuana cigar to Tatum and exhaled. "I've seen some terrible shit. Good people in bad spots. This shit takes souls, but it hasn't taken his."

Tatum took a puff of the cigar and coughed a bit. After a moment, he responded, "No, he sold that a long time ago."

"Your pop's seen some dark days, bro. I've seen him at rock bottom. He's not there. Far from it, in fact."

Tatum glanced at his friend, Stone's excitement peering through his words. Something he corrected as he saw Tatum's cold-slated gaze. Still, Stone was the kind of man to press a point until he felt he made one.

"He's...staying in rehab. He's not even moving with the same junk fiends. He's close to the man we knew growing u—"

"Kenley! Let this go," Tatum said as sternly yet as politely as possible to his best friend. Who nodded, acknowledging Tatum's seriousness. *This is the longest fucking drive,* Tatum, he thought. The only way to end this conversation with Kenley was to not be around him.

"One last thing, and I'll let this go, I promise. Solomon being born has made a difference to all the Clarke men."

Tatum said nothing. Instead, he took another hit of the blunt and handed it back to Stone before looking out the window. The conversation had run its course, and just in time. He was almost home. Stone wasn't going to talk about it anymore, even if pressed.

As they pulled up to the Savoy Apartments, Tatum felt a wave of relief. He loved his friend but had enough bonding time for today. He nervously started to tap his foot as they entered the apartment gate. He wasn't going to be able to spend a lot of time with Solomon, but he wanted to at least pick him up and play with him for a spell which trumped taking care of his aforementioned urges, that would have to wait until later. They parked in front of the first apartment on the right. As Tatum was about to get out of Stone's car, he looked for his own. It was nowhere to be found.

"Now she knows I have to get to class."

"Maybe she parked around back."

"I guess."

"Yo, Reverend, I appreciate you taking that ride with me. I know you ain't gonna take the money, but if your other hustle is dried up, maybe you can take a few dollars to supplement."

"Stone—"

"I know, I know."

"I'm good, bro. It's time for me to level up."

"Alright...well, at least take this."

Stone moved a blanket in the back seat. Sitting on the leather were four boxes of diapers and three large canisters of formula."

Tatum couldn't believe it. His friend had been hiding the gift in plain sight. That was Stone—always planning, even when it didn't look like it.

"I respect the fuck out of you, Tate, and I'm not gonna lie. I wish we were doing this thing over here together 'cause we've always done everything together. I know getting married and having Solomon wasn't part of the plans, but we're here now, and you've been a stand-up dude from day one. That mailroom job ain't gonna cut it, bro, but until then, I got your back."

"I know. That's why I gotta clean up. I'm gonna do this pharmacy thing and make some real cash. This job shit is just part of me paying dues. It's no mistake I got in Dr. Peterson's department for a reason. I'm gonna work my ass off so they can't deny me. I'm—"

Tatum paused midsentence and adjusted the rearview mirror toward the road. A blue diaper bag with Bob the Builder on the front was sitting near the parking space where Tatum parked the car last. "Is that Solomon's—"

"Tatum?" Stone asked, but it was too late. Tatum jumped out of the car and jogged over to the bag on the asphalt. He lifted it and looked around, racing to the house as Stone caught up to him.

"Say, fool, don't just take off and—"

"This is Solomon's diaper bag. It was just sitting in the driveway."

The two men ran over to the front of the building and stopped at the apartment door. It was partially open.

"Hold on," Stone said, reaching behind the small of his back to retrieve a .9-millimeter Glock pistol. Tatum nodded as Stone moved to the front of the door with the pistol in hand. Tatum stood behind him and moved quickly to the kitchen to grab his machete. He scanned the room. The two cleared every corner of the two-bedroom apartment. Tatum was sweltering—it felt every bit of ninety degrees, which concerned him even more. Why would Monique cut off the A/C?

"Mo, are you here?" he shouted as he turned on the A/C, verifying the temperature as Stone moved to the hallway. Tatum followed with the cutlass in his hand and pointed at the door to the master bedroom. It was closed.

"We going in," Stone said as he positioned himself on one side of the door, Tatum on the other. Stone threw open the door. As they entered the room, Tatum stopped in his tracks and dropped the machete.

"Oh God!" he yelled as he dropped to his knees, scrambling toward a car seat with Solomon still strapped in. He was covered in feces, formula, and urine from a soaked diaper that hadn't been changed in what had to be hours. He'd stopped paying attention to see if anyone else was in the room.

"I gotta get him out of this thing. Solly? Solly, are you okay?" he said nervously. He tried to check for a pulse, but his hands were shaking with panic too badly. He decided to jostle him to wake up. The child was unresponsive.

"Solomon!" he yelled as he removed the car-seat buckle. It was warm to the touch, the child thoroughly soaked between his own fluids and sweat.

Tatum picked him up and rushed to the restroom as Stone secured the rest of the bedroom; but Tate was unaware of his efforts, stripping his son and turning on the faucet to wipe his son's saturated body.

"Is he okay?"

"I don't know."

"Do you want me to call 911?"

"I don't know!" Tatum yelled. He didn't have a clue what to do. Right now, he just needed to make sure his son was okay. As he poured room-temperature water on his son, he heard the most beautiful sound—his son's loud cry.

"Okay, it's okay, Solly."

"Stone, get me a water bottle out the fridge."

"Bet."

Tatum continued to wash his son and clean him. There were no bruises or wounds of any kind, but he sensed he was thirsty.

"Stone!"

"I'm coming!"

Tatum pulled Solomon from underneath the water, drying him with a hand towel from the bar near the sink.

"It's okay, big boy, daddy's got you."

Relief flowed over him once he sensed his son would survive. He knew 911 wouldn't be necessary for his son, but there may still need to be a call for his wife. There was an avalanche of thoughts in his mind, for starters, where in the hell was Monique? Was she OK? Why would she leave the baby alone? Did something happen to her? He needed answers, but for this moment, the only thing that mattered was how his son responded to the water. Stone came in with four bottles, only one of which was water.

"I just brought everything I could carry," his friend said as Tatum took the blue bottle marked *water* out of his hands. He placed it in the crying Solomon's mouth, his boy settling down once he received the bottle. He usually would fuss before taking it, but there was no resistance this time. He consumed the water as if dehydrated.

What in the hell is going on? Tatum wondered. He worried about Monique, tragic scenarios seizing his mind for a few seconds—at least until he heard a very large burp.

"Good job, big man! You finished the whole thing!" Tatum said, receiving a smile from his son with some awkward arm movements. The panic for his son's welfare receded, allowing it to return to his wife.

"I'll get you another water."

"Yeah, good."

Stone jogged off to get another water bottle while Tatum took his son to the changing area to dress him. The stifling air in the apartment was cooling down by the time Stone came back with the water bottle. Once again, Solomon put up no resistance in drinking the water.

As he lotioned the baby, he pictured Mo dead in a ditch or gasping for air in a hospital room somewhere. He turned to the closet to grab a onesie for Solomon only to realize that most of Monique's clothes were missing. The hair on the back of his neck stood up.

What in the fuck is going on?!

"Yo, Rev, you need to see this." Stone said as he handed him a note resting underneath the car seat on the floor. Tatum steadied the baby and took the note from Stone's hand, Monique's unmistakable handwriting scrawled across the page.

I'm sorry.
I can't do this anymore.
Good luck to the both of you.
Monique

HIS KNEES BUCKLED.

"This can't be real," he said aloud.

"Rev…."

"Maybe someone snatched her and didn't know she had the baby back here."

"Rev, she left a note. It said both of you. She knows what she's doing."

"I need to call her."

He picked up the phone to call Monique, his mind bursting with theories about why she would write this letter. He hadn't given up on the idea that maybe she was forced to. His mind even flirted with the idea for a brief second that that bastard Gustavo was behind this. He'd kill him if he was, but he knew Stavo was too big a loser to pull this off, no matter what kind of revenge he wanted. Monique would have kicked his ass.

Tatum turned his thoughts inward, blaming himself. He knew it had been a struggle since getting back together. When he found out about her pregnancy, they were already living apart, but once Solomon was born, they tried to make it work. They hadn't been fighting as of late. He felt the baby brought them together.

Damn it, Mo, Pick up!

The call went to voicemail, amplifying his apprehensions. He called again and again, but it always went straight to voicemail.

"You might be blocked," Stone said.

"There's no wa—"

"What's her number?" Stone said, pulling out his phone.

Tatum showed Stone the contact information and watched as he dialed the number, hit send, and put the call on speaker. On the second ring, a woman's voice picked up.

"Hello."

"Monique, please tell me you're playing some kind of warped ass joke you've taken too far!" Tatum yelled as he realized he was indeed blocked.

"Tatum, I don't want to do this anymore."

"Do what exactly? This marriage? Be a mother? Show goddamn compassion and leave the AC on for our child you left in this hot ass apartment?"

"This! I don't want to do this anymore with you."

"And you think I want to be doing this right now with you? Having this conversation? Unbelievable. I'm working two jobs, busting my ass to provide for you, and getting married? That was your idea, and I did it; now you owe me an explanation. Why are you doing this?" Nothing. Just silence. He couldn't even hear her breathing. "Monique! Talk to me!"

"It's too much. You, the baby...Look, just tell Solomon I love him. Don't call me back."

Click. The phone disconnected. He had all the confirmation he needed. She was leaving them—the experiment was over. He looked at Kenley, who did his best to avoid making eye contact. The situation was as awkward as it came. The silence was lingering to the point they just had to address the issue. Stone, never being one to bite his tongue, took his most gentle approach.

"I know you're not good, Rev. Man... I'm sorry."

Not good was an understatement. He was devastated. He left this morning with a plan for the future and came home to a brand-new reality.

"Man, fuck that shit. I gotta study. One monkey don't stop no show, right?"

It was his attempt at bravado. It was all he could muster, but it wasn't working. He was hurt. He was hoping his friend would take the message he wanted to be alone. For the first time, Stone obliged. No offers to get drunk, get stoned, or get laid. There was no blowing this off. No forgetting it for a night. Not with a baby boy sitting there as a permanent reminder.

"Cool, bro. I'm gonna head out then. You're gonna be alright, Reverend?"

"All day," Tatum replied half-heartedly. He was still in disbelief and wanted to be alone.

"I'm gonna hit you up later, Stone. I need to study. Get this shit situated. You know."

"Yeah, I feel you," Stone said, his eyes saying it all. He felt sorry for his friend. And as he reached the front door, he turned around. "If you need me—for anything—I'll be around."

"Bet."

The moment Stone closed the door, Tatum wanted to yell. He wanted to unleash his anger in the most visceral, damaging way possible. Punch a hole in the wall. Destroy anything that used to belong to Monique. Anything that even reminded him of her. Set it on fire and forget it forever. But that was no example for Solomon.

He walked to the master bedroom and pulled his journal out of the top drawer of his nightstand. He opened the bronze book with the magnetic flap and started to write feverishly. Each word made the pressure subside ever so slightly in his chest. He was halfway through the page when Solomon whimpered. It was his feeding time. He closed the book and walked back into the other side of the bedroom where Solomon, lying on the changing table throughout the ordeal, started to get cranky. His plans to go to class had changed. His life had changed. He needed to figure out how to operate for the foreseeable future without Monique. He grabbed one of the bottles of formula Stone brought when they first arrived and fed it to his son, who again put up no resistance.

"It's okay, Solly; I got you, son."

His pain further dissipating when he looked into his son's eyes. Those deep eyes soothed his soul more than his writing ever could. He was a father, which had nothing to do with having a mother in his son's life. He was determined to be the best father he knew how to be, no matter who was in their lives.

"It's okay. Everything is gonna be okay, Solly. We'll be fine; I promise you that."

He carried Solomon into the living room, bouncing him in his arms as he walked, burping him before rocking him to sleep. He continued walking with Solomon from room to room, afraid to put him down for fear he'd wake the baby, clinging to him as much as his son clung to his father. Once back in the bedroom, his eyes were drawn to the journal. He nestled his infant boy on the bed and picked up the book, which was nearing the end of its life. With determination, he flipped to the last page and wrote:

I brought you into this world, so I'm going to bring you through this world. I promise.

2

ANOTHER AGAIN

"As you know," Dr. Peterson, an elderly, medium brown-skinned gentleman began, "the winner of the Wilcox Award is chosen through a variety of criteria: dedication, discipline, outstanding service to class and community, not to mention academic excellence. We also consider the improvement a student makes throughout pharmacy school. All resident professors have a vote, but the final decision is at the discretion of the dean. Well, let me say, the dean has had to make no such decision. This is the first year in this school's history that we have had a unanimous vote for one student, and the dean wholeheartedly agrees with their choice. Your personal growth has been phenomenal, even off the charts. I can't say I've ever met a student who matured right before my eyes as swiftly as you have. For that, you deserve this award more than anyone else. So, congratulations Tatum Clarke. You're the recipient of this year's Wilcox Award. We'll announce it sometime before graduation, but I'm too old to be sneaking around working on surprises, so I'm telling you now. You earned it; you should know about it. Plain and simple. Congratulations."

Tatum shook Dr. Peterson's outstretched hand. He couldn't believe it was his last year of pharmacy school and that he'd won the award that would essentially launch his career.

"Thank you, Dr. Peterson. I can't tell you what this means to me."

"So, you're in the final stretch of university. How do you feel?"

"Well, today I feel great. This U of H has been a part of me so long I don't know what life looks like without that chunk of time being spoken for but it will give me more time to spend with my son. I know he's glad he's not up here as much these nights."

"I bet he is. Hell, the boy was up here so much he deserves partial credit. Probably qualifies as a pharmacy tech," Dr. Peterson joked before turning serious. "But I gotta be honest, Tatum. I didn't know if you were going to make it when you suddenly found yourself a single dad. I'll never forget the first day you showed up with him in class. It looked like you'd had the worst possible day. You were disgruntled and distracted and didn't seem to know what to do with your newborn."

"Oh, I'll never forget that day either, trust me. I was just glad the class didn't turn on me. I didn't think I could take it."

"I think a couple of students wanted to say something after class, but they saw how much trouble you were having with getting him situated and didn't have the heart to say anything. I certainly didn't," the professor said as he adjusted his black metal glasses then smoothed his salt-and-pepper mustache.

"I think that's the first time you noticed me at all," Tatum responded, only half-joking.

"There's a good chance that's true," the professor responded. "I never gave you much thought before that. You were just another student. But when your professors started to speak highly of you, and I saw your grades, I finally connected the dots and realized you were the same kid who Solomon made us pay attention to."

"I was so embarrassed."

"You shouldn't be, son. I watched as you sat outside Dr. Mavis's classroom, taking notes in the shadows, trying to hide while keeping Solomon quiet. Yet, you aced every test. A lot of parents—hell, a lot of people, wouldn't have been able to do the same thing if they were in your shoes. Of course, it doesn't hurt that Solomon is just a heart-breakingly good kid with the biggest cartoon-character eyes. Just a joy to be around and to look at. Must get that from his mother, though," the professor joked.

"Ouch, Dr. P."

"I'm serious. He was your secret weapon. I'm sure it worked with the ladies. He was such an angel, and you were so focused and driven it's no wonder you're here receiving this award. You should be proud."

"I'm just glad I made it. You don't know what I had to go through, and you don't know what you're recommending me to Simmons Pharmaceuticals has done for me. I can't thank you enough."

"You did the work. We just were there to root you on. How old is your son now? Four?"

"Almost."

"Four years! Where does the time go?"

"Hopefully, I'll be able to tell you. You have no idea how much I'm looking forward to just being able to go to work and go home."

"Work-life balance, my friend. Where is Solly today?"

"Oh, you didn't hear? The work daycare extended their hours, which means my mom can pick him up after work. It gives me some breathing room for my final year of school."

"Well, at this rate, you have a mastery of the knowledge and a handful of classes left. Nothing should derail you. Just pace yourself. It's all going to be fine. With that being said, I'm sure you're not looking forward to spending your newfound time with me, so tell me, what are you going to do with your newly acquired luxury?"

"Now that's a good question. My life has been diapers and phar-maceutical studies for so long, I'm not even sure where to start, but I'm desperate to get some of that work-life balance you mentioned."

The doctor placed his hand on Tatum's shoulder and smiled.

"Always the fast learner. I'm going to miss seeing you in these halls. You don't know this, but a young black man walking up and down these halls getting an education while raising his son, well, that was inspiring for all of us to see."

Tatum smiled, and recognizing how close he and Dr. Peterson had become, decided to ask some of the questions that had long preoccupied him.

"Is that why you brought me into your department all those years ago?"

"It's precisely why, as I said, I didn't know you, but I asked Dr. Mavis about you, and he told me, and I quote: 'Tatum Clarke would be hell on wheels if he ever got his shit together.' Well, now, you had my attention, and the way you were operating on campus, it looked like you were trying to get said shit together. You never missed a day of school. Never missed a single class or turned in a single assignment late. And one day, I was getting on the elevator here in this building, and you were leaving your job in the mailroom here, getting ready to work your night job at UPS. Well, that was the kicker because that meant you were working just as many hours as me, only with a more grueling workload, and you didn't complain. Then, when you had Solomon, your workload doubled, but you still didn't complain and still didn't miss a day of school or a class. I mean, here you were working the same fourteen hours as me, only harder because I wasn't changing diapers. Well, that was when I knew I made the right decision about recommending you to our department. And nothing you've done since has ever made me regret that decision."

"Well, I can't thank you enough, Dr. Peterson. That changed my life."

"Young brother, it was my duty to help you along the path. It takes a village— never forget that. And besides, helping a guy like you was easy. You flat out earned it. We all looked good because of your drive. That's why I have something else for you."

The doctor rubbed this hands through his graying hair and smiled the kind of smile that insinuated he was plotting something.

"What's bigger than the Wilcox Award?"

"I told you I'm not good at surprises. I know you're going to be looking for gainful employment after school, but what if I told you that you didn't have to."

"I'm not following."

"All those brains, and you can't connect the dots?" The doctor smiled and walked over to his desk. Tatum was apprehensive as he remained silent so the doctor could finish his thoughts.

"There is a principal agreement for you, Tatum Clarke, to become a pharmacist at the largest pharmaceutical company in the state of Texas. I talked to the CEO this morning. Simmons Pharmaceuticals is offering you a job as soon as you graduate."

Tatum was overwhelmed. "Oh my God! Don't play with me, Doc."

"Son, I know how hard you work, and I know you'll work even harder as a pharmacist. Like I said, you make it easy to root for you."

"I can't thank you, Dr. Peterson. This is incredible."

"Incredible things happen to incredible people, and you, my friend, are just that."

Tatum smiled awkwardly. He respected Dr. Peterson and wanted him to know that his words meant the world to him. Still, it made him feel uncomfortable knowing he had stolen from the company, risking the reputation of the man who stuck his neck out for him so long ago. And although it had been years since he needed to run a con of any kind, there was no way he could come clean now. He decided it was best to change the subject.

"Dr. Peterson, on the midterms, do we—"

"No, I'm not gonna let you do that. Take the compliment, son. This is your victory lap. Take a bow. Smell the roses. They wilt sooner than you think." Tatum nodded his head nervously to agree with his mentor. He valued the doctor more than he could ever express—and all the man asked for in return was for Tatum to embrace the moment. He owed him that much.

"Thank you, Dr. Peterson. It means everything you think that highly of me. I mean it."

"Now that's how you do it!" the elder gentleman said, resting his hand on Tatum's shoulder again. "And yes, to answer the question you were going to ask--midterms happen during the first week of December because you know I don't like to grade papers during the holiday season. But, I've wasted enough of your time, get out of there and do something before you find some work around here to do!"

"Okay, okay, I'm leaving," Tatum said as he shuffled the papers into his book bag and shook his mentor's hand one more time.

"I'm headed out. Thank you again, Doc."

"Sounds good, son. Enjoy your time to yourself."

Tatum left Dr. Peterson's classroom thinking it felt good to know someone believed in him the way he was starting to believe in himself. Becoming a pharmacist would ensure he could provide a quality life for his son, which was all he wanted to do. He had long hoped Simmons would offer him a job, but he was never sure they would. Now he knew where his next step was and was convinced he'd land on solid ground. As he walked out of the building, he turned around and studied the campus. There were oak trees in every direction standing tall along the pathways and in between the buildings, the famous Towers dormitory rising above it all. Everything seemed as tall and strong as he did at that moment. His journey from this school was in its final stages. There was nothing left for him to accomplish here.

*Buzz...Buzz...*His Android cell phone rang, and his eyes widened. "Okay, before you get mad, I got held up at school and totally forgot."

"T.C., now you know I only have a few hours."

"I know, I know, I'm on the way."

"Come on now, T.C."

"I'll be there in thirty, Pops, I promise."

His personal time would have to wait. He had promised his father, Johnny Clarke, that he would come by and visit with Solomon, and there wasn't a lot of time before the rehab facility where he was living stopped accepting visitors. He sent a text to his mom, who wouldn't be happy he was picking up Solomon to see her troublesome ex-husband, so he decided not to mention it.

Hey mom, I'll pick up Solly. I have something I have to do I forgot about.

Tatum had thirty minutes to make it to the front door of the Santa Anna Rehabilitation Center. Walking to the blue parking lot took about ten minutes, and he was ten minutes away from his son, whose daycare was ten minutes away from the facility. He could shave some time off by getting out of campus before the next wave of students came in looking for parking spaces.

"Gotta book it," he said as he jogged quickly to his car. Thinking this would never do, he strapped his laptop bag on his back and sprinted toward the parking garage. This shortened his walk by a full four minutes but left him winded by the time he reached his car. He hit the button on his black Toyota Camry and opened up the trunk, tossing the bag in while still catching his breath. That's when he realized he was blocked in by a blue Nissan Maxima, its driver door open, leaving him no way to get out.

"You gotta be fucking kidding me."

He looked at his watch, knowing he was about to lose all the time he saved. "Shit!" he said to himself.

Tatum scanned the parking lot and discovered students were already looking for parking spaces, but he didn't see the Nissan's driver. There was no one around but a girl talking to someone fifty yards away from the car. He initially thought no one would leave their car door open and be this far away, yet there was no one else in sight, and he was out of time. He had to leave and now. He jogged over to the two people talking. One was a light brown-skinned woman wearing cream linen pants and a peach tank-top with a bag slung over one shoulder, its contents half-in and half-out. She was talking to a pale-skinned white man in a checkered red and black flannel shirt, a gray skully, and a gray T-shirt. No question, these were hipsters. Tatum directed his question towards the pair.

"Excuse me. I hate to bother you, but does that blue Nissan belong to either one of you?" he asked, lightly agitated that his time was dwindling.

"Oh, it's mine." the woman responded, going back to the conversation.

"Well, your door is open."

"Yeah, I know; I'm waiting on a parking spot." It was the most awkward and egocentric thing he had heard all day.

"Well...I'm in a rush, and I'm right behind you. You think you could move your car so I can get out? You get that parking space, and everyone is happy."

"That sounds great! I'll be over in just a minute."

He was taken aback. The nerve to not only park your car in a manner that blocks someone in and then leave your car so you couldn't move it was insulting enough but to then finish what you were doing when approached about it was a line too far. He saw her car keys dangling out of her purse and grabbed them, swiftly walking back to the car. He knew she only was half-paying attention and wondered if he could move the car before she even noticed her keys were gone. He was halfway to the car when she realized what he'd done. He heard in the background the hipster male say aloud.

"Hey, did he just take your keys?"

He continued towards the Blue Nissan. It wasn't long before he heard footsteps followed by the woman's voice screaming, "What are you doing?" He picked up the pace, climbed in her car, and turned it on. She was now in a full sprint behind him. He pulled the car out of his way and parked it, leaving the keys in the ignition. She reached the car just as he got out.

"What in the hell are you doing!" the woman screamed.

"Like I said, I have someplace to be soon, and since you don't own the fucking parking lot, I moved your car so I can pull out like I asked you to. Now, here's your goddamn parking space. Try not to be an asshole next time."

Tatum slammed her door and walked to his car. He pulled out without any incident, though she flipped him off as he drove away. Tatum returned the favor and sped off.

Fucking asshole. The nerve of her. He might have told her off a little more, but he didn't have time for that shit.

He was able to make up some ground at Solomon's daycare by picking him up in the drive-through line. As his son entered the car he, heard the innocent high squeal of his voice.

"Daddy!"

"Hey, Solly! How was your day today?"

"It was good. I thought Nana was going to get me today."

"Well, she was, but we have someplace special to be."

"More specialer than Nana's house?" Solomon asked. Tatum chuckled at the way his son was trying to say *more special*.

"Well, maybe not that special, but it's pretty special."

"Where are we going?"

"It's a surprise," Tatum said as he waited for his son to be buckled in. When the door closed, he looked at the time. He had twelve minutes to get ten minutes down the road. He headed toward the Santa Anna Rehabilitation Center, driving slightly above the speed limit in the hopes of shaving another minute off his time. His efforts were dashed when it felt like he was running into every traffic light he came across. "Damn it."

"Dad! Language!"

"Sorry, Solly."

He replied to his son. His frustrations were getting the better of him. He was cutting it close on time, and he was apprehensive because of it. His father had been trying hard over the last few years to correct his life and all but kicked his crack cocaine habit, something Tatum never thought possible. Still, he was deliberate about making sure people who couldn't be fixtures wouldn't be present in his son's life. Johnny was no exception—at least until he proved he could be consistent. Even then, Tatum would move with caution.

Yet, he was excited to see his dad pull it together. He recalled Stone telling him a few years earlier that his dad was getting it together, and he was right, although he'd never admit it to him. The man he was about to visit was different than the man he'd come to label as his dad. This man was more like the father he remembered before the drugs.

"Dad, are we there yet? What's the surprise?" Solomon asked, growing impatient.

"Yes, we are," Tatum said, pulling into the Santa Anna Rehabilitation Center.

Two minutes too late.

"Shit."

3
OUT OF THE BLUE

"*W*hat's wrong, Daddy?"

"Hey, big guy, everything is fine. Let's get out the car," Tatum said as he unbuckled himself before going around to the back seat to get his son. He knew the facility had a strict policy on curfew. You could stay for two hours after the cutoff time, but you had to be punctual. No exceptions. It was written vividly on the wall as well as on the website. But he figured it wouldn't hurt to try. Maybe they would be lenient with his son in tow.

"Come on, Solly," Tatum said as he took the toddler out of the car and carried him partly before placing him on the ground to walk.

A black metal barred gate allowed entrance and exit into the cream-colored building. There was an old Texas feel to the structure, the exterior a remolded fort from the Texas Revolution. This area of town had a heavy Spanish population; in fact, the facility was named after the famous Mexican general who fought against Texas during the great war.

Tatum caught the door as someone else was leaving and ushered his son into the building. They walked up to the front to find the administrative clerk in charge of admittances, a short and portly Hispanic man with steel-framed glasses.

"Um, excuse me, I'm here to see—"

"Sorry, sir, it's after visiting admittance time. You'll have to come back between the hours of eight and four-thirty," the orderly said.

Tatum looked at his son and started to walk back to the car. As he passed through the gate, he heard his name.

"Hey, T.C.!"

A six-foot-two, well-defined yet older dark-skinned man, accompanied by a full-figured woman in dark blue FedEx uniform and skin the color of mahogany, had spoken.

"Pop-Pop," Solomon screamed as he ran to hug his grandfather. Tatum watched as his father, Johnny Clarke, hoisted his son in the air.

"Hey, Pops, shouldn't you be on the other side of this gate?"

"Yeah, but I ain't visiting—I live here," he replied, dismissing his son's statement. He motioned to the woman who was standing back slightly, waiting to be introduced.

"Hey Darlene, real quick, I want you to meet my son, the big shot at Simmons Pharmaceuticals."

"Oh, you're T.C., your dad has told me so much about you." Tatum shook the woman's hand. She was attractive at any age, but the lines between her eyes and the heavy makeup she wore to hide the fact, indicated she was around his dad's age. "And you must be Solly!"

"Solomon, say high to Darlene," Tatum said to his child. He didn't like anyone calling his son Solly but him. It was his nickname, but he figured his pop wanted to impress this woman, and she meant no offense, so he let it slide.

"Oh, you're Ms. Darlene! You're the person my Pop-Pop always talks all about." The comment made Darlene blush.

"Oh, does he now? What does he say?"

"He says you have a pretty smile, a big heart, and...um...he can't wait to take you dancing."

Darlene paused. "Wait—he really says that about me?"

"Every time we FaceTime."

The woman shifted her eyes to Johnny, who looked at her with a confident grin as if to say I told you so.

"Well, maybe my big heart will give him a chance. What do you say, Solly?"

"I say a pretty lady like you can do anything she wants and my Pop-Pop better like it!"

Darlene smiled, as clearly charmed by Solomon as she had been by his grandfather.

"Well, I have to get back to work, but it was nice to meet you, young man."

"Nice to meet you too," Solomon said as he hugged Darlene while Tatum rolled his eyes. The woman stood back up and looked at Tatum. "It was nice to meet you as well, T.C."

"Same here."

"J.C., I'm gonna leave you with your family, but let me talk to you for a second," she said.

"Come on, Solly, grown-up talk."

Father and son took a step back as Johnny ushered the woman toward her truck. His father whispered in the woman's ear, and she began to giggle, her broad smile obvious even from where he was standing.

Oh, she's falling for it, he thought as he watched her take a sheet of paper out of the truck and write something down. It was no question. It was her phone number, by the way, his father smiled. She climbed in the truck and waved goodbye to Tatum and Solomon, the young boy waving back emphatically. Johnny smiled as he approached the two of them.

"So you got her number, huh."

"Son, I'm done with cr...substances, not women," he said, looking at Solomon and choosing his words carefully.

"Apparently. Just quit pimping out your grandson in the process. How did the two of you work out that scam anyway?"

"It's called game, son. I got tons of it, and so does S.C. over there. It just skipped a generation with you, that's all."

"Whatever, Pop."

"All that Nintendo you played and no game with the women. This is just what men do, and I'm not pimping out my grandson—I'm showing him the first order of business in the fraternity of men."

"Which is?"

"When it comes to women...lie."

"Pop." Tatum didn't like his father taking that approach, but he knew it all too well from his own experiences with his father. He watched as his father resumed tossing his son in the air as they both laughed. "So, how much are you paying him?"

"Ten bucks."

"Ten bucks! When I was his age, I only got a dollar."

"I was in my prime back. I didn't need your help as much. Plus, there's inflation. And let's be honest, son, you weren't this cute of a kid."

"Just quit pimping out your grandson, please."

"Now T.C., I'm teaching the boy two valuable things. Number one is how to work for money, and number two is always to think quick on your feet and have a good alibi. You should be proud, son! The boy already good at something!"

Johnny always had a quick wit. It was a comeback Tatum had no reply for, so he shook his head and moved on.

"The delivery woman was nice-looking, though."

Who Darlene? Yeah, she bad, and if she keep playing with me, she gonna be receiving packages instead of dropping them off real soon."

"Pops," Tatum smirked as he shook his head. He looked at Solomon, who was smiling, but not at the joke. He had something else on his mind. "What is it, Solly?"

"Why does Pop-Pop call you T.C., but everybody else calls you Reverend?"

"Boy, they still calling you that?" Johnny said, placing his hands on his son's shoulder. "See, his knucklehead friends started calling him Reverend back in school, and that's an amazing story. See, your dad—"

"Pops, please not now," Tatum said, still embarrassed by the story even now.

"Okay, okay. I'm gonna tell you one day how he got that other nickname, but I always called him T.C., like I'm gonna call you S.C."

"Really?"

"Yeah, I will! You're a Clarke. They gotta know you're my grandson. So I'm J.C., your daddy is T.C., and you're S.C. But we'll talk about it more inside. Come on."

The group started to enter the building until Tatum looked at the same attendant who denied him entrance earlier.

"Hey Pop, I don't think we can get in now. We didn't make it on time," Tatum said, pointing at the sign about the entrance. Johnny looked at the sign and smirked.

"Son, come on in here." They walked into the building. Tatum looked at the attendant, who looked back and forth between him and his father.

"Ol' Miguel denied you? Man, next time you see him, you just keep moving; he ain't nobody."

The portly Spanish man's tone went from entirely professional to playful. "They're with you, J.C.?"

"Yeah, this my son, the big shot over there at Simmons Pharmaceuticals. And this is his son Solomon, now and forevermore known as little S.C."

"Oh, it's nice to meet you both," the man said, walking from around the booth to meet Tatum formally and extending this hand to greet him and Solomon.

Johnny placed his hand on Miguel's shoulder and said, "Hey, we're gonna go to the game room for a little while so I can play chess with my son."

"You can't go in there, J.C."

"Now come on, Miguel, you gonna make me look bad in front of my grandson over here?"

Tatum watched as the Spanish man raised his hands in a calming fashion. "Come on, J.C., you know me better than that. I'm not trying to be a hard-ass, I swear. But Dr. Mallard is using it right now."

"Shoot. Okay, well, see if you can go in and get me a chessboard and a football for the youngin. We can sit outside in the atrium."

"Yeah, I can do that. I'll meet you over on the patio."

"My man."

Johnny Clarke did what he was best at—making friends and using them to his advantage. Tatum suddenly questioned why he was worried about being late at all. As Miguel walked off, Tatum and Solomon followed J.C. to the atrium. It was quite stunning for a rehabilitation center, with benches covered in positive sayings and freshly groomed exotic flowers spread around the room. The stargazers were particularly attractive, and he wasn't alone in thinking that as his son sprinted over to one of the more colorful flowers.

"Wow, these are so cool!"

"You think so? Well, you can take one, but you gotta give it to your Nana for me."

"Or not, Solly," Tatum interjected. It was bad enough he had taken Solly away from her to see her ex-husband—he was about to bring her gifts from him.

"But Dad, Grandma will love these," Solomon said.

"You're right; she will. We'll talk about it before we leave, okay?"

"Okay," he said with certain dejection in his voice.

Tatum sat on the bench that said: *Nothing is impossible. The very word is spelled 'I'm Possible.' You can do it!* It was a moving statement. One he personally identified with. Something his father picked up on as he sat down opposite Tatum.

"Yeah, I like that one too."

"I feel like I've been living that one lately." Tatum looked over to Solomon, who was running back as Miguel brought in the chess set, a football, a long plastic object, and what looked like all he could carry in snacks.

"I figured you guys could use something to drink, so I brought a couple of sodas and some cookies and chips. Whatever you want. Oh, and I know you like your music, J.C., so I got you one of the portable speakers."

"Miguel, you're the man!" Johnny said as Tatum watched *the man* place all the items on their bench. Tatum wasn't surprised by the response his father was getting. He was actively breaking what appeared to be a hard-fast rule and had Miguel feeling good about doing it. He'd learned growing up that rules were just suggestions to his father. A lesson Solomon was now starting to understand. As Miguel went back to his desk, Solomon, still inquisitive about the exchange, asked the question that seemed to be bothering him.

"Pop-Pop, that man said Daddy and I couldn't come in here. Why did he let us come in with you?"

Johnny picked up Solomon and placed him on his knee.

"You see, S.C., all these flowers you like and this building are like a jungle, and your Pop-Pop is the king of the jungle."

"Wow, that's so cool! Are you really the king, Pop-Pop?"

"I most certainly am! In fact, they call me The Lion."

"The Lion?"

Tatum swiftly responded, "No, Solomon, don't. Please don't ask that qu—"

"Say what, S.C.? Ya daddy didn't tell you they use to call me The Lion?

"Here we go," Tatum said, rolling his eyes and looking around for help that wasn't coming.

"Oh yeah!" Johnny said with a devilish grin, pulling his grandson in closer to continue a story Tatum had heard for what felt like a literal thousand times. "See, S.C., what your nana and your daddy don't want you to know is before you were born, your Pop-Pop didn't live in a place that had a gate. He was out there in the str—"

"Dad..."

"Uh...yeah...your Granddaddy was real. He was so real they use to call him The Lion. T.C., tell the boy the truth."

"They called him The Lion," Tatum murmured unenthusiastically, praying the story would end and knowing there would be no such reprieve.

"So, The Lion is so big and so bad he has to live somewhere they can watch him, and that's why I live here—so people can make sure I don't do no liony shi...stuff."

Johnny playfully snuggled with his son, and when they were done,

Solomon, still putting it all together, looked over at Tatum and asked, "But Daddy, I thought Pop-Pop lived here, so he won't smoke crack?"

"Solly!" Tatum shouted, looking at his dad awkwardly. He was slightly embarrassed by his son's response but not by much. His father, however, was stunned.

"I didn't tell him. I mean, he spends a lot of time with Nana," Tatum said, shrugging his shoulders. Johnny cut his eyes at his son and smiled back at his grandson.

"Well, it don't matter why I'm in here. The point is a place like this can't hold a lion, so real soon I'm gonna move out and be the best Pop-Pop you will ever meet. You hear me, S.C.?"

"Yay! I love you, Pop-Pop."

"I love you too, S.C.," Johnny said as he hugged his grandson.

Tatum watched without saying a word, settled in spirit as his father and son's relationship bloomed right before his eyes. A sliver of him realized he couldn't remember a similar moment between him and Johnny, and a twinge of sullenness struck him. He wanted to know what that felt like. Still, he was happy his father hugged the child affectionately as if the hug itself were nourishment replenishing his energy. He was grateful that his son got the one thing he never got from his own childhood.

"Alright, S.C., I'm gonna whip your daddy in chess, and it ain't gonna take long because he's terrible. But soon as I'm done, we're gonna throw the football, okay?"

"Okay!"

"You ain't whipping me, old man," Tatum said defensively, setting up the board. While his father connected his phone to the portable speaker and put on what was no doubt one of his many playlists. Most of the songs were familiar to Tatum, with just a few exceptions.

"You ready to get this whooping?" Johnny asked Tatum before he made the first move. It was true his father was a much better chess player than him, something he had a hard time accepting since his father had no formal education of any kind. Still, he was determined not to lose in front of his son. Despite how determined he was, his skill level just wasn't up to speed. He lost convincingly in seven moves.

"Checkmate," The words irked Tatum's soul.

"I don't get it. You have an eighth-grade education and sold dope for a living. I've got two college degrees. How are you beating me?"

"Because nothing beats the school of hard knocks," J.C. said as he opened a pack of cookies. "You know, there's an old saying: some of us got it, and some of us don't. Well, I got it, and you well, there's always next time," he said, laughing at Tatum, who was still a bit upset about how quickly he lost. They played two more times with the same results, the last time being enough for Tatum to concede defeat.

"That's it. If I didn't know better, I would think you were cheating somehow. Where did you learn to play?"

"Prison."

"Are you serious?"

"As a heart attack. See, you've always been good at the books, but the one thing I wanted you to get was if you don't learn life's lessons, it's gonna be hard."

Tatum watched as his dad looked at Solomon, throwing the ball in the air by himself.

"T.C., I'm proud of you. I know it had to be hard. Shit, men don't know anything about raising kids. That's women's work. But you stood tall."

"Chauvinist much?" Tatum responded to his dad's insinuation about women only being capable of parenting kids.

"Now, son, I think you got me all wrong. Everything is made better by the input of a woman. I can't even think of one thing in history that a woman was involved in and say yeah, she really fucked that up. Men just too stupid to realize it. So yeah, raising kids is women's work because God knows you always put your best employees on the toughest job, but don't get it twisted, so is everything else in the world, including leading it, and I mean that. I mean, think about it, ain't that many women as leaders of countries, and that's why shit is all gone to hell right now. Truth is we need them, and they accept us."

Tatum was startled by his dad's candor and nodded his head in disbelief.

"Wow. I gotta admit I wasn't expecting this conversation to take that turn."

"They say God looks out for old people and fools. Well, I'm a bit of both, but I learn," J.C. said with a chuckle. As Tatum put the chessboard back together for one last game, his father continued. "Saying all that to say you've done a good job raising this boy by yourself. I know it had to be hard, and I don't know if it means much or not, but I'm proud of you. You stood in the gap like the man I should have been. But if at all possible, boy needs his mot—"

"Well, all he has is me, Pops. We all don't get a chance to go off to deadbeat-parent school," Tatum fired back. He knew his words hurt just as equally as his father's words hurt him. He knew it wasn't a condemnation of his parenting. In fact, Johnny made a point to let him know that wasn't the case. Still, the mitigated gall of J.C. to say anything about parenting, something he knew firsthand the man knew nothing about, was a trigger for him.

"Alright...my bad. I didn't mean anything by it, Mr. Clarke."

"It's all good," Tatum said, cutting his father off, his wounds reflected by the term 'Mr. Clarke'. He decided to let this be the end of it.

"Let's just change the subject," Tatum said. Seconds later, a song came on he was familiar with but didn't think his father knew about. "I see you liking a bit of my old school."

"Who?"

"That song *Who Can I Run To* by Xscape. When did you—"

Johnny looked at him and chuckled. Tatum knew he'd made a mistake, something when it came to music, and his dad would have no mercy roasting him about. He watched as he threw his hands in the air and exclaimed, "Man, you youngsters. I swear y'all don't know shit —which is crazy since you all walk around with James Bond phones glued to your ears. But I'm not gonna get on you about this one because your mother loved Xscape, so I could see how you'd be stupid enough to say something like that. You know, all that water behind ya ears, maybe you don't hear the difference in the chords. But those women right there are The Jones Girls."

"Are you kidding me? They sound like Xscape."

"T.C., you're embarrassing yourself today, son. Just be quiet and nod your head and fake the words like you use to in Sunday school. The Jones Girls don't sound like Xscape. Xscape sounds like The Jones Girls," his father said jokingly.

"Dad, I—"

"See, this is why you should've stayed up with your piano and guitar lessons. You'd have a better ear for music than you do now."

"Pops, I still know a thing or two about music."

"Boy, you don't know shit," Johnny said. "And I had such high hopes for you. I never forget how much you loved listening to music when you were a baby. You went to sleep to it; you woke up to it. You'd smile at anything I played. Prince or Michael Jackson, and you'd go to sleep to Luther Vandross. Even as a child, you only did your homework to *Kind of Blue*. You remember that?"

"Yes, I remember, Pop. Miles Davis redefined music with that one album. Can we please move on now?" Tatum said, wanting to hear the end of the song but knowing his Dad would never stop this assault. He lived for moments like this.

"Okay, okay, T.C.," Johnny replied, "but let me say this, sloppy mistakes like that is why I'll always be the master of music in this family. You got it?"

"Dad, look at me!" Tatum turned to witness his son catch a ball in the air he'd thrown to himself. It was his way of saying it was time for him to get some attention. Both Tatum and Johnny recognized that they better pay attention to him. The pair got up, and Johnny called for the football from Solomon, still trying this best to make an impression."

"How's that pharmacy school going?"

"It's going. I got a big award today."

"It's crazy. I still can't get over the fact you're not making music. Remember when you were nine you taught—"

"Myself to play the guitar, I know."

I'm just saying you had a ton of potential," Johnny said as he threw the ball back to his grandson.

"Dad, you know how hard it is to get into music?"

"Life is hard. Might as well die trying doing what you were meant to do."

"I can't sing."

"I'm gonna leave it alone. It's just I thought you'd at least try. You used to write some really good songs."

"You mean my childhood ramblings?"

"I liked them."

"Trust me, Dad, you'd be the only one. It's hella hard to do anyway. I don't think you recognize that enough. Like, do you have any idea how hard it is to be in music?"

"Not really, but if I had to guess, I'd say just as hard as being a single dad working a full-time job and going to school and winning some big award," Johnny said with a smirk. Tatum rolled his eyes.

"I'll admit I walked right into that one."

Johnny walked closer to his son and put his hand on Tatum's shoulder, and said quietly.

"Son, The Lion never sleeps."

"Do you have an answer for everything?" Tatum asked, truly curious about his father's quick responses.

"Only the easy questions." As they finished taking turns throwing the football to Solomon, Tatum asked his dad a question he wasn't sure he was prepared to know the answer to.

"So Pops—"

"Yo."

"—When did you become this life-guru guy?"

Johnny stopped throwing the ball to look at his son. "You know, son, I'm gonna be honest with you. When you told me you were having the little guy over there, I was proud. But when you told me Monique left you with the baby, I was worried. Hell, I ain't never been good at nothing, but I wanted to be there for you. You were a young man still trying to figure out what being a man was, and now you had to figure out how to be a mom and a dad, and you never had a good example of a dad. I had to do something to help out, so I read this book. And in it was some of the most powerful stuff I've ever heard, really. So if I have to say anything changed, it was my mindset after reading that book."

Tatum nodded. Somehow his father was present but far away at the same time.

"Sounds like a hell of a book."

"It is. You should read it. I'm gonna give you my copy."

"Pops, I can buy my own copy."

"Let me give my copy. Please. It's the least I can do for you."

T.C. had never heard his father say the word please unless he wanted something. Now he was using it to give something away. Maybe he had changed, if only a little.

"Okay.

"Our time is almost up. Meet me at the front. I'm gonna go upstairs and grab my copy."

Tatum nodded and waved his son over.

The book had him intrigued. His father was always a varying degree of a bad man. When he sold drugs, he was violent and cold, and arrogant. When he got hooked on them, he was distant, erratic, and violent. The man in front of him was a work in progress, but from what he could tell, the progress was moving in the right direction.

Tatum and Solomon got to the front and stood near the wall across from Miguel. The floral stucco walls felt appropriate for the building. There was a water fountain that had a design of a dove nesting in the flowers, the sign above it reading *Let Your Peace Flow*. He thought it was corny but still nice. Overall, it was honestly better than he thought it would be, considering the neighborhood. He looked down the corridor to see his father coming down the hall empty-handed.

"I looked all over the damn room. I couldn't find it."

"It's okay; I'll pick it u—"

"Son, I *want* you to read this book." He could tell his father was adamant. "It's all about finding your best self, your happiest self. You need it. Just hold on."

J.C. walked to the desk, beckoning Tatum and Solomon to come over. As they walked up, Johnny asked the attendant, "Hey Miguel, I need a copy of that book from the library for my son to take with him."

"J.C., you know the books are for the residents. We have to make sure we have it in stock for anyone who wants to read it. If we did that for all the residents, there wouldn't be any books."

"But you're not doing it for any resident, Miguel—you're doing it for me."

"J.C."

"Come on, Miguel. Look at the way the kid is dressed. He got on— what's that? Brooks Brothers?"

"Ralph Lauren."

"Ralph Lauren! The kid got on goddamn Ralph Lauren shoes! You think he's gonna steal your book? 'Scuse my language, S.C.," Johnny said, realizing he cursed in front of his grandson.

Miguel came around the counter, shaking his head at Johnny. He couldn't believe it, but he was going to break the rules again. "Okay, what's it called?"

"*The Alchemist*. Ask Brenda. She knows where it is."

"Okay, J.C., and I wasn't trying to—"

"We'll talk about that later. Now go get the book. My son's a man on the move!" J.C. responded, cutting Miguel off mid-sentence.

"Okay," Miguel said, heading for the library.

Tatum smirked at his father. "I could've gotten the book from the store, Pops."

"That's not the point. This ain't got nothing to do with the book. I'm teaching S.C. a very valuable lesson."

"And what's that?" Johnny turned to face his son and grandson, looking them squarely in the face.

"Lions don't take orders from sheep."

Solomon's face lit up. "Pop-Pop, you're so cool."

As Johnny picked up Solomon and swung him through the air, Miguel came back and extended the book to Tatum.

"Thanks, Miguel, I owe ya one."

"Of course, J.C."

The man went back behind the counter to give Johnny time to say his final goodbyes. J.C. shook his son's hand while still holding Solomon. He then gave the child a giant hug and put him on the ground.

"Pop-Pop?"

"Yeah, S.C.?"

"Where is my ten dollars for saying that stuff to that woman?"

Tatum laughed, happy his son didn't forget the original agreement. J.C. looked somewhat caught off-guard by the question as Tatum continued to chuckled. His laughter at J. C.'s expense was cut short when his father responded to Solomon's question.

"I gave it to your daddy. He's going to give it to you when he gets home."

4

E X

he Jones Girls. Unbelievable, Tatum thought. It had been a full day, and he was still a little miffed he didn't recognize *Who Can I Run To* as the version by The Jones Girls. *I could've sworn it was Xscape.* The old man always could pull a rabbit out of his hat.

He decided to put up the rest of his stuff, find a nice spot on campus, and do something he hadn't done since he was an undergrad: read for pleasure. Now that pharmacy school was just a formality, he could finally stop and smell the roses. He looked at the students and wondered what they were studying and what did they set out to become—and how none of it truly mattered. He was graduating with no student loans to speak of, thanks to his job at Simmons Pharmaceuticals, and his mom was watching his son. Today was his first day of freedom, and the best thing he could think to do was read a book. He walked back to the parking garage to retrieve the copy of The Alchemist his father lent to him.

"You've got to be fucking kidding me." The same Nissan Maxima was sitting in front of his car, blocking the entrance again.

Motherfucker, he thought. He wasn't leaving, but that wasn't the point. If he wanted to leave, he couldn't. He scanned the area and found her in almost the same spot she had been in before. He headed in her direction, ready to argue. Yesterday he had someplace to be, but today he had time.

"What in the hell is your problem? You blocked me in yesterday and now—"

"Look, here are my keys. Whatever you want to do, just do it. I don't give a damn. I'm quitting school because my asshole ex-husband is cutting off the funding we agreed on because, well, he's an asshole. I said that already but it just feels good to call him that. Kaleb Washington is an asshole!" she yelled, letting her words echo off the parking garage for all to hear.

Tatum didn't say anything. He wanted to get out of there but could tell she was hurt. The woman, lost in her own thoughts, persisted.

"You know, I was there for him. I wasn't perfect, but I was there. And he has the nerve to call me crazy. Me! Can you believe that?"

"Miss, I just want you to move your—"

"And to think I put up with all his cheating and his bullshit lies, and then he fucks around and gets another woman pregnant, and I'm supposed to forgive him again? And that's just the hoes I know about. I didn't find out about this one until she was knocking at the door eight months pregnant. So yeah, I guess that makes me crazy. Or stupid, at least. Stupid, as fuck! And now I have to drop classes because I can't afford this shit. I bet you probably think I'm crazy too, but the only thing crazy would be staying there while he has a whole 'nother fucking kid. That would be crazy—staying with the legendary Kaleb Washington."

What in the fuck? Tatum thought, his eyes wide open as she continued her barrage of emotional epithets against her ex-husband. He did think she was crazy, but at this moment, he realized exactly what she was—a woman hurt by revelation. She was rebuilding, and he was in the middle of it.

"You know, the thing is, I'm not even upset. I'm glad it's over. When I found out he fucked up again, I felt a wave of relief, like, good God; this nightmare is over. He didn't even put up a fight for us. Oh no. But his money he fought tooth and nail for. I guess because he's going to be on child support for the next eighteen fucking years, he's going to need all the cash he can find."

"Miss, I just need you to move your car." None of this was his problem. As he was speaking, the same white guy from yesterday came up wearing glasses and a gray flannel shirt.

"Autumn, here are the last of them. I'm going to hate to see you go."

"Thanks, Charlie. I'll be alright. Charlie, this is...um..."

"Oh...uh...me? Tatum. Tatum Clarke," he said, caught off-guard by the awkward introduction.

"Yeah, Tatum. He's going to help me move all this stuff to my car so—"

"Wait, wait...what did you just say?" Tatum stumbled, again caught off-guard.

She put one of the paintings down and looked at him with stern determination, like a poker player holding all the winning cards.

"You want me to move my car, I gotta move this stuff, and we're both walking that way. Just grab what you can and bring it with you."

This motherfucker here! Tatum thought to himself. He didn't even want to move his car—he was making the point on principle. Now he was stuck helping a woman he wanted to strangle move a bunch of paintings to her car. Still, he thought if he could get this done, he could go on about his life. For now, his book would have to wait.

"What are we moving?"

"Just everything that you see here."

Tatum examined the haul. There were several paintings—all oil-canvas-based and all very impressive. A couple of them looked freshly painted. He wondered if it was a good idea to handle them.

"Yes, they're all dry. That's just the sheen setting in to seal the painting, so don't worry. Your lovely powder-blue sweater is going to be fine.

Tatum looked stunned. He was indeed worried about getting paint on his sweater. It was his first time wearing it, but he didn't think he was *that* obvious. He decided to defend himself from her baseless accusation.

"I wasn't worried about the sweater."

Autumn glanced up as she fumbled with the paintings.

"A fitted cashmere sweater? Looks expensive. I'd be worried," she said as if it were the most obvious thing in the world. She picked up what she could and headed toward the car, leaving Tatum to carry all that remained, including two freshly minted paintings, and proceed to the car. When he got there, he put them down as she opened the trunk. Several trash bags, which looked like they contained clothes, nearly filled the space. Tatum thought this might be all she had left after her divorce and was now living out of her car.

He regretted being so hard on her for her atrocious parking.

As they loaded the paintings, Tatum caught a glimpse of one: a stirring portrait of an Egyptian priestess.

"Did you paint this?"

"Yes, Tatum, I, the art major, drew a painting that we're now loading in my car. Astute observation," she said clearly being sarcastic, which Tatum ignored.

"Well, before you cut me off, I was going to say it's dope, and I was wondering how much it cost."

"It's not for sale."

"Well, in case you...look, if you need money, I know a guy."

"I don't sell my art," she replied. Her shortness caught him off-guard. She was, after all, working on a master's in art.

"So if you don't sell your art, why are you in art school?"

"I... look, it's complicated. Can we just change the subject?"

"Uh, sure."

It was a topic she wasn't going to divulge freely, so he had no choice but to move on. But before he could come up with a new topic or shift gears in some way, she hit him with a bombshell. "Ready to help me unload this stuff at my apartment? It's right up the road."

Tatum's gut told him to run. Never get involved with a woman on the verge of a breakdown or who might just be flat-out crazy. Still, he was just helping her move some things, and having done this much, he felt obligated at this point.

He looked at the woman who was barely holding it together and nodded his head. "Yeah, I can do that. I'll follow you in my car."

"Great! Thank you!"

He hadn't expected a thank you. It was the least she could do, but it was the first sign of kindness he'd seen from her.

The two got in their respective cars, and Tatum pulled out of his parking spot as Autumn drove ahead. The trip didn't take long as she lived in a newly developed condo not far from the college.

She pulled into the driveway, and he followed her through the gates. He waited as she parked in front of what he presumed to be her condo. He got out of his car and met Autumn at her already open trunk.

"This is such a big help. Thank you," she said.

"It's all good," he replied. He hoisted two of the paintings and followed her to the front of her condo, and waited as she opened the door. It was a disaster zone of chaos— unorganized papers, clothes on the floor, and paint canvases against a pastel yellow wall. There was an openness to the room, even if the mess made it feel cramped, and the cherry hardwood floors were strikingly rich and freshly shined.

"How long have you been divorced?"

"Over a year, but we just now stopped fucking each other."

"Are you this blunt about everything?"

"I don't think it's blunt at all. You asked me a question, and I gave you an answer. You can put those paintings over there in the corner." Tatum looked at the paintings that hung on the wall—four pictures of what appeared to be the same woman. One, in particular, stood out to him: a woman exhaling the universe.

"I haven't figure out what to call that one. It's either *A Divine Eye* or *Purple Haze*," she said as he marveled at the painting.

"This is the dopest thing I've ever seen. You do all of these?" The more he looked at the portrait, the more it looked like her, but in a different way than the other paintings.

"Yes, Tatum, I, the art major, pai—"

"Okay, okay, I get it, stupid question," he said, conceding to her response.

"So... what does it symbolize to you?"

That question piqued her interest as she stopped picking things up off the floor. She walked toward the painting.

"It's multiple interpretations. The hair kind of reminds me of Jimi Hendrix, and I was listening to a lot of *Purple Haze* when I painted it, but my favorite is, you know, people think they got the universe figured out when they don't even got earth figured out. Like, we think a black hole destroys matter, but what if it's not that? What if it's just a blotch, and we can't see it because it exists on a divine light spectrum. Maybe when we're looking at a black hole, we're looking at God herself. So I call it *A Divine Eye* or *Purple Haze* depending on what mood I'm in."

"*A Divine Eye*," Tatum said, now understanding the dual interpretation and appreciating it even more after hearing the artist's thoughts on it.

"Is it for sale?"

"Hell no! I mean, I don't sell my paintings and definitely nothing on my wall. Because those are the most meaningful pieces, I've ever made."

Tatum scanned the remaining three paintings, each a marvel in its own right. How he felt about the woman had nothing to do with how he felt about the artist. He admired the paintings, each evoking a different yet powerful emotion. He wondered if the paintings he just brought in would be going on the walls. The four paintings on the wall were magnetic, and in his untrained eye, the others just didn't stack up. He had to get the artist's opinion to see if he was right.

"What about these? Are they going on the wall?"

"Oh no, those were assignments. The ones on the wall have meaning. The far one is *Sun Goddess*, next to it *is Winter Queen*, and next to it is *Scarlet*. You've already met *Purple Haze*. They're for me and me only, which is why I won't sell them. I put a piece of my heart into each one of them. They'll probably be the only four paintings to ever be on the wall because I'm never giving that shit away again, so soak it up."

Tatum chuckled at the statement, at least happy he was right. The paintings on the wall were heads and shoulders above the others. Reflecting on her words about giving away her heart, though, finally gave him a way to change the subject.

"You know, I use to think my world would never be the same after my wife walked out on me and our son. I thought I'd never love someone again, but I know that's not the case. Keep a space on your wall open," he said as he picked up another portrait to examine it.

"So you're divorced?"

"Sorta. We've never gone through the proceedings, but we're not getting back together. I just haven't had time to get around to it since I've been raising our son, going to school, and working."

He paused in his tracks. There was a large green smudge on his cashmere sweater. Apparently, one of the paintings was still wet. Something Autumn also picked up on.

"Shit, I'm sorry. I didn't know."

"It's okay," he said to keep the peace. It wasn't okay. In fact, he was downright pissed that his sweater was ruined. He went to the sink to rinse the paint out, but there wasn't a lot to be said. He knew the stain wasn't going to come out. Nonetheless, he kept his mouth shut and moved the final paintings as well as her garbage bags of clothes. When they finished unloading the trunk, he looked at his watch.

"I need to go pick up my son right now," he said as he continued taking swipes at his sweater in a futile effort.

"Okay. Well, thank you again for helping, and sorry about your sweater."

"No problem," he said, slightly irritated by the entire exchange.

He went to his car and pulled off his sweater. The moment he got out of the driveway, he noticed Autumn waving him down in his review mirror.

"No thanks, buddy," he said to himself. For the last two days, he'd been derailed by this woman, and he didn't want one additional second to be wasted by her. He pretended he didn't see her and stepped on the gas. The drive to his mother's house wasn't long, but his week wasn't off to a good start. All he wanted to do was read the book his father let him borrow. And, as always, that would have to wait.

When he got to his mother's house, Solomon was waiting at the front door.

"Daddy!" the boy screamed as he ran over and wrapped his arms around his father's legs. He was followed by his mother, Savannah Clarke, who was wiping her hands with a cloth she used to wash the dishes.

"When I told him you were coming, he was checking the window every time he heard a car." the five-foot-two West Indian woman with chestnut skin said before her son kissed her on the cheek.

"Thanks for watching Solly, Mom," he said to his mother for watching Solomon. His kiss was greeted with a slap to the back of the neck.

"Ow, ma!"

"Did you take my grandson to see that piece of you know what yesterday?" Tatum's eyes widened. He looked at his son, who, even at this young age, realized he probably shouldn't have hit the hornets' nest.

"Ma, I've had an exhausting day. I don't want to do this with you now."

"Look, I don't have a problem with you having a relationship with your father, but the child right here is an extension of my efforts. You don't take time away from me to give to him. He needs to find his own damn time to fit into your life the same way he had to find time to fit in when you were growing up."

"Momma, I don't want to get into this right now."

"I bet you don't 'cause you done slid down a razor blade and ended up in alcohol river." She swung at Tatum again, who braced for a gentler slap to the back of his neck.

"Did he eat?" Tatum asked.

"Did he? That's all the boy do! He eats like a grown man. He ate rice and peas, and then he wanted curry goat, then he wanted johnny cake, then he wanted fried shrimp and potatoes. Let me tell you, son, you can't go on *Maury* 'cause you are definitely the father of this child."

Tatum laughed as he picked up Solly.

"You ate all of Nana's food, Solly?" His son buried his face in his father's shoulder as if to be embarrassed. "Oh, don't be like that, son. Nana likes cooking for you. Now, go get in the car. I'll be right there."

He put the child down and looked at his mother. She wasn't done with this conversation about his dad, and he knew it.

"Ma."

"I don't want him to break the boy's heart, Tatum. Johnny Clarke has only ever been good at two things: selling drugs and disappointing people."

"You don't think I know that?"

"Then why are you wasting your time?"

"Because he's...he's different. And I know what you're gonna say, but I'm telling you with my own two eyes he's trying."

His mother cut her eyes and folded her arms, looking over the shrubbery in front of her one-story home.

"Well, you're a grown man, and I can't tell you what to do. If you want to have a relationship with your father, that's fine, but I wish you'd leave my grandson out of it."

"I would never do anything to put Solly in harm's way. Believe me when I tell you if there is even a tiny slip-up, I'm cutting all ties."

"Okay. Well, I packed you a plate because I know you haven't eaten. I had to hide the rest of the curry goat from your son."

"Thanks, Ma. I hope he goes to sleep early so I can relax a bit and actually get a bite of it."

"Oh, I'm sure he'll have the 'itis soon. He'll be asleep before you pull into your driveway."

"Thanks again, Ma. I really appreciate it. Have a good night."

"You too, Tatum. I love you."

"Love you too."

He gave his mother a hug and a kiss on the opposite cheek and got back in his car to head home.

The short drive gave him just enough time to think about the whirlwind of the last few hours. He'd seen literal works of art—the most compelling pieces he'd ever laid eyes on—painted by a girl who was all but certifiable. He wasn't even into art, but her paintings spoke to him. It was uncanny. Still, all he wanted was to read at least one chapter of the book his father asked him to read. When he pulled into the driveway, he looked in the back seat. His mother was right. Solomon was fast asleep. He got out of the car, picked up his son, went into the house, and laid his son in his room. After kissing him on the forehead, he walked back to the car to grab the book, except it wasn't there. He searched the entire car and even went back into the house to see if he'd brought it in but forgot. It was gone. The last time he could remember having it was when he was helping Autumn move. "Shit, I must've dropped it over there."

That's when he remembered her coming back outside as he was driving off. She was only doing it to get him to come back for the book. He breathed a sigh of relief, glad she wasn't interested in any more of his time, or worse, romance.

But now, after helping her move a few things, he'd lost his father's book.

No good deed, he thought as he turned on the television set and settled in for a bite of his mother's curry goat.

5

FOR REAL

"'m telling you, Stone, it was crazy. And on top of all that, I left the damn book at her house. That's why I'm leaving the fucking bookstore right now. But she can paint—I won't front," Tatum said over the phone. Stone laughing at the situation made him laugh himself.

"So you ruin a 100-dollar sweater, didn't get anything you planned on getting done accomplished, and oh yeah, you lost your book too. Rev, you got the worst luck when it comes to women," Stone said, continuing his laughter.

"Well, that's why I'm not coming through today."

"Aw damn, Reverend. Again?"

"Dog, I swear—"

"Now you listen to me, Reverend Clarke, and you listen good, I don't care. Read that fucking book another time. We, the fellas, need to link up. I met this chick name—"

"Brother, I don't want to hear about your thot-a-thon," Tatum said as he listened to his friend snicker in the background.

"Now hold on, Rev—you just got through telling me about some art B-A-E who is already literally a drain of time and money, but when I want to talk about a bitch who gonna drain my nuts for real, now you want to cut the convo."

"First of all, she's not some art B-A-E. She's a crazy paint lady. Secondly, draining your nuts? Did I need to hear that? Third, I don't want to hear about your latest victim because it's always the same story."

"That's not true."

"Stone, every story since we were twelve goes like this." Tatum imitated his friend's voice.

"Yo, Rev, check it out. I met this freak with the fattest ass named—insert freak's name here. Man, I'm telling you, she got a fat ass, and when I say fat, I mean '80s Luther Vandross with the S-curl fat. I'm talking 'bout the Fat Boys with the pizza on the cover fat. I'm talking about her ass has its own ZIP code, files a W2 at the end of the year, and checks off Head of Household fat. Dog, soon as she let me slide in, I'm finna be in that thang like the Lone Ranger riding nonstop from New York to California." Tatum's tone and cadence were so perfect; Stone could barely stop laughing on the other end of the phone.

"So tell me, Kenley Stoneridge, is there anything remotely different about the story this time?"

"First of all, I would never say the Lone Ranger. I'd say Bass Reeves cause black cowboys matter. Secondly, this one got some real fat titties too."

"You are a nut."

"Naw, but I'm trying to catch one. I'm serious, Rev—them joints look like two coconuts about to fall out a grocery bag fighting with each other."

Tatum laughed at his friend's crude analogy. "I have to admit, that is a new wrinkle...but they will *always* have a big ass."

"Well, of course, they will, Reverend. Haven't you heard? Everything is bigger in Texas."

The two laughed again at the entirety of the conversation.

"Rev, she got a friend, and her friend got some thick-ass lips. I'm saying we could Hulk Hogan/Macho Man Savage these hoes and—"

"Some other time, Stone, I promise you. I'm just really determined to read this book."

"Goddamn, Rev! See, that's why nobody like yo' ass. Always fucking up a good time with responsible shit. You really finna choose a book over some pussy? Well, go head, tell me what this book about that's keeping us from winning the tag team title tonight."

Tatum shook his head as he located the spot where he wanted to sit and read. Summing up the book for Stone, even if it was only what he read on the back cover, would just keep the conversation going and give his friend another reason to talk about pussy. His friend's true mission was to get him to come through the neighborhood, and he wanted to—just not today. He decided to be a bit more forthcoming too.

"To keep it a buck fifty, don't know what the book is about. But the way I see it, anything that had J.C. looking, walking, and talking the way he was the other day makes me want to know what's between the covers."

"Man, you're not gonna remember this, but I tried to tell you a few years ago right when Solomon was born—"

"I was waiting on that shit. Okay, okay, you were right," Tatum said reluctantly. "I'll be honest, I was a bit skeptical, but he's been solid. Conned me out of ten dollars with Solomon, but besides that, it was good. Oh, and did you know that the song *Who Can I Run To* was a cover?"

"Yeah, The Jones Girls. I'm surprised you didn't know that since y'alls thing has always been music."

"Damn, you knew that?"

"Bruh, I sit around here and watch the news, *Unsung,* and *Power* reruns. Life selling white isn't exciting until it's exciting, and usually, that's some bad shit."

"True that. Alright, bro, I got to my spot. I'm gonna hit you up when I'm on the way home."

"Alright, fam. Keep it 100."

"Always."

Tatum got off the phone and was finally able to sit down with his copy of *The Alchemist*. He was irritated he lost the book, but he hadn't let that stop him. He normally would've lost interest in reading a book at this point, but if it impacted his father to the point he'd at least attempt to kick his habits, he wanted to know what it was about. Today he was going to read. He found a tree not far from the spot he wanted to sit yesterday and sat down. He looked at the campus for the first time through a fresh set of eyes. This moment he was at peace again. His mother was looking after Solomon, and he had a pocket of time before he had to go and become a dad. He wanted to savor it. He pulled out his wireless headphones and connected them. He turned on *Superstar*, a classic song from Usher off of his *Confessions* album. It was the first song on his reading playlist. When Usher hit the first note, he read the first words on page one.

"The boy's name was Santiago," he said aloud before reading the rest of the page to himself.

He heard a muffled noise over his headphone, which seemed off. He took out one of the wireless headphones to see if he could make out the voice.

"The boy's name was Tatum Clarke." His eyes widened. It was art B-A-E, err, crazy paint lady. He pulled the other earphone out of his ear and looked up. "Hey Autumn...uh...you know what, I think I left a book at your house yesterday."

"Hello to you too, Mr. Clarke. And yes, I know. I tried to wave you down to give it to you."

"Oh, you did?" Tatum said, now regretting he didn't stop when he saw her.

"I'm sure you were just upset about that sweater and ignored me."

"NO, that wasn't it at all." That was precisely it, but he didn't want to concede the fact he was upset because, after all, she did note he should've been worried about the sweater. Of course, he hadn't made a big deal out of then, so it couldn't very well make a big deal of it now.

"I had to pick up my son. It's all good. I bought a new one today."

"Oh, that's good. Then I can keep this one." She pulled the book he'd dropped out of her purse and wagged it slightly. He tried to reach for it, but she snatched it back, which annoyed him greatly. "Hey! You know what, keep it, it's yours," he said. Other than giving it back to his father, he truly didn't care at all.

"What's it about anyway?" she asked, plopping down next to him.

"Well, I wouldn't know because up until an hour ago, I didn't have a copy of the book," he said, putting the book back up to read as if not to be disturbed, something Autumn didn't seem to notice.

"Oh, so you don't know Santiago has met the fortune teller yet."

Tatum closed the book. "Autumn, don't take this the wrong way, but for the last two days—three, if you count this very moment—you have been one giant inconvenience. All I want to do is read this book. So if you didn't come to do the right thing and return the copy I left in your apartment, then please leave me alone."

He was silent as she shivered in jest at his cold response.

"Well, that was frosty."

"Autumn, I—"

"I wanted to give you back the book, but I also wanted to say thank you for yesterday. I know the last two days I probably haven't made the best impression, but I've just been trying to...I just...I just wanted to get you some coffee, if that's okay."

"I don't drink coffee."

"Okay then, how about tea?"

Tatum paused. She was determined to erase the poor impression she'd made, and that was commendable. Maye some tea would warm his icy demeanor.

"I could probably drink some tea."

"Okay, well, come on. I know this great place not far from here. It's quiet, and you can read your book."

Tatum nodded, and the pair got up, walking across campus in what Tatum assumed to be the direction of one of the nearby coffee houses surrounding the school. He was dying to ask her why she didn't sell her paintings—really, why such a talented artist wouldn't share her gift with the world and make a buck at the same time—but he knew it was a sore subject. Also, knowing that she was probably having the worst week she'd had in a while, he didn't want to press her. Instead, he asked about something they both had in common, at least until a few days ago.

"I know it's a big campus, but I've never seen you on it."

"I transferred from Reno."

"Is that where you're from?"

"No, I'm from Houston. My parents lived in Bellaire until my dad moved us to Austin when I was in the 7th grade."

"I feel you. So what are you going to do about school?" He watched as she looked at the trees as if to find the light between the leaves.

"You know, I honestly don't know. I mean, I'm probably too old to still be in college, and hell, I can't worry about that now. I just need to get my place together and figure out my triumphant return to the art world," she said, her sarcasm still intact.

He wanted to say something about how she could make a big splash in that art world. Maybe she hadn't conquered the art world, but he was sure she could. Hell, he'd be the first one in line to buy one of her paintings even if he didn't understand it. But he could tell the wound was still fresh, and so he said nothing more. Before the conversation turned awkward, they reached the coffee house. The Sutra. A place he'd passed before but never been inside. As he opened the door for her, he was impressed by the minimalist design. Everything was off-white, with a trace of gray in the middle of each design. The floors to the marble tables matched the tile on the floor and the paint on the walls.

"This is sweet."

"You have to download the app to order, but since this is my treat, take a look." He leaned over the woman's shoulder, inhaling the fresh remnants of lavender and vanilla in her curly jet-black hair.

"That's a nice shampoo."

"You like? Thanks. It's the one thing about having this natural—it doesn't look like it takes a long time to put together. Of course, it does."

"I'm sure of it. I'll have lemon and ginger tea."

"Okay, lemon and ginger for you and pure Colombian for me," Autumn ordered the beverages as the two took a chair next to one of the windows that captured a beautiful angle of the campus. For the first time since in the seven years he'd been here, he felt like a college student.

"So why *The Alchemist?*"

"Huh?"

"Why are you reading this book?"

"My dad recommended it."

"Are you two close?"

"We're working on it," Tatum said without offering a further explanation. His dad's life was hardly first-time-having-coffee-together conversations. "What about you? When you're not parking illegally, what are you doing?"

"Well, right now, nothing. I'll be honest—I just took a few classes to defer my student loans. I didn't care about a degree. I'm just trying to kick the can down the road. Other than that, I work in the museum district. There is a black art project I'm helping put together, which I guess I'll have more time to do since I don't have college to worry about anymore."

"Ok, where do you work in the museum district? The museum of fine arts? Is it the event going on with the Egyptian art because I-"?

"OK, damn it! I work at Paint & Sip."

"The Paint & Sip in the third ward? That's not really the museum district."

"I know. I don't know why I even said that. I just feel with school being gone, I needed a win. I didn't think you were going to press me on it. And how in the hell do you know about an Egyptian art exhibit?"

"It's the only one I wanted to go to. I'm sorry I pressed you, but no need to lie to me. I ain't nobody special."

"I know. I just feel like I'm too old to have this much spare time, you know? I liked having this time carved out. The campus always inspired me, and I don't want to leave. Not the classes. I could give a shit about them, but the camaraderie. I had really good people in those classes; now it's just me. So now I have to figure out what to do with this time. Hell. Maybe I'll get a dog or something. Maybe I'll actually spend my time and read this book again. It appears I have a free copy."

Tatum could tell the woman had a lot on her mind and needed a distraction.

"I tell you what, why don't we read it together? You said you've already carved out this time, and I've always wanted to be in a book club, so why not?"

He examined the woman, happy he made that offer no matter what her decision. Her smile was soft and her eyes earnest. He felt familiar with her.

"Cool. We'll do it. But next time you're buying the coffee."

6

LIFETIME

"Tatum, can you believe we finally did it?"

"Oh man...we're done."

Autumn and Tatum laughed as they realized they finally finished the book they started six weeks prior. Since their book club of two began, they found themselves doing less reading and more talking about everything from their views on politics, prior relationships, family history, just about anything of relevance two people could discuss when they were getting to know each other. They also realized they had a lot in common. While neither of them was looking for a relationship, their friendship had been catapulted above most friendships in their lives. Tatum truly enjoyed talking to her and developed a comfort level that allowed him to share his past and the past of his parents, son's mother, best friend, and his future plans. All that mattered was having the company of another adult, though both considered it a bonus to meet a person who saw the world as they saw it. She was funny, bold, and above all else, honest. He enjoyed talking with her about her current dating life and his lack of one. He laughed at the idea that the woman he wanted to strangle six weeks prior happened to be one of the coolest people he'd ever met.

"What are you thinking about over there?" Autumn said as he realized he was drifting.

"Oh man, I was just thinking this book isn't that long. If we would've just read three pages a day, we would've probably been done weeks ago."

"That's because you're long-winded," she replied, sipping the coffee she ordered from the third place they'd starting hanging out at since their club began. Tatum, caught off guard by her statement, had to respond.

"Oh my God, now you know you are Queen Chatterbox, right?"

"Are you serious? Now you know that out of the two of us, you're the talker."

"How am I the talker when I can't even get a word in?"

"Well, whatever you think, you're right. I know I'm right. We're moving on. So what are we going to read next?" she asked, overruling the option for any further debate.

Tatum scoffed at her smugness and replied, "Woman, I'm not reading anything else with you!"

"Why not?"

"Need I remind you your loud mouth got us kicked out of our spot?"

"What, Sutra? Please, that place was stupid. The only way to order your coffee is from an app. How dumb! I hope they go out of business. Now Elvin's was our spot."

Tatum glared at his new friend. In the last six weeks, he realized she was a master at deflection. He wasn't going to let that statement stand without adding a little truth.

"Elvin's didn't even have brown sugar. And as far as Sutra goes, you got to be kidding, right? When we first met, all you could talk about was that place!"

"Sutra? Please, that place was *your* idea." Tatum's eyes widened at the false accusation.

"Autumn, you know that shit's not true! We—"

"Okay, fine, whatever. It was my idea, it sucks now, and their coffee always sucked. How damn hard is it to make black coffee?"

"Making it for a normal person? Not hard at all, but making it for you? The hardest damn job in the world."

"And what is that supposed mean?"

"Autumn, we have never been anywhere, where you haven't either changed the order to something off-menu, or sent the drink or food back, and might I add, the only reason Sutra began to 'suck' is because they got that life-size Connect Four game, which you got the bright idea to challenge me in, and after a perfect thirty-and-o strea, finally realized you could never win so you decided to get us kicked out."

"A, you're a liar, and B, that had nothing to do with it!"

"Now you know that had everything to do with it! You probably have nightmares about me beating you in Connect Four. You're terrible. It's like you didn't even have a childhood."

"Excuse me, guys," their dialogue was interrupted by a member of the wait staff.

"My manager told me to inform you our other patrons have made a couple of comments about the noise over the last week or so. If you can't keep it down, we're gonna have to ask you to leave."

Tatum looked at Autumn blankly, who had already started to gather her belongings. She turned to the waiter and said.

"Tell your manager he never has to worry about our coins again and that you constantly undercook eggs."

Tatum stood up, fighting the urge to laugh as the two walked out of yet another coffee shop they had effectively been kicked out of. Without saying a word, the pair looked down the row and found the last coffee shop they hadn't been put out of. Brewers, a shop also within walking distance from campus. Without a word, they headed to the shop, although Tatum was dying to point out how they yet again were hoisted. It wasn't long before they were inside Brewers sitting at what would now effectively become their new spot ordering their usual drinks. Still, not a word was said, although Tatum's smile said it all. A point Autumn picked up on as the coffee arrived, and she finally said something.

"Go ahead, say it. It's all over your goddamn face."

He could hold it in no longer. He finally said something.

"Damn, you are really bad at Connect Four."

Tatum couldn't help but laugh, which made Autumn turn playfully defensive.

"Oh fuck you, Tatum, you weren't playing Connect Four as a kid. You were playing Connect Crack."

"Well, whatever we were playing, we knew how to put four in a row together," Tatum fired back as her bruised ego turned jovial. The two laughed at the shared memory. It *had* been six weeks since they first sat in that first coffee shop, and it was sinking in that they'd talked every day, often for hours. Then they'd call each other and talk until one of them went to sleep. She had proved once over she was not the person he first met—that rude, inconsiderate, and dismissive hipster. She was more than her first impression. He truly enjoyed her energy and intelligence, however sporadic it might be. She was also a good sounding board who knew all about Tatum's relationship with Johnny—to the point that she could joke about it.

"So—and I can't believe I'm saying this—but what do we do now that the book is finished?"

Tatum rubbed the bristles on his goatee. "I guess it's time for us to do a Q&A on what we took away from the book. That is if we're a legit book club."

"Well, since we are a legit book club with one book already under our belt, let me ask the first question. What do you think was the meaning behind the book, Mr. Clarke?"

He grinned at her playful imitation of a journalist asking a thought provoking question and rested his head on his chin as if to go along with the bit. The answer didn't hit Tatum until he started to respond. "I think...that's a layered question, but if I had to give one answer, it would probably be a synopsis of the human experience. Is God trying to see what true love would do if faced with impossible situations?"

"I got some of that, but I got more of a follow-your-heart vibe," she responded as she sipped her coffee.

"What about Fatima?" Tatum asked, taking his turn to ask an official book-club-like question.

"Oh man, she was the original ride-or-die chick."

"Facts."

"She told this man, don't worry about it, go to Egypt. I'll be here waiting on you, and he was riding a fucking horse. How long did that shit take?"

The two laughed as Tatum responded to Autumn's perspective on the book.

"She had his back, no question."

"She's a better woman than me 'cause soon as that horse galloped out of town, I'd have been at the well with someone else."

"Aww, that's messed up. You wouldn't wait for the love of your life?"

"Please, you think he's riding to Egypt from wherever the hell they were and not stopping to get his willy wet? These hoes ain't loyal."

Tatum laughed at the statement. It was the kind of honesty he'd come to expect from her.

She took a bite of the toast that came with her coffee and asked, "In all honesty, you think those relationships are real? Like, do people ever find each other like that?"

"Not with women like you running to the watering hole for the next guy soon as the last one hops on his horse."

They both laughed, ignoring the slight truth in his statement. She took another sip of her coffee and asked.

"So, final thoughts on *The Alchemist*?

"Whatever you put your mind to, put your grind to."

"And don't be a bitch."

The two laughed hysterically. As they laughed, she circled back around to making a point about the book.

"No, seriously. I think that the book taps on the point that we all limit ourselves by what was before us. And the truth of the matter is, we're here now. The rules from 1970 or even 1990 don't apply. That was then. We have to put things together and go after what we want actively."

"Which is why you need to submit your work to the art exhibit."

"Not this again."

"You are insanely talented you're going to get into that Egypt exhibit if you just app- "

67

"Not doing this shit with you now, Tate." Tatum shook his head. He knew she wanted no parts of this conversation, but he felt now was as good a time as any to have this conversation."

"Autumn, we just read a book that's all about chasing your dreams. You are a talented artist. Annoying, but talented. Seriously, you're incredible. So why aren't you giving yourself a shot for the rest of the world to know what everyone around you already knows?"

Autumn took a sip of her coffee and looked out the window. He knew there was more to the story, but none of it made any sense.

She put the cup down and said, "Remember the paintings on the wall at my loft? They all mean something to me. Years ago, I was going to sell the first one you ever asked me about, *Purple Haze.*"

Tatum was stunned. It was by far his favorite painting of hers and one he thought she should sell. But it was also her favorite, and he couldn't believe she ever considered parting with it.

"I was pregnant at the time. I had just got out of my first trimester —the 'scary' part—and the baby would kick and wake me up in the middle of the night. And since I was up, I would paint. It was uncanny. She was only calm when I was painting. So every night, or rather the wee hours of the morning, I worked on *Purple Haze* until it was done. I was so excited. I couldn't wait to show her when she got old enough. I mean, this is the painting we worked on together. When I finished that painting, I was over the moon, but Kaleb thought we should sell it. I told him I wanted to keep it because our daughter helped me make it. He agreed at first, or so he said because what I found out two days later is he made a few calls , and I come home to find out an art broker in our living room that was interested. Kaleb had the deal all set up and I reluctantly agreed but miscarried three days after I finished the painting." Autumn fought back the tears. Tatum had never seen her like this. He'd seen her upset, but that always came out as anger. Now she was sad, recalling the immense pain of losing her baby, and paused before she continued.

"I had a lot of hospital stuff I went through, but I don't want to talk about that. I'm just saying that to say when it was time to sell that painting, I couldn't. It was the only thing I've ever done with my baby.

It took me a year to pick up a paintbrush again and even more to gain the confidence to sell my paintings, so that's where I am. I keep thinking I could've shown Ezri this one or that one, and I can't let go of them."

Tatum reached out and took her hand, a sign that offered more support than anything he could say.

"I won't sell anything on my walls. Those are literal pieces of my heart. I draw inspiration from them daily. I know I should sell — hell, I need to sell. I got bills to pay. I just can't sell the important ones."

Tatum sat back and nodded. He didn't know the story behind the paintings on the wall, but he always knew they meant the world to her. Understanding why made him instantly regret all the times he pressed her to sell those paintings. She couldn't exchange fame for cash. She couldn't let a piece of her heart hang on someone else's wall.

"So *Purple Haze* was for the baby?"

"Ezri. We were going to call her Ezri."

"Ezri...that's beautiful. A name like that should inspire a beautiful painting. What about the others on the wall?"

Autumn took a sip of the now-cooled Colombian coffee.

"One me and my dad kind of worked on. One reminds me of my mom, and one— probably TMI—but I painted when I lost my virginity. It represents me becoming a woman."

"I see. So losing your virginity, Ezri, mom, and dad. That's four."

"Very good, Tatum. You can count. Now let's work on your primary colors and shapes," she said coyly.

"Okay," said Tatum, following her lead and trying to lighten the mood. "Um...what shape is an asshole? Oh, that's right. You're an asshole. Must be Autumn shape," he said with a broad smile before turning serious again. "The reason I was asking was you didn't make a painting for Kaleb?

"Fuck no! That clown wasn't important enough for me to waste paint on. He wanted me to make paintings of Tupac and sell them for 9.99 at the barbershop. I mean, I might not be the best artist in the world, but I'm worth more than 9.99."

Tatum laughed at the idea anyone would think the masterpieces he saw were worth only ten dollars.

"That's insane. The amount of work alone is worth ten times that."

"He's an idiot."

Tatum didn't doubt that. The supplies alone were worth ten dollars, and if the labor was worth ten times that, the sentimental connection to little Ezri made one painting priceless.

"What about the ones we brought in from school? And all the ones that were sitting on the floor."

"Why would anyone buy those? I don't give a fuck about them. They're assignments. I didn't breathe life into them like I did the others. I had to paint them," she responded bluntly.

"So that's why you don't sell those. I mean, we just got through reading a book about following your dreams, and all your work is dope as hell, and you just said you could use the money. Sell the pieces that aren't heirlooms."

She paused and looked at him, still uncertain why she hadn't already been selling her work. But his confidence in her work gave her the confidence to do it.

"You know, I never really put any thought into it, but yeah, I'll think about it. I'll go home tonight and organize them. But that's enough about me."

"Perfect. We can get you an Instagram profile and post all your artwork. You'll be straight."

"You're kinda useful, Mr. Clarke."

He nodded in a way to concede her statement. She was teasing him, but he remained focused on the compliment. He was kinda useful.

"What about you?" she said, reversing the question.

"Me?"

"Yes, Mr. Clarke, what is your dream? Isn't that what we were talking about? What would you be doing in a perfect world? Like if money wasn't an issue. You could just do something from the heart."

Tatum thought long and hard, taking a sip of his lemon-ginger tea.

"I think I don't know."

"Bullshit," Autumn said matter-of-factly.

"How are you going to say that?"

"Because I've been an artist all of my life. The one thing I know is that anyone who writes in his journal as much as you do has dreams." The words were blunt and off-putting but true. He wasn't sure how she was able to read through his façade so easily, but he respected the fact she paid close attention to detail.

"That's a good point. No one ever asks me about the journal. I don't think they notice."

"So before you take me all around the world with your answer, just tell me directly—what's in that notebook?"

Tatum's phone rang, interrupting his thoughts.

"Shit! It's already six o'clock? I'm supposed to be meeting Stone and my pops to hang out for a while with Solly."

"Now, wait a damn minute. You just gonna ignore the question? And what about crawfish? You said yesterday we were going to get crawfish today."

"I did say that, didn't I?" he said as Autumn cut her eyes in his direction. "My bad. I totally forgot. I'm—"

"I had my mouth all set on some crawfish, and you gotta cancel."

"Tomorrow?"

Autumn rolled her eyes playfully, picked up her phone, and began typing. Within moments, he got a notification on his phone. He unlocked the phone and read *Eating Mud Bugs with A.E. @ Kajun Kitchen 5 pm Central Time*

A second later, he got another notification. *Cancel, and you die.*

He smirked at the notion she already had the place picked out and laughed harder at the ensuing threat. She had a way about her as if every day were an adventure he had to appreciate.

"We'll leave from my house. I have an interview at this bar, but it shouldn't take long," she said as he gathered his belongings.

"Cool. Alright, I'm gonna head out to pick up Solly and get over there. I'll hit you later on."

"Peace," she said as she started to doodle on a napkin.

7

NOTHING EVEN MATTERS

*T*atum headed out of Brewers, walked a decent distance to his car, and drove over to pick up Solomon, who wasn't far from their new coffee shop. To his surprise, Solly was ready to go. He was always excited to see Pop-Pop.

When they reached the Santa Ana Rehabilitation Center, he found Stone parked out front talking to his hero, Johnny Clarke. Tatum watched Stone, a hardened drug dealer, act like a twelve-year-old kid in front of his father. As they approached, Stone turned to Tatum enthusiastically.

"Yo, Reverend, did you know that J.C. use to work with those Spanish construction boys back in the day?"

"Oh yeah, T.C. knows I know those Mendoza boys real well. Is Ernesto still wearing that Joop cologne? I had to stop wearing that after he bathed in it one day."

"Oh man, Rev, he is right. This dude been wearing that stank-ass cologne ever since I met him." Tatum chuckled along with the other two. It was good to see them both in good spirits.

"So where you coming from? Hanging out with art BAE?" Stone said.

"Art BAE? What the hell is that?" Johnny said, jumping in.

"That's what they call girlf—"

"Nothing, Pops. That's what they call nothing," Tatum said, cutting off Stone. He wasn't concerned about them teasing him for hanging out with Autumn. She was cool. But he didn't want Solomon to know he was dating anyone. He was determined not to introduce another variable into his son's life that way.

Johnny, picking up on the unspoken eye contact, followed along. "So... you um...painting now?" his father asked as Stone snickered.

"Not that it's any of your business, but it's not like that. It's strictly platonic."

"If you say so, Rev. All I know is I'm your friend—hell, I'm your best friend—and I ain't seen you in weeks. So must be more than that," Stone replied as he gave J.C. a high-five. Tatum fired back.

"I'm ignoring beige Kevin Hart over there and answering your question. No, I am not painting anything. We read the book you gave me in a mini book club. We finished this book you gave me," he said, handing back the original copy he had reacquired from Autumn.

"How many people were in this mini book club?" Stone interjected, pressing the issue as he always did.

"Two. It was just me and her."

"Rev, that's not a book club. That's a book couple." The two men laughed at Tatum's expense. He knew this wasn't going to ever end unless there was another topic.

That wasn't going to happen.

Tatum's eyes widened when he noticed J.C. examining a blue spot on the book a bit further.

"Yep, he's painting."

The two men laughed at Tatum while he postured to explain himself further, making him look guiltier in the eyes of public opinion. Stone, catching his breath, said, "Might as well fess up, Rev. Ain't nothing wrong with a little... artwork."

"Yeah, T.C., we're all men here. I need some paint in my life." The two laughed again until Solomon spoke up.

"Daddy, why does Pop-Pop call you T.C. and Uncle Stone call you Reverend?"

Tatum looked at both men. Stone and his father were excited by the question. There was nothing he could do to stop what was going to happen next.

"Aw, Rev! You didn't tell S.C. how you got the nickname, Reverend Clarke?" Stone said excitedly, kneeling to make eye contact with the child.

"You see, nephew, a long time ago, me and your dad were in high school, and on the first day, there was this bully who used to mess with all the little freshmen at the school, and he decided to pick on your dad. So—"

"But your daddy learned how to fight from a Marine and—" Johnny interrupted.

"It ain't your turn in the story yet, J.C. Can I tell it?"

"My bad, my bad. You got it, Stone."

Stone looked back at Solomon as Tatum rested his hands on his head and continued.

"So anyway, the bully wanted to pick on your daddy, but your daddy could fight real good—"

"Because a Marine taught him," J.C. interjected.

"Yes, because a Marine taught him, and so the bully tried to take your daddy's journal he's always walking around with because it looks like a bible, and he said, 'What are you, a reverend? What's in this book?' Well, all the kids laughed in your daddy's face. He was sad, but as you know, nobody touches your daddy's journal, so he got big, big mad, and your daddy slapped him around like, Tatum, what's that game we use to play with the big Sumo wrestler with the hands?"

Tatum rolled his eyes. He didn't want to be a part of the story, but he was in it now. Stone persisted.

"Rev, you hear me talking to you! You know the one, the big boy on that game. You know the one."

"E. Honda."

"Exactly! E. Honda. He slapped that boy one hundred times just like that," Stone said as he playfully punched Solomon in a ticklish fashion. "And when your daddy won the fight, the crowd went wild.

So I stood up on the table and said, "Who else wanna fu...I mean mess with Reverend Clarke?"

Stone was full-fledged tickling Solomon.

"But wait, that's not the end of the story. So then your grandpa J.C. said—"

"I'll take it from here, Kenley. You telling it all wrong."

"Okay," said Stone, who knew that when he got called Kenley, it was time to step aside like a little kid who'd done wrong. Johnny walked over to his grandson and rested his hand on his grandson's shoulder.

"So your dad got suspended from school because of this fight and by now, me and your grandmother had broken up. She started dating this sorry fake Nation of Isl—"

"Nothing to do with the story, Dad," Tatum said before this got out of hand.

"Right. My bad. So, well, your nana didn't know what to do. Tatum had got in trouble, so when I talk to your dad, he tells me all of what you just heard, and I realize he was defending himself. Now I haven't been around but ain't nobody gonna tell my son he can't defend himself. So, I go up to the school the next day and tell them I'm dropping off my son and am looking for principal, what's his name."

"Mr. Allen."

"Right. Old punk motherfucker."

"Dad!"

"My bad, my bad. You didn't hear that, S.C."

"That's the end of story time, S.C.," Tatum said, irritated by his father's outburst.

"Come on, T.C. You can't cut me off now. It's the end of the story!"

"Daddy, I want to know what happened."

Tatum buried his hand in his face. "I went back to school. The end."

"I want Pop-Pop to tell it."

"Yeah, he wants Pop-Pop to tell it," Johnny replied with a devilish grin. "He knows a good storyteller when he hears one."

"Daddy, please?" S.C. said, looking at his father with pleading eyes he didn't have the will to resist. Tatum let out a giant sight.

"Fine."

Tatum glanced at Stone, who was doubled over laughing as Johnny continued.

"Okay, so I gets up to the school, and that pu...uh...wimp, Mr. Allen, was like, 'Your son was punished for his actions. We have rules!'" J.C. said, impersonating the principal in the stuffiest voice he could muster while shaking his fist in the air as if he were in charge.

"Now, right about that time, a couple of the football coaches came up to try to be his little back-up like they was intimidating somebody. So there I was surrounded by a pack of hyenas—the principal and his two goons."

"Were you scared?"

"Heck no, I wasn't scared. I'm The Lion, and ain't no lion scared of no stinking hyenas." see what you don't know is that they use to call your Pop-Pop, The Lion."

By now, Solly was smiling from ear to ear.

"So you're a lion, like in *The Lion King*."

"Yeah, I'm like—who's the biggest, baddest lion in that movie? What's his name?"

"Mufasa," said Solomon, happy to know something his grandfather didn't.

"Yeah, I'm Mufasa. And you're my Simba," Johnny said with a proud smile as if ready to earn his title.

"Pops, you can't be Mufasa."

"Boy, how you gonna tell me who I can and can't be?"

"Dad, in the movie—"

"See, that's what I'm talking about. You always trying to tell somebody what to do."

"Dad! In the movie, Mufasa was Simba's father, not grandfather."

Oh. Then I'm Mufasa's daddy. Is he in the movie?"

"No, Dad, he—"

"Who the one that slapped those hyenas?" Johnny asked.

"That would be Mufasa."

"Then I'm Mufasa. You're gonna have to be someone else."

Tatum rolled his eyes and threw his hands in the air. "I can't believe we're debating movie consistency. Fine, in this imaginary world, you're Mufasa, Pops."

"Wait, I got it! You can be Mufasa 'cause they couldn't kill me. I'll be Mufasa's very handsome, very strong daddy. Yeah, I'm Mobutu. That's Mufasa's daddy, and he is bigger and badder than all the lions that ever was, so they couldn't even let him in the movie! 'Cause if I was in the movie, I would've slapped nine hyenas."

"Dad!"

"What?"

"Finish the original story!" Tatum said, trying to focus his father's attention back on the point before his tirade.

"Oh, right. Okay, so there I was, S.C.; me, Mobutu, the legendary lion, surrounded by these three measly hyenas. And this clown says to me, 'Mr. Clarke, please leave campus before you are forcibly removed.' So you know what I did?"

"What did you do, Pop-Pop?" Solomon's eyes were huge as he waited for the conclusion of a story Tatum figured he'd heard more than a thousand times. At least his father's part in it.

J.C. puffed his chest out and growled, "I looked all three of them dead in the eye and said, 'The only way I leave this campus is my son going to class or in handcuffs for breaking two jaws. So you got a choice—you can let my son go to class or you can figure which two of you is about to get some free dental work. Choose wisely.'"

He walked over to Stone, who was laughing at the top of his lungs as if he was about to give him a jab to confirm his truth.

"You really said that, Pop-Pop?"

"Damn straight, I told you, ya Pop-Pop is real! And your daddy was there! Tatum, tell the boy!"

"He said it, Solomon," Tatum said dryly, not wanting to add to the dramatic way the story was going.

"And you know what happened next??

"No."

"Your daddy went to school every single day!" Johnny said as Stone started laughing again, this time joined by S.C., who probably didn't entirely know what he was laughing at, but it was funny.

"When your daddy got sick one day. The principal called to say if he wanted to, he could come to school and get all the kids sick, just please don't send Pop-Pop up here."

Now even Tatum had to laugh. It was the truth. He couldn't understand then why the principal would call to check on one sick student, but he understood now why Mr. Allen never made eye contact with him in school.

"Pop-Pop, you think you could've beat up all three of those men?" Solomon asked inquisitively.

"I do. Like I said, your Pop-Pop was real, Solly," Johnny answered, still chuckling at the story.

He picked Solomon up and held him in his left arm.

"S.C., I'm not saying I haven't gotten lucky in a fight or two, but I was never worried about those chumps. You see, Pop-Pop was a Marine. We trained to handle at least a couple of guys, but that's not my secret. You wanna know why I know I could've beat up all three of those chumps?"

"Oh dear God," Tatum said, throwing his hands in the air.

"Yeah, Pop-Pop, tell me."

"'Cause when it's all said and done, I'm an old Louisiana boy, and that's all we do. Shit, we fought alligators."

"Dad!"

Tatum barked as Johnny went to dab up Stone with his free hand while still holding Solomon with the other. Stone was howling at this point and did a semi-dance jog to embrace J.C. Tatum had to laugh at his dad's analogy. In reality, he remembered the day very vividly, and his father's story was highly accurate. He mostly remembered his father had no fear in his eyes. In fact, he had an eagerness in his eyes, or as Johnny would put it, he was in full 'I wish a motherfucker would' mode. He also remembered all of the men looking visibly shaken, even though he thought Coach Haynes could have taken his dad. He outweighed J.C. by at least thirty pounds of muscle and stood two inches taller. Tatum learned what fear looked like in a man's eyes that day. When The Lion was in the building, no one was safe.

"I want to learn how to fight like you, Pop-Pop, so I can beat the bad guys up like 'Pow!'" Solomon said, swinging his little fist in the air.

"You won't need to fight, Solly," Tatum said.

"What the boy gonna do—read them to death?" Johnny interjected, objecting to his son's statement. "Yeah, S.C, I'll teach you. When I get out of here, I'm gonna teach you everything about everything."

"Don't get your hopes up, S.C.," Tatum said jokingly, something that clearly upset Johnny.

"What does that mean, son?"

"Nothing. It's just, you know, you got a way of letting people down." There was a silence after the statement.

"Hey nephew, why don't you hug Pop-Pop, and we'll go to the car and get some corndogs," Stone said, trying to cut the tension.

As Solomon hugged Johnny, Tatum remained behind. He knew his father had something to say, and it wasn't long before J.C. spoke his mind.

"You needed to say that right now?"

"Say what?"

"Oh, come on, T.C. You were a man when you said it, so own it."

Tatum repositioned himself squarely. He knew exactly what this conversation was about, and if Johnny didn't want to ignore the elephant in the room, neither would he.

"Okay, Pops. I don't appreciate you filling my son's head up with false hope."

"And what false hope, son? That I'm getting out of here?"

"No. That you'll be there for him," Tatum said.

Johnny shook his head and smirked.

"Yeah, I get it. You're upset, and I ain't expecting you to just be gung ho. But I'm going to be all I can to that boy—if you let me."

Tatum realized his father's words had sincerity. He was punishing him needlessly. It was time to move past it.

"I'm not upset, Dad. Just...look, I'm sorry I shouldn't have said it.

Can we get together this weekend and head over to Herman Park and throw the football?"

Johnny, the strongest man Tatum ever knew, become ginger.

"It's all good, son. Yeah, we'll get together."

Tatum decided it was time to let his own issues go. He gave his father a hug. It took a second, but Johnny returned it before the two men parted ways.

Tatum walked over and caught up to Stone, who had just gotten a corndog for Solomon from the food truck that remained in the area.

"Bro, you apologize to your dad for being a dick?" he said with a smirk.

"Stone, I don't need that shit from you," he said as he walked to his car and let his son into the back seat. After strapping him in, he closed the door and turned around to see Stone in front of him.

"You're too hard on him, man. Whatever kind of father you think he was, you can't just deny he just told a low-key *Lion King* prequel we'd both watch."

Tatum shrugged his shoulders as if to dismiss the statement. He started to move when Stone stopped him again.

"Rev, I know he wasn't the dad he could've been but trust me, he was better than not having a dad at all. Man, Johnny Clarke put money in our pockets and made sure nobody messed with us. To me, that's a dad."

"Johnny Clarke was a lot of things, but dad was never one of them."

"I guess I can't see him the way you do. In my eyes, the man is a legend, and if you pay close attention to his rehabilitation. He ain't smoking or drinking; he's reading. You should at least acknowledge he's trying. And if not for your sake, for Solomon's. Give him credit, my brother." And with those words, Stone shook his friend's hand and went to the car.

The words stuck with Tatum. Stone was right—he'd ruined a good afternoon that had nothing to do with his emotions. After he got home, he put Solomon in the tub and pulled out his phone. He searched his contacts for J.C.

My bad earlier, we good?

There was no response. He thought about his friend's words; maybe he was being too hard.

"We're good, son. I ain't no bitch, see you this weekend. Kiss my grandson."

He smirked at the comment. He didn't want to let his guard down, but his friend was right. His father was different, and it was time for him to recognize that. He got Solomon out of the tub and put him down for bed before laying down himself. As he laid down , his phone buzzed again. This time it was Autumn.

Crawfish! Tomorrow! Do. Not. Forget.

8

OLD TIMES

*T*he next day, as promised, he went to Autumn's loft, leaving Solomon with his mother. He figured he would be drinking a little tonight and didn't want to wake up early and be a parent first thing in the morning. As he parked next to her car, he noticed her car door was open. This was a peeve of his. She often left her car door wide open. He even found her asleep in her car late at night and didn't understand how or why she could be that reckless. He chalked it up to artistic creativity but still wished she'd pay attention to her surroundings more.

"This girl is crazy," he muttered to himself as he closed the car door. Then he discovered the loft door was partly open. "Oh, she's just trying to end up on *Law & Order* at this point."

He walked toward the loft's door and knocked. The force of his light rap moved the door open. Although he knew the door wasn't closed all the way, he was still surprised at how easily it opened. He decided to walk in since she was expecting him.

"Autumn?" he said aloud, slowly entering the loft. There was no answer. *Damn. Maybe something is wrong,* he thought as he crept into the living room. Half-worked paintings sat along one wall, but on her purple couch, one painting had been purposely destroyed, its canvas cut with a knife. He found this disturbing. In the almost two months he'd known her, he'd never known her to destroy any of her completed work. Something was wrong. He pulled his phone from his pocket and called her. Within seconds he heard the ring, but it was not through his phone. He scanned the area and saw her phone on the kitchen countertop, inches from the sink.

Tatum instantly raised his guard. She was usually glued to her phone. That was another of her annoying qualities. As he reached to pick it up, he detected movement out of the corner of his eye. He spun, ready to fight, when he breathed a sigh of relief and relaxed. She was in the backyard jumping on the trampoline. He headed outside to find out what was going on. She saw him and waved, never breaking stride. The closer he got, he could see redness in her eyes. Her hair was all over the place, and it appeared at least from what he could tell in between jumps her nose was red as if to indicate she'd been crying. She was clearly disheveled.

"Yo, Autumn, you okay?"

"I'm great," she responded, a statement that couldn't be true. He knew her well enough by now to know she was anything but *great*.

"Are you sure? Because you left the front door wide open."

"I'm fine. Why wouldn't I be? I'm a divorced college dropout with no direction who works at a Goddamn Paint & Sip to pay my extensive student loans. I'm living the dream!" she said. The fact that she jumped through all of this all just confirmed something was wrong.

Tatum walked closer to the trampoline, but even that failed to stop her. Instead, she spun, turning her back to him.

"First of all, you're not a college dropout. You are a graduate school dropout. There's a difference. Secondly, if you say nothing is wrong, like a good friend, I'm gonna pretend with you, but just know if you need me to be a *real* friend, I'm here to listen."

She said nothing. He took that as an indication to let it be and be the good friend he promised to be. He took off his shoes and got on the rectangular trampoline. Not saying a word, they watched the sunset. As the night's skyline took over, he decided to get her mind off of whatever was troubling her.

"So, I take it we're not eating crawfish?"

"You'd be correct," she responded, jumping more forcefully as if shutting out everything else. "Where is Solomon?"

"He's...with my...mom...She's gonna keep him for the weekend," he said, struggling to catch his breath. He wondered how long she'd been jumping and how long she'd continue to jump at this pace, but above all else, he wondered why they were jumping at all.

"Kaleb had his baby."

"Oh..." he said, realizing he now had the answer to his question. He also realized that now more than ever, she needed a *real* friend. He stopped jumping as she continued.

"I know you're not okay, but what can I do to help you get there?" he said, gingerly hoping she understood his true desire to help, to be available for her.

"I'm fine. All this time I spent trying to conceive with him, taking all kinds of hormones, fertility drugs, and whatever the hell they inject black women with, and he goes out and pops out a child. Another child."

Autumn stopped jumping and looked away in the distance as she continued to express what was troubling her.

"I mean, I was even okay with having his baby even though we weren't together. Fuck marriage, right? But the bastard wanted to do it right on paper, so we got married a second time even though we were living separate lives, and like a dummy, I went along with it. I knew marrying him again was a mistake."

"Wait...did you say again?" Tatum asked, caught off guard by her statement. "Are you telling me this is your second divorce from Kaleb?"

"Yep. I married him twice—once because we were young and didn't know any better, and I realized he was just gonna be an asshole. And the second time I had a hard time getting over losing Ezri. I didn't want to be out in these streets sexually. Honestly, I wanted a baby, and I think he did too since he felt it was his fault we lost her."

Tatum, confused by the last revelation, pressed the issue. "How was it his fault?"

Autumn laid down on the trampoline. As Tatum joined her, they looked up at the night sky's first few stars.

"When we were married the first time, I found out he was messing around, so I confronted him about it and—"

"He hit you." He watched as she traveled to a place in her mind he couldn't access and maybe never would. She looked distant, the pain on her face leaving her cold and distant.

"You'd think after that shit I'd be done with him forever, but I couldn't stop thinking about the nursery and the joy I had painting with her in my stomach. So somehow, I went from hatred to forgiveness to wanting another baby with this awful, nasty motherfucker. I felt owed, you know?"

Tatum was silent. He had empathy for her, but he knew, even that he had no idea where her pain began or ended even as a single parent. He put his hand on her shoulder as she continued to talk. A tear rolled out the side of her eye. He hesitated before gently wiping it away. That single act of kindness encouraged her to open up.

"The day you met me, I'd come from the fertility clinic to have another round of in vitro he was paying for. And then he told me he wasn't. It wouldn't be necessary. He said he was having a baby with someone else and wasn't interested in this arrangement anymore, which was completely on-brand for that selfish asshole, but I didn't see it coming."

She shifted her body weight to curl away from him. Tatum said nothing, waiting until she resumed her train of thought.

"You know what's so crazy? I asked him if he was sleeping with anyone else, and he'd say no, and I'd go take my STD test, and everything would come back clean, so I believed him. I told him I'm only sleeping with him for the baby, and if he decided to sleep with someone else, just let me know because, at this point, we had no reason to lie to each other. I didn't want to get back with him, and he didn't want to get back with me even if we were married."

"So you felt it was a violation."

"Him having a whole fucking baby while sleeping with me is a serious fucking violation! So if anything, that's why I'm mad. But you know what? If I'm mad at anyone, it's me because this is who the fuck Kaleb Washington has always and forever will be. Somebody said a long time ago, if someone shows you who they are, believe them, and he showed me who he was years ago." Another tear rolled from her eye. She sniffled, wiping it away and rolling onto her back to once again stare at the stars and allow Tatum to see the side of her face.

He didn't know what to say, but he knew he needed to say something. The best he could do were words of wisdom he'd heard from someone else. "Sometimes we forget the devil you know...is still a devil."

He slid over and hugged her as she buried her face in his chest to process her pain. He said nothing, and soon she was better, at least on the outside.

"It's a beautiful night," she said, composing herself. The stars were crystal clear against the sky, even though the chill of the cooling air on the trampoline mat and the evening breezes pressed against their skin to say hello.

"I messed up your sweater," she said as the tear-streaked makeup smeared his burgundy cashmere sweater.

"It's so dark I can't notice. Besides, I'm used to it with you."

The two chuckled.

"Autumn, I wish there was something I could say to make it all better, but there's no such thing. I do know that you will be okay in time."

She nodded and established her own space again. "I don't know why we were ever together."

"Well, it had to be something. I mean, you married him twice."

She chuckled, conceding Tatum's observation.

"If I think about it, I married him because he was the first guy to show me any real interest, and well, marriage was the endgame. You know, you're with someone for a while; it's not long before people start asking, 'So when are you tying the knot?' Or buy a cow, drink some milk' or whatever bullshit they come up with. And like idiots, we just nod and agree. I guess I did it for my parents."

"Did you love him?"

"I liked him, but *love*...I didn't know what that meant. Hell, I still don't. Does that make sense?"

Tatum studied the stars above them for a few seconds, but there were no answers there. Whatever she needed was here on earth. And he realized what she needed was more than a friend—she needed a confidant.

"Total sense. I didn't want to marry Monique. We dated for a few years prior, but by the time we got married, most of the life was gone from our relationship,"

"Then the better question is why did you get married?"

"Hell, I don't know, Tyler Perry," he responded, referencing the producer's movie *Why Did I Get Married?*

"The crazy part is we weren't even together. I was moving on, dating someone else, when one day I get a knock at the door, and it's Mo, telling me she's pregnant."

"And you believed her?"

"Not to sound like an ass, but hell no! As I said, we were over for a few months at that point. I never said anything during the pregnancy, but I knew she knew I thought it. Hell, the entire reason behind our split was some questionable texts and absent locations. I could never place my finger on it, but it never felt right. You know what I'm saying?"

"So why didn't you just wait?"

"I didn't have to. She was more than willing to take a blood test, and once I knew there was no question, I had to be a dad. You combine that with us going to her mother's church every week and the good reverend preaching every week about children out of wedlock—"

"The black guilt wedding."

"Exactly!"

"I feel that. Kaleb was kind of a black guilt wedding. It's crazy how we let people who already ruined their lives tell us the best way to ruin ours and blame it on God."

"Can't front. That was a mouthful you just said right there!" Tatum said as the pair chuckled at their misfortune when.

After a brief spell, Autumn asked, "So how did y'all meet?"

"Me and Mo? Oh man, we've known each other since high school. I went to high school for health professions and—"

"Wait, there's a high school for health professionals?"

"Yeah, it was if you wanted to go into some medical field, you would test, and that's the school you'd go to."

"So you've always known you wanted to be a pharmacist?"

"Well, not really..." Tatum replied with a puzzled look. It was the first time he'd thought about the question.

"You know, I think I didn't feel like I had a choice. I come from a hard-working family, and we had to get ahead, so my mother just wanted us to be professionals."

"Ha, the expectations of a hardworking black parent."

"What?"

"You know when parents kinda impose their will on you because their life was so hard, and they want you to have more than they did. You sacrifice what will make you happy for what pays well."

"Yeah, exactly. I hadn't thought about it like that, but it fits. I don't know if I ever thought about being anything. Medicine was just the only option. Hell, I hate blood. I even hate science, but I had to wear that white coat because everyone always said you can be anything. But then they only give you a few options, the first two being doctor or lawyer," he said, pausing to think about the new tangent they were on. As far as he could remember, being a doctor was the only option. He settled on pharmacy because he needed money sooner rather than later.

"So, how did you end up with Solomon?"

"She walked out one day. It was my first year of grad school. I came home, and she was gone; he was there, the rest is history. What was I supposed to do, you know? I bring you into this world. I'm gonna bring you through this world. Hell, I named him Solomon cause the original was supposed to be the wisest person who ever lived. I guess I wanted God to protect him in the event I couldn't. It might sound crazy, but maybe if he has a fondness for the name

Solomon, I figured if he hears Solomon Clarke, maybe my son gets blessed off the overflow."

Autumn sat up and looked at Tatum.

"What?" he responded.

"Tatum, that's...pretty fucking thoughtful."

"That's my cub. I protect him with everything I do."

"Are you ever mad at her for leaving?"

He watched as a shooting star passed through the sky and briefly diverted both of their attention before resuming his response.

"I used to be. But mainly now, I just feel sorry for her and Solly. It's like here I am every day getting to hang out with the coolest person on the planet. I get to play with him, feed him, watch him learn, and listen to his crazy jokes. She has no idea how truly dope her son is. If she did, she'd love him just as much as I do."

Autumn sat up and looked at Tatum, positioning herself to get off the trampoline.

"You know what? Fuck love, let's get drunk."

9

THAT'S WHAT I LIKE

It wasn't a long drive to Lucky's, an upscale bowling alley located in the heart of downtown, not far from Autumn's loft. While many people showed up to bowl, it was the drinks that brought people through the doors. They were strong, well made, and cheap. When they walked in, the dark ambiance was offset by the red neon lighting. There was a whimsical theme mixed with a nightlife vibe in the bowling alley, with all the floors in some way referencing getting "lucky" in sexual overtones. The example they were currently reading said, "Let her win if you want to score." Tatum and Autumn both laughed at the sexual innuendo. There were sayings like this all over the walls, each written as graffiti inside painted bowling pins.

Screwdriver?" he asked, referencing what he had come to know as Autumn's drink of choice.

"Make it a double," she replied. He nodded and went to the bar to pick up their drinks—a Screwdriver for her and pineapple, lemon, and vodka cocktail called A Day in Paradise for him. He ordered the drinks and located Autumn, who was securing a bowling lane. She waved him over to make sure he saw her. He carried the drinks over to lane ten just as she finished setting up the game. Tatum was first to bowl. He shook his head because, once again, she challenged him to a game she had no chance of winning.

"Autumn, you're already having a bad day. Are you sure you want to get your ass whooped in bowling?"

A statement that made her scoff. "The question is, are you ready to get embarrassed. This isn't Connect Four," she said, taking the drink out of his hand to take a large gulp. He shook his head and smirked. He wasn't a good bowler by any stretch—he just believed she had no competitive talent. It wasn't long after the first game and their third drink apiece that Autumn arrived at the same conclusion.

"We're gonna call that 3-0 my way," Tatum said, rubbing in his victories.

"You suck! Didn't you read the sign—Let her win if you want to score?"

"And if I was dating you, you'd be undefeated," he replied sharply.

He watched as Autumn took another sip of her Screwdriver and flipped him off. He could tell she was feeling good. Maybe too good.

"Are you sure you're okay?" he asked, slightly concerned.

"Tate, if there's one thing I can do, it's hold my liquor. You just worry about this ass-whoopin' you're about to take..." she said as she almost stumbled. Noticing he was watching, she added, "I'm feeling really good, though."

"Maybe you should slow down. You've already had two double shots, and this place makes their drinks really strong."

"I said I can hold my liquor, Tate! You just...get...bowl," she stammered.

He shrugged his shoulders and slid down the lane to start game four. He rolled, then got a strike.

"Not looking good for you already," he said, walking back as she looked off in the distance.

"You know...Kaleb never took me on a date. All those years we were together. Sure we ate, and we went to functions. But a date—I'll pick you up at 7:00 pm—it never happened."

"Damn, not even to the movies?"

"Not even to the fucking movies," she replied. "Why did men stop taking women out on dates?"

"I can't speak for all men, but I took my ex out."

"I'm sure you did. You probably had date nights and shit, and she never appreciated it. Probably just took it for granted to have fun with no expectation. I'm not saying this is a date, but this feels good just to have someone to have a good time with...to talk to. I'm just saying the extent of every conversation with your spouse shouldn't be what we gon' eat tonight."

"I hate that fucking shit!" Tatum yelled in excitement.

"That is the most unimaginative, overused statement in all things relationship! I could see Adam asking Eve, 'Ugh, what we gon' eat?' And that bitch was like. 'This apple, motherfucker! Here, don't ask me that no more.'"

Tatum laughed as he chimed in. "It's like all we do is eat and argue."

"Hell, sometimes you even argue about what to eat."

"And what's the point of that when we both know we're gonna end up eating tacos?"

"Because we just had tacos!" Autumn said. Tatum started laughing about the tangent they were on.

"My pops always says any good relationship make sure you have food, have fun, and have sex. When you lose those things, that's when the problems start," he said as he sipped his liquor.

"Your dad's important to you, isn't he?"

"Who, J.C.? I wouldn't go that far. But you know, every now and then, he'll have a point."

"You quote him a lot."

Tatum nodded, realizing what she said was probably true.

"Like I said, he'll make a valid point now and then." He watched as she rolled yet another gutter ball. At this point, the competition segment of this night was over.

As she came back and sipped her drink, she said, "I wish I had that connection with my dad, you know?"

Tatum picked up the drink he had been nursing since this started as Autumn searched her thoughts while waiting for her ball to be returned.

"It just feels like I could never please him. Like, I love him, and I know he loves me, but he judges me for-I don't know—maybe not being him and getting into structural design and working a nine to five. Or maybe even because I'm not as good an artist as he was, or is. I don't know."

"Your dad was an artist too?"

"Yeah, he was an amazing artist. Growing up, all of us painted. I used to beg him to take me to the art galleries with him, but he always gravitated towards my siblings, especially my sister. She's an art critic now, and I'm proud of her, but he treats her like royalty."

"And you're jealous of that?"

"No, not really. It's just out of the three of us, she and my brother have all been able to find their way, but with me...hell, I'm not even sure if he thinks I have talent. All I can hear him saying is, 'How much longer are you going to be working at this Paint & Sip?'"

Tatum was silent. He often wondered why she was so enthusiastic about working for a place that limited her ability so much, but he could tell this wasn't the moment to interject his thoughts. Instead, he asked a more probing question.

"Is that why you don't sell your art?"

"I don't know. I want to sell my work, but deadlines, expecta-tions...Let me say this—I'll never sell the work on my walls. *Purple Haze, Water Queen, Sun Goddess,* and *Scarlet*—I call that collection pieces of my heart, and they are the most meaningful pieces I've ever created. They are going to my art studio when I make it one day. But if I had to put my finger on it, I would say that's why I don't sell the rest of my work. I'm sure he'll criticize it or tell me I need to go back to school so I can get into structural design like him. Which is crazy because he's so talented. But he spent all these years basically being an engineer building buildings and never seemed happy doing it."

"You know, it was a different time. We didn't have the opportuni-ties we have now. I'm sure he was just doing the best thing he could do to feed his kids. Hell, I'm not sold on pharmacy. I just took it because I knew I could take care of Solly."

"I get that, and believe me, it worked. My siblings are all very accomplished. My brother's a lawyer, and my sister is a big-city art critic, and then there's me: the wayward child always making the wrong decision and wasting her talent as a Paint & Sip bitch."

"Autumn, you know you're more than that."

"It's okay with me if I'm not. I like what I do. Art is in my blood, just like it's in his; he's just forgotten that. If you ever see his buildings, the ones he's designed, they're beautiful. I just don't know why we don't connect on this level. When I try to share that with him, all I get is scorn and rejection."

Tatum nodded, processing her words. This was a sensitive subject, and he wanted to tread lightly. After a brief spell, he responded.

"I think all parents want their kids to be some version of what they have found to be successful. Maybe he wants what's best for you. Maybe he's jealous because you have the freedom he's always wanted. Both seem plausible." Tatum leaned against the wall near their bowling station, giving her time to roll her all and knock down two pins on the end. At least it was better than a gutter ball.

"Yeah, well, he doesn't have any reason to be jealous. He's amazing! He designed this recreational center in Austin. I was in high school when it opened, and it was so awe-inspiring. I tagged it with graffiti to show my love for it, you know, like I was big into graffiti back then. When he found out, he was livid. Told me that it was an embarrassment and that I need to do better things than play with crayons. Which is crazy because he used to work on art all the time when we were young."

"But only you know that. How many works of art has he never had time to finish because of some work deadline? Because his kids needed him to be somewhere. You can love somebody and want the best for them and still be envious of their circumstances, and parents do it a lot. They often see their kid doing things they dream of and want to know what it's like. My pops always wonders what it's like for me working for a corporation. It wasn't his path, but he talks about it more than me. It wasn't my dream or anything—just what paid my bills."

Autumn took a final sip of the drink she was working on. As she put it down, she responded, "Well, it's always been my dream that I put my artwork in a studio so my dad can see it, and I can show him 'Look, I'm not a fuck-up, and you're gonna have to accept that I'm a great artist...' but he'd probably just find another way to criticize me. I know he loves me, but why doesn't he love me the way I feel like he should? Everything is just contrary, and sometimes you just want a win, you know? There are no wins with my dad." The playful atmosphere had become tenser. Still, this was a long cry from thinking about Kaleb. Tatum decided to press the issue.

"I feel that. Do you think you're in some ways looking for your father's approval?"

Autumn picked up her bowling ball and rolled her first strike since they started playing. That small victory fired up her competitive spirit and made her more combative.

"I don't know. Do you think in some ways you're looking for yours?"

The statement made him pause. In his mind, he was numb to his dad's antics, yet there was a thread of truth in her statement. The longer he thought about it, the more he began to agree with Autumn.

"In some way, I'm always looking for my father's approval. I think whenever he left the house, it just did a number on me."

"And my dad being in the house every day did a number on me."

Tatum smirked at her last statement and took a sip of his drink that was now taking its effects.

"It's ironic. You grew up with your dad in the house, and I grew up never knowing if my dad was alive, and we're both looking for something from them. I don't know what that's about, but I do know this. You're a hell of an artist, and the world should see your work, even if your dad can't see it."

Her emotions were all tangled. Everything she'd been through with her ex-husband, losing the baby, and still wanting a relationship with her father bothered her deeply. Tatum wanted to console her, but he wasn't sure if that was possible—or that she'd let him.

He decided to break up the emotional entanglement by rolling the ball.

"Boom! Strike! Game over! Now, do you want to concede the fact I beat you in every game we play?"

"I'm having a whole episode over here, and you still couldn't let me win?"

"Hey, this is Cobra Kai. No mercy," he said as he smiled. Somehow that lifted her spirits—at least her relationship with Tatum was consistent, if still frustrating.

As they finished the game, they signed their tab and were going to leave when Autumn saw a life-sized Connect Four game. She looked at Tatum.

"Autumn, you do not want this smoke."

"Best two out of three," she said anxiously.

"You just got mopped up in bowling; now you want another ass-whooping?"

As he was talking, he spied a bar across the street—a lounge called The Blue Lion.

"Let's go over there. Save you some embarrassment and listen to some music," Tatum suggested, pushing an alternative to beating her again.

"What?"

"Come with me. We gotta go there."

He grabbed her by the hand without thinking and headed toward the exit. He had not been to a lounge in years, but since he didn't have to watch Solomon for the whole weekend, he wanted to make the most of the night. He'd thought that ever since the trampoline, and he didn't want the fun to end just yet. There was an excitement in the air he hadn't felt before. For the first time in a long time, he was carefree.

One look at Autumn, and he knew he wasn't alone in that feeling.

After stopping to show the bouncer their IDs, Tatum tugged her forward with child-like enthusiasm. Once inside, Tatum was pleasantly surprised by its spaciousness. It looked much smaller from the outside. The lighting was true to the name—the entire ceiling was made out of blue fluorescent light bulbs, patterned in the shape of a lion, that gave the entire club a blue hue.

"Sweet," Autumn said as they made their way into the middle of the lounge.

The furniture was a series of modern black couches spread around the walls and metallic blue barstools near the drink area. Drink tables surrounded the black hardwood dance floor—also shaped like a lion's head and accented by dozens of blue lights. A stage for live performances sat near the rear of the club adjacent to the bar, where a ginger-brown-skinned man sang an up-tempo neo-soul song.

"He sounds incredible! Who is that?" Tatum asked rhetorically, impressed by the artist's stage presence and talent. He was caught off guard when Autumn provided an answer.

"That's Preston Cole. He's kind of the hottest thing in Houston right now."

Tatum replied as he nodded to the man's voice, "Man, he sounds really good."

"Well, enjoy him while he's around. He's supposed to be working on an album, but my girl Lawanda told me that his record label is about to drop him because he hasn't turned in any good music. He's great at the covers of Jodeci or Boyz II Men, or even Brian McKnight, but his original stuff isn't cutting it."

Tatum listed as the man started singing *Stay* by Jodeci, a throwback to the '90s.

"Well, while you have your man crush, you want anything to drink? My treat," Autumn said.

"Yeah, I'll take a Crown on the rocks." Tatum watched Autumn walk over to the bar and started flirting with a guy who shortly after bought her two drinks. After he handed them to her, he headed off.

"Here you go." Tatum took a sip of the drink, still processing what just occurred. He watched the man glance over in their general direction as Autumn handed him his crown and coke.

"Did you just get drinks off that man?"

"Sure did. I can't afford these high-priced ass drinks."

Tatum's eyes widened at her candor. "Autumn, what in the hell is wrong with you? "

"Oh, please. Anyone in this club is here to fish. Sometimes you catch one, and sometimes you don't. He knew the risk."

Tatum couldn't help but chuckle at her rationalization as she sipped what had to be her sixth Screwdriver of the night, now in a taller glass than what she was downing at the bowling alley.

"Autumn, are you sure you should be drinking?"

"Should you be, lightweight?" she said, guzzling from her glass as if to make a point. Tatum shrugged his shoulders.

"When in Rome," he said as he finished his drink. He reached the bottom of the glass when Bruno Mars' *That's What I Like* came on.

"Oh, this is the joint right there!" she screamed.

Without hesitation, she grabbed Tatum's hand and pulled him onto the dance floor. Tatum glanced as the man who bought the drinks staring at the two of them, more than slightly agitated. Tatum didn't care—he was having fun. The two danced as if the night was theirs, and for a moment, time itself was theirs. He couldn't recall having this much fun with anyone. The longer the song played, the more he loosened up. His friend embraced the moment too, forgetting about the worries that brought her out for a night on the town in the first place. She was finally relaxed.

"Let's take a shot!" she yelled in his ear over the music.

"Cool. What do you want?"

"Cuervo." She replied. Tatum left the dance floor and ordered two chilled tequilas at the bar. As the drinks came, he looked over and noticed Autumn dancing between two men. He made eye contact and was slightly annoyed.

He wasn't jealous. After all, they were friends, but being left to hold a drink for a woman he wasn't dating partly bruised his ego. He now understood fully how the guy who bought his drink felt. He was about to drink his shot when he heard a soft sensual voice in his ear.

"Well, that's awkward."

He turned around and saw a beautiful, deeply melanated- woman about five-foot-seven with high cheekbones, full rouge-colored lips, and the complexion of dark mahogany.

"You saw that?"

"I did. The second you turned around, one of those guys asked her to dance. She didn't say no." Tatum brooded on that statement for a second before the woman continued. "Is that your girlfriend?"

"If that were my girlfriend, she wouldn't be my girlfriend anymore...but nah, we're just friends."

"Good. Then it won't be awkward if I have that shot in your hand with you."

Tatum examined her again. Taking in her striking dark ebony frame in a fitted spaghetti-strapped blue dress, his male instinct kicked in. He turned back to Autumn, who was still dancing with the two men and having a good time. She had clearly forgotten he was gone. Or coming back.

It was every man for himself.

"Yeah, we can do that."

Tatum handed the vixen the other shot of Cuervo, and they lifted their hands in the air to commemorate the shot before drinking it.

"Whooo, that burns," the woman said as Tatum ordered another round while watching the woman tap her neck rhythmically to indicate the alcohol burned her throat. He watched her watch him as he looked at her lips. He looked up and smiled.

"So now that we've had this shot, you care to tell me your name?" he asked.

"I'm Nairobi. It's nice to meet you—?"

"Tatum. And the pleasure is mine. Nairobi, as in Kenya, I'm assuming?"

She smiled as she responded. "On my mother's side. My daddy's from Georgia."

"Kenya, so, that's where this overflow of melanin comes from."

The woman smiled, taking in his compliment.

"You know, every time I tell a man in a club my daddy's from Georgia, they say, so that's where that peach comes from, but you went the other way. Kudos. I like it. Guilty as charged. And you?"

"Well, I'm a good ol' mix of West Indian and Louisiana plantations, so take your pick," he said, smiling as she returned the action. They both took the second shot, and she performed the same rhythmic motion to the neck. Tatum started to lean in as she picked up the flow of conversation.

"So, Tatum, have you've gone to Kenya?"

"I've gone several places."

"Really, like where?"

"I'll tell you that on the condition that I tell you on the dance floor."

"I've never danced with an island man before. It's fabled that you really know how to move your hips."

"Only one way to find out."

Nairobi smiled, offering no resistance. Tatum extended his hand as the woman gathered her clutch purse and led her to the dance floor. He pulled her in close enough to put his hands on the Georgia side of her family while looking into the eyes of the Kenyan side and told her about the places he'd been. She moved in closer, allowing his hands to fall naturally on the full crest of her backside. "Mmm, Georgia on my mind!" he said, causing her to laugh at the Ray Charles song reference.

As they danced, he saw Autumn had now gone from two men to one, and she was already disinterested in him. She looked at Tatum, crinkled her nose, and rolled her eyes to show her displeasure. Tatum chuckled and suggested with his eyes she examine Nairobi. Autumn made the same face she had a second ago. He ignored it and danced. He couldn't help it. Nairobi was sensual, pushing her body on him as he moved his hips into hers as Preston Cole crooned *Get to Know Ya* by Maxwell. The song was extended by the band, and Tatum soon started to feel a connection between himself and the dark-skinned beauty. When the song ended, he wanted to continue the conversation. He leaned in to whisper in her ear.

"I want to get to know you better. If you'd like to do the same, I'd love to buy you another drink. Will that work for you?"

Nairobi smiled, put her hand on his chest, and leaned forward.

"I'm not going anywhere," she said and headed toward the bar. She was feeling him the way he was feeling her, no question about it. He headed to the restroom and thought about making sure he was freshened up from the heavy amount of drinking he'd already done. He went to the bathroom and examined himself once over.

I'm trying to tap that ass tonight, he thought to himself. *I just need to get her out of here and... oh shit. Autumn!* He'd forgotten all about her in his hunt. No sooner had he had that thought than his phone buzzed

Kinda messed up you left me.

His eyes widened. "Oh, this heifer," he said as he replied to her.

You were doing you, so I did me. I'm just doing it better than you do you. :-)

There was no response. He smirked at his punchline and cleaned up in the bathroom to go talk to Nairobi.

When he came out, he headed to the bar, and to his surprise, Autumn was talking to Nairobi.

What in the hell? If this woman fucks this up for me...

His worst fears were confirmed as Nairobi's face soured, and she walked off before he could reach the bar. Tatum, confused, looked at Autumn, who picked up the drink intended for Nairobi and handed him the other one.

"What? I was thirsty," she replied. Tatum looked at her and looked at Nairobi as she walked off.

"What did you tell her?"

"We were just having girl talk."

He motioned towards Nairobi walking out before looking at Autumn with contempt.

"Okay, so just what in the hell did you say to her in this girl talk?"

"She asked if we were together, and I said no, but neither were you and your wife."

His eyes widened. He looked at her with agitation and bewilderment as she continued to sip the drink intended for his would-be catch of the night.

"Motherfu...Autumn...I don't think...there is a... *dick*...big enough on this entire earth to handle the amount of cock block you just applied to that situation!"

"She wasn't your type, no way."

Tatum looked at Nairobi, taking the entire state of Georgia with her, and pointed in her direction.

"Autumn, that ass in that dress is definitely my type. Why do you care anyway? Where are the two-step twins?"

"Those guys I was dancing with? Were you jealous?"

"Please. First of all, it took two men for you to get over the moves I put on you out there, so not worried in the least."

"Okay. Liking the confidence and the jealousy."

"Not jealous. Why would I be?"

"'Cause you missed my dance moves," Autumn said playfully as she started to dance in his direction. As she moved, she stumbled, spilling the rest of her drink and almost falling before Tatum caught her.

"Okay, the room is starting to spin," she said.

"Wait, what?"

"That liquor was stronger than I thought. I need some food."

"So you want to go?"

"I do, but I want to get that guy's number."

"Well, which one do you want to do more?"

"Leave because if I don't, I'm gonna probably throw up."

"Yeah, probably over that guy's number. Alright, let's get out of here." He took her arm to escort her out before he realized something. "Wait, I'm gonna have to order an Uber. I'm not good to drive either."

"Tatum, I..."

The liquor was catching up to her quickly. She was drunk, alright. He looked over to see one of the guys she was dancing with start to head in their direction like a wolf circling for the kill. Tatum waved him off as if not to play games. The man paused as Autumn regained her balance.

"Tatum, I'm not feeling good."

"I know. Let's get out of here," he said, assisting her to the exit. Their good time tonight had come to an end.

INTIMATE FRIENDS

"What did you do to me?" Autumn moaned in the back of the Uber. After the amount they had to drink, he decided it was better to just pick up his car later and get home safely. But as Autumn started to feel the effects of eight Screwdrivers, he realized nothing about this night was going as planned.

"Me? What in the hell are you talking about?"

"Yes, you. What did you put in those drinks?"

"You're kidding, right? I didn't put anything in those drinks. You just had eight of them, that's all."

"Then why did you let me have eight?" she bellowed.

The conversation had caught the attention of their Uber driver, who decided to investigate if everything was okay instead of paying closer attention to the road. This driver clearly could not do both at the same time.

"My man, you want me to drive?" Tatum asked, an insult the driver let slide, still hoping for a good tip.

"Hey buddy, is she gonna be okay?" the Uber driver asked as Tatum fed her more water.

"She's fine. She just needs some food," he responded, somewhat annoyed by the inquiry.

"Oh my God, Whataburger biscuits sound so good right now. I need some Whataburger." Autumn interjected in a drunken stupor.

Tatum looked around. They were sitting at a light, and to his good fortune, a Whataburger waited for them at the next intersection.

"Hey, pull in to the—"

"Sorry. If you want changes, you have to add it to the route." The driver's cold response flustered Tatum who decided to let it be known.

"Oh, just thirty seconds ago, you were concerned for her well-being, but now you can't just pull in right here?"

"You gotta add it to the route, bud."

"Unbelievable," Tatum said, pulling out his phone. The alcohol was also weighing on him, but his thumbs managed to change the route on his blurry screen.

"What do you want?"

"Um, get me the biscuits and a gravy and sandwich combo...Oh and...and pancakes and hash browns. And...um...a regular Whataburger combo with...with a sweet tea!"

The amount of food caught him off guard.

"Uh, you eating for two?"

"Just get the fucking food."

Fuck, he thought. This night was going so well. It wasn't long ago he was about to line up a potential rendezvous with a chocolate bombshell. Now he was in an Uber with an attitude, and a drunk woman hung up on her ex-husband, cursing at him for hash browns. *Not the night I planned at all.* He thought to himself. As they pulled up to pay, the driver pulled to the back window. The cashier handed Tatum the food and asked for payment.

"That will be $31.72."

"Okay, one second. Hey, Autumn, where is your card...Autumn?"

But Autumn was fast asleep.

This motherfucker...

Tatum looked at the Uber driver, who clearly regretted taking the ride, and halfheartedly grinned. He pulled out his card and paid for the food.

"No eating in the—"

"Wasn't planning on it, sir. Just get us to the address. Thanks," he said, cutting the guy off. While Tatum knew the man was agitated, he was still paying him and didn't want or need his two cents about anything. The ride was much more subdued now that she was knocked out, although the driver still glanced back several times to make sure Tatum didn't violate the rule he'd just informed him of. Tatum rolled his eyes and looked at his phone. It wasn't long until they were at her loft. He grabbed her purse and took the food inside, and came back to help her out of the car,

"Autumn, you gotta walk, homie."

Ding. He got a notification from Uber.

Terrible customer. One star.

"Oh, this night went from awesome to aw hell real quick," he said as he decided to just carry Autumn since she was struggling to get to the door. With her in his arms, he walked into her living room and placed her on the couch. He looked at her with the contempt of an annoyed friend.

"I can hold my liquor, she said," he murmured, even though he was starting to have a hard time holding his own liquor, but at least he had thirty-one dollars of fast food no one would eat. He decided to make the best of the scenario. Since she was passed out and wouldn't need the food, he headed to the kitchen. That's when he heard a thud. He turned around and scanned the living room. Autumn wasn't on the couch anymore.

"Autumn?" Getting no response, he followed a noise coming from the bathroom. She held her liquor as long as she could but was now letting it all go.

"Aw hell," he said. She was lying on the floor, heaving up whatever she had left.

She mostly made it to the toilet, but he was certainly going to have to clean up, starting with her.

He helped her off the tile and turned on the shower.

"Okay, sis, I need you to undress and put some water on you. I'm gonna get you a BC powder, make you some lemon and ginger tea, and we're gonna eat, and maybe that will settle your stomach. While you're doing that, I'll clean up this mess."

As he helped her up, her eyes glazed over, and she asked, "Tatum, why haven't we hooked up yet?"

The question unnerved him. She was obviously drunk, and this was no time to act on that question. He responded as directly as he could.

"Well, let's see...Such a long list, but if I had to choose, I'd say:

A) because we're friends.

B) because I'm married.

C) because up until two months ago, you were still sleeping with your ex-husband, who you just found out is having a baby, and you're hurt beyond measure.

And D) all of the above."

He checked the temperature of the water for her as she continued to wander in her drunkenness.

"You haven't been married in years," she said stammering.

"I haven't been with my wife in years. I'm still married."

"It's a formality."

"No, it's...Why are we talking about this? You don't want me, and I don't want you."

Autumn looked at him in the way she always did when her gears were turning. It typically meant she was either on the verge of genius or a terrible idea.

"Whatever it is," Tatum said, hoping this wouldn't go any further, "it's too late, and I'm too tired and—"

"But what if, okay, just hear me out. I mean...I don't want you, but I'd fuck you. The way you were salivating over that girl at the bar, you're horny as fuck, and I'm horny as fuck."

"Autumn, you know the only turn-on happening right now is one for the shower and faucet. Now wash your ass and brush your teeth and we're not gonna speak of this again," he said with authority. This night had run its course, and he was ready for it to end.

"Okay, I just need some water."

"Get in the shower. I got you."

He walked out of the bathroom and turned on the tea. Once she was done and in her bedroom, he came back to clean up the mess she made. As he was giving the tile a final wipe down, she walked in, apparently feeling better.

"I got some sweats and a T-shirt you can fit. I was gonna give them to Kaleb, but...they're yours if you want to shower," she said, tossing them in, slightly embarrassed.

He smiled and replied, "Soon as I'm done cleaning up your insides, I planned on it. Drink that tea and take your ass to sleep."

A shower would clear his mind, so he agreed and took the gray sweatpants and white muscle shirt and placed them on top of the newly cleaned toilet. After inspecting the area, he jumped in the shower and allowed the entire day to roll off of him. He was still hungry, but more than anything, he regretted not getting Nairobi's phone number. He knew he should be mad at Autumn, but for some reason, he wasn't. In fact, he was chuckling about it all.

"A day in the life of Reverend Clarke," he said as he got out of the shower and began to dry off with one of the towels he found in the hamper. After putting on the sweatpants and T-shirt, he walked out of the bathroom, refreshed but tired. He wasn't going to Uber home tonight. He opened the bedroom door, expecting to find Autumn asleep.

"Hey, I'm gonna cra—"

He heard what sounded like a muffled moan coming from her beneath the large blue blanket she was under. She was drinking the tea he gave her, but she was hiding something else. He wasn't sure what, but he knew she was startled by his presence. *Was she watching porn?* He wasn't sure if she was. Nor was he sure what to say as she looked blankly at him.

"Did I interrupt something?" he asked.

"Um...no, I was just um..." The moans under the blanket got louder and faster. She was definitely watching porn.

"Having a moment? I get it. I thought about the same thing ever since you cock blocked Nairobi."

"You think you could've gotten her to sleep with you tonight?"

"I would've liked to have tried. Thanks for that, by the way."

"Like I said, she wasn't your type."

"Well, whatever type she was, it don't matter now—I got blue balls and... look, I'm gonna grab the couch so you can do what it is you were about to do," he said as she laid in bed, embarrassed about the muffled sounds coming from her phone. She took it from underneath the covers and turned it off.

"You made it all weird now," she said as the two laughed. As he was about to walk away, she called to him. "Tatum?"

"Yeah?"

"I'm sorry about earlier. As you can tell, I'm just drunk and horny."

"Woman, I know how it is when you're drunk. We're good. Have a good night." He didn't get a step before she called to him again.

"Tatum?"

"Yes, Autumn?"

"Could you...just lay next to me? I don't want to sleep alone."

Her words gave him pause. He looked at her. It all made sense—the excessive drinking, the desire for quick sex. She was hurt and needed an outlet. He thought about how he felt the first night Monique left and how lonely he felt. Right now, she just needed to be reassured everything was going to be okay. He nodded and climbed into the bed. As she made room for him, she gave him the smile of a deeply happy person. She hugged him and lay on her back, looking toward the ceiling. Her breathing was slow and regular, the sign of a person at ease.

"I'm gonna have a headache in the morning," she said, showing signs of sobering up.

"You didn't take that BC powder I put next to the tea? You're gonna need it."

"I did. Is it gonna work?"

"Part of my post-game ritual. You'll be fine," he responded.

She repositioned her curly, jet black hair on the bed and turned to face him. "Tate, you're a hell of a friend if I've never told you that. Nobody would've done for me what you did for me tonight. And I mean all of it—you're here listening to my problems, you helped me move, and you just let me talk and talk. And I appreciate that because you just care. You're decent. What I'm saying is thanks for coming out with me tonight."

He felt the sincerity of her words and used his hand to punch her in the arm playfully.

"You would do the same for me."

"Hell no, I wouldn't. That's why I'm saying thank you now. I don't ever expect to return this favor."

The two laughed, recognizing the truth in her words. Not only wouldn't she return this favor, but he also hoped never to put her in the position where she had to.

"I'm just thankful, that's all," Autumn said. "I know you got your own problems—you don't need mine."

"I needed to blow off steam too, you know."

"Yeah."

The pause in their conversation allowed Tatum to push it a bit deeper.

"Do you still love him?" Tatum asked. She shifted closer to him before responding to the question.

"No, not at all. I've been thinking about this. Now, don't get me wrong—this really upset me—but do you know what the one thing I've been feeling all night, and I couldn't put my finger on it until just a moment ago, was...relief. I just don't have to deal with his shit ever again."

"I know that feeling. When Mo first left, I was hurt, but I felt the same way."

"Why don't you think she's asked for the official divorce?"

Tatum shifted his body weight; it was a question he'd asked himself from time to time but never put too much thought into. He looked into his friend's eyes and responded.

"I don't know. Just one of those things we haven't gotten around to. I think there was a time I thought maybe we'd work it out, but that's passed. I've just been focused on school all these years. She shows up every now and again to see Solly, but I think she's just trying to figure it all out. To keep it real with you, I'm not even mad anymore. It hasn't always been easy, but you realize once you have a kid, there's nothing more important you could be doing but raising them. I get a joy every day that no parent, no person, should miss out on."

"You love your son, don't you?"

"Oh man, with all my heart. There are just moments you can see him figuring it out. He's smart for any age, and he's funny. I get to laugh every day. I feel privileged to be raising him. It's my only real duty," he said. Looking into her eyes to see if she understood, he noticed she was distant. She was thinking about something heavy—he just wasn't sure what. "Hey, where are you at this moment?"

She made eye contact with him.

"I was just wondering if my dad ever would describe being a dad the way you just did. I wonder if he cares that much about me."

"He does. We're just not good with this emotional stuff. I mean, personally, I'd rather just fight than feel any kind of emotional pain. At least I know it will heal. You feel me?"

She never answered. It would be a question for another day, he guessed. Her eyes were closed. The liquor and night's air had won.

"'Night Autumn," he said with a gentle kiss on her forehead.

FUNNY HOW TIME FLIES

Damn, what time is it? Tatum wondered. The light beamed through the faux wood blinds to his right.

Wait, where am I? He was trying to get his bearings, but he couldn't fully remember the night before. He did remember meeting a dark-skinned woman with an ass he wanted to bite.

Did I go home with her?

He moved his hand and touched someone next to him—definitely a woman. Soft and warm, he hoped it was the woman from last night. *What was her name? Kenya? No, Nairobi. Yeah, please let it be Nairobi.*

Tatum rolled over, opened his eyes, and found Autumn lying next to him.

Now the night was coming back to him.

The sun laid against her skin, almost kissing it. Her eyes were locked on his. It was different. She was different. She was beautiful. He watched as her eyes unwaveringly told a story in exchange—a story of them.

Neither one of them wanted to look away.

"Hey," she said.

He'd seen her every day for the past six weeks, yet never saw her—or any woman before her—look the way she looked at him at this moment. He admired the way the slivers of sunlight shimmered on her light golden brown skin. He could smell the scent of lilacs and Shea butter that moistened her hair. It was intoxicating, but it all paled in comparison to the immeasurable depth of her light brown eyes. A beacon to the dawn of creation; a gateway to a soul filled with passion, understanding, empathy, and life. She was beautiful by that definition, and he couldn't look away.

"Hey," he finally said, keeping his eyes fixed on hers. The pair looked at each other as the energy-filled all but the space between them. She smiled and bit her lip.

"How did you slee—"

His lips met hers at the end of her sentence.

The kiss filled the room with an unrelenting passion he didn't know he had been suppressing. He abandoned the notion of friend-ship without reservation. He wanted to kiss her again, and she welcomed that. They'd passed a boundary neither one of them antici-pated crossing, and there was no turning back for either of them. As they continued to explore each other, he moved down her neck and bit into her with the aggression of a man's nature. He rolled on top of her and took off the white muscle shirt she had given him.

"Damn," she said, running her hand across his dark, chiseled chest and down his bulging deep bronze arms. Her eyes examined his physique, followed by her fingers. She ran her fingertip across each cut of definition in his chest and abdomen. Her eyes approved, and she looked him in the eyes again. There was a language being spoken without words, one that gave him permission to continue. He took off her shirt, exposing her golden light brown C-cup breasts and dark perky nipples. He leaned toward her left breast and slightly bit her nipple, gently pulling it into his lips, not ceasing until he held her entire areola in his mouth. She put her hands on the back of his neck, slightly burying her nails into his flesh. The twinge of pain excited him, and he applied more pressure to her nipple, something she welcomed with a low, appreciative moan. He continued to hold the nipple for as long as it took his tongue to memorize the texture and every ripple of her areola. After a spell, he released it as she moaned again, directing his lips to her right breast. He gladly obliged, giving it the same treatment. She moaned louder and pressed her nails into the back of his neck deeper than the first time, signifying her approval. After releasing her right breast, he came up to connect with her eyes, only to be met by her lips as she reengaged their passion. They kissed as if their souls understood that nothing around them mattered. All that was important was the deep desire in their kisses. It was life.

The kiss evolved into Autumn sliding her hands into his sweatpants. He was fully erect, hardened by her presence and the passion they were experiencing. Without hesitation, he pulled off the pants, leaving her to stroke his rock-hard nine-and-a-half-inch cock. Autumn's eyes widened as she ran her hands across the shaft of his manhood. The excitement of the morning had built up a trickle of precum, which Autumn touched before licking it up with her tongue. She looked up at him and smiled.

"You got a big dick, Mr. Clarke," she said. He chuckled. Even now, she was still her outspoken, funny self. He had to admit it—he wanted her, and she wanted him.

She slipped out of her crimson lace panties and laid in the center of the bed as he climbed on top of her. He entered her—not with haste or lust, but with the purity that comes with caring. Regardless of what happened next, she was important to him, and touching her in the most intimate way possible required his respect.

"Oh my God," she moaned, arching her hips to fully receive the length of his hardened cock.

When he could go no deeper, he stopped to enjoy the oneness he'd never felt before. He stroked her as she moaned, her eyes indicating the pleasures or pains of the specific contour of his cock inside of her. He took it slow and slid in again.

"You feel amazing," he whispered in her ear as the two kissed again. He controlled his stamina, sliding into her with a rhythmic motion as she asked for more; nearly begged for more. Her legs shivered as he pushed harder, encouraging him to push faster until reaching a pace of passion that consumed them.

"Oh shit!" she screamed. He'd found her G-spot. With persistence, he rubbed his hardened dick against the walls of her moisture. He could tell she was close when she dug her nails into his back. Her eyes widened as she thrust her pelvis toward him to receive his maximum girth. 'I'm cumming!" she screamed, a powerful orgasm flowing through her body, and with it, a burst of fluid that caught Tatum off guard, leaving her panting and breathless even after her orgasm passed.

"I didn't know you squir- "

"How...are you...still..."

She wanted to know how he was still hard. He'd always had stamina but pleasing her was a turn-on. As bad as he wanted his own release, he relished pleasing her. Something he quickly proved as she came a second time, even more intensely than the first.

"Oh God!" she yelled. Another seizing orgasm shot through her body, followed by an even more visceral release as she clenched him to brace for the experience. After her third orgasm, she looked him in his eyes with a penetrating look as if the two were connecting in a way neither had done before. Her eyes glazed over as he descended into her again. As the sweat from his forehead dripped onto her breasts, he pressed his rock-hard dick inside her with authority, confident he was satisfying her. She bit his nipple in a painful tease, the pressure sparking his first orgasm.

"Oh my God!" he yelled as he released his seed deep into her, his savage thrusts picking up the intensity until he surpassed his climax. He had lost all stamina and strength, but she wouldn't let him recede now. She wanted more, and her moisture and desire gave him the strength to pick up his pace and bring her to orgasm once more.

Laying there with this man inside her, Autumn took a moment to catch her breath, hoping he somehow had the energy to keep this going.

"It's noon—I can't believe you're still hard," she panted.

"I can't believe you still want it."

"Is that so?" she said, rolling him onto his back and climbing on top of his still fully erect cock. He loved the way her breasts bounced in the air as she straddled his dick, matching his energy as she rocked from side to side, bouncing on his shaft, swelling the head to a critical mass. It was his turn to have another orgasm. He allowed the pleasure she provided to course through him. The pair made eye contact, appreciating what they were doing for each other in this bedroom and beyond. He marveled at how well their chemistry in other areas heightened their connection in the bedroom. Sleeping with her felt natural, and with each thrust, he felt the freedom to pursue pleasure. It was the sort of carefree connection that comes when truly connecting with someone for the first time.

Now at ease and thoroughly exhausted, the two of them curled up together. Autumn snuggle against his chest until both, sated and satisfied, drifted off to sleep.

"It's fucking three o'clock," Tatum said, waking up with a jolt.

"In the afternoon?" Autumn replied, the still-drawn shades darkening the room.

"Oh my God, what's wrong with us." The pair laughed, though Tatum, sitting up, scanned the room.

"Looking for your journal?"

"I was. How did you know."

"You're always looking for that thing," Autumn said, shaking her head. "Can I ask you a question?"

"Yeah, sure."

"Why do you think you write in that thing?"

"I don't know. One day I had one, and before I knew it, I was just writing in it."

"What do you write?"

He let out a sigh that said, "Are you serious?"

"You made a fuss about this notebook. I've never looked in it even when I could have, so tell me what you write."

Tatum looked at her as she positioned her head on his shoulder. There was a slight hesitation in granting her request. He didn't necessarily feel comfortable talking to anyone about the contents of his journal because of its content. Yet he trusted Autumn, and he now knew her in every way imaginable it was only right he shared.

"After my dad left, I didn't have anyone to talk to, so I started putting my feelings inside a journal. At first, it was a bunch of angry—yeah, it's gonna sound stupid—but rap lyrics. You know, 'fuck dad, I wish you were dead.' Shit like that. But after a while, I just found myself making melodies, mostly songs. I was listening to *Purple Rain*, and that line where Prince says, 'maybe I'm like my father, and maybe I'm like my mother' just hit me different. I started writing there and never looked back. You know how you have your paintings on your wall? Well, my journal is just like that to me. It's the only place I'm ever truly me."

"So it's a piece of your heart."

"It's my whole heart."

He watched as she nodded in agreement with his feelings. After a spell, she leaned into his chest and asked.

"So, you like Prince?"

"I love Prince. He's the greatest musical artist of all time. I mean, think about it: he can play every instrument, sing like he does, and take your girl all in a pair of stilettos. And according to Dave Chappelle, he might drop thirty on you on the basketball court. He's the GOAT, man."

"Goat?"

"Greatest of All Time."

"How am I just now finding this out about you?"

"We've never had sex before."

The two laughed as they began to kiss again.

They had been intimate for hours, and their appetites were not satisfied. They wanted more, and they graciously provided for each other. That entire Saturday, he laid in bed next to her, their sexual session evolving the more they connected. They eventually stopped to order take-in Chinese and shower again, only to end up having sex in the shower.

By the evening, they understood each other's bodies with impunity. Tatum was surprised Autumn's appetite matched his own, which only made him want more of her. Their lovemaking fell into nightfall, and they were different for the experience. As they exhausted their energies, they mutually agreed their collective appetites were finally satisfied.

"I have to admit, Tatum Lavelle Clarke, when we first started, I didn't know what to expect, but there is no way I could've expected what you were."

"And what's that?" he said, gasping for oxygen.

"A freaky motherfucker." The pair laughed in mutual admiration, recognizing how similar they were.

"I'm not alone because you're insatiable."

"Good enough to get in that journal of yours?"

"My mind is already jotting notes," he said. She didn't press the point any further, only hoping that someday he would share those notes—maybe even those melodies—with her. Comfortable, they held each other and watched Eddie Murphy's *Boomerang* on Netflix.

They had spent the day together and connected in a way that made both of them believe that things could revert to normal.

Exhausted, he fell asleep holding her in his arms and would not let her go until morning.

1 2

AGAIN

"Hey, beautiful..."

It was his first words of a new day. Autumn lay next to him, naked, comfortable, and attentive.

"Morning, handsome man," she replied. He kissed her left breast and nibbled his way from there to her neck, culminating in a peck on the lips as she giggled at his actions.

"Eww, stop! I don't know where your mouth has been..." she said playfully.

"You know exactly where my mouth has been, and if you keep playing, I'm gonna give you a few reminders." The two laughed as he climbed on top of her naked frame.

"Oh no, you not gonna have me in here chained to this bed today. Come on and get up. Acting like you fresh out of jail."

Tatum rolled over and sighed playfully. "I didn't hear you complaining yesterday morning, yesterday evening, or last night."

"You didn't hear me complain just now. I was just making an observation. Men with jobs don't have a dick like that."

"And what kind of dick is that?"

"You know that 'I'm gonna sit around and play 2K all day on the new PlayStation while having no direction in life and can you bring me something to eat kind of dick," she replied.

Tatum laughed at her analogy. He could tell she'd put thought in it.

"I'm gonna take it as a compliment."

"You should cause if you ask me to get you a sandwich right now, I would. Hell, I don't have another pair of sheets to put on the bed if we get started," she said, pointing to a corner in the room where two piles of soiled sheets resided. There were cartons of Chinese and Mediterranean takeout on the side of the bed and an empty bottle of wine. The room was in upheaval.

"Well, shouldn't we at least clean u—"

"I'm not falling for that shit Tatum. I fell for that shit nine orgasms ago. Remember the 'Oh, we'll just go get Mediterranean, but let's clean up.' And the second I bent over to put these sheets on, you were trying to put your dick in my ass."

Tatum laughed and slapped her on her left butt cheek. "It's amazing how quickly we've progressed to the ass-slapping cheek level. I'm such a slut."

"Don't sell yourself short—you a whole hoe," she said as she licked him on his nipple.

She crawled underneath him and kissed his exposed chest.

"It was great sex, much needed."

"You're not just saying that cause-"

"Tate, I'm telling you if you want me to, I'll go make that sandwich right now! Gold star for Tatum. If it were trash, I'd tell you just as honestly because the most annoying thing in life is to spend a whole lot of time fucking not to cum."

"Yeah, that's some exhausting shit. But trust me, I knew you came. That's why we're on your last pair of sheets."

The two laughed at the comment but then moved closer to each other, Autumn resting on his chest. Tatum enjoyed her intuitive nature and, in return, held her with his arm, his hand across her golden-brown buttocks.

"Well, I'm gonna tell you if you want to go anywhere, getting closer to me ain't gonna do the trick."

"Well, I know we're gonna at least get your car."

"Oh shit! That's right. Damn, we didn't do anything yesterday, did we?"

"Oh no, we did something. You know what we did, and we did it very well."

She kissed him on his neck as he rubbed her back and took a sigh weighing his options.

"Well, if I had to choose between getting my car out of the pound and making my toes curl, I'm taking the toe curl for three hundred, Alex." Tatum laughed and kissed her on her neck. The fact that the way they talked to each other didn't change through this encounter was the most rewarding thing he could've hoped for. This new wrinkle in their relationship felt very natural. He was enjoying being nowhere in particular—and being there with her. He didn't want it to end. Yet, he didn't want to take up her time. Maybe she needed him to leave. He decided to give her an out.

"Hey, so it's been a while for me, and I don't know standard booty call protocol, but if you need time to do something else, I'll call an Uber to get my car." Autumn pushed away from Tatum and looked at him sternly; the intensity in her eyes surprised him as she said.

"Whoa, booty call? Tate, that sounds re-occurring. I hate to break this to you, but this was just a one-time thing. We're friends. Nothing more."

The words caught Tatum off guard. Could she be serious? He'd been so consumed by Autumn, and he never stopped to think she didn't feel the way he did. Her statement drove him to play it off.

"Oh. Um...I—"

"Psych! You're such a dumbass, Tate. For the record, we're fucking at some point today. I just need the sunlight and maybe a waffle."

A wave of relief rushed over him. He grabbed the pillow he was lying on and playfully hit her in the face with it as the two started to wrestle, Autumn quickly ending up on top of him.

"But if you don't recall Mr. Clarke, we were gonna hang out today anyway, so—"

"When did we say that?"

"Don't try that shit. Last week you told me we were going to the museum today."

"Did I?"

"You know I'm not even playing with you like that."

Autumn tried to get off of him, but he held her waist, to which she didn't put up any real resistance. She did, however, sigh, and she rolled her eyes. Tatum playfully scanned his thoughts.

"Wait...let me think. That's right. You lost an absurd amount of Connect Four games, and if I won, we agreed to go to the Museum of Natural Science this weekend."

"And if I won, we'd go to the Museum of Fine Arts, so you cheated."

"How can you cheat at Connect Four? You're just really bad. Seriously. What's the deal with you and that game? It's just four in a row. Can artists not count?"

Autumn moved away from him and folded her arms. She never liked the ribbing Tatum did when it came to this game, but he either didn't pick up on it, or he enjoyed it. He leaned over and started kissing her on her neck.

"I'm sorry...you're...so bad at that game," he said, letting out a chuckle, causing her to hit him with the pillow.

"Whatever. I'd tell you to kiss my ass, but I know you'd like it." He continued to laugh as she joined him. It was funny that less than twelve hours ago, he had never seen her in a sexual light, and now he couldn't believe he'd missed it for so long. She was beautiful, she was sexy, she was exciting, and above all, she was already comfortable with him. She allowed him to be who he was, and that was refreshing. In return, he provided the same sanctuary to her. This was the foundation of their friendship, and it only seemed to be growing. He didn't know where this would lead, but he liked exactly where they were. He slid Autumn to the side and jumped out of bed, catching Autumn off guard.

"Well, come on—sunlight, waffle, sex. Chop chop!" he said, laughing as he shuffled over to the shower.

Tatum got in the now-familiar shower. As he washed his muscular frame, the shower door opened.

"Room for one more?"

"We'll make it work," he replied. The two relaxed as the heat from the water matched the temperature radiated by their combined auras. Tatum took the soap and washed Autumn's caramel frame. She returned the favor as the two made eye contact. Tatum moved his hand lower when he stopped himself.

"Sunlight, waffle, sex," he said, getting out of the shower.

As he dried off, he put on the clothes he'd worn Friday night, which they washed yesterday in a half-hearted attempt to go home. Autumn, having full access to her wardrobe, wore a soft blue top with a pair of fitted black tights and blue tennis shoes to compensate for all the walking they'd be doing.

"How does this look? Is this okay?"

"It's...perfect."

"Are you sure? You don't know how much I obsessed over this outfit. I—"

"You thought to yourself, 'Is this a date? We agreed to it a while ago, but we're clearly fucking now.' So you want to make an impression, but you don't want to try too hard, so you made your best attempt at crazy/sexy/cool/homie/lover/friend."

Her mouth dropped wide open. "How did you know?"

"Do you know how many times I've been on the phone with you while you've gotten ready? Or waited on you while you got ready? Plus, it's Sunday. You'd normally be deciding if you're going to take a spin class or go bike riding at Allen Park right about...now actually."

She nodded and said nothing. She gathered her things, once in a while peculiarly making eye contact. He knew his friend, but he wasn't privy to what she was thinking.

"Hey...where are you?" he asked. It was their way of saying "share with the class" when one or the other had drifted off for a spell. Something Autumn realized once he asked the question.

"You...are too much, you know that?"

"What?"

"Nothing. It's just...are you always like this?"

"Like what?"

"Thoughtful."

He didn't respond. It was awkward to receive a compliment, particularly from her. They were friends, and as friends, they always had each other's backs and were even there for emotional support. But this compliment was different. This one was formed out of attraction. The way a man tries to impress a woman and the woman then conveys she's impressed. This was new. He took it in stride.

"I'm just thorough."

"That's cool you listen to me like that. That's all."

"This is touching you feel that way, but if we're going to hit the museum and get something to eat, we need to step on it."

"Fine."

Tatum headed to the door as she followed him, locking up the house. The pair drove downtown to pick up Tatum's car. To his surprise and relief, it was in a parking lot that charged by the day, something he hadn't remembered. From there, the two drove to Hermann Park, home to the museum district. When they walked to the counter, Tatum pulled out his card.

"Two for the Museum of Fine Arts, please."

He glanced out of the corner of his eye to see Autumn's giant grin. She was ecstatic. She hugged him and asked, "But you won?"

He looked at her, her smile so contagious he couldn't help but smile himself.

"Well, it's like the sign at Lucky's said if you want to score, let her win, so we'll call this one a draw."

She kissed him, and they collected their tickets. Autumn was in her element as she walked into the main hallway with wonder in her eyes.

"You're going to love this. I'm telling you, you won't be sorry. They have an Egyptian exhibit with local artists. It's so dope, I promise you," she said as she grabbed him by the hand and walked as rapidly as a child about to get a treat.

The museum had been totally renovated from the last time Tatum visited it. Every school year, they were bussed here for a day, and it always gave off an '80s vibe. This was all remodeled. The floors were a gray marble, the widows massive, and the paintings vibrant.

"We just missed the Soul of a Nation exhibit, but I've been dying to see Rise of the Pharaohs. But first, I want to see the Local Artist spotlight. There's a guy, Pasha Hammond, whose work I'd like to see. We were classmates, and oh, I'm sorry, Tate. You must be bored as hell. I'm just talking your head off and dragging you to all this stuff."

"No. In fact, I just thought I've never seen this side of you. I've never really been in this part of your world, so I'm curious. Lead the way."

She smiled the same way she did earlier, and it again made him happy to see it.

"Well, come on, it's this way."

He followed her lead as they walked into the exhibit. Tatum wasn't an art critic by any measure. The only thing he truly knew about art was the Mona Lisa, and that Autumn was an artist. Yet, he was impressed by how magnificent some of these paintings were. More than that, though, he enjoyed the education Autumn provided. She marveled at the artwork, interpreting the meaning of each painting before breaking down the techniques the artist must have used. Between the paintings, she would stop to ask if he was comfortable or bored, to which he always reassured her he was fine and engaged. In earnest, he genuinely was having a good time.

Tatum was again impressed when they left the local artist display and entered the Egyptian exhibit. The museum spared no expense. Everything from the tile on the floor to the markings on the wall catered to their perception that they were in ancient Egypt. Tatum's eyes widened as he finally had something to contribute to the conversation. They exchanged dialogue about why the noses were blown off each statue and how immaculate the designs had to have been to build such artifacts. He enjoyed the mutual understanding they were gaining as their thoughts ran deeper than either knew. He marveled at her beauty, which was enhanced by the fact that she was truly a master of her craft.

"Tatum, come check this out."

He joined her in front of a large painting of the city of Tel el-Amarna in its glory.

"I'm not sure who painted this one because I haven't seen it in school, but it's good. It's more than good. I gotta find out who painted it!" Autumn said. Tatum walked closer to the painting, and his eyes glazed over in its splendor.

"This is the city of love," He said, still in awe. Autumn delayed her inquest and turned to her lover.

"City of love, what are you talking about?"

"Well, the legend says this city was built out of love itself."

"I'm not following."

Tatum looked at the portrait and continued.

"See, the pharaoh had fallen in love with this princess, but she was supposed to marry the king of Ethiopia. Naturally, he didn't care, and neither did she. They started an affair, and things were good until the king of Ethiopia found out. He immediately went to war with the Egyptians to bust that ass. But the war got out of hand when people realized they were all basically dying behind some pum-pum. Both sides wanted an end to the war, so Pharaoh agreed to leave the king's wife alone in exchange for peace. Eventually, the pharaoh marries someone else and has a son. The princess gets married to the king of Ethiopia, and they have a daughter. Time passes, and back in Egypt, on the pharaoh's deathbed, he tells his son to deliver a very important message to the queen of Ethiopia. The son agrees, but a couple of hundred miles outside Cairo, they run into a royal entourage from Ethiopia. Come to find out, the queen of Ethiopia died and also had an important message to tell the pharaoh. The new queen meets the new pharaoh, and they exchange their important messages: *Even in death, there will be US—I love you.* They both had the same message for each other. The new pharaoh and the new queen decide to honor their parents' love and built Tel el-Amarna in that very spot."

"That is a beautiful story."

"This was a beautiful time. Can you imagine? Thousands of years before all this, the kings were black."

"And the queens were the mothers of civilization."

He looked at her and then the painting and nodded. After a spell, she said, "You would have liked to live there, wouldn't you?"

"No, I like central AC too much. But I'd love to have gone back in time to see it. How cool would it have been to see it all being built, just standing in Cairo looking at the newness of it all, like in that book we just finished."

"*The Alchemist?*"

"Yeah. If it was anything like this, it was beautiful. He chose this over love."

"So... you think it was hard for him to leave Fatima?"

"Damn near impossible. Like I just said, he loved her."

He turned to her, pulling his eyes away from the portrait.

"So you know how in the book the pyramids represent his dreams, but on some level, Fatima represents everything he already had that he loved? It must have been hard to give up everything for the unknown."

"It wasn't unknown; it was his dream. He had to pursue his—what did they call it?"

"Personal legend."

Autumn nodded. "I mean, that's one way to look at it. Where are you going with this?"

"Man, I'm saying look at this picture of Egypt. It's paradise. It was worth it."

"You know what I just noticed?"

"What?"

"How much of a turn-on you make books and ancient black culture sound. This is some sexy shit you're doing right here."

"Girl, you so crazy," he said, laughing at her,

"I'm serious. The more you talk, the more I feel like the Nile River. Wanna feel?" she said, pulling him into a dark corner of the museum near the exhibit. He welcomed it as he slid his hand into her tights and slid a finger across her swollen clit, making her shiver.

"You are so bad," he said almost in a whisper, fighting back the urge to take her right there.

She smirked, still welcoming the pleasure he was bringing.

He smirked in return. A moment ago, he was talking about Egypt, and now he was dipping his finger in the Nile. He lifted his hand and extended it toward her as she licked herself off his finger. The two kissed passionately as he pulled her closer to press against his growing manhood.

"Now show me yours," she said. He pulled down his sweatpants to expose his cock, nearing full erectness. She rubbed with consideration.

"Just put it in one time."

He turned her around and slid down her tights. Without hesitation, he slid inside her.

"Oh shit, I missed you already," she moaned as he slowly pushed inside of her. Their intensity was about to pick up when Tatum heard a noise.

"Ahem."

The pair separated as an older white lady approached them. Very gingerly, the woman walked over and said, "Excuse me...um...I'm looking for the Pasha Hammond collection?"

The pair made sure they were decent, although Tatum was sure he couldn't hide his erection, and Autumn felt uncomfortable in her wet tights. Tatum looked at Autumn. She was just as stunned as he was. Did the lady not see them at all? Her question indicated maybe she didn't.

"Pasha Hammond?" Tatum said, recalling him as one of the local artists Autumn praised. "You're looking for the local black artist collection. It's—"

"No, I've been there. He's supposed to have more work in the Egyptian exhibit."

Tatum, now fully clothed and adjusted, walked over to the painting they were just looking at. He examined it closely.

"I think this is one of them."

Autumn walked over briskly, and her excited face became sullen. "It is," she said, confirming Tatum's guess.

"Thank the both of you so much...and... look, I don't want to be considered one of those Karens everyone is talking about, and believe me, I know it's none of my business I know, but..." she looked around and leaned in even closer. "...I just don't think you should be doing *that* here."

She had seen them. A wave of embarrassment rushed over Tatum's face. He glanced at Autumn, who was suppressing a laugh as the older woman continued.

"And it's not because you're black and because...well, you're also black. It's...it's because we're in a museum, it's public, and... oh my Lord, this is the art museum! Is this art? I'm so, so sorry! Please don't make me go viral!"

She turned to walk away but not fast enough because Autumn stopped her.

"I just wanted to let you know that you're right. We were being perverts and should not be doing this here, so we're going to leave promptly. No one's going to make you go viral. Thank you for talking to us like reasonable humans and not calling the police."

The two nodded and hurried away. Tatum was excited by the carefreeness of it all. It made him giddy inside.

"That was crazy!" he said as they left the museum. Autumn, however, was somber.

"Hey, what's wrong? Where are you?"

1 3

WHO CAN I RUN TO?

"*H*ey, did you hear me? Slow down."

Tatum wasn't sure what happened, but something wasn't right. Autumn never broke stride until they got outside the museum. The temperature had cooled, but that didn't slow her down either. She bundled up and walked faster.

Tatum matched her pace and asked, "Autumn, you gonna talk? What did I miss back there?"

"Nothing, it's just..."

Tatum jogged in front of her and gently grabbed her by her shoulders, stopping her in her tracks.

"Take a deep breath. Rela—"

"I'm fine."

"Don't do that. Tell me, what's going on? Where are you in your mind right now?"

She paused. "Pasha Hammond, my ex-classmate. He's in the museum of fine fuckin' arts."

"Okay...and this bothers you?"

"I mean, it's one thing to be a featured local artist, but to be on tour with the museum's exhibits? That's major. I know Pasha Hammond. He graduated two years before me. Let me tell you he couldn't hold a candle to me in school, now he's blowing up, and I'm a dropout that works at a goddamn Paint & Sip."

"You can't look at it like that, Autumn. Let me tell you something. I just spent the last few hours looking at some pretty incredible art, but nothing is more breathtaking than the work on the floor in your loft. You are incredible. You just have to let the rest of the world know you're here, and hell, they'll come to you."

She looked at the museum as Tatum kissed her on the neck to reassure her.

"You think so?"

"I know so. And I'm not just saying that because you were just giving me some goodness in that museum over there—I'm saying it 'cause it's true."

She turned and kissed him in exchange for lifting her spirits even more. As they crossed the street, they walked through Hermann Park and looked at the bristling leaves, the cool air keeping them close together.

"You know people are going to think we're a couple."

"How did Eddie Murphy put it in *Coming to America?* Oh yeah... 'Then let them see.'"

She giggled as he held her hand, and they walked through Hermann Park, watching the cascade of folk of all creeds riding their bikes while children clamored for funnel cakes at the nearest vendor. For a moment, he thought about his son and realized it was the first time in a while he'd not been so wired into being a parent. It felt good to be with a beautiful woman walking nowhere in particular, just happy to be together. Tatum truly enjoyed her company—the laughter, the way her cheeks crinkled when she smiled, and her passion. He thought about her straddling him, and his eyes went somewhere else.

"Hey, where are you?" she asked. She looked into his eyes. He tried to shake the thought, but it was too late.

"Oh...you're still in my pussy, are you?" she said with a smile.

"Autumn..."

"Admit it."

He smirked. *Why the hell not?* He was having the best time he could think of in recent memory.

"I was there." He kissed her on the cheek and resumed walking.

After a few paces, Autumn asked, "What did you call it?"

"Excuse me?"

"You heard me. What did you call my pussy?"

"I... didn't."

"Now, I find that hard to believe. Since the beginning of time, the one thing men have consistently done is name shit they think belongs to them. Hell, the first man's entire job was just walking around naming shit."

He laughed as she hunched her shoulders over and did a deliberately terrible rendition of a caveman. "Duh...boy, cat, bird, water," she rattled off as she pointed at several examples in the park.

"Okay, okay, I get your point, but I'll be honest. I hadn't...wait...you said men name what belongs to them. You think I think your...cookie belongs to me?"

"Do you want it to?" She smiled and walked ahead of him as he stood in his tracks.

"Autumn, wait a second."

She turned around and stuck her tongue out. He chuckled as he jogged over to her.

"So, have you named mine?"

"Nightcrawler."

"Excuse me?"

"You asked if I named your...deluxe Hershey bar, and I named it Nightcrawler, like in those Marvel movies. It pops up out of nowhere and is always ready for action."

"I'm serious! I came so many times last night and this morning. It was gluttonous."

"Oh, I was there for all the waterworks."

"You never been with a squirter before?"

"Not one as in tune with their body as you are."

"Oh honey, let me tell you—I didn't have a choice. You *made* me cum... hard. I'm just glad you didn't make me cum in the museum. They would have had to get a mop."

The two laughed at the exchange. They were friends who'd crossed a line, but it wasn't taboo. In fact, it was completely natural to have this kind of conversation. Tatum smiled and provided the answer to the initial question Autumn asked: what would he name her treasure?

"Jubilee."

"Like the X-Man?"

"The one and only. I figured if we're doing an X-man theme, let me choose the one with the fireworks." Tatum nodded as they laughed again. They held each other for a moment in the middle of the park, unbothered by anyone around them. Tatum thought this was as good as it gets. It was time for the sunlight, waffle, sex itinerary. He looked into her eyes and asked, "Okay, but seriously, what are we eating?"

"You know I love Italian."

"Woman, you love food. I'm serious—I don't know anyone who eats like you."

"Look, all I know is whenever I die when I meet the other spirits from other worlds, and they ask, 'Where are you from,' I'm gonna say, 'Yeah, I lived on Earth, and the food was delicious.'"

While she was talking, Tatum spied the light rail directly across the street. "Well, if you're up for a little ride, I know this Italian place not too far from here. We can go and grab a bite."

"I'm game."

The two crossed the street and boarded the light rail as it came. Tatum sat next to the window, and Autumn sat next to him, nestling her head on his shoulder. Looking out the window, he took out his wireless headphones and handed Autumn the other earbud as he put on a playlist. The first song that came on was, *Who Can I Run To?*

"I love this song; this is the original, right?"

"Original? You knew this was a remake?"

"You're kidding, right?"

He said nothing as she rested her head back on his shoulder, and they enjoyed the rest of the playlist.

It wasn't long before they arrived, stepping off the light rail just two blocks from a trio of Italian restaurants hidden to the rest of the world but a place Tatum went frequently. He learned of it only because the sales reps at Simmons Pharmaceuticals took clients there.

"This is amazing! I didn't know Houston had anything like this."

"You have your choice—Nino's, Vincent's, or Grappino's."

The feel of old-world Italy emanating from each place made it hard for her to choose. She felt transported to another world as if they'd gone from the streets of Cairo to the roads of Napa in a single day.

"Ugh! It's so hard to choose, 'cause I don't know anything about them."

"Let's go to Nino's. I'm sure you're going to like it."

The pair walked into the restaurant. Of the three, Nino's was the best known for traditional Italian food, something they could both enjoy. As they walked in, the stone architecture and light brown hardwood floors brought the feel of an Italian vineyard to life, and the smell of basil and pesto sweetened the air. The whole place was brought together by the heat from a crackling fireplace.

They sat at a table near the window where Autumn thought they could see the world go by. Once settled, Tatum couldn't help but smile. He couldn't recall the last time he'd been this relaxed.

The waiter, a short Italian man in his early twenties with jet black hair and a black uniform with a white apron he'd recently stained, greeted them in a light nasal tone.

"Greetings! Welcome to Nino's. Have you dined with us before?"

"I have. The lady hasn't."

"Well, ma'am, you're in for a treat. This is a traditional Italian experience. Before
we begin, may I interest you in our wine selection?"

Tatum nodded. "Let's get a bottle of wine. Wild Horse if you have it."

"Coming right up, sir," the waiter said before walking off. Autumn looked around the restaurant, taking it in. They practically had the place to themselves, which added to the ambiance and romantic atmosphere.

"You're different, aren't you?"

"I'm not sure what you mean."

"I mean...who goes to art museums and knows about a trio of restaurants nestled off in the heart of Houston and goes there for lunch on a whim? You're different."

"I'm...not even sure how to respond to that."

"No need. It was more of a statement than a question."

The conversation was interrupted by the waiter bringing over their wine and pouring the couple a glass each. He took their order, returning with two heaping plates of steaming pasta. They talked and ate and never seemed to run out of words to say. Tatum listened as she described her ambitions as an artist, and he talked about life after pharmacy school. When the meal was over, the two took a slow walk back through the restaurant to examine all the photos of Italy and copies of Renaissance masters' paintings before heading back to the light rail.

There was no question things were heating up between them. It was very early in their relationship, but Tatum knew he wanted to do this tomorrow. And the day after that. She was that important.

"What are you thinking?" she asked.

"I'm pretty buzzed; you know that. That wine was strong as fuck. What about you? What are you thinking?"

She smiled as they arrived at the light rail. "I think you don't know what my favorite color is."

"Bullshit. It's blue."

"How did you—"

"You have it on right now. But besides that, you paint a lot with it."

Autumn studied his face, searching his eyes as if to understand his words. After a spell, she smiled and said,

"Yeah, you're different."

The conversation shifted once the pair got back on the light rail. Tatum took his same spot next to the window with Autumn next to him as they rode back to Hermann Park watching the sun begin its descent. They watched the city pass them by.

She kissed him on the cheek when he glanced at her. It was her turn to play a soundtrack to their ride. She put her wireless earbud in one of his ears while she kept the other. *Let's Wait Awhile* by Janet Jackson streamed out of the headphone as they locked arms. Tatum couldn't determine if she played the song on purpose or if it was a random shuffle, and he wasn't sure he wanted to ask. At the same time, the melody was perfect for the short ride, and he enjoyed it for what it was—a perfect nightcap to a perfect day with what was becoming more and more a perfect woman.

"Blue is my favorite color," she said as she tugged at her sweater. He kissed her on the forehead as the two continued to enjoy the song, neither one of them wanting to talk for fear of breaking up this moment. A moment they both understood, but neither would admit, scared it was too soon.

They had arrived in love.

Once they exited the light rail, Tatum gave her back the wireless headset and walked over to a park bench overlooking the lake, where he and Autumn sat to watch the sunset's final moment. The wind rustling the brightly colored leaves and children laughing became their new soundtrack.

He looked at her. She had a tear rolling from her eye.

"Hey, something wrong? Where are you?"

She wiped the tear from her eye and took a breath.

"You know I've been in bad relationships, and sometimes I'd look over at couples in places like this and think I'd like to be happy like that. And today, right now, I'm that person. We're those people. I don't know...I mean, I'm happy. We started off the day with you lying next to me, and it felt right. We go to the museum, and you let me talk about everything. I get down about Pasha, and you pick me up. Then we had lunch in a beautiful Italian restaurant, and now we're just in the park being ourselves. And the thing is, we probably would've had the same day without ever having sex. It's just the way you are."

He pulled her closer and nibbled her earlobe as he squeezed her.

"I could feel like every day," he said, realizing that she was in sync with him. They had overcome a rough spot in a parking lot garage to learn about each other. This would not be their last date or even the last time they saw each other because this was something that had been building for weeks, and neither one of them could deny it.

"It's funny. A few days ago, I was upset about Kaleb having a baby. Now I barely remember why I was upset."

Tatum grabbed Autumn's hand, but then his phone went off. He pulled it from his pocket and read the text from his mother.

Hey Son, when are you heading to pick up Solly?

"Shit."

"Something wrong?" Autumn asked as he turned to her.

"I don't want today to end, but I have to go get Solomon."

"It doesn't have to. We can go get him together." Tatum sat up and looked at her. He wasn't sure how to say what he had to say next. He grabbed her hand and looked her in her eyes with all the sincerity he had in his heart.

"I am having a wonderful time, so I hope this doesn't kill the vibe. Try to understand this—I've never let anyone meet my son until it's serious, and it's not that this isn't—"

"No, I get it," she said, shifting to the opposite end of the bench.

"I'm sorry. It's an awkward ending to a beautiful couple of days."

"No, it's fine. Duty calls." The pair stood up and began their walk back to the car, ending what was a wonderful day. Tatum felt it was also time to address the elephant in the room.

"Since we're talking about it...Autumn, I... you know I've had an amazing weekend. You also know my situation—I'm still mar—"

"Let's just enjoy each other. Hell, for all we know, we just ruined our friendship. So let's just hang and see where it goes."

It was unconventional for him. He lived his life by plans and structure. He had to for his son's sake. But he was also having more fun than he could recall in recent memory. The fairytale weekend was over. Tomorrow morning he'd be back to being Dad. But for now, he was in bliss.

"Okay, we'll try it your way," he said before kissing her on the lips, both relieved and perturbed and still thinking he needed a plan.

14

FOOL FOR YOU

"*T*atum, what are you doing?" his frustrated mother said over the phone. Tatum wanted to respond honestly but knew it would be pointless, so he kept his mouth shut.

"Bringing that boy around your daddy is just gonna break his heart. You of all people should know that."

Tatum listened to his mother go on about the dangers of spending time with Johnny Clarke. It was part of their usual conversation. Every time he took Solomon to see Johnny, he knew he'd hear from Savannah.

"Ma, he just wants to get to know him. Like it or not, they are blood. Why would I stand in the way of that?"

"You know what? I'm just gonna give it to the Lord because clearly, you can't see a brick wall when it's right in front of your face."

The conversation was interrupted by a phone call. Tatum looked at the screen to see a picture of his best friend holding up a middle finger.

"Hey, Mom, I love you, but I gotta take this call."

"Well, I was just going to—"

"Talk to you later. Bye," he said as he hastily got her off of the phone and switched to the other line. "Stone, are you there?"

"Excuse me, sir. I was wondering if you could help me out. I'm looking for my brother. His name is Tatum Clarke, but he goes by the name Reverend. He was last seen about four months ago when he found a magical vagina, and we haven't seen him since."

Tatum chuckled at his friend's comment.

"My bad, bro. It's just been busy. Me and Solly are just walking in from seeing J.C. and—"

"Yeah, fuck all that, dog. Let's hang tonight," Stone said eagerly, even though Tatum hesitated. He already had plans with Autumn, but he knew he couldn't say as much. It didn't matter. His friend sniffed out his hesitation.

"I don't want to hear it, Rev. You've been busy every weekend for damn near four months. You gotta come through tonight. Tell Art BAE she's gotta take a rain check."

"I'm just swamped, bro, between work, school, Solly, and dealing with my crazy-ass parents. I'm just keeping my head above water."

"Bitch, pull that violin out for someone who doesn't know you. You ain't got time 'cause of Autumn. I'm not tripping, though. Bring her through. 'Bout time I put a face with the name."

"We might, bro, but it's tight. I got something I've been working on for her."

"Reverend, you're working on gifts for her? Dog, what are you doing? This chick gonna have you color-coordinating her socks if you keep this simp shit up."

"Stone, if I need advice on how to treat a bitch with a bullet wound, you'll be the first person I call but—"

Beep. He looked at his phone. To no one's surprise, it was Autumn.

"Damn, man, speak of the devil. That's her, bro. Let me hit you back."

"Dog, you can't eat the pussy through the phone."

"Bye, fool. I'ma hit you up."

"Fuck that, Rev, just come through."

"Alright, Stone, whatever," Tatum said as he clicked over to answer Autumn's call.

"Hey you, how's it going?"

"Baby, you won't believe this shit today," Autumn began, complaining about her job at the Paint & Sip. Tatum was microwaving pizza for Solomon, who was also vying for his attention, meaning he was only half-listening.

"Are you even paying attention?"

"No, to be honest."

"Well, that was rude."

"Baby, you complain about work all the time. And what you're getting paid there, we've already done the math. You could be getting twice that if you just sold one painting a month. But have you built your Instagram profile to showcase your work? No. Real talk, you probably got about thirty beautiful portraits just in crates in your loft that could solve all your financial problems, and you want me to feel bad because Amanda at the Paint & Sip wants you to paint by numbers?"

"You sound like my dad right now."

"Because you need to hear it. I've never met the man, but if this is what he's saying, sweetheart, it's the truth."

"Well, I feel like you're a terrible boyfriend. You're supposed to be on my side regardless if it's not making sense."

"You're an artist, baby. The best one I've ever seen. Step out there and let the world see you."

"Says the man who won't even let me read this book of songs he carries around with him everywhere he goes."

"Well, now you worried about grown folk's business."

"Whatever, are we on for the movies tonight?"

"As soon as I get Solomon over to my mom's house. I—" Tatum paused. He thought he heard something. "Tatum? Are you there?"

"Yeah, I'm here."

"What are you doing?" He heard it again. He was certain there was a knock at the door. He walked over to answer it.

"Baby, someone is at the door. Let me call you back."

He hung up and opened the door. A dark-complexioned woman with silky, jet black natural hair, wearing a white and teal patterned sundress, stood in the doorway. Tatum's eyes dulled over; he only had five words for her.

"What are you doing here?"

"Hey, Tatum, how have you been?"

"Busy. Now, what do you want?"

"I'd like to come in."

Tatum blocked the door with his body. He looked over his shoulder at the kitchen table where Solomon ate his pizza.

"Solly, Daddy's gonna be right outside, okay?" he said as he stepped outside, partly closing the door behind him. He turned his attention to the woman in front of him.

"What do you want, Mo?"

"I just want...to see how you guys were doing."

"We're good, anything else?"

"You don't have to be like that Tatum, I just want to talk to you. I mean, like it or not we're still a family, and I- "

"Let me stop you right there, Monique. It's clear you've moved on with your life, and it's time for me to move on with mine. I want a divorce."

"You...you want a divorce?"

"Don't you think it's past time?"

"I hadn't thought about it."

"It's been four years, Mo," he said, surprised by her genuine reaction to the news. It was not what she expected.

"So, what does this mean?"

"It means you can go on living your life, and I can start living mine."

"What does that mean? Are you doing this because you met someone?"

"Look, Mo, if you came over here to play 20 questions, I'll save you the time. I'll get the papers drawn up so we can both just move on."

She stood motionless, barely able to lift her head.

"Tatum, I'm not the same girl anymore."

"Well, that's good to know. Hopefully, the next man will reap the benefits of whatever changes you've undergone. When can we get this done?"

"I... I was hoping to talk about trying...it doesn't matter. I will sign the papers, but I want to spend more time with my son."

"What son?"

"Tatum, don't—"

"No, I'm serious, Mo. What child are you talking about? Surely not Solomon."

"He's my child too."

"Really? Because for the last four years, he's been, my child. My child alone. Hell, I thought a stork left him in that car seat. You remember the last time you two were together, right? You left him strapped to a car seat in an apartment with the AC turned off. So forgive me if I'm not quick to rush to let you two have some quality alone time."

There was silence after his statement. He had no idea why she was even suggesting this or why he was still listening to it. It infuriated him, but he knew he had to refrain from going any further. The fact of the matter was until Monique signed the divorce papers, his life was in flux. If he needed any more proof that he had to back off and let the lawyers settle this, Monique began to weep.

"Do you remember that morning? I woke up after three hours of sleep. I got dressed, put on my oversized panties, and brushed my teeth. When I came out, there was the smell of bacon in the air...eggs, toast...it was quick. I walked over to you, and you were about to go to work. I asked, 'Did you make any for me?' You let me have it. You said that every time you got home, I was asleep, which was crazy. I wasn't sleeping at all."

"I'm not interested in your revisionist history, Mo. I took Solomon to daycare. I took Solomon to my mom's. And when I got home, I still had to come home and wash bottles and a sink full of dishes I didn't use, and then make myself something to eat for dinner or breakfast because you were tired all the damn time."

"From your point of view, I guess all I did was sleep because when you'd take Solomon to school or your mom's, I'd lay down. But I had to fill those bottles, and that was physically taxing and—"

"Look, the past is the past. Why are we reliving this today?" Tatum said, cutting her off. The feelings were still raw. It didn't matter how far he buried those emotions; they were right beneath the surface.

"That morning, I got Solomon dressed. I guess I forgot to pay the internet bill, so we didn't have Wi-Fi, which means he couldn't watch his shows, and so he didn't have a good morning. But it was okay. We were going on a field trip. It was the highlight of my week—leaving the house to go to the OB/GYN and the pediatrician. Now, when I first started to go to that OB/GYN, there was a guy who I knew just found me attractive, and I'll be honest, I liked the idea of watching him squirm when I walked past. One day I heard him talking to another guard and him calling me juicy ass. It was cute. It got to the point I would look forward to him hitting on me when I went to the doctor.

"But after I had Solomon, I saw him, and he saw me, but it was as if he didn't even remember me. My body had changed so much. I picked up all this baby weight, and when I was driving home, I thought to myself, *is this going to be the rest of my life?* I could just hear Solomon crying in the background. He was cranky because he'd gotten his shots, and he didn't watch his shows, and he let me have it on the way home. It was the soundtrack to my life at that point. I got here, and somehow the whole day had passed. It was like I just woke up and got dressed, and now it was four o'clock.

"I knew you were off doing God knows what with Kenley, and then you had school, and I just needed him to stop crying...but he kept on crying, I put him in the house still trying to calm him down, but he just wouldn't calm down. I walked back out to the car to get the diaper bag. I had one more bottle, and I was going to feed him. I remember putting the diaper bag down on the outside of the car and getting in just to feel the A/C blow. It was so goddamn hot that summer, and I closed my eyes, and somehow the door closed shut. And it was quiet. For the first time in four weeks, it was quiet. And the more I thought about how peaceful it was, the more I remembered what it was like before the...noise. I could go anywhere, I could do anything, and I was desirable. I just had this overwhelming urge to do that, to be that person again. I knew it was wrong, so I shook my head, grabbed the bottle, and walked back into the house. And when I got back inside, he was still crying. So I started yelling at him like a crazy person at the top of my fucking lungs to show him, see, I can yell too, and I can cry, and I can scream, and it doesn't get you anywhere in life, so just stop it right now goddammit."

She yelled at the top of her lungs. Tatum watched as she recalled the day she left Solomon in their apartment. She took a breath and continued.

"I had had enough. And then something, as if out of thin air, whispered to me. 'Just get back in the car.' I looked in the mirror and couldn't even recognize my body. I was sore, tired, leaking from places I didn't know I could, and it could all just stop if I got back in the car."

She caught a tear rolling from her face as she continued to talk. "And so I wrote a note, grabbed a few essentials, and left. And I remember looking at the diaper bag, thinking I needed to pick it up. But I felt that if I picked it up, I'd go back, and I just didn't want to hear the goddamn crying anymore. So I got in the car, closed the door, and pulled out the driveway. I didn't learn until maybe a year ago it was post-partum depression."

At this point, Tatum had begun to suppress tears of his own. Maybe Monique was dealing with post-partum depression at the time, maybe she wasn't. It didn't matter.

"He could've died, Mo."

"I know. I have to live with that, and believe me, I know it was wrong, but not as wrong as me not trying to fix it by coming back into his life. I love Solomon, and I know you don't believe it, but I love you too, Tatum. I just had a really, really bad day, and I don't think you can ever forgive me for that."

"Monique, that was four years ago. If you felt that way, why didn't you say something then? I don't know what to say. Maybe I should've been more present. Maybe, but I was working two jobs trying to make this all work."

"Daddy, who's at the door?"

He looked at his son walking toward the entrance and knew Monique was trying to peek around him. And he couldn't blame her. He knew she wanted to know what her son looked like now.

"Solly...um..."

"Mommy?"

"Hey, Solomon. I'm your—"

"Mommy!"

Solomon rushed and hugged his mother, to which Tatum, at a loss for thought and words, stood back and observed. The interaction between mother and child was a bond so strong that, despite her absence, remained undeniable. As the pair hugged, Monique looked at Tatum.

"Please...just give me a chance to get to know him."

"Come inside."

He looked at his son, the unbridled joy on his face unmistakable. Despite it all, he couldn't help but feel concerned. He could only think one thing.

Tatum, what are you doing?

15

SAY SO

"Well, let's just get it out the way—did you fuck her?"

"No, Stone."

"I mean legally, she's your wife."

"I wouldn't touch Monique."

"I'm just saying if you fucked her, I wouldn't blame you. Not after what she put you through."

Tatum rolled his eyes as he exited the highway. It had been a while since he'd caught up with his friend Stone and he was starting to regret calling him. Monique had come back, and he wasn't quite sure how to handle it. However crude, he needed his friend's counsel.

"Reverend, it's just...tell me the truth. If you need an alibi, I'm here for you."

"Stone, I'm keeping it one hundred. All we did was go to Party Pete's with Solly."

"Well, that can't be all you did because if it was, you wouldn't be on the phone with me like a little kid worried about getting detention."

Tatum became squeamish as he turned onto Autumn's street. Stone was right. He did nothing; why was he so concerned?

"Man, I don't know. It wasn't a big deal but..."

"But what, fool? She give you head?"

"No. It's just after the Party Pete's outing, I didn't tell Autumn. I was going to, but when we were out, I ran into this friend of hers from school. I'm sure this is going to be a problem."

The phone fell silent, causing Tatum to respond.

"Stone, you there?"

"Bitch, I'm on the highway right now looking out for the Federales, and you call me 'cause you got caught having a lunch date with your baby momma? Rev, get off my goddamn line with this low-stakes problem!"

"I'm serious, Stone."

"Rev, I'm serious too. You better walk in there and tell art BAE tha—"

"Her name is Autumn."

"Whatever. You better tell *Autumn* you saw your baby momma, and she lucky you didn't fuck the shit out of her fine ass on some pussy-reparations shit."

Tatum shook his head at his friend's suggestion. He knew Stone well enough to know he wasn't joking however it sounded.

"Stone, you're a toxic motherfucker, you know that?"

"I'm a foster child. What do you expect?"

The pair laughed at the exchange. Stone wasn't one to mince words. At the same time, he always had a perspective Tatum could never arrive at on his own.

"Seriously, Rev, let me be a good friend, even though you been a shit one lately. Ask yourself the question your conscience is asking you: why didn't you tell her?"

It was true his conscience was asking him that very question, nagging him. That didn't mean he had an answer for it.

"Man, I don't know! I didn't think there would be anything to tell. It's Mo! You know what I'm saying? When does she ever follow through? Hell, a part of me didn't even think she would show up. I didn't even tell Solly so he wouldn't get his hopes up. When she showed up, I was like...cool. I just didn't want to stir a hornet's nest unnecessarily."

"Now these hornets about to tear your ass up," Stone said emphatically. Tatum smirked as his friend laughed heavily at his own joke.

"Are you finished? I just don't know what to say. Her friend, Charles, from U of H, saw me and Monique eating, and I know it looked weird."

"I feel that, but let me ask you—how did it feel sitting across from Monique? Did it feel weird? I know she had them titties out."

"Did you talk about her like this when we were together?"

"What? You are my brother. That would be disrespectful. But were they out?"

"Stone."

"Then answer the original question—how did it feel sitting across from her?"

It was a good question. Tatum thought for a bit before finally responding.

"Man, if you want to know the truth, it was weird. Like we have history, you know...but the more I sat there, the more I realized it's just that—the past. I don't want anything from Monique. I already asked her for a divorce, and now I'm gonna ask her to sign the papers so I can be done with it."

"Rev, that's kinda major. You think she's gonna go for that?"

"It's time. Solomon was excited, and that's all that mattered to me. Eventually, I had to just forget this woman walked out on us and let her spend time with him. Once I did that, things started to flow pretty good."

"You a better man than me, Reverend, I'll give you that. Because if this chick would've shown up at my door after leaving me with our baby—"

"Trust me, this ain't for the faint of heart." He turned into the driveway. A second later, Autumn walked outside. Her expression said it all. "Damn, Stone, she knows. Let me hit you back."

"Men everywhere should be ashamed of how you running behind this woman."

"Whatever. I'm out." He hung up the phone and got out of the car.

Autumn stepped back inside but left the door to her loft open. It wasn't the friendliest invitation he'd ever received.

He found Autumn working on her latest piece, aggressively striking the canvas with her paintbrush.

"Hey, ba—"

"So I'm not good enough to meet your son, but you're out here with some random thot drinking tea? Let me guess—lemon ginger."

"Baby, it's not like that at all."

"What I don't get is when did you have the time to meet this hoe?" She slammed the paintbrush on the floor. "Who is she, Tatum?" Tatum was put off by her reaction; he walked closer to assure her.

"Is that what you think? Baby, I haven't met anyone. That's Solomon's mom. She...came over one day asking to reconnect with him and... look, she wants to spend time with Solomon, and the boy really could use a woman in his life." Autumn resumed her painting processing his words. After a spell, she said.

"Well, that's just pretty damn funny because here I thought that I would eventually get to be the female in his life, but you two are out on dates and shit."

"It was not a date. Your friend saw us laughing for a second. The entire moment had been awkward until that point."

She slammed the paintbrush and looked at him.

"How fucking convenient."

"I'm telling you the truth, Autumn."

"I don't give a damn about you telling me the truth now, Tatum. You didn't tell me about it then! You didn't tell me about it before-hand. That's my problem."

She was right. It wasn't something he was proud of, and he honestly didn't have a good answer. He tried to share his mind as best he could.

"I... I didn't know how you would respond."

"Why? Because you were spending time with your son's mother, who, by the way, still happens to be your current wife? Or because you hid it from your girlfriend, who, well, I guess I'm your mistress at this point because she had no problem flashing that ring? Or is it because you have been telling me that the reason I can't meet your son is that you don't want him to get attached to a woman unless it's serious, yet here you are on a Sunday date with a goddamn stranger!"

"Woman, stop it now!" he barked as he moved closer to her. He took her hands, and although she put up some resistance, he wouldn't budge.

"Now I didn't handle this well, I'll admit. It wasn't my intent to sneak around and do anything. It's been awkward, but I... look, I asked Monique for a divorce."

Autumn's anger subsided if only slightly, her eyes shifting to curiosity.

"The one condition on the divorce was she gets to spend time with Solly."

"When did you ask her?"

"A few weeks ago, but she pushed back, saying she'd give me one provided she could see her son. I told her that was a non-starter because the last time they were alone, it didn't go so well. So we're doing some supervised time together until I feel comfortable enough to trust her with Solly. That's it. I don't want her back or anything like that. I'm just doing what I need to do so I can bury that part of my life and be fully present in my current one."

Autumn pulled away and walked into the kitchen to pick up a cup of coffee. She slowly stirred the coffee, no doubt Colombian blend, as if she were processing information miles away from here. After a spell, she responded.

"Do you still love her?"

"Love her? I don't even like her." He walked over to her and wrapped his arms around her, reassuring her of his presence in her life. He kissed her on the back of her neck and turned her around to establish eye contact.

"I only care for one woman. And despite what she may think at the moment, I'm truly doing this out of love for that woman."

"Oh yeah? And which woman is that."

"Jurnee Smollett."

"Tatum, get off of me!" she said as he chuckled. Refusing to let her go, she halfway pushed and relented with little effort.

"Yeah, I mean, she just came back on the market. I gotta shoot my shot."

"I hate you."

"No, you care for me too, and to prove how much you do, I'm about to slide this dick inside of you and touch your backbone until you make a mess on this newly mopped floor of yours."

"You think you deserve Jubilee after what you just said?"

"No, I don't. Thankfully, Jubilee is mine, so I can have my kitty anytime I want. It is my pussy, isn't it?"

She smiled as she pressed her hips against his hardening dick. He wrapped his hand around her neck ever so slightly, starting to squeeze.

"It is," she said as the last walls of her defense went down.

Tatum slid her peach boy shorts down and placed his fingers between her thighs. He wasn't sure if it was the gentle kisses on the neck, the sternness in his voice, or the fact she enjoyed being grabbed by the neck that made her moist, but she was ready to welcome him into her. An opportunity he would not waste. He slid his gray sweatpants down to expose his hardened dick. He gently saturated the head of his cock with her nectar, something that aroused her even more, as he continued to squeeze her neck with his other hand. After the head of this cock was fully glistened, he heard her moan.

"Quit playing, daddy. Give it to me."

He released his hand from her neck and slid it toward the small of her back. Pushing her forward, she bent over to receive his thick cock. He pressed between her lips to enter her as she exhaled pure pleasure.

"Right there," he said as all nine and a half inches bellowed inside of her.

"This is the feeling I have when I say we're one, Autumn. It feels like this." He pushed his dick even further into her, something she welcomed.

"Oh baby," she moaned.

"But I don't want to make love today. You haven't been fucked in a while, and I want to do that," he said as her legs trembled. He pulled his cock back, leaving just the tip in, and then he slammed the entire muscle back inside her. She cried out in ecstasy. He repeated the motion with power and punishment until she bent all the way over to receive him. He gripped her buttocks and pushed with more intensity. The apartment's acoustics made the clapping of their bodies echo as she begged for more.

"Please, daddy," she moaned.

He obliged and thrust his pelvis against her with no regard for anything but pleasure.

"Oh yes, fuck me like you mean it!"

He continued, never breaking stride, his dick pressing hard against her G-spot as his balls slapped her clitoris, bringing added pleasure to her. She was building up to an ecstasy she could no longer hold back.

"I'm cumming," she moaned as he continued to fuck her mercilessly.

"That's it, let that pussy go," he barked as she came on every inch of his now rock-hard dick buried inside her, making her pussy even wetter—something that brought him to his own powerful climax.

"Oh shit, oh shit!" he yelled as he erupted deep in her core, his explosive cum firing against her walls, leaving her dripping, their mixture dripping on the floor. He could go no more. He had given her his essence.

As the two regained their breaths, Autumn relished the moment, inhaling the ecstasy they just experienced. After a brief moment, Tatum turned to her and kissed her passionately. She pushed away from the kiss and locked eyes with him, and spoke from a vulnerable space.

"I... went through a lot with Kaleb. In the end, it was the lies that broke us up. I know your situation, and maybe this was stupid of me, but...just don't hurt me."

"Autumn, I won't let you hit the ground, even if I'm falling myself. I love you too much for that."

Her stunned reaction brought her to face him directly.

"You...love me?"

"I do."

"Since when?"

"Since the moment we went to Egypt," Tatum said, referencing their first weekend together.

"And you're just telling me now, why?"

"I've been too busy showing you."

Her grin grew into a full-blown smile, and she repositioned herself to get closer to him. Autumn responded.

"It was Italy for me. I mean, Egypt...well, that just seems fast— but then again, you are a slut."

He chuckled as the two kissed, sealing the moment. Tatum thought about the entire day. What had started as a dilemma was met with their ability to communicate and be there for each other, and nothing could stand up to that because it was the power of love.

----

1 6

A COUPLE OF FOREVERS

"*B*abe, you sure you haven't seen it?"

"I told you if you keep just putting it anywhere, one day it's gonna—"

"I know, I know, but...that's not helping right now, love. I just need to find my phone."

Tatum rolled his eyes while fighting back a grin. He'd been talking to Autumn on video chat through the computer since she'd once again lost her phone. It was a ritual of hers he loathed. She'd always been careless, except this time, it wasn't entirely her fault. He took it earlier in the day when they had coffee to aid in his plan for the evening.

"I know you had it today because you called me earlier? Can you recall if you had it after that?"

"I... think so," she said, not sounding confident.

Tatum chuckled. It was funny to watch her squirm, particularly when he was the cause.

"Well, I'm going to be leaving here any minute, so I'll swing by and help you look for it. I'm sure it will show up," Tatum said through video chat.

"Okay, I'm gonna check the back to see if I dropped it on the floor; see you soon. Bye, babe."

Tatum logged off of his computer and was fixing his blue button-down shirt when Dr. Peterson came walking down the hallway.

"Oh, there he is!"

"Hey, Dr. P. You going to be teaching the class tonight?"

"Oh, no doubt. The question is will I see you there?"

Tatum conceded his mentor's point. He had missed a lot of class time as of late. Nothing to affect his grades but certainly enough to catch his professor's attention. Tatum grabbed his bag as the two headed for the door.

"You know, Doc, I've just been busy with Solomon and the job and-"

"Your love life."

Tatum froze up as he looked at Dr. Peterson, who fixed his glasses and smiled.

"Doc, how did you—"

"It's a pharmacist's job to detect variances, and you not being at school is about as varied as it gets," he said.

"You're right. She's wonderful. Smart, funny, talented—total package. She's the one I think I'm going to marry."

The doctor shifted his weight and looked at Tatum, who could tell he was aging. His full mustache, once jet-black, was beginning to develop some salt and pepper against his brown skin. He pulled a hand out of his gray pants pocket and placed it on his pupil's shoulder.

"Well, that's funny because I thought you were married to someone else who used to be *the one* unless it's been that long since we talked."

"Well, yeah...I'm...working on that."

"So you talked to your ex-wife?"

"Yeah, she came back around a couple of weeks ago wanting to spend more time with Solomon. We had a few civil discussions. We're getting divorced provided she gets a good visitation schedule with Solomon."

"So she's back in his life! Man, I'm glad to hear that. Unless it's dram-"

"So far, so good," Tatum said, cutting his mentor off. "Seems like her intent is only to spend time with Solly."

Dr. Peterson leaned in as he responded. "Just make sure you do what you got to do to get the Wilcox Award. Not only is your tuition secure, but it's going to make sure you have a job here for at least a year. There's an unspoken rule; every Wilcox winner has a home at his company for life. You're a good young brother. I just want to see you succeed."

He finished as he and Tatum both reached the parking garage.

"That means a lot to me, Dr. P. I want to thank you for all those years ago when you took a chance on me. I had no idea what the possibilities were. Thanks for taking me under your wing."

"Tatum, I was always told it's better to be prepared for an opportunity and not have one rather than to have an opportunity and not be prepared. You made yourself known by being the hardest-working person in the room. Didn't matter who was in the room—including me. So, I didn't give you an opportunity. I just recognized you'd earned one."

Tatum acknowledged his mentor's truth but was still glad someone believed in him. And he knew he would have to do better. He reached out to shake the professor's hand, but it turned into an embrace.

"I'll do better, Dr. P."

"So I'll see you tonight?"

"Not tonight. It's been exactly six months since...well..."

"Ah. The variance. I understand. Well, if I have taught you anything, I've taught you that you can't disappoint a pretty woman. Go do what you have to do."

Tatum smiled and walked off with his mentor's blessing. After several steps, he stopped and turned back.

"Hey Doc, how'd you know she was pretty?"

"Aren't they always?"

The two men shared one final laugh and parted ways. Tatum got in his car. He respected Dr. Peterson even more now that the two had become more than student and teacher, employee and employer. Dr.

Peterson was his friend, and he decided to defer to his wisdom and finish strong.

Buzz. He checked his phone it was Autumn; she sent an email

R u on ur way? I still can't find it!

Be there soon.

Tatum had plans, but he knew the first thing he had to do was give Autumn back her phone. The joke had gone on long enough. It wasn't long before he got to her job at Paint & Sip, a franchise that allowed its patrons to drink recreationally while painting by numbers. Autumn enjoyed the job, but it seriously underutilized her talents, something he told her all the time. She could be making real money painting, not helping a bunch of people who didn't have the talent to make it.

He walked into the boutique studio with its multi-colored walls. *I feel like I'm standing inside a Rubik's Cube*, he thought. None of it mattered when he saw her, though. She wore a pair of red spandex tights and a fitted white top, and if this hadn't been her place of work, he would have taken her right there. She was distracted, still searching for her phone, which Tatum saw as the perfect chance to hide the pink box, complete with a white bow, that contained her phone near the trashcan holding several used canvases.

"So you haven't found it yet, huh?" Tatum asked, hoping to contribute to her quest. The place was empty at this time of day, leaving her to mainly do administrative work, which didn't take up a lot of her time. As a result, she had become comfortable in more ways than one.

"I think I must have left it at home."

"Well, did you call it?"

"You are so handsome and stupid. Of course! It's the first thing I did."

"Says the woman who can't find her phone. I'm gonna call it right now." Tatum picked up his phone to dial her number. Within moments, the two of them heard a buzzing noise. Autumn, stunned by the sound, spun around and walked toward the trashcan.

"I swear I called it and... oh, you asshole," she said, retrieving the phone from the box Tatum had wrapped it in. As he chuckled, she unwrapped her phone and charged at him to lightly punch him in the arm.

"You had my phone this whole time?"

"I did. Hell, you don't pay any attention anyway," he said, laughing as she continued to punch him playfully.

"Why did you take it?"

"There is a note on your phone. Open it."

Autumn put in her pin and opened the phone, and she read the following:

Happy six-month anniversary. Welcome to Autumn's Song!

"What's Autumn's Song?"

"Why, it's just the hottest online art gallery for black art on the internet, also known as your new business."

Autumn was stunned by his words as her mouth dropped wide open. He continued,

"Since you were never going to do it, I took the time to upload pictures of all of the paintings you're willing to sell to your newly built website and attached your new email address to your newly created business Instagram profile and put them all on your phone for you to manage. Anyone can now reach out to you to buy the paintings because they're all online. You just have to, well, do nothing. Now you have no more excuses," Tatum said as he kissed her on the cheek while she scrolled.

"Holy shit, babe, there's like one thousand followers already. People are asking for prices!"

"Sounds like Autumn's Song is officially in business. Now your first step is to...Autumn?"

He watched as she teared up. She leaned into him and wept openly. It caught him off guard as he tried to console her.

"Baby, what's wrong?" he asked.

"Tate, nobody has ever believed in me like this. When I tell my dad my dreams, he's the first to point out what could go wrong or shoot them down. I don't have anyone that would be this proactive for me."

"That's not true—you got me. Baby, I believe in you."

She pulled back and wiped away the tears running down her cheeks. After a breath, she said, "I know you do, but...it's different from someone saying the words and walking the walk. Like...you already got the pussy. Why are you trying so hard?" She said, trying to laugh through her tears. Tatum chuckled in response as she continued, "Seriously, you always go above and beyond like...you work at making sure I'm happy. Who does that? I don't want to go on and on, but it's just...I never feel like you won't be there for me. I trust you. I trust you with my heart."

"You're just saying that 'cause you don't have anything for me, huh?"

The two laughed. Everything she was saying was true, and he knew it. He also knew that Autumn didn't know it was their six-month anniversary because she didn't make a big deal out of those kinds of events, and why should she? She'd never had anyone to enjoy them with.

"It's been busy. You're not mad, are you?"

"Not at all. You're gonna feel guilty, so you'll be extra freaky in the bedroom; everyone wins!" he said, kissing her on the neck.

"Come on. We are going to eat."

"Wait, where are we going?"

"Grazia's." Autumn smiled and hugged him intimately. She'd been talking about eating there for weeks, with Tatum always putting it off. What she didn't know was that he'd been putting it off for just this purpose. For tonight.

"Oh, you're gonna have to call in tomorrow—you're getting all the Jubilee you want." She started to take off her apron.

"Woman, get your shit and get in the car."

"Okay, let me lock up."

Tatum walked out to his sedan and waited until Autumn closed down the shop. She came outside having changed her top to a green earth tone, off-the-shoulder number with black tights and jet-black, ankle-high boots. She threw her bag in the back, and the two headed to Grazia's in a suburb south of Houston. While they were on the highway, Autumn stared at him curiously. It was as if she wanted to ask a question. He wasn't sure what it was. As he parked, he turned to her.

"Hey, where are you?"

She looked at him endearingly and replied, "I'm here."

It was all the confirmation he needed. It meant she was with him no matter where they were.

They walked into Grazia's, and Tatum could see why she was eager to try it. He was impressed by how the modern design fused with an Old World Italian feel, complete with sandstone tiles and cobblestone walls. The silver-doored brick oven was the center of attention, and the warm lighting made the ambiance the perfect place to celebrate anything. The hostess ushered them to a seat right near one of the large double-pane windows overlooking a nearby lake.

"So, is it living up to your expectations?" Tatum asked.

"This is beautiful." As they took in the ambiance, the waiter approached. Tatum ordered lasagna, his go-to Italian meal, while Autumn went with baked fish in Alfredo sauce. It wasn't long before they finished their meals and sat, enjoying each other's company over a cup of coffee and tea. That's when Tatum pulled out another box.

"You're just showing off now."

"Hate the game, not the player." He smiled. She opened the box and started bouncing in her chair.

Inside of the box was a silver necklace with a customized gem attached to it—a paintbrush made of diamonds and sapphires.

"This is beautiful, baby. I am speechless."

Tatum smiled as she put the necklace on and looked in the mirror. He adored her smile, and she couldn't help but smile at this moment. She was happy, but he wasn't done. He took out another box and handed it to her, and said,

"But wait, there's more." As if to imitate the old infomercials that would come on late-night television. Autumn opened the other box and dropped the box in excitement.

"Oh my God! We're going to see Preston Cole?" she said excitedly.

"He's the one that got us in this mess, right? Figured we could dance to him again, but in Austin."

"Oh, you know I love me some Preston. But what about Solomon? Didn't you say your mom was working most weekends?"

"I've worked it out with Monique. She's going to watch him that weekend."

"Wait, he's spending the entire weekend?"

"Like you just said, mom had to work, and I wanted to do this. Besides, Monique's been consistent over the last couple of months, and he wants to meet his grandma on that side of the family. I have to get out of my own bias. It's time." Autumn placed the necklace on her neck and smiled with the enthusiasm of a six-year-old child at Christmas time. She then turned her attention back to the matter at hand.

"Okay, but I don't want you to feel uncomfortable. I know how you are with Solomon."

"I'm good. I haven't had a break—like a whole weekend—since, well, hell, six months ago, and since we're doing it up, I figured maybe you'd stop by and see your pops while you're there. You've been talking about it and..."

"Why do you love me?" The question caught him off guard. He looked at her as her mood became serious. She continued. "Why do all of this? Get me this beautiful necklace, tickets to my favorite artist, build an Instagram profile—hell, a business—and try to get me to reconnect with my dad. I need to know. Why do you care? Is this real?"

Tatum smiled and looked out the window before returning to her beautiful brown eyes.

"If you would've told me six months ago I would even be talking to you after the day we met, I'd have laughed in your face. But, I mean, you've been here. We've had moments better than any I can remember in my life, and I think about you all the time. I want you to be happy. Seeing you smile makes me happy. I think about your smile, and it...it fills me. When you ask me what I'm thinking about—I'm thinking about you. The answer is always you. You're in my dreams. It's you when I'm awake, and it's you when I'm happy, sad, lonely, horny, and when I... breathe."

She covered her lips with her hand as he continued.

"I wear my heart on my sleeve, Autumn. I think you don't show your heart because you're afraid someone's gonna break it."

He watched her as the moonlight glistened off her mocha cheekbones. "I won't break your heart because I'm giving you mine to keep. And I like my heart. I need my heart...but not as much as I need you. And yeah, it's been six months on paper, but I feel as if I've loved you over several lifetimes. Hell, I don't know if I could stop now if I tried. You ask me why do I do this; why do I care. To me, the answer is simple. I was born to. You are my Fatima."

A tear rolled from her eyes. She understood the significance of the name: Fatima, one of the two soulmates from the book that started this whirlwind love affair. Autumn pointed at him as he extended his hand, and she leaned in to kiss him. She took the napkin and wiped her face. After a spell, she looked up and smiled, another tear rolling down her cheek.

"I can't stand you, Tatum Clarke. You got me crying over here and shit. I love you for it, but not just for that, for everything you have been. You're good to me, and you're smart. When you look at me, it's like you see someone else. You see who I could be, who I'd like to be. It makes me strive to want to meet that version of myself I see looking back at me through your eyes. You shower me with compliments and confidence, and every time I listen to you speak, I feel like I'm gonna have an orgasm." She looked into his eyes as if to connect with his spirit. He was silent as she continued.

"You're humble, but at the same time have high-reaching confidence, which could be confused for arrogance if you're not paying attention. But that's just because the average person can't match your ambition. Achievement is a lifestyle for you. You're not just an alpha; you're an apex predator. You hit life with a sledgehammer, and all the while, go unnoticed until it's too late because you're comfortable in your role as *the* alpha. Regardless of who's in the room, they gravitate to you, and you carry it. You seek responsibility almost to a fault in a world full of fuck boys who run from it. All of this while somewhere searching for yourself. So, yeah...I love you. You make it easy to love you. To me, loving you is art."

It was heartfelt; it was sincere; it was Autumn. He was falling in love at a rate that could only end in beauty or disaster. He was about to kiss her when she stopped him.

"And I know you don't think I remember a bunch of things...but I remembered today."

She opened her bag and pulled out a royal blue gift bag, and handed it to him. He smiled as he removed the card.

You're hot, I'm in heat, we're a match...so let's just ignite already.

He laughed at the signature. He went into the bag and pulled out the last item: a bronzed notebook with a blue and bronzed floral design and a metallic flap to seal. He opened the notebook and noticed there was an inscription.

To Blue — I hope you find the inspiration to fill these pages. —Autumn

He smiled. It was perfect. He'd been close to filling up the contents of his old notebook. Yet, there was something about the inscription that puzzled him.

"This is beautiful, but why did you say, To Blue?"

"Because when I think of you, that's what I call you."

"Okay, but why Blue?"

"Because it's my favorite color...and you're my favorite person."

17

UNRAVEL ME

"*I* can't believe that for the first time in ten years we missed the car show. And for what? For some new pussy you're gettin'."

"Stone, I'm gonna make it up to you, brother, I swear. We've just been on a whirlwind since Autumn started selling her artwork online. She was posting, and an art buyer hit her up on the Direct Messages. I checked out the buyer, and he was legit. His shop is on the outskirts of Austin. It just so happens we were coming to see Preston Cole up there anyway, so she hit the dealer back to see if she could meet during the day, and he agreed. The original plan was to get on the road after me and you hit the car show, but since the dealer agreed, we're going the night before."

"Aw, fuck you, Rev, I swear."

"My bad, bro, but I swear I'm gonna figure it out."

"Your word don't mean shit these days, Reverend Clarke, but I still got love for ya. So where is Art BAE now?"

Tatum looked around to see if Autumn was in sight. He resumed his conversation.

"Alright, Stone, this between me and you. So, she's tweaking, right?

She didn't like any of the paintings she brought up here. She's been moody, but I realize she's just nervous, so I—"

"So you dicked her down, didn't you? Nah... you been acting like a whole placenta lately, so knowing you...you went down on her."

"Point is I took care of her."

"I knew it! You're a nasty motherfucker, Reverend Clarke."

"So, the thing is this. I put it down. She's screaming and yelling and all that, but almost as soon as we're done, she just pops up and starts painting,"

"Wait, she just popped up?"

"She popped up."

"You had her leg shaking 'n' shit?"

"All of that, Stone, and so it got me thinking. Like, damn, was it trash?"

The two were silent on the phone. Tatum could tell his best friend was deep in thought.

"How long before she got up?"

"It was like an hour later, and she been up all night since."

"Did she sleep a lot the night before?"

"Probably about normal."

"Sounds like it might have been trash. You should've dicked her down."

"Damn. I was tired too."

"Getting old, bro."

"Fuck... man, I'm gonna go talk to her."

"And say what? I'm sorry my tongue game was trash last night?"

Tatum conceded the point.

"Then what do I say?"

"Nothing, fool. Go in there, have a pep talk with your boy downstairs, and tell him he gotta show up for your ancestors' pride. For Wakanada."

"Alright, bro, I appreciate it. Soon as I get back, we'll link up."

"Enjoy Austin."

"Hey, check on my pops for me."

"I just saw him yesterday."

"How's he doing?

"Well, he's not looking at power lines if that's what you mean. He's actually the life of the party. You need to go see him when you take your face out of Art BAE's crotch. Anyway, do your thing. We'll be here when you get back."

"Alright, brother. Peace."

Tatum hung up the phone. It was their first day in Austin, and it wasn't starting out the way he planned. Since they'd been together, they always had incredible chemistry, yet her one action made him doubt himself. *Fuck it; I had a bad day, it happens,* he thought, accepting he might have given an off- performance the night before. He walked down the stairs to find Autumn in the kitchen. He wanted to know what time they were going to see her father, considering they needed to swing by the art buyer's shop, all before the concert.

Tatum turned the corner and saw and Autumn looking at what was a newly finished portrait. It stopped him in his tracks. Her self-portrait was the most majestic thing he'd ever seen. To call it beautiful would be understating its mastery. She'd sculpted her eyes, her lips, and her afro perfectly. The brown-skinned woman with jet black hair in the picture wearing a white tank top was, without question, the most impressive painting he'd ever seen. He stood in awe of how skillfully she captured the strength and vulnerability of the woman in the image: her beauty, her poise, her joy, her pain—all of it on display.

"Autumn, this is-"

"Beautiful," she said, finishing his statement. She walked over and, with confidence, kissed him and looked deep in his eyes.

"When we made love last night, I saw you, the way you looked at me. I saw myself through your eyes, and it was like I was someone who wasn't here yet. And I saw how madly in love you were with her, and I started imagining the way she sees you. The way I see you—a good man with a good heart with a purpose in this life. I wanted to let you know that if you ever needed to go to the pyramids in Egypt and I couldn't go with you, I'd be at the well. I'm *your* Fatima."

Her smile felt like a kiss from the sun. He shook his head in disbelief. She was his Fatima, but he had no plans of going anywhere.

"Is this what you were working on?"

"Yes."

"So my tongue game wasn't trash?"

"What? No, it was amazing. It was inspirational head." She kissed him on the cheek, both still looking at the portrait. He held her as he wiped paint from her cheek.

"No disrespect to your Purple Haze painting, but I think it's the most beautiful painting I've ever seen." He wanted to keep it for himself, but he also knew how important it was for her to present her best work to the buyer.

"Are you going to show this to the art buyer while we're in town?"

"I'm considering it. I took a picture to add to my portfolio. I at least want him to see it for—"

"Validation. I get it. Well, it's as good as sold. Now hurry up. We're about to be late to see your father."

As Tatum continued to get dressed, he noticed Autumn hesitating.

"Blue..." she said, calling him by his newly minted nickname.

"Yes, baby? What's wrong?"

"My dad. There's a reason it's been years since we've seen each other. He's a good man, but he's harsh. I'm going into this meeting with this art buyer and—"

"Autumn, I told you I won't let you hit the ground if I'm falling my damn self. You're gonna have a wonderful day today with your dad, and selling your biggest commission, and seeing Preston Cole. I'm gonna make sure of it."

"What if he doesn't like it?"

"Then he shouldn't be an art buyer because he has no taste. Now hurry your ass up because we've gotta go meet your father."

The trip to her father's house was scenic. Autumn pointed out the architecture in the city that her dad had contributed. Tatum watched her pride swell as she talked about him, yet the closer they got to the home where she grew up, the more apprehensive she appeared. By the time they arrived, she was all but silent. As Tatum parked the car, he looked at her.

"Hey? Are you okay? Where are you right now?"

"Um...my dad has done a lot of great things, and as a result, sometimes he doesn't know how to talk to people. I'm—"

"Oh, you think I'm gonna say something to your dad? I'm about to be a pharmacist for the rest of my life. I'm gonna be able to deal with a... Autumn?"

It was then he realized she wasn't concerned about what her dad would say to him but rather to her. Tatum unbuckled his seatbelt.

"Autumn, we don't have to go in if you—"

"No, I want to. It's time. Just...if he starts—"

"Here," Tatum said, cutting her off and giving her the car keys. "If you feel uncomfortable in any way, just squeeze my hand two times. When you do that, I'll politely interrupt whatever is going on, and you head straight to the car, okay?"

She nodded, but she was still uncertain. He lifted her chin.

"Fatima, look at me. I got you. It's us, always." Reassured by his statement, he got out of the car to open her door. Tatum stood in front of the concrete, gray-brick, two-story home accented by green shutters.

They walked to the front door and rang the doorbell. An older man, about six-foot-one with the same cinnamon-brown skin as Autumn, answered the door.

"Hey baby, come in, come in," her father said as the two walked inside the home. From the moment Tatum walked in, he was impressed. The home itself was aesthetically appealing. Wall-indented cherry wood shelves displayed his architectural awards, and large slates of marble accented the walls. This was an artisan's handiwork, and you tell her father took personal pride in it.

"You like it, huh? Took a long time. Maybe you'll get a house of your own, Mr... I'm sorry—what's your name, son?"

"Tatum Clarke," he said, the two men shaking hands. He glanced over at Autumn, who was already apologizing with her eyes since she knew the word son rubbed him wrong. Nonetheless, Tatum was cordial, and they carried on into the kitchen, another astonishing room. Stainless steel appliances with grayish-blue paint against walls that bled into white cabinets. The marble countertop looked identical to the marble protruding from the walls in the hallway.

As they turned the corner, a woman about the same height as Autumn's dad turned around.

"Hey, Momma."

"Autumn, baby! How are you doing?" the woman said warmly.

Autumn embraced her mother and introduced her to Tatum. As they all sat at the kitchen table, Tatum couldn't help but be impressed by the authentic architecture of the home. Every room had striking details.

"This home is one giant piece of marble. I got it at auction from the old Enron building. They were going to use it for God knows what. I got it for considerably less and used it to weave in and out of every room in our home.

"It's pretty impressive."

"Thank you," her father said, running a hand through his curly gray hair. He turned to his daughter and said, "So, Autumn, how's my favorite soon-to-be graduate?"

Tatum glanced at Autumn, who clearly hadn't told her parents she dropped out.

"Things are good. I'm just in town, thought I'd swing by. How have you and Mom been?"

"We've been great. Your mother's been nagging me about my diet, but other than that—"

"Autumn, take this man. He don't listen to nobody for nothing. Honey, I tell you the man needs to go back to work."

"Constance, they can't afford me no more. That's why I'm consulting."

"Well, you need to do something. All you do is sit around here complaining about your headaches and constipation."

"Constance, that ain't nobody's business but me and the Lord's, and I'd appreciate it if you'd keep it that way."

The couple's back and forth sparked a chuckle from Tatum.

Constance looked at Autumn and said, "But you didn't come out here to hear a bunch of old people problems."

"In other words, what do you need?" her father said, getting to the point.

"I'm actually out here selling a painting. And me and my friend Tatum stopped by."

"I didn't know your little paint-by-numbers job allowed you to sell any real merchandise."

Tatum instantly understood Autumn's apprehension. He glanced over at her, feeling her uneasiness. But he wasn't alone. Constance leaned over and rubbed her daughter on the arm.

"Don't mind him. Autumn, that's good, honey. I'm proud of you. Do you sell a lot of artwork?"

"Well, I-"

"Hell, she needs to, as much money as that degree cost."

"Keith!" her mother interjected. "You hush. Now, Autumn, honey, what were you saying?"

"Well, actually, it's my first painting for my online business. Wanna see?"

She pulled out her phone and showed it to her mother, who put on her glasses to examine the picture. She then exited the phone so Keith could look at the photos. Autumn's face shifted from excited to hopeful. She wanted his approval.

"I don't want to see those pictures. What I want to know is how are you going to run a whole business with your busy work schedule, your school, and a dog?"

"Keith, now you know she don't have that dog anymore."

"That's right; you killed the damn dog. And now you're gonna try to run a business and go to school? Oh, I see, so now it comes out—the real reason you're here. Tell me, how much money do you need?"

"What, I...no, I don't need money. That's not why I came, and as far as school goes, I dropped out."

Her father stood up in frustration. "You did what?"

"I believe in this business. I want to see what it can be. I'm really good and-"

"Autumn, just stop! Because all I hear is Dad, I pissed away your money yet again!"

Autumn squeezed Tatum's hand twice. He'd been expecting it and stood up.

"Excuse me, I need to use the restroom. Autumn, can you show me where it is?"

"Okay," she said, the pain between the cracks of her unraveling armor obvious. He helped her to her feet and walked to the front of the house. He opened the front door.

"Go outside and start the car. I'll be there soon." She was in tears as she walked out of the house she'd always had trouble calling a home. Today's events only proved that it could never be a home to her.

As the door closed Tatum, heard footsteps behind him. Keith and Constance were walking up to the living room door. Keith scanned the area for his daughter, ready to continue his tirade against her.

"Where is Autumn? Did she go outside?"

"Mr. Elders, we're going to head out. It was nice to meet you both."

"Boy, just who in the hell do you think you are talking to me about my child?"

"That's the other thing. I'm not your son or your boy. I'm the man who came to support your daughter, and when she felt uncomfortable, I'm the man who's going to make sure she's okay. That's all I am. Right now, I need you to see that."

Keith pushed Tatum in the chest, causing him to budge slightly. Tatum couldn't hold his instinct to react and shoved Keith backward, causing him to stumble slightly. After he regained his balance, he fixed his glasses and barked at Tatum.

"Oh, so you supposed to be some kind of tough guy?"

"You put your hands on me again, and you'll find out the answer to all your questions."

Tatum responded with a coldness so bitter it brought a chill to the room. Mr. Elders stood motionless. Tatum wasn't looking for conflict, but he wasn't going to run from it. He saw the concern in Constance's eyes and decided to be more ginger.

"Look, Mr. Elders—and I say that with the respect you've earned thus far—we're leaving. But before we do, I've gotta say this. You know what's sad? I came over here to meet this great man Autumn told me about. This kind and compassionate man, and the thing she loved the most about him, was when he used to be this amazing artist. It's what inspired her to paint in the first place. It's too bad I never got to meet him. I would have liked him. You have a nice day."

Tatum opened the door to walk out.

"Oh, but before I go, the headaches and the constipation are typically a side effect from acid reflux medication. Tell your doctor to lower your dosage. It was a pleasure to meet you both."

Tatum closed the door and never looked back.

18

MAKE THE MOST

*T*atum opened the door and walked out to see his lover in the car, wiping tears from her eyes. He glanced back at Keith, who had come outside by now. He stood on the steps and nodded, clearly receiving the message Tatum expressed. Tatum got in the car and started to drive. He watched Autumn as she silently stared out the window. He wanted to say something—he just didn't know what.

"Oh shit, the art buyer. Baby, we gotta go there." It was the best he could do. He wanted to be there for her but also understood to a great degree the complexities of the father-child relationship.

"Am I a fuck-up?" Autumn said after a spell.

"What? Love, of course, no-"

"Are you ashamed of me?"

Tatum pulled to the curb in front of a house before exiting the suburb.

"I could never be ashamed of you."

"Oh really? Because it's been over six months, and I still haven't met Solomon. You think I'd fuck that up somehow?"

"What? No... you know that's different. It's not that I don't want you to meet him. I just...look, my mother only dated my dad and this guy name Osmond since I've been alive. Now, I'm sure there were more men, but I have nothing to indicate that and I respect her for it. I'm just trying to make sure the woman in his life isn't passing through."

" Like his mother?"

"It's his mother. I won't go there with you. What's this really about?"

"It's about trust, Tatum. You trust her but not me. Hell, you don't trust me with anything. You won't even let me read your journal. Nobody trusts me."

He wanted to respond, but she was hurting. More than he could solve right now. Still, he had to try.

"He didn't mean it, Autumn. Any of it."

"Let's just go home. I'm not responsible enough to run a business."

Tatum picked up her phone and got the address to the art studio, and set directions on the map.

"What are you doing? I said let's go back to—"

"Woman, I'm gonna tell you this one time—whatever your emotions, however you feel, the one place we will not the fuck go, is home. Now you might have valid points about all of this, but the bottom line is this: We don't have time for you to have a pity party. We'll do that when we're off the court. Your dad got under your skin, but he can't take your gift away from you. You have a talent the world needs to see. Hell, there's a man willing to pay for that talent just down the road here, so take all the time you need to brood and weep until you get there, but the next time that car door opens, be prepared to sell some art."

"I'm not in the headspace to sell any art."

"Then get in the headspace to sell some art. You feel like no one trusts you? You want to prove your father wrong? Go do your thing, Fatima. You showed me every building your father designed, and I saw the home he put together, and none of it even comes close to a portrait you did this morning on a whim. This ain't time to die; it's time to ride."

"But I-"

"End of discussion."

He knew she was afraid, but he wasn't going to let her give in to her fears. She was silent as he drove. By the time he got on the highway, she extended her arm to hold his hand. When they got to the building to park, Tatum unbuckled his seatbelt. Before he could climb out, he heard, "I'm always the punchline in my family, I can't seem to do anything right, and my dad doesn't let me forget that. But today...today was the first time anyone defended me. No one has ever protected me like that. And even now, when I wanted to run, you made me come here. How do you know what I need when I need it?" Tatum held her hand as she was struggling to regain composure.

"I listen," Tatum responded.

Autumn looked him deep in his eyes.

"When you met me, I was in the middle of a storm, and I want to thank you because anytime I feel overwhelmed or lost, I just need to find you to course-correct. You've been a light...a beacon...a—"

"You've done the same for me. We're each other's lighthouses."

"Thank you." She leaned in and kissed him.

"I love you," Tatum said. "And as far as Solomon goes, I ju-"

"I get it. You don't want to confuse him. But your journal—that's a different story," she said, her smile wiping away the remnants of her tears.

"Well, with that being said, we're here. Should we sell some art?"

"Let's go conquer Studio 21," Tatum said aloud, waiting a few seconds for Autumn to finish applying foundation to her face. The pair got out of the car and walked into the red stone building, where they were immediately taken aback. The inside was totally renovated, a contrast to the retro feel on the outside of the building. They realized Studio 21 was a technology company that, by the look of things, had nothing to do with art. Tatum thought they must have the wrong location.

"Is this the right place?" Tatum said.

"I think so..."

"Welcome to Studio 21. My name is Davis. You must be here to meet Shead."

"Yes. Montrice Shead."

"Right this way," Davis said as the pair followed him. They looked at each other, confirming they were both confused as to why a technology company would be interested in art.

"Hi, I'm Montrice," said a stocky, brown-skinned man about five feet nine with a warm smile. "You must be Autumn. I'm sorry I didn't meet you out front. This is my partner, Russ. We were just talking about your work."

"Hi, I'm Autumn, and this is my business partner Tatum Clarke. It's nice to meet you."

While Autumn spoke, Montrice gave her a long look. Something that was promptly picked up by Tatum prompted Montrice to finally share what he was thinking.

"Excuse me for staring, but did you go to Austin Liberal Arts and Science Academy?"

"I did."

"I knew it!" Montrice said as he pounded his desk in excitement.

"You made the black angel mural in the cafeteria for the nativity scene."

And got expelled in the process, Autumn wanted to remind him but thought it best if she found out where he stood on it first.

"Holy cow, man. That was an amazing mural. Russ, check it out. Christmas week, the Arts Department painted a nativity scene. Only issue was everyone in the scene was white. Well, you know, all the black kids had an issue with it. But the principal says it's just art, it doesn't mean anything, and we're sensitive. Well, the day before Christmas break, we go into the cafeteria. Autumn over here apparently breaks in the school in the middle of the night and paints over the entire nativity scene with an army of angels. Black women, all of them. Afros poppin', melanin poppin', hips poppin', and underneath the mural was the inscription—"

"All black women are angels," Montrice and Autumn said in unison, laughing at their shared memory. Autumn had now relaxed, her spirits lifted by this conversation.

"Man, after that, you were a legend at school! All the black kids protested after you got expelled. We all wondered what happened to you."

"I ended up graduating from Austin High. My dad was furious."

"Well, he's got to be proud of you now. You're doing your art thing!"

"He's still...my dad. But forget about that. What about you?"

"Oh, man. Well, I know you don't remember me, but I was on the science side. I went to UT after high school, met Russ, and went to work for Dell. He went to work for Apple, but after a while, we decided we should go out on our own. So we created Studio 21, which stores all your digital records for a lifetime for a small fee."

"Montrice is modest," Russ interjected. "Right now, we're in negotiations with Amazon to use our services. If they do, it's game over."

"That's amazing!" Autumn said. "But I don't understand what it has to do with art."

"Nothing. But like I said, we went to the same high school. There was something inspirational about walking in the hallways and seeing art along the corridors. One of your paintings popped up in my feed, and I reached out to you."

"So, we want three to five paintings, and I'll be honest— there's a guy named Pasha Hammonds. He's got a collection and a name that's heavy in art circles, so we feel his art is going to increase in value."

Tatum watched as Autumn became deflated. He had to step in.

"You know, it's interesting you have that point of view. I think too many people misunderstand genius because it's uncommon. Now, I've seen Pasha's work, and it's amazing, but I've also seen Autumn's. I'm biased, but I'm also a straight shooter." Tatum pulled out his phone and went to the Instagram profile that featured Autumn's work. He handed it to Montrice, who began to scroll through the profile.

"THAT IS THE WORK OF A GENIUS. SHE'S PLAYING CHESS WHILE HER competition is playing checkers. The way I see it, you're a bleeding-edge company. You need a bleeding-edge artist. That's not Pasha. That's the woman standing in front of you. The one who got kicked out of school for her bold vision. The one who stirred an entire community with a single painting. More importantly, we as a company are doing the same thing you guys are doing, blending the digital world with the artistic—just from a different angle. That's why all of our paintings are uploaded on Instagram direct to our customers. Because no disrespect to Mr. Hammond, I think what he's done is amazing. I could never think as he does. But the one thing I've learned working with Autumn is light moves at a different speed."

He waited for Montrice to scroll through her collection.

"I like these four paintings. Let me know what the cost is and send me the invoice."

Autumn's eyes widened.

"They are five hundred do- "

"As a down payment. The total cost of the paintings themselves is four grand apiece," Tatum said.

"Sixteen grand. Cool. I'll get with Accounting and cut you a check. But I still want that invoice."

Autumn took the phone and examined the pictures.

"I'm sorry, this one isn't for sale."

Tatum took the phone and looked at the profile. It was the image she painted that morning—the portrait of Fatima.

"Autumn, are you sure?"

"Yes, I'm sure. I need to take it off my profile."

Montrice leaned over to examine the painting that wasn't available.

"Oh, man, I like that one the most. Is it money? Because I'll pay more."

No, it's not money. It's...just not available. I'm sorry."

Tatum wanted to ask why, but he knew now wasn't the time. Montrice nodded as if to concede.

"Me too. I'll still get the other three, but if this one becomes available, let me know. It would be perfect outside my office. I could look at it every day."

"Montrice, thank you," Autumn said as the teams shook hands.

"I'll get you that check, and we can celebrate. What are you two doing for dinner?"

"Oh, we're supposed to be seeing Preston Cole at Midtown Live."

"No way! We're going there too. We keep a reserved table. Feel free to come through."

"That sounds like a plan."

The pair walked out of the building. The two said nothing until they got in the car. As Tatum turned on the engine, Autumn screamed.

"Twelve thousand U.S. American Dollars!"

19

BEST PART

"*B*aby! I just made twelve thousand dollars. Can you believe that shit?"

Autumn screamed excitedly as they sat in the car. Tatum smiled for Autumn, who was as happy as he'd ever seen her. In the course of a day, she'd gone from being doubted by her father to selling not just one but three of her paintings for a price he negotiated.

"I can't believe you were going to sell those masterpieces for five hundred dollars."

"I know, I know, I don't know what I was thinking."

"You weren't thinking like a business owner, that's for sure. I don't know anything about art, but I know how much Pasha Hammond sells his paintings for."

Autumn paused.

"How do you know that?"

"Because I went on his website and sent him an email about several paintings, and he responded."

Tatum followed the directions to Midtown Live while Autumn was stunned.

"I didn't know he was making that much."

"And you have to know stuff like that, Fatima—you're a business owner now. This is, on some level, your competition. You can paint, but you need to know the market prices. It's about balance."

"Damn, what do you want from me, Tatum? I have a sharp tongue and some good pussy. That's balance."

"Autumn."

"Okay, I get it! Geeze, let me enjoy the moment. I'm rich!"

Tatum rolled his eyes and parked the car. The pair got out and walked into the darkly lit lounge. Tatum, who was already exhausted from the day, wanted to move on from hanging out with their newfound friends, but he knew he had to stomach it a bit longer. To loosen up, the two ordered the first of several vodka-based drinks. Autumn had her usual screwdriver while Tatum stuck with vodka and cranberry for the remainder of the night. They took the shots and started to head to Studio 21's table. Montrice waved them over. They walked into the VIP section, where Tatum and Autumn were both surprised by a slender, light-skinned man in an emerald shirt sitting at the table.

"Autumn, Tatum, I'd like you to meet Preston Cole."

"What's good with you?" Preston said as he extended his hand to greet them.

A giddy Autumn responded, "You're so awesome! I know you hear this all the time, but we're some of your biggest fans. We started dating the night we saw you in Houston."

"Oh, that's cool. I'm from the H, so I appreciate the love."

As Russ and Montrice started talking amongst themselves, Autumn continued. "When is the album dropping?"

Preston winced at the question.

"Real soon. I'm working on it."

"Well, if you need some material, Tatum here is an excellent songwriter."

The words caught Tatum off guard. He looked at her in astonishment.

"What? Wait...no, I... dabble. I'm..."

"He's modest. He keeps a journal, and all he has in there are songs."

Tatum leaned in and muttered in between his teeth so only Autumn could hear. "What in the hell are you doing?"

Smiling, she turned to him and muttered back, "The same thing you did for me."

"You write songs?" Preston asked.

"I um...yeah, I do," Tatum said after downing his drink.

"Cool. Well, we're both from Houston. Maybe we can link up. Hit me up on IG. Right now, I gotta get ready to go on stage. Enjoy the show."

"Will do, man. It was good to meet you." The two shook hands as Preston said goodbye to the remainder of the table and headed backstage to get ready to perform. Autumn sat down and sipped her drink. She turned to Montrice and said,

"I can't believe you know Preston Cole!"

"Yeah, he comes here twice a month. Has a great voice."

Autumn let out a giant sigh. "Oh, I miss Austin for things like this. You can meet anyone doing anything."

"Have you thought about moving back?" Montrice asked.

"Sometimes. My parents are here, so I'd like to be closer to them."

Montrice looked at Russ, who nodded. He turned back to Autumn.

"Damn, we were just talking on the way over here about what to do with the building we're in now that we're going to Silicon Valley, and it occurred to us thinking how cool it would be if it was an art gallery."

The words shocked Autumn and Tatum, who were still slightly star-struck.

"Are you serious?" Autumn said, trying to hold in her excitement.

"I mean, the interior is nothing to write home about for what you'll need but—"

"What Montrice is trying to say is it's a real shithole. On the inside at least," Russ said, chiming in.

Montrice resumed his train of thought, still trying to be a little less blunt than his partner.

"Well, we didn't do much with it. We bought this place before they started renovating downtown Austin, so we were anxious to be right on the edge of Lake Travis. It's turning into good real estate. We get several offers a month for the spot, but we thought what could we as a company do to keep a presence in Austin while supporting local culture. An art studio sounds perfect."

"Plus, we'd make a grant that doubles as a tax write-off," Russ said, only half-joking.

"Russ."

"I'm just keeping it real."

Montrice ignored him. "Like I was saying, the kids from our old high school could get free tours, and we get our name placed as a sponsor on the walls and the literature. We could give it to you for scratch change."

Autumn looked at Tatum, who was just as shocked as she was. She turned back to Montrice.

"An amazing offer, but my life is in Houston. I don't see myself lea-"

"What Autumn is trying to say is...can we take a little time to think about it?"

"Sure thing, man. We're going to eventually set up shop in California, and we don't need the overhead. If you want it, it's yours."

The music was about to come on. Montrice and Russ both looked at their phones.

"Hey guys, work emergency. If you see Preston again, tell him we're sorry we had to leave. Feel free to come in and out of VIP for the night. My man Tony over there will hook you up." The two men stood up and shook their guests' hands before taking off. Tatum turned to Autumn, who was riddled with excitement.

"Baby, this day can't get any better. And why didn't you tell Preston Cole about your songs?"

"Fatima, how do you know my songs are any good?"

"I snoop your journal. Well, your old journal. I haven't seen this new one."

"Ain't that some-"

"Baby, we're on fire today. Let's not worry about such minutia. It's shot time."

Tatum shook his head.

"You know what? Fuck it. Let's celebrate."

"Oh yeah...that's what I'm talkin' 'bout,'" Autumn said, doing her best impression of Della Reese in *Harlem Nights*, causing Tatum to chuckle.

"I'm going to the ladies' room. I'll meet you at the bar."

He walked over to the bar and signaled to the bartender that he wanted another round. While waiting on two shots, he watched Autumn walk to the bathroom. She blew him a kiss before disappearing through the door. He smiled, pulled out his phone, and shot her a text.

Yeah, I'm punishing that thang tonight.

Baby, Jubilee been ready since we left my parent's house.

Is that right?

The bass in ur voice when you barked at me, "we're selling art, end of discussion" on the one hand, I wanted to cry. On the other my pussy was so wet. But then you put that large chunk of change in my pocket. We might have a baby tonight.

He laughed as Beyoncé's *So in Love* came on.

He looked at his phone and responded, *-your song is on.*

Bing! His phone came back with her response.

You don't even know! I'm gonna ride you until the sunrise.

He chuckled and thought about their connection. She was only going to the restroom, but it felt like an eternity. He was about to respond when he heard his name.

"Tatum?" The voice was familiar, but he couldn't identify it. He turned around and turned pale as if he'd seen a ghost. A five-foot-two almond-skinned woman with a dark pixie bob stood next to him, smiling. It was Raylene Carter, one of Monique's closest friends. At least she was when they were married.

"Raylene? What's up? What are you doing here?"

"I thought that was you," the woman said as she embraced him for an unwanted hug.

"I haven't seen you since—"

"Since the baby shower," he responded as she smiled and shook her head.

"Yeah, it's been a minute. How are you doing? You look good. Picked up some muscle, I see." She grabbed one of his biceps.

"Thanks for saying that," he said, chuckling.

"And from what I'm hearing, you're working things out with Mo?"

"What? No, we're just getting comfortable with co-parenting."

"Yeah, Monique is something else. Of course, had you hooked up with me, maybe all of it would be different. I'd be Mrs. Clarke...still," Raylene said, laughing.

Tatum knew she was flirting but ignored her.

"How's Darren?"

"You know, we're still together, and he's still trying to figure it out, but forget all that. You here by yourself or what?" she said, moving closer.

"Actually, I'm here with my...um—"

"Oh shit! Tatum Clarke has moved on from Monique Harrison? I never thought I'd see the day."

Tatum nodded to concede her statement. "Well, it was bound to happen at some point."

"True. I'm just kinda shocked it wasn't with me," she said jokingly. Tatum laughed along with her. "Well, where is she? I'd love to see the woman who hit the jackpot."

Tatum looked back at the restroom, relieved that Autumn was walking toward the bar.

"Here she is. Baby, this is Raylene. She's a friend of Solomon's mom."

"Hi, I'm Autumn. Nice to meet you."

"It's good to meet you too, although that introduction was a little misleading. I'm a friend of yours too, Tatum. You just too busy for us now." He was caught a little off guard by the statement. He wasn't terribly close to Darren, and he only ever dealt with Raylene through Monique.

"Yeah... I guess so."

"Oh, did you and Mo finalize your divorce?"

"It's okay. I know all about his marital status," Autumn replied, hoping this didn't get ugly.

"Oh girl, I'm sorry. You know I didn't mean anything by that, but you know these brothas be out here perpetrating."

"No, I totally understand, girlfriend. Now, if I was Tatum, I don't know how I'd feel if my friend just snaked me, but I appreciate the heads up as a sister. Babe, you ready?" The frostiness in her voice indicated that Autumn lost interest in the rest of the night.

"Uh, yeah. It was nice to see you, Raylene."

"Alright, Tatum, have a good night. It was nice to meet you, Autumn."

"Bye."

Tatum closed out his tab, and the pair left the lounge. When they reached the Airbnb, Tatum poured them both a nightcap. He had Hennessy while she had a glass of wine. He noticed Autumn was a little quiet, which meant Tatum needed to get her talking to find out why.

"Hey, where are you?"

"Raylene was nice."

"Oh yeah...she's cool. I guess."

"She wants to fuck you."

"She wants to fuck everyone."

"No, not everyone—just you."

Tatum smirked. "I've known Raylene since she was sixteen. She's just a flirt."

"She may be a flirt, but that don't change the fact she wants to fuck you. And she had to be let it be known you were married, or did that just slip? She knew what she was doing. That was some snake shit."

"She didn't mean anything by it. And might I point out that you did the exact same thing to me the first night we went out dancing—unless you're really Nairobi and I didn't know—"

"Fuck Nairobi, and fuck Raylene."

"That's exactly my point. They're not here. You are. So why are we even talking about this?" Tatum asked. Autumn fell silent, which made him think the conversation was over. He took off his shoes and started to pour himself another shot. Autumn made sure he didn't get too comfortable.

"It's just you're so naive when it comes to women. You don't know if a woman is flirting with you until her pussy is right in front of your face, and it's annoying. How don't you see that?"

Tatum finished his last shot of Hennessy. He took off his shirt. His rock-hard chocolate abs glistened in the pale of the moonlight beaming through the window. He walked over to her.

"I don't see it because I'm not looking for it. I am looking for you. I've spent the whole day looking for you. Now look, we can argue, or we can fuck, but we're not gonna do both. I got a dick full of that Hennessey, and I told you I'm gonna punish that thang, so what I need you to do is...You know what? Why am I even talking to you?"

He lifted her up, carried her into the bedroom, and tossed her on the bed. Once again silent, her state shifted from agitated to submissive.

"Take them fucking clothes off," he said with authority. Autumn in no way resisted.

"Okay, daddy," she said.

He grinned as he took off his pants to expose his fully aroused dick. He climbed on the bed as she hurried to remove her burnt orange dress and silky matching thong. He buried his face in her pussy as if hugging a long-lost friend. She moaned in ecstasy. He raised his head, her nectar already saturating his full, soft lips.

"Let me tell you something. About an hour ago I was thinking to myself I was with the most beautiful woman in the city. I don't give a fuck about Raylene or anybody else. The only woman I'm ever going to want to fuck is in my bed right now. You're everything to me."

He swore she almost came right there.

Tatum hoisted her in the air and pressed her body against the sheetrock beyond the headboard. He buried his face into her center as her caramel thighs rested on his dark, broad shoulders. He kissed her pussy with the kind of authority and confidence that no rank amateur possessed. He knew how to make her cum and what to do when she was close. He licked her clit with precision, touching a spot in the top right corner of her clitoris that had her bucking her hips. The more he licked, the harder it got and the louder she moaned. He tried to take a deep breath, but it was too late. She was feeling the ecstasy. He knew she wanted more, so he shoved his face deeper into her being. He couldn't breathe, but he couldn't resist. He had made the decision she was going to cum, or he would pass out. He persisted in pleasing her, sucking her moisture with whatever oxygen he had left. His passion took over as she pressed his head harder and harder against her frame.

"Oh my fucking god!" she screamed. She dug her nails deep into his shoulder blades as she moaned savagely. The orgasm flowed from her body onto his chin, finally hitting the mattress. He tasted the warm sweet nectar saturating his palate as he persisted through the first spasm. She howled as she moved her nails to the back of his scalp. She was penetrating the flesh underneath, causing a slight trickle of blood. He didn't care—he took that as confirmation she was satisfied.

He finally took a deep breath once her body went limp.

"Oh...my...God. You...I... this..."

He licked his lips, still enjoying her taste. She moaned in the pleasure of aftershock.

"Tatum Clarke...you...are..."

"You need to consider moving back here."

Autumn looked at him blankly while still trying to regain her breath. Tatum continued.

"Just hear me out. This city is an art town. You're an artist. Everywhere we go, there are murals and graffiti. Hell, you went to an art high school, and this man is interested in giving you the opportunity of a lifetime. You can't turn it down. If you want to move back home to get close to your parents once you get your name out there and are selling art all over the- "

"Baby, we just had—well, I just had a mind-blowing orgasm. Can we-"

"I'm serious."

"I don't want to talk about this now. Can we just—"

"Why does this scare you?"

"It doesn't. I—"

"Fatima, where are you?" He looked deeper into her eyes, speaking to her spirit at this point. Their connection allowed him access beyond her defensive walls. Still, she said nothing. He knew she needed reassurance, so he wrapped her in his arms even tighter, letting her know he was right there for her.

"You're right, I'm scared. There's a lot that goes into running a gallery." Tatum rubbed his hand across the necklace he'd given her for their six-month anniversary.

"Baby, you are the most gifted person with a paintbrush in your hand God has ever created. That's why I gave you this necklace. I believe in you. Montrice believes in you. And soon, the rest of the world is gonna have to play catch-up."

"But what if I fai-"

"You won't."

"But what if I-"

"Let's not talk in what-ifs, baby. Why are you afraid?"

Autumn tried to pull away, but he wouldn't let her. He pulled her closer, looking down into her beautiful brown eyes and unlocking the final walls of her uncertainty. She smiled, a tear falling from her eyes.

"You always see me, Tatum. How do you do that better than anyone else?"

"Because I'm looking. Because I want to see you," he said as she began to cry.

"My parents don't believe in me. They think I'm just this screw-up who can't get it together. My ex-husband always told me I wasn't going to do anything because I wasn't as good as I thought I was. He'd say I can't focus long enough to have what it takes. Can you believe that? Of course, you can because it's true. I just want to paint. Having my own spot sounds good, but what if they're right? What if I get out here and I fuck it up? What am I gonna do then? I'm almost thirty. It's time to have a direction." Tatum lifted her chin and kissed her gently near her earlobe.

"Fatima, listen to me. Anyone can teach you how to be content, but no one can teach you how to be happy. You know, people laughed at me when I told them I was going to pharmacy school, but just because they aren't capable doesn't mean I'm not. You say I'm fearless, but I'm just not letting someone else's doubts be the foundation I build my house on."

He kissed her on the back of her head and turned her around to look into her eyes.

"If you don't want this, you don't have to take it. We will find something else. But if it speaks to you, then I'm here to tell you this: you will not fail. I won't let you because that's what love is."

His words had never meant more. He knew she was afraid. He knew all the doubts that swarmed inside her head as if they were his own. And he could smell the fear in the air, even though he was unafraid. He wanted her to know she could finally be vulnerable because he was the guardian there to protect her most fragile thoughts. He needed her to know that as long as he drew breath, she would always be safe. He needed her to know it was okay to dream.

"Alright, I'll talk to him," she said gently.

Tatum smiled. "You will?"

"Yeah. I mean, what I just heard was, 'If it doesn't work, I can blame you. It's your fault.'"

The two chuckled as Tatum pulled her in and kissed her as if nothing around them existed. He savored the taste of her tongue until he finally pulled away reluctantly.

"Baby, you just paint until there's nothing left inside of you. We'll figure out the rest. I want the world to know how beautiful you are inside and out."

He looked at her and wiped her tears, although he couldn't catch them as fast as they were falling.

"You ever meet someone," he said, "that you've never met before, but they are familiar to you? You have a connection, even if you can't put your finger on it? That's how I felt when I met you. I didn't know it at the time, but something in my spirit told me you were going to be around for a while. You're like a cool night in the heat of summer...something to look forward to. I first thought as a good friend, but now I see all along that this is how destiny shows up in your life unannounced with all the familiarities of home."

Autumn's eyes filled with fire, encouraging him to speak from his heart.

"I know you've never met someone who feels the way I do about you, and that might be arrogant enough to say, but I'll continue to prove it. No one is in love with your spirit, who you really are, more than me. When you ask why do I believe in you—Fatima, you got it all wrong. I believe in us."

She smiled and laid on his chest as he rubbed her curly hair.

After a spell, she turned to him and said, "This morning, I woke up, and I was inspired. As I painted, Ne-Yo's *Good Man* came on, and before I knew it, I had this painting. It was marvelous. The last time I felt like this, I was carrying Ezri, so I couldn't sell today's painting. When you were negotiating the price for the portrait, I realized that painting is a piece of my heart because you are a piece of my heart."

The words were powerful. He wanted to kiss her but holding her in the dead of night after their exchange of love was all that mattered.

"When we get back home, I'm going to call Montrice about his offer and make space in my loft for the newest piece of my heart." Tatum had nothing to offer in exchange, but no exchange was required. They had the kind of love that didn't keep score.

20

CHOCOLATE

"*Y*ou like it?" Autumn said as Tatum put her self-portrait on the wall.

She leaned on his shoulder as the pair stood back to look at the painting

"It's beautiful but not as good as the real thing. And that painting is one of the most beautiful things I've ever seen."

They drove back to Houston early in the morning, portrait in tow, and hoisted it on the wall, never to move.

"You're so talented, you know that?"

"Are you talking about my skills with a paintbrush or my skills with your paintbrush?"

"Both," he said as he chuckled. The two held each other, intimately knowing reality was on the other side of the door.

"I had an amazing, life-changing weekend. Thank you, Blue," she said as she turned to give him a peck on the cheek.

"Is that all you got?" he asked.

"You're so bad." She giggled as he pulled her closer.

"You know that's not going to fly with me."

He kissed her with the full weight of his passion. The flick of his tongue was beyond physical, as if it was the only way he could communicate that his love was the kind you could hold onto forever. Only the heavens themselves could tear them apart. They were one.

He wanted to harvest her mind, protect her body, and cradle her spirit. For all the days he had left on earth, he wanted their souls to be singular because, for the first time in his life, he wasn't alone. He was understood. To worship her extraordinary physique with all of his energy was a gift to him. This act of love was just that—a manifestation of the most powerful emotion in physical form. In one kiss, that was anything but simple.

"That was...amazing..." she replied, catching her breath.

He stroked her caramel cheek as he looked into her dark brown eyes.

"That is how a man is supposed to kiss a woman. And with you, that is the only kiss I'll ever be interested in."

She nodded as her eyes turned to passion, pulling him toward the bedroom.

"Oh no, you don't—I'm off to work," he said as he slapped her on her right butt cheek.

"You don't have time for—"

"Aw, hell no, I don't have time! You said that an hour ago and ended up with a dick in your mouth."

"You liked it, didn't you?"

"I loved it, baby, but I got bills, and so do you, Ms. Business Owner. Now I gots ta go." He pulled away from her as she tried to massage his dick through his charcoal slacks.

"Okay, fine. You're no fun. But it's cool. Maybe we can do lunch. You can order the pussy."

"Fatima, it's already lunchtime. Besides, I haven't been to class, spent any time with my dad. Stone is kind of being a bitch right now, and I know Solly misses me. I've probably got a full night of action heroes ahead of me."

"Okay," she said with an exaggerated pout. "Call me, I guess. I'll do some administrative stuff for my twelve-thousand-dollar business."

"It's going to be worth more than that, you goofball. Have fun."

He kissed her one more time, then walked out the door. Feeling the bliss that comes with a lover's touch, he got in the car and put on the '90s R&B station. *Pretty Brown Eyes* came on by Silk, and he smiled, thinking about Autumn. Getting on the highway, he called Monique to make sure she had no issue dropping off Solomon but was unable to reach her. He decided to call his dad, who answered the phone right away.

"It must be my lucky day."

"Hey, Pops, how's it going?"

"You tell me. I haven't seen or heard from you in a while."

"I've been busy, man."

"I bet. Stone tells me you been chasing around some young trim."

Tatum rolled his eyes. He imagined his best friend telling his dad just that. "I did meet someone."

"The artist girl?"

"Yeah. She's cool. We went to Austin this weekend. It was incredible."

"Well, I'm glad for you, but when am I gonna see my grandson again?"

"Real soon, Pops, I promise. As a matter of fact, I'll pick him up, and we'll swing by tonight."

"Sounds like a plan, man. Bring the football."

"Stays in the car with us. But say, I just got to work. I'll hit you back when I'm leaving."

"Okay, T.C., love you, man."

"Okay, I'll talk to you later."

Tatum hung up the phone. He had just arrived, parked in his usual spot, and headed toward the main entrance of the building. Seconds after stepping through the front door, the receptionist flagged him down.

"Tatum, um...there are some men in conference room B that need to talk to you."

Tatum turned and saw two officials in disheveled suits—one, a light brown skinned man with a heavy mustache and the other, a middle-aged white male wearing a brown suit with a blue shirt.

"Thanks, Tory," he said as he curiously walked into the conference room to greet the men.

"Hi. I heard you were looking for me."

"Are you Mr. Tatum Clarke?"

"Uh...who are you, and what's this about?" Tatum said defensively. He wasn't sure who they were, but he started to develop a knot in the pit of his stomach.

"Are you Mr. Clarke?"

"I am." The man in the gray suit approached Tatum and handed him a set of stapled papers.

"Okay, sir. We are with the attorney general's office. This is a protective order filed by Monique Clarke ordering you to stay away from her and Solomon Clarke."

"Wait, what? Is this about the divorce?" Tatum asked, still processing the statement.

"No, sir. Please read the paperwork. If you have any questions, call the attorney general's office."

"Hold on, sir! What is going on?"

"Mr. Clarke, I advise you to read the paperwork. If you have any questions, please contact the attorney general's office."

Tatum's chest sank when he read the headline.

TEMPORARY RESTRAINING ORDER AND ORDER SETTING HEARING FOR *Temporary Orders*

"WHAT IN THE FUCK?" HE SAID ALOUD. HE GRABBED HIS PHONE AND found the contact *MO*, and hit dial. The call went straight to voicemail. Frantically he called again.

"Did she block me?" he said loud enough to catch Tory, the receptionist's attention. He started to walk toward the back of the conference room and called Solomon's daycare.

"Happy Kids Daycare, this is Amanda. How can I help you?"

"Hi, Amanda, this is Tatum, Solomon's dad. Is Solomon at school today?"

"Um...hi, Mr. Clarke. No, he isn't. He didn't show up tod-"

He hung up the phone and sprinted out of the office. He wished he had told Dr. Peterson, but he would have to deal with that later. He got in his car and screeched out of the parking lot. As he drove, his pulse raced. He continued to call Monique, who realized by now must have blocked his phone number.

"This motherfucker comes back in my life for a couple of months and wants to keep your son for a weekend and you're okay with it? What in the fuck is wrong with you, Tatum?!" he screamed at himself. He could not shake the feeling he felt when she first knocked on the door. He punched the steering wheel in anger. He wanted to believe in Monique, but that faith was coming back to kick him harder than ever. He sped as fast as he could into 5th Ward, an area on the North-side where his ex lived. When he pulled up, an officer was waiting at the house. Monique was outside talking to a six-foot-one black constable of Harris County. Tatum didn't care. He was glad the police were there. This was kidnapping.

As he opened the door, Monique said, "There he is."

Tatum ignored her theatrics as he entered the yard. The dark-skinned officer with the buzz cut approached him.

"Sir, you need to stop moving. We want to talk to you."

"Officer, this woman is kidnapping my son, and I am here to take him home!" he said angrily.

"Sir, we can't let you do that."

"Let me? I'm the only parent he knows. How can you stop me?"

"Sir, I'm—"

"Daddy!" Solomon raced out of the home, moving swiftly toward him.

"Solomon!" He screamed as he took two steps up the driveway before the first officer stopped him.

"Sir, we need you to call—"

"I don't know what this viper has told you, but this is *my* son, goddammit! He's lived with me his whole life! This is his first weekend with that woman! Arrest that motherfucker!"

"Sir, I'm not gonna ask you again. We need to finish this conversat-"

"Solomon!" he yelled, but as he proceeded up the driveway, the cop shoved him.

"Sir, final warning. I need you to-"

"That's right, arrest him! Arrest that motherfucker! He's on private property with me and my son!" Monique clamored. Tatum saw red. He tried to move past the officer again, but he wouldn't take another step. The officer wrestled him to the ground, pushing his arm behind his back. Solomon, who was still outside, became inconsolable.

"Daddy!" Tatum realized this was making things worse and decided not to resist.

"Solly, it's okay! I'm not resisting, officer," Tatum said, switching between screaming and remaining calm. He watched as his son tried to run toward him, only to have Monique grab him.

"Get off of me, lady!" Solomon yelled as he wiggled past his mother and ran to his father on the ground, face-first with his hands pinned behind his back.

"That's right, Solomon!" Monique shouted. "Say goodbye to your daddy! He's going to jail!"

"That's enough from you, miss. Be quiet, or you're coming with us!" the officer barked. Tatum wanted to resist, but he felt a strong twinge in his left shoulder. He had to remain calm for his son to let him know everything was okay. He went numb because he also knew better than to resist an officer under any circumstances. His heart started to beat profusely. He was breathing heavily as if he were in the middle of a panic attack. He decided to calm himself by taking deep breaths and closing his eyes. He started to think about melodies to add to his journal. *Focus on the music*, he said to himself. It wasn't long before he was humming.

"Mmm Hmmm Mmm Hmmm," he hummed aloud. He heard his son in the background crying his name at the top of his lungs. Tatum looked up and saw the tears in his son's eyes, and his heart broke, but he couldn't let his son see him cry. He had to be tempered at this moment.

He took a deep breath and said, "It's okay, Solly. Just go back inside, son. It's gonna be okay. Daddy's fine."

"Let me go! I wanna go home! Daddy, let's go home!" Solomon pleaded.

Tatum closed his eyes as his son screamed. The officer hoisted him up and cuffed him. He looked at his son and saw a look in his eyes that was all too familiar—it was the look he had on his own face almost twenty years ago when J.C. was locked up for selling drugs. It was a look of powerlessness. In his mind, he was now Johnny Clarke. It was almost too much to bear.

"Everything's gonna be okay, Solly, I promise you. It's gonna be okay, little man."

"Daddy!" Solomon said as he hit the officer carrying his father away in the leg.

"Ma'am, get your son inside!" the officer snapped at Monique.

"Officer, she's kidnapping my son. He doesn't know this lady!"

"Fuck you, Tatum, he's my son! I gave birth to him."

"You're a sick, twisted bi-"

"Everyone quiet!" the officer barked into the p.a.

Tatum didn't resist. So much damage had been done, he willingly walked to the police car. As he got inside, the other officer picked up the now sobbing boy and walked him inside the house, closing the door behind him. Tatum resumed his calming technique, writing a new song in his head.

"Her body's like alcohol..." he said, breathing as he thought about the events that just happened. He was put in the back of a police car in front of his son. *Unbelievable.*

The officer came out of the home and crossed over to the cop who handcuffed Tatum. After a brief conversation, the officer went back inside. His officer got in the car and turned on the ignition, then turned toward Tatum.

"Mr. Clarke, I'm Officer Greenwood. Do you want to tell me what happened?"

Tatum ignored his question and countered with one of his own. The only one that mattered to him at the moment.

"What am I being charged with, officer?"

"Well, that depends. Tell me what's going on."

Tatum was silent. If he knew anything from growing up with his father, it was that talking to the police never ended well. Apparently, the rationale behind his silence was something the officer picked up on. The officer leaned in.

"Look, man, I'm not trying to pop you. If I wanted you in jail, we'd already be talking about assaulting an officer. What I want to know is, does your son live with you? I'm not going to use anything against you, I swear. I'm trying to help you."

He looked into the officer's eyes. The man was sincere. Tatum took a deep sigh. In spite of himself, he decided he had nothing to lose.

"That's my ex. Well, that's my wife. She walked out on us four years ago, and I've been raising our son by myself ever since. About two months ago, I asked for a divorce. She told me she'd sign the papers if she could spend time with our son. I agreed. This past weekend I asked her to keep him for the weekend, and she agreed."

"Why did you need her to keep your son?"

"Like I said, we'd been working on her rebuilding a relationship with our son. I was taking my girlfriend on a getaway. Everything was fine, but we ran into her friend Raylene in Austin and... man, I don't know. Look, all I know is I get to work today, I get served papers. I'm thinking maybe it has something to do with the divorce, but it was an order of protection against me for my son."

The officer nodded but remained silent. He turned his car on and pulled away from the house.

I knew I shouldn't have trusted this motherfucker.

Tatum was going to jail, and what was worse, he fell for the officer's convincing nature.

"Thanks for the help. This is real fucking helpful right now."

"Quiet!" the officer shouted. Tatum slumped in the chair and looked back to see if he could see Solomon.

Fuck!

He started thinking about who he needed to call and how much bail would cost. *I can't call Dr. Peterson. I damn sure can't call Stone. My dad won't have the money...I'm gonna have to call my Mom. Shit!*

As Tatum became lost in his thoughts, the officer pulled into a gas station convenience store. He looked out of the windows to see his partner pulling up behind them. He started to panic.

Oh shit, they are going to try to fuck me up. He did try to push past the officer, and he did just call him useless in so many words. Maybe he was about to be taught a lesson.

Officer Greenwood parked the car, got out, and walked over to his partner. They talked for a second, then the other officer got back in his car and drove away. Officer Greenwood opened the door and pulled Tatum out of the car, and to his surprise, uncuffed him.

"Look, we're not arresting you. We just needed to get you off private property."

Tatum couldn't believe it. No one would've believed it. The officer continued.

"But let me say what you did was reckless. Are you paying attention to the way things have been lately? Listen, man, you don't do anything but comply if a cop tells you to do something. Hell, even that'll get you killed in some places."

"But my son—"

"Is with his mother who, at this moment, is within her legal rights to not only have you removed from the property but also restrain you from your son."

Tatum's nostrils flared. He wanted to attack anything, but he'd already avoided jail once and didn't want to push his luck.

"You know what? This is insane! If I was a woman right now, there would be twelve Amber Alerts and nine police warrants behind this shit, but no, I'm just the parent that's been doing the job for the last four years. The one thing I never wanted my son to see was his dad being arrested and hauled off by the police. And now for no other crime but being a dad, he gets to live with that image."

"Look, man, do I believe you? Yeah. I saw the way that kid looked at the both of you. He didn't know her. But no one gives a shit what I believe. All I can do is enforce the law. The bottom line is if you go back there, the next time, we'll arrest you. You're going to have to get this resolved through the courts. Get you a lawyer—a good one—and this should all get resolved. Now the tow-truck driver followed my partner to this gas station. You'll have to pay him for the tow, but you're free to go. Good luck."

Tatum looked at the officer.

"So... yeah...thanks." But he had a feeling he would need more than luck to win this fight.

21

DAMAGE

"So, according to Texas law, since we are legally married, I can't interrupt the order of protection until we see the judge. The best I can do is visitation right now."

"Wait a goddamn minute. Solomon has been with you this whole time, and they just give her custody without a fight?"

"Stone, I've replayed this in my head countless times. This entire thing is a pile of bullshit, and now I'm sitting outside her house knocking on the door for the last forty-five minutes of the hour I got to spend time with Solomon."

"Damn, Rev, you want me to go kill the motherfucker?"

"Don't tempt me, Stone...please."

Stone took a drag off the blunt he was smoking as Tatum sat in his car video chatting with him. He glanced over to see if there was any activity in Monique's house.

There was none.

"I got a lead on a good lawyer. Problem is the retainer is steep."

"How steep?

"About fifteen stacks."

"Hold the fuck up," Stone said, astonished by the price tag. "You're talking fifteen thousand American dollars?"

"Yep."

"Shit, Rev, for half that price, I know some motherfuckers that will take out a whole city block! Now I'm gonna ask you again—you sure you don't want to kill the bitch?"

Tatum scoffed at the notion in frustration.

"Bro, right now, I just want to make sure my son is good," Tatum said, rubbing his hands across his face.

He glanced at the time. It was 6:48. Legally he only had twelve minutes to see his son, and he wasn't going to leave until he was forced to.

"You got the bread?"

"I do. I had it saved up to pay off my student loans when they come due and some emergency cash I had on the side. I got right about fifteen."

Stone rubbed his goatee and looked at him. "Bruh, ain't that award you're gonna win pay for school?"

"The Wilcox Award? Well, yeah, it's supposed to, but-"

"Then what we even talking about? You just said you got the bread between that and some emergency cash. Well, if this don't qualify as an emergency, I don't know what does."

"Yeah, no shit," Tatum said.

Stone took another hit off the cigar he was smoking and, after exhaling, said, "What I don't understand is why ain't there a mother-fucker to make sure the woman is there with your kid? Like, who's refereeing this shit?"

"Man, I don't know. I'm learning all this shit on the fly, and the way this shit is going, I'm gonna have a law degree by the time I figure out what my actual rights are." The two laughed at the statement.

"Rev, if you need some bread, we could move some prescription pi-"

"I can't do that, bro. I appreciate what you're trying to do, but I'll be straight."

"I feel you. Well, when you come through, we'll grab a bottle to sip on and none of this FaceTime shit."

"Yeah, my bad, bro. I've just had—hey, Stone, let me call you back. I think I just saw someone at the door."

"Good luck, brother."

Tatum hung up the phone. He got out of the car and sprinted over to the front door, and started to knock. The door opened.

"What do you want, Tatum?"

"I'm here to see Solomon."

"Well, you're late. It's seven o'clock. You were late for your child visitation."

"Monique, you know goddamn good, and well, I was sitting outside knocking on the door the last hour."

"Not my problem. The state says you can have visitation between six and seven. It's 7:01."

Tatum balled his fist in aggravation and started to turn around but stopped in his tracks.

"What in the fuck is wrong with you?"

"What's wrong with you? You think I'm supposed to be your fucking babysitter while you fuck some other bitch? Yeah, Raylene told me she saw y'all in Austin."

Tatum's eyes widened at the inflammatory statement.

"Are you fucking kidding me right now? You're barely a mother."

"I made a mistake, Tatum!" she screamed. "You never made a mistake before? All the hard work we put in before Solomon was born —you just want to throw that away?"

"Monique, you threw it away! What is this you need—closure?"

"No, I...so that's it," she finally said. "You don't want anything to do with me? I get it, I fucked up, but I thought we had love."

"You just sat in the house while I banged on the door for nearly an hour, and when my legal time is up, you answer, and you call that, love? Right now, it's hard to respect you, let alone love you. You know what's funny? I thought I'd never have to deal with your ass again."

"You don't mean that."

"Let's keep it real. What we had was never going to work. You weren't ready—hell, I shouldn't have been ready. When I found Solomon alone like that, I was sad, but the biggest feeling I felt was a relief. Like, thank God I don't have to deal with this manipulative, deceptive, never-met-a-lie-she-didn't-want-to-tell-ass woman. We were done when you found out you were pregnant with Solly, and we both knew that, but like a dumbass trying to do the right thing, I rode with it. And you think I want to get back on that roller coaster? I'm never going back, Mo. I'm here for our child, period. There is no love here, and I don't think there can ever be love here again. The best we can do is like one another, and right now, I'm struggling to do that."

After Tatum said his peace, Monique didn't say anything. There was nothing to say. There was just a stillness in the air as Tatum turned to walk away.

"Solomon, come here."

Tatum paused in his tracks and spun around, catching a glimpse of his brown-skinned curly-head son. His eyes lit up until Monique slammed the door in his face. An instant burst of rage ensued until he realized who he was dealing with.

"I see what you're trying to do. The Queen of Manipulation is alive and well. Fuck off, I'll see you in court."

Tatum stormed off, got in his car, and did his best to drive away calmly. When he got out of the neighborhood, he parked the car and angrily punched the steering wheel. This was a nightmare, and he felt responsible. His world was torn from its roots. The last two weeks had been hurting more as each day went by. He wondered if Solomon was okay. He wasn't sure if Monique was feeding him right, taking him to school, or buying him any clothes.

Tatum didn't know who to talk to, but he found himself driving in one direction.

Twenty minutes later, he pulled up in front of the Santa Ana Rehabilitation Center. He found his father outside in a white muscle shirt and olive-green pants playing dominoes with Manuel and a couple of men he'd seen before.

"Hey, J.C., you busy?"

"Yo, T.C., I'm in the middle of whooping Manuel in some dominoes. Man, what's going on? What brings you this way?"

"I was..."

"Hold on, T.C. I gotta show this clown here you don't need a big six when you holding a quarter! Domino, motherfucker! Give me my twenty-five points!" Johnny said, slamming the domino on the ground. Tatum tried to be composed but was unraveling.

"Dad, I..."

Johnny stopped to look at Tatum, and his eyes widened.

"Oh, I see. Hey fellas, y'all deal me out this game. I'll be back."

Johnny stood up out of the chair, and the pair started to walk to the street. Tatum tried to get his thoughts together but was struggling to do so. The two men got far enough out of earshot for them to speak.

"What's going on, son?"

"I'm sorry I haven't been by here."

"Oh, you're a young man. I know how it is. But I also know that something serious is on your mind."

"How do you know that?"

"I don't think you've called me dad since you were about seven. So talk to me. What's going on?"

"You know I went to Austin a few weeks ago."

"Yeah, with the art girl, right? What's her name... Amy?"

"Autumn."

"Yeah, Autumn. Okay, did something happen?"

"Well, that weekend, I let Monique keep Solomon, only I ran into one of her friends. When I came back, Monique lost it. She got a restraining order against me, and she has temporary custody of Solomon now."

"What? When did this happen?"

"Two-and-a-half weeks ago. She filed for custody—full custody—of my son. Can you believe that shit, Pops? And then, after all of that, she has the audacity to suggest we get back together. Like, what are we going to do—go to counseling to figure out why it took her so long to get around to being a mother again?"

Tatum looked at his dad, who was looking up at a power line, then glancing up and down the street. After a spell, he spoke.

"Robert Frost has this poem about the road not taken. Basically, some shit like you can't look back at the other road. I read it as a young man, and it stuck with me. But the older I get, the more I realize that the road not taken—if you let it— will take up a lot of real estate in your mind. It did for me. I finally decided the only way to enjoy my life was to focus on the road I was on."

"Dad, what in the hell are you talking about? Are you using again? Because you're looking at power lines and reciting poetry that has nothing to do with what we're talking about."

Johnny folded his arms and gave his son the kind of look that commanded his undivided attention.

"Now, T.C., I give you a lot of latitude because you're my son, but I'm gonna tell you this one time and one time only. I wasn't shit as a dad, but when I put my mind to something, it's done. I decided I won't let hell or high water stop me from being a grandfather. Drugs have no place in my life anymore. The time I got with this boy is all that matters. So when I tell you I swear on my grandson's life I'm not using drugs anymore, then that's the way it is because he's too valuable to me to mess that up. So don't ever question it again."

His light-brown eyes were stern, cold, and filled with sincerity. In an instant, he recognized his father was as serious as he would ever get. A slight comprehension of what his three teachers must have felt vaguely passed his mind. This wasn't his dad talking—this was Johnny Motherfucking Clarke, aka The Lion. He wasn't asking to be believed; he was decreeing the way things were. He was telling the truth. He'd never seen his father more serious and was forced to accept this truth.

"The poem—maybe Monique is trying to get back on the road she turned off of. She wants to be a wife again. Your wife."

"Whose wife? That part of my life is over."

"Not legally, and for her not at all. Apparently, she's been stuck on that day. So for you, it's been four years, but for her, it hasn't been a week. If you don't believe anything I say, trust me when I tell you people can lose track of time."

"I'm not even sure why we're talking about me getting back with Monique. It's a non-starter of an idea."

"Let me tell you something son, what did that L.L. Cool J song say?

Tina might got a big ole butt, but Monique's got a *case*. If you thinking about moving on with Autumn, you better get used to paying child support and seeing that boy every other weekend because let's keep it real. A black man versus the State of Texas in regards to getting custody is an uphill battle that started below sea level. I'm not gonna say it's hopeless, but you got a hell of a fight on your hands, and that don't include the internal fight."

Tatum cocked his head. "What do you mean internal fight?"

Johnny looked back up at the power lines for a second. "The world's different from up there, man. I'm looking at your problem from one of those things right there. The internal fight is this. See, you're the kind of dad that's gotta wake up and cook breakfast and be there to see him skate, talk to the teacher. That kid goes everywhere with you. Since you've been with this Autumn person, that's the most you've ever been apart from him. But can you do that for the next fourteen years? Can you live without being in the house with Solomon? And say I'm wrong about Monique trying to get a second chance. Let's say she is just as batshit crazy as you think she is. Can you sleep at night knowing she has prime influence over your son for the next fourteen years?"

"It won't come to that."

"I hope it doesn't, but if it does, you gotta be prepared. Just imagine that was the case, T.C., could you live with it? Meanwhile, you're dishing out money to raise a kid you were already raising. Your kid the one you know better than anybody. He's gonna get older, and you're gonna miss things. Things you would've caught if you were there. And one day, you're gonna turn to Autumn, and something's gonna be different. You'll start arguing more, and you won't know why. A seed is gonna plant itself, and that seed is going to ask what kind of woman would let you walk away from your son? And that seed is going to turn into a weed that will strangle your relationship. If you do it, son, you'll resent her. I'm telling you right now. Because if you have to choose and you don't choose Solomon, you'll feel the pressure. And being there for pressure ain't the same as being there for love."

His words, however bitter, made sense. Tatum didn't want them to. He had no interest in any other option but being the primary parent. He also knew, after talking to his father, however brutal it was, made sense. That man had lived a life and had his regrets no matter which road he said he was focused on. Tatum didn't want that life for himself but somehow felt himself heading down that road.

Johnny took out a Camel cigarette and lit it. After he inhaled, he spoke.

"Your mother was the finest thing Barbados had to offer. I mean, the woman brought life to everything. I loved her and wanted to give her the world. When I think about her even now she...she does something to me, ya know? I was living the dream being with her. But when you feel an obligation, sometimes the woman of your dreams gotta wait. At least that's what I thought. I didn't want to hustle, and I damn sure didn't want to be a junkie. Hell, you'd laugh if you knew what I wanted to be in life, but I owed the streets. But when you get my age, you start to realize what's really important. Solomon is as important as they come. And I know you're still young enough to think you got a good woman over there, but I'm gonna let you in on a little secret—they're all good women. You just gotta pick one and work like hell at it. And the thing about it is this one, Monique; she has your son. She's doing it all wrong, but she's telling you she's willing to fight for you. The both of you."

"Pops, I—"

"Damn it! Just listen to me for a second, T.C.," his father said, flustered. He took another drag of the cigarette and exhaled.

"Man, I know you love Autumn. You wouldn't be talking to me about this if it wasn't serious. But you also came to me for the real, and the truth of the matter is if you chose to be with her, she might make you happy. She might be the same headache you're dealing with right now, but one thing's for sure: your son's life changes. You might get custody, but again you're leaving that to the U.S. Justice System, and we know in great detail their relationship with the word justice for black men, so take your chances there. Or you could raise your son in a household with a mother and father. A good father sacrifices for his kids, something neither one of us ever had. Don't be me."

Tatum watched as his dad, who was noticeably more slender, studied the light poles. It pained him to say these words, but Tatum wasn't sure why.

"Look, son, you a smart man. Always have been, and I ain't got no place to say what I'm about to say next. Autumn might be the love of your life, but Solomon is your life. And if it comes between this woman or your son, there is no choice because I know this much about you: you may or may not regret having a life with this Autumn, but I can guarantee you will definitely regret not having a life with Solomon. You're not a weekend dad; you're not even a half-a-year dad. You're every day, all-day, I-have-to-see-every-moment-of-your-life dad, and if you don't believe me, just ask the people at your job or your college because they all know S.C. He goes with you everywhere. Blood is thicker than water, son."

The words both settled and hurt Tatum. His father was such a different person now, a man he could admire. But he didn't understand why.

"That sounds good, Pops, but why didn't you take your own advice? I needed you, man. I'm glad you're there for Solly. I love that, but I... needed this growing up. I needed you. Why weren't you there for me like this in the house? Maybe I'd know what to do right now. But I'm figuring it out. Ain't no examples to pull from for me, man," he said, fighting the tears that were building up. He was torn and needed answers any answers at this moment. If he couldn't get the ones he had to deal with, he could at least get the one from the man in front of him.

Johnny nodded and beckoned his son to walk with him to the end of the street before he responded.

"You go down about four blocks to the left. You're off of Scott Street. There's pimps, prostitutes, drugs...anything you're looking for. Now, if you go down about four blocks to the right, you're in the heart of downtown. There's a mosque, a church, a gym. This is literally that fork in the road from that poem I was telling you about. And

I've seen people come in with good hopes. But eventually, you start seeing them turn to the left, and when they do that, you know it won't be long before you don't see them again. See, I know what's on both of these roads, but I didn't always know. You asked where was I? The better question is, how does one of the biggest drug dealers in Houston get hooked on his own supply? I mean, nobody selling dope with any good sense goes and tries this shit. We know what we're doing out here."

Johnny put out the cigarette as the two turned around and headed back to the facility. Tatum listened attentively as his father gave him the perspective he was longing for.

"I smoked herb growing up. Now, ya momma knew I was in the life, and the plan—well, her plan—was for us to get out. I'd always give her some money, and she'd hide it. She was a good woman—a woman I took for granted because I could. I was J.C. Money. Everyone respected me, especially the women. So I fucked around. A lot. One night drinking, I meet this badass little thing from El Salvador. I fell in love with her. Hell, I wasn't never home, and your mother stayed there to take care of you guys while I was running the streets. She raised you, changed your diapers, helped with your homework, and put food on the table— and she did it all without my help or input. It made me mad she was doing it in spite of me. So one day, I'm drunk or high or both, and I asked her why she was even here. I'll never forget what she said. She looked at me with those deep chocolate eyes of hers and said the kind of wife and mother she was going to be had nothing to do with what kind of husband I chose to be, and it's only a matter of time before they won't need either one of us. Whatever they think of us is because of what they saw. She said it and went right back to cooking for you guys like I wasn't even there. Fucked me up, man, and then I realized it was because I wasn't there. That woman had cried her last tear over me some time ago, and I wasn't even around to see it. I realized I wasn't shit then, and I swear this is true. I decided to end things with Claudia. Now, she took it hard over the phone, so I was going to meet her. I was gonna have one last romp in the bedroom to get it out of my system. When I got there, she had a pre-rolled blunt waiting for me. So I walk in, and she's sitting there naked. Beautiful, a glass of Crown Royal in one hand, a joint in the other. So I take a hit, and this shit is strong, and I'm coughing, but it's good, you know? And so I go ahead and finish the blunt while she's doing...well, grown-folk shit, and I am higher than I've ever been in my life. I mean, this feels incredible. I don't know the strand of this weed, but it's an I-gotta-have-it kinda high.

"So the next morning, I wake up and leave, but now I can't stop thinking about her and how good she made me feel, especially the weed. So I gotta go back that night. I need that blunt again. I need that feeling. So I go back, and it's almost as good but not as good. We do the same thing until I pass out.

"The next morning, I'm gonna go ask her for the strand of that weed, and I walk in the room, and Claudia is cutting up crack rock and hydro into a blunt. She had been packing the weed with finely crushed crack cocaine. My life has been a downward spiral ever since, and all I could think about was I had everything I'd ever wanted at home, so why was I looking anywhere else?"

They arrived back in front of the rehabilitation center. Johnny put his hand on his son's shoulder and quickly embraced him. Tatum hugged his father back, understanding the pain and remorse attached to his story. After a spell, he let him go and shook his head in disappointment.

"I wish I could give you what you're looking for, son, but I can't. I wasn't there for any good reason. All I got is a bag of regrets and wishful thinking. I know them two things mighty well. I thought everything I was looking for was on the other side of the life I built. I married your mother, I had you and your sister, and then I took it all for granted. Got to a point, I wanted out of it all, and so I took off, chasing a fine El Salvadorian woman who lived in New Laredo with a bad coke habit and a life full of chaos. And she took me high, man, so high that—well, hell, I'm in rehab right now trying to come down from those times. And after all them years and all that fun, you know I don't know where that woman is or what she is doing, and I don't want to know. But I do know I miss Savannah's oxtails, and I wish I could've seen the game; you had six sacks in high school, and every time your sister talks, she sounds like an angel. I missed all of this. This was the important stuff. This was true love, the thing I was looking for. See, people think the heart is a fool. That's not true. You get older and realize your heart isn't foolish at all. It just ages at a different rate than your brain. You're a better man than me, Tatum. Be a better father. Don't make my mistakes. Nothing is worth losing the relationship you're building with your son."

Tatum recognized in his father's words that Johnny, at his core, was a good man who made bad choices, and he wanted Tatum to be better than him, as any friend, mentor, or father would. Still, despite it all. He knew there had to be more.

"I'll have to cross that bridge when I get to it, Pops. I'm gonna fight for custody. It's different with Autumn, Dad. I love her. She makes me happier than I ever thought possible."

Johnny nodded, but after a spell, asked a question. "You'd give your life for Solomon?"

"In a heartbeat."

He turned and looked Tatum in his eyes.

"If you'd sacrifice your life for him, why wouldn't you sacrifice your happiness?"

22

SESSION 32

"*A*nyway, brother, I paid the lawyer, and we have mediation in a week or so. But this is a newly elected judge, so we don't know his views on this."

"Rev, I swear we could just ride through Fifth Ward packing that you know what and have a conversation that will straighten out everyone and everybody."

Tatum laughed at his friend's statement.

"It might come to that, but for now, I'm gonna trust this lawyer to do his job."

"Reverend Clarke, you gotta come through the hood a bit more, homie. You don't even realize how soft you've gotten. We don't handle stuff like this the way you're going about it."

"It's my son, Stone. Besides, it's time to get all the paperwork out of the way. I want to be free of this witch."

"The only way to get rid of a witch is to drop a house on 'er. It's strength in numbers. Cuz, you done left the pack an-"

"Stone, right now, getting Solomon back legally is all that matters to me. I can't afford no fuck shit. Say, man, I gotta go. My boss just sent me an email to come to his office."

"Peace."

The phone clicked. Tatum was gathering his things, and he could see Dr. Peterson waving him over to his office from his workstation. He gathered his belongings and headed to the office. When he got closer, he realized Dr. Peterson wasn't alone. He was with someone Tatum hadn't seen before.

Dr. Peterson stood up and ushered Tatum to the round table in his office, where the other man joined them.

"Hey Dr. P., what's going on?"

"Hey, Tate..." Dr. Peterson responded. Tatum noticed he was visibly disturbed. He pointed to the man next to him. A white man with green eyes and soft red hair, wearing a solid gray suit and a pinstripe blue tie.

"This is Ron Bigsly, the head of Human Resources. Have a seat."

Tatum took a seat at the table, concerned about why his mentor was so upset.

"Okay, so what's this about, Dr. P.? If it's about the Wilcox Award, I've been in every class since our talk."

"It's...it's not that, Tatum."

Dr. Peterson was silent. Tatum could feel his struggle to get out any thoughts as a sinking feeling began to grow in the pit of his stomach. Ron shuffled some papers and placed one copy in front of Tatum, keeping one for himself.

"Perhaps I should go. Mr. Clarke, as Dr. Peterson said, I'm Ron Bigsly. Every few years, we perform an internal audit to comply with the FDA and account for all of our inventory. And while everything has been pristine over the last few years, we went back four years and discovered there was a high level of irregularities in Dr. Peterson's department, most of which happened when you first joined his team."

"What does this have to do with me?"

"We have it on good authority that-"

"Can we just cut the bull for a minute?" Dr. Peterson interjected. "We're talking theft of a controlled substance through forgery. Some serious allegations, but we're not going to the cops. I just want to know is why'd you do it, son?"

Tatum wanted to tell Dr. Peterson the truth, but he knew he had to deny it all. He had too much riding on this with his mediation coming up, and now being penniless, he needed to be able to get another job. He also couldn't take the chance Dr. Peterson was lying to him.

"I'm not sure what you're talking about, Dr. Peterson. I followed protocols from the day I got here. I've always respected you."

Dr. Peterson pounded the table and stood up in frustration. He turned his back to Tatum and continued.

"Your position is terminated effective immediately. Security has already packed your things and is waiting for you outside. Additionally, we're revoking your nomination for the Wilcox Award, also effective immediately. It's pretty safe to say you won't be able to work here or any of our subsidiaries again. That is all."

It was an embarrassing, unceremonious end to his career at Simmons Pharmaceuticals, a place he'd grown to love as his second home. But more than that, he'd left a look of disappointment on his mentor's face he'd never seen before.

He walked to the exit and waved bye to the receptionist, who had been trying to pretend she wasn't eavesdropping. She waved in return. He gathered the box from the security officer and walked out the door. He was numb to the pain. He wasn't sure how to feel. He'd gotten to his car when he heard his name.

"Mr. Clarke!" Tatum turned around to find Dr. Peterson walking up to him hastily. Tatum put his belongings in the car and waited on the man he still considered his mentor.

"I realize that you probably didn't trust me in there. You don't have to worry about any legal ramifications. But I need to know why? I've never seen anyone work as hard as you. There's never been a unanimous Wilcox Award winner. That should tell you how much this feels wrong. Why?"

Tatum wanted to tell him his story. How he was just trying to make ends meet when he first found out he was a father and how misguided he was before he started working at Simmons. But all he could muster up was his pain.

"Dr. Peterson, I've always respected you. I'm sorry I put you in this situation."

Dr. Peterson took his glasses off and wiped them with his handkerchief.

"I trusted you, and you betrayed that trust. If I find out that you were selling to other students..."

"I'd never do that, Dr. Peterson."

The old man smiled and put his head down, sighing in disbelief.

"A day ago, that would've meant something to me. Now I don't know what to believe." He turned around to slowly walk off, but before he did, he stopped.

"You'll graduate on time provided you pay your own tuition. There's no sense in you coming to class. I also can't write you a letter of recommendation for another job, but I can guarantee you this incident won't show up on a background check. Best of luck to you, Mr. Clarke."

With that, Tatum's mentor, his second father, walked away.

Defeated, Tatum got in his car and drove aimlessly for an hour, thinking about his state of affairs. He decided he couldn't afford to waste gas any longer and went to his lover's house. He knocked on the door as Autumn was getting ready for work.

"Hey, Blue! What are you doing here?" Autumn said while putting her Paint & Sip apron in her bag. "I was just about to leave. Melissa called about an acrylic paint shortage, so now I have to drive halfway across town to Texas Art Supply and find a quick fix; when had she told me two days ago I could have ordered it then. I swear I need to just call Montrice and tell him yes, I'll take the gallery. I hate this place. Babe...are you okay?"

Without saying a word, he walked into the bedroom and slumped onto the bed. Autumn walked over, curious about his state of mind.

"Are you missing Solomon?"

Tatum looked up at Autumn.

"Yes, I am... but..."

He covered his face and let out a deep sigh of frustration. Autumn sat next to him as he tried to gather the strength to say the words.

"Hey...where are you?" she asked. He looked her in the eyes, fighting back the pain he'd been repressing.

"I lost my job today."

"What? What happened?"

"I... I just fucked up." He looked at her, realizing he never shared this part of his life with her.

Autumn got up and walked into the kitchen. He started to ponder his next move when she showed up with a bottle of Crown Royal and an already-poured glass. She then walked into the bathroom with the bottle and turned on the water for the tub. Tatum sipped on the glass. It was what he needed to ease the pain of today's events. Without saying a word, she took his hand and led him to the tub. The pair got undressed as Tatum sat in the back and Autumn sat in front. He held her in his bulging dark arms and instantly started to feel better. He was ready to tell the entire story.

"Before Solomon was born, I ran the streets. A lot. I told you what Stone does; what I didn't tell you was I used to sell prescription pills. Xanax, Perc, codeine, whatever I could get my hands on. Today they found out about that and let me go."

Autumn said nothing, and he wondered if she viewed him differently. After a spell, she said, "You were trying to survive. You did what you knew in order to do that. I get it."

A wave of relief rushed over him, and he held her closer.

"Thing is, that place was home to me, you know? I knew everyone, and they knew me. They watched me—hell, helped me become the kind of man I want to be, and now I'm not even sure if I can graduate. And if I do, who will hire me?"

"Wait, what do you mean about graduation? I thought it was a done deal."

"They rescinded the award, which means I have to pay for school, which is money I don't have since I just paid the lawyer," Tatum said as the effects of the Bourbon started to settle in.

"I've been working since I was eight years old, sometimes two, sometimes three jobs. I got mediation in a week and... for Dr. Peterson to think I'm just some...some thief..."

"You know that's not who you are, right?"

Tatum nodded, unable to say any words for fear of breaking down.

"It's gonna be okay. You know that, right?"

He looked away. He did not know that because right now, there was nothing about what was happening that was okay.

"Have you written about this in your journal? Maybe there's a song there. I know with my art; extreme emotion makes me do my best work."

"I'm not feeling terribly creative. Besides, I'm not a songwriter."

"Your spirit was born for the arts. The only person who doesn't know it is you. Maybe now's a good time to work on some songs."

Tatum got out of the tub. Autumn got up after him as he walked into the bedroom.

"Hey, what did I say?"

"I need a goddamn job, Autumn. I can't think about pipe dreams right now. I gotta-"

"You need to believe in yourself, Blue. There is always going to be something. Look, we don't have to talk about it. I'm sorry if it came across as insensitive, just lay down."

She took him by the hand and led him to the bed. Naked, he laid on his stomach on top of the goose-down blue cover. She took an herbal essence oil—scented coconut, hibiscus, and lavender—and rubbed it across his naked body. She focused on his shoulders, breaking down his tension.

"Autumn, I-"

"Shhhh...close your eyes, King. Let me take care of you." She turned him over and rubbed his heavily melanated naked flesh with the same oil, starting with his chest and shoulders and eventually settling on his hardening manhood. She rubbed the oil on his cock as it became stiff.

"You know, I always wondered how this oil tastes."

She lowered her head, licking the tip of his dick as the precum began to spill out of the side of his throbbing cock. It wasn't long before she engulfed his entire package. He moaned in ecstasy. She worked her head up and down, twisting her hands to slowly slide down the shaft, controlling his dick with her lips and tongue. She picked up intensity as he moaned.

"Damn, that's good. Don't stop."

She stopped anyway, straddled him, and descended upon him like the fantasy he'd grown accustomed to. As he gripped her caramel buttocks, with each thrust, his dick hardened, touching her G-spot in the most pleasurable sensation.

"Oh shit," she moaned.

This further swelled his rod until his seed exploded into her core.

"I'm cumming!" he said, his body shuddering uncontrollably, his seed running down her pussy onto his cock and balls.

"Keep going," he said as she looked at him for confirmation, he was ready for more. He had not gotten soft at all. His dick was just as hard, though twice as sensitive, as when his sweet nectar entered her temple. She continued to thrust her caramel body onto his chocolate rod.

She said, "Damn, baby, you like it?"

He kissed her with such intensity that she could not doubt his answer. Biting her lip, she continued to bounce on his dick as she moaned, "I feel it getting harder again, daddy." And within moments of her sliding on his cock, he was back to the point of orgasm.

"Oh my God. I'm cumming again!" he said, releasing a second round of semen into her soft, tight pussy. She was turned on by feeling his hot load inside of her for a second time and began to rock on his cock as he continued to pump her full of his seed. The sensation of her pussy being even wetter—to the point she was slipping on his dick almost recklessly, unable to tell what was her own moistness and what was his—made her ride him even harder. She would not give his dick a chance to settle in sweeping the ecstasy. Within several thrusts, he was back pushing his dick against her G-spot. All that lubricant and the fact he had come twice inside her made her unleash an orgasm of her own.

"Oh fuck!" she screamed, her orgasm flowing down her body and out her pussy, adding to their cocktail of essence.

"Damn it," she said, holding her face with her hands before collapsing on his chest. Usually, she could go multiple times, but today she could handle only one.

Their session had come to an end.

As the two lay there exhausted, she turned to him as he breathed heavily, regaining his awareness.

"How do you feel?"

He turned to answer her question. "A lot better." The pair chuckled. Autumn leaned over the side of the bed to grab something. When she turned back, she handed him his journal.

"Now...take that hurt, take that pleasure, and write a song."

He looked at her. He was exhausted but inspired. He took the journal and jotted down the notes floating around his head. It wasn't long before he had something he liked.

"Oh shit. This is...this is..."

"Dope, huh? The funny thing about my job is I get to see people and see what they need to bring the best out of them. Sure, it's just a paint-by-numbers gig, but every now and then, someone comes in with real talent. They don't know it, or maybe they do, and they need a nudge. That's the one thing I've learned out there. I may not know a lot about some of what you're going through, but I know an artist when I see one."

Tatum kissed her on the neck and turned back to his journal to finish his thoughts. After a spell, he was satisfied.

"Hey, Fatima, I think this is the first song I've ever actually...Fatima?" He turned over, and she was fast asleep. He kissed his lover's sleeping frame and put his journal on the nightstand, and settled in next to her.

"Thank you," he whispered in her ear as he closed his eyes, holding her until he joined her in slumber.

23

BLAME GAME

"*J*'m serious, Stone. I've been writing some music, and the shit is fire."

"Oh, you back on that shit again, huh?"

"What's that supposed to mean?"

"Nothing, Rev., I'll check out the lyrics if you come through tonight."

"Bro, didn't I say I was coming through?"

"You say a lot of things. Your word ain't what it used to be."

"Dog, I ain't got time for this shit."

"Really? I figure time is the one thing you got. You got fired two weeks ago."

"Oh, okay."

"It don't matter, Rev. Good luck today."

"Peace."

Tatum hung up the phone. He wasn't sure what Stone's attitude was about, but it would have to wait. He was standing outside the hallway while his lawyer went to the restroom. He paced the floor until he returned, and they were called into court.

It wasn't long before the judge came in. An older white lady sat down and shuffled through the paperwork nonchalantly, barely noticing the clients. She moved a sliver of her dark brown hair into the bun it fell out of as she pushed her glasses against her nose.

"This is in the interest of Monique Clarke asking for primary custody of the child Solomon Clarke against the defendant, Tatum Clarke, who is counter-petitioning for full custody and divorce. Counselor for the counter-petitioner, present your argument."

"Thank you, Your Honor." Tatum's lawyer, Mark Anderson, from the prestigious firm Anderson and Doyle, stood up to present his case.

"Your Honor, my client was trusting his son's mother when she turned around and abducted the child, using the court system to facilitate a legal kidnapping. She has not been in this child's life for the last four years. We ask for immediate dismissal of the restraining order and for Tatum Clarke to have full custody of his son."

"Your Honor, if I may." Monique's lawyer, a young Latina, stood up and presented her case. She stood and cleared her throat.

"My client has always been in her son's life. These allegations are baseless. She, along with her mother and several witnesses in her family, are here to testify that she felt threatened by Mr. Clarke, who has a history of violence in his family. His father is notorious drug kingpin Johnny Clarke, commonly known as J.C. Money, whose reputation in this town precedes him. Mrs. Clarke is concerned for not only her safety but her son. Solomon will be exposed to the same violent and drug-infested lifestyle that the defendant was exposed to as a child."

Tatum's eyes opened wide. It stunned him that she used his upbringing against him. He looked over to her and lost his composure at the statement.

"You evil bitch!" he yelled.

"Order!"

"My client also does not understand that if Mr. Clarke was so determined to see his son, why did he miss his last supervised visitation?"

Tatum stood up and raised his hand. The judge paused Monique's lawyer.

"Mr. Clarke, I'll indulge you this one time since there's clearly something you need to share with the court. But no more after this."

"I understand, Your Honor. I just want to say, and I've thought about any other words I could use to convey this point, but all of this you're hearing is grade-A bullshit. She keeps my son in the house until the last ten or fifteen minutes of every visitation and—"

"I've heard enough. Mrs. Clarke, is this true?"

"Your Honor, my client will concede that she's had a hard time adjusting her comfort level for her son to be around Mr. Clarke, but last week he said he wouldn't be able to make visitation because he had a job interview. Apparently, Mr. Clarke was recently terminated from his job, which makes us wonder how would he be able to support a child if he can't support himself?"

The judge raised his head from the paperwork and looked at Tatum.

"Mr. Clarke, do you have a job?"

"Not at this time, Your Honor."

"Do you have any leads on a job?"

"No, Your Honor. My work history has been steady but-"t

The judge waved him to stop.

"Mrs. Clarke, have you been denying visitation?"

Monique stood up and, as innocent as a newborn lamb, said, "No, Your Honor. I was late once, I think, but I even allowed him extra time as a result. I just want what's best for my baby."

"Oh, this is a goddamn lie," Tatum said, stunned by the performance he was witnessing.

Bang! The judge slammed the gavel and pointed it toward Tatum.

"Counsel, I suggest you get a hold of your client."

Tatum's lawyer tried to calm him down, but it was too late. His character was being attacked, and he was fighting for the most important person in his life. He ignored the statement.

"Your Honor, none of this is-"

"I said order! Now another outburst from you, Mr. Clarke, and you're going to have bigger problems than mediation on your hands." The judge turned to Monique. "Continue, Mrs. Clarke."

"Our background was complicated. There was a brief while he stayed with his father, and I'm ashamed to say I... I stayed away from my son. I was scared of the criminal element his father associates himself with. We've been married this whole time, but he became increasingly violent and agitated, and I was afraid for my life. Why, not long ago, he actually came to my house and had to be escorted away by the police."

Tatum sat, losing his mind. He bit his tongue so as not to make his situation any worse. He looked up at the judge, who didn't want to hear anything else. He realized what she had done. Monique, after all these years, was still able to push his buttons.

"This can't be happening," he whispered to himself. He looked at his lawyer, who barely said a word, and rolled his eyes. *I just wasted fifteen thousand dollars.*

After a spell, the judge spoke. "Mr. Clarke, this court does not care about a person's past or upbringing. We only care about taking care of the well-being of the child. Now I don't doubt you may be an outstanding father, but we have to look at the facts. At the moment, you don't have a job; no means of providing for your child. You haven't provided any information to indicate the child isn't being properly taken care of, and you missed your last visitation. It is the opinion of this court that the temporary order for Monique Clarke be granted primary conservatorship over the child remain in force until the divorce proceedings are finalized."

The bang of the gavel felt like a nail through his heart. He'd lost, and there was nothing he could do about it. Tatum began to hyperventilate. He couldn't move. His feet became as heavy as cinder blocks. He glanced at Monique, who was smiling as she walked out. He composed himself. He could not give her the satisfaction of seeing him so defeated. His legs found their strength as he heard the words his lawyer muttered. He needed air. As he walked out the door, his lawyer stopped him.

"We got blindsided, but this is far from over."

"Oh, you have a voice! I was wondering what I spent fifteen thousand dollars on."

"Listen, they caught me off guard with the way this went, but you never said anything about losing your job. And the one thing I know about this judge is that the moment you had an outburst, she all but stopped listening. Right now, you're no good to your son if you can't get control of your emotions."

Tatum's emotion was rage. He didn't want to hear what the lawyer was saying. Still, he listened. He felt he had no other choice.

"What's the plan?"

"I've got some work to do. There's no way she can win, but it's going to take time. Time and money."

"You want more money?"

"No, what you have should cover it, but you have to get a job and quickly if we're going to come back with a better defense."

Tatum nodded. He was angry at his lawyer because he felt vastly underrepresented, but he also knew not working didn't help things. He shook Mark's hand and walked out the door. When he got outside, Monique was on the phone, waving to him as she got inside her car. He flipped her the bird and headed to his car. There was no boundary to the pain he was feeling. He was hurt, afraid, and scared.

A few moments later, his phone rang. He figured it was Monique calling him to bust his balls and taunt him over his performance in the courtroom. But it wasn't. It was his father. Tatum decided not to answer it. His father would give him some speech about being The Lion or getting things done, and he didn't need that right now.

He turned on the car and drove to Autumn's house. He got to her condo, and as usual, her door was unlocked. He didn't care. He wasn't going to chastise her over that now that he had bigger fish to fry. Autumn was listening to Marvin Gaye's *Got To Give It Up* as she painted a portrait of the late singer.

"Hey baby, how are you doing?" she said as she danced over to him and kissed him on the cheek.

"I lost in mediation today..."

Autumn turned off the music and stopped painting. She walked over to Tatum.

"I'm sorry. I know this has been hard on you."

"You should've seen her in there lying 'bout all kinds of shit. Talking 'bout I got a history of violence. Used my dad against me. Fuck, man!" Tatum barked as he poured himself a double of Hennessy he kept at his lover's place.

"Maybe the silver lining is you wanted him to get to know his mother eventually. Maybe this is God's—"

"She's not a mother. A mother doesn't abandon her child. She's an egg donor, and I can't believe you're saying this right now!" Tatum took another large gulp of the liquor as if willing himself to drunkenness. Autumn inched closer.

"Blue, this isn't going your way. It's taking its toll on you. I'm just saying we can figure it out."

Tatum took a final swig of the liquor and put the glass on the table.

"Fatima, I can't believe you right now. If I were a woman, would you tell me to leave my kid?"

"That's not what I'm saying."

"That's all I'm hearing. Would you respect any woman who left her kid for a man? Then why in the fuck would you think that's easy for me to do? Why would you think it's even an option? He's *my* kid! I'm the primary caretaker! I sat through the colds and fevers and scared nights, but you wouldn't know anything about commitment because you barely follow through with anything you do."

His venomous words hit Autumn directly in the jaw, at least judging by her visceral reaction to them.

"Excuse me?"

"What, we hard of hearing now? I'll say it again: You barely follow through with anything you do. Sure, you will build up someone else's dream and fortune so that a place like Paint & Sip is doing fine— which is just fine for you because it's safe. But what are you working for? What's the meaning of sacrifice to you? You hop from art gallery to art gallery begging someone to tell you what to do, and you give them your entire soul because you don't want to figure out how a spreadsheet works. Someone comes along and gives you an actual studio. All you claim you dream of, and you haven't acted on it yet. The truth of the matter is you're afraid to do that for yourself."

"Fuck you, Tatum. I've been in your corner all this time, and you think just because you fucked the wrong bitch you get to take it out on me?"

"I'm not taking shit out on you. Anybody that can sit there with a straight face and tell me to abandon my child has a serious problem. But once again, it's a one-way street."

"And what does that mean?"

"It means I'm always here for you. You need help selling your artwork? Fine, I help. You want to own a studio; I tell you I'm willing to relocate with you to get it started. You need help dealing with your daddy issues? Fine, Tatum Clarke's your man. But I've lost my job, my scholarship, and now custody of my kid, and you're sitting there like, 'Look at the silver lining.' Fuck the silver lining!"

Tatum paused. He knew he was losing control of not just himself but everything around him. The life he'd spend the past four years building. He was lashing out at the wrong person. He was in the mood for a fight, but he didn't want it to be Autumn. He took a deep breath and pushed his liquor glass to the other end of the counter. He shouldn't drink anymore. Not when he was like this.

"Look, my bad. I lost my temper. You want something to eat?" he said, dismissing the carnage he just unleashed. Something that wasn't missed by Autumn as she was now upset.

"Tatum, I understand you're going through a lot, but we have to talk about what you said."

"I'm not in the mood to talk about that or anything else right now. Now, do you want something to eat or not?"

"And I don't understand why you have to be such an asshole right now."

"I'm an asshole right now because if you weren't paying attention, I lost my scholarship, I lost my job, and I lost my savings all to lose custody of my son. It's a lot to deal with at one time, so forgive me if I'm not Mr. Happy-Go-Lucky. I got too many problems to be worried about hurt feelings."

His words reached their target, and the fallout was already on full display as her face soured. He couldn't look at her. He knew those were the kind of words they never used, and he instantly regretted saying them. But it was all too much. He was dealing with the very real fallout of his decimated life, and she chose to walk through his minefield of thoughts and emotions in large boots with high heels. Collateral damage was unavoidable.

"Well, I guess that's what I needed to know," she said, her voice giving a clear indication his words were effective. "I don't have an appetite."

Say something, he thought. He was caught in a snare between his heart and his brain. Allowing her to walk out the door would create irrevocable problems, but his pride wouldn't allow him to say anything. He couldn't figure out if his head was telling his heart to be quiet or the other way around. She said nothing, which angered him even more.

"I just told you I lost custody of my son, and you wanna talk about forgetting about him! I hate this shit. I'm so fucking sick and tired of this double-standard society that thinks men can't be parents too. I just lost my fucking kid! Do you have any idea what kind of state of mind I'm in? I'm not in the mood to talk about paint!"

He fought back the tears as he screamed at her, but it did not slow his unfiltered anger.

"If I was a woman, there'd be a task force aimed at bringing justice to this situation, but instead, it's 'Oh well, now you're free.' But I don't wanna be free! Because heaven forbid a father—especially a black one —gives a fuck about his child."

"Tatum, I didn't mean it like that. I was just saying, look at the silver lining."

"There is no silver lining! Was there a silver lining with your miscarriage? This isn't a puppy. This isn't a fictional child who lives in my spirit for artistic inspiration or some other bullshit. My child is real! I don't have to imagine him. He's flesh-and-blood real, and I'm the only parent he knows, and nobody seems to give a fuck about that but me!"

Tatum was seeing red. He couldn't believe she was so cavalier about his pain. He watched as her face went from sensitive to hurt, her eyes welling up. *No, fuck that,* he thought. *She doesn't get to cry at my pain.*

He reached for his glass and poured himself another shot of Hennessy. It was only when she began to cry that he realized the magnitude of his words.

Shit...Ezri.

Between his own hurt, alcohol, and pent-up aggression, he'd gone too far. He'd hurt her to the core.

"Autumn, I wasn't even thinking about Ezri. Not like that. I was just—"

"Get out, Tatum."

"I'm sorry, Autumn. I—"

"Get out!" she screamed.

Tatum looked at her and glared.

"You know what? Fuck this. I don't need this on top of everything else. I am out. Who needs this one-way street shit? I got bigger problems," he said, walking out the door to the sidewalk. He didn't want to drive. He'd been drinking heavily, but he couldn't stay there. He walked outside and decided to Uber his way somewhere else. Anywhere else. He didn't even realize what he said was what he was actually saying, but he realized it hurt and he was wrong. He needed her support—he just didn't know how to apologize at this point. He'd been trying to cope with the circumstances of the day and failing as miserably as he felt the courts failed him. He couldn't believe that after almost five years of single parenting, a judge just handed his son to a complete stranger. It was unreal. He was living a nightmare he couldn't wake up from. That Hennessey hadn't been enough to calm his nerves or keep his shit together. He needed something stronger.

It wasn't long before Uber pulled up. He sat in the back and picked up his phone to see another missed call from his dad. He was in no mood to tell him he lost. He called his best friend, or rather his only friend in the world at this moment.

"Yo, Stone, I'm coming through."

24

SHOES

*T*atum pulled up to Stone's home in Sunnyside, Texas. He looked at the Uber driver, who was slightly nervous to be dropping him off in this neighborhood, and scoffed at him.

"Thanks, man," he said as he left him a decent tip as he started to walk up to the front door. Several men were standing outside, none of whom he recognized. One of the men—a dark-skinned, heavyset man with dreads and several neck tattoos walked up to him.

"Hey, you lost, homie?"

"Nah, I know where I'm at," Tatum said as he continued down the driveway.

The man blocked his path and briefly examined Tatum.

"Oh, my bad, pastor. We not giving out donations."

"I ain't no pastor."

"What's with the suit and the book then?" the man asked, referring to Tatum's journal and the suit he wore to court today. He stuck out like a sore thumb in this part of town. He didn't care.

"Motherfucker, I ain't gotta explain nothing to—"

"Yo, Rev!"

Tatum looked over as Stone walked outside. He waved him in. Stone made eye contact with the dread-headed man indicate Tatum was fine to come in as Tatum sized him up. He dismissed him as no threat and disappeared inside the house to shake his friend's hand.

Stone was nonchalant about the experience.

"I see you got some new faces around here."

"Nah, they been here for a minute. You just been missing."

Tatum always joked how Stone had the nicest trap house in the neighborhood. Slum on the outside but a mansion on the inside. He walked in the house to a freshly painted gray interior with charcoal hardwood floors and a nice navy-blue sectional with two men playing games on the 85-inch flat-screen TV mounted on the wall. Stone walked into the kitchen and sat on one of the barstools as Tatum sat on the other.

"So you slumming with us since you and ya girl on the outs?"

"Dog, I know it's been a while. The shit with Monique, the shit with Autumn, graduation, my job, Solly—it's been a lot, bro."

"Nah, I get it. You gotta make time for what's important."

Tatum detected a hint of sarcasm in his friend's response and decided to address it cautiously.

"I don't have time for your shit neither. I lost in mediation today."

Stone took a puff off a blunt he lit and handed it to Tatum, who took a hit of the blunt as well.

"Damn, Rev., I told you we shoulda just walked in there and took my nephew back months ago. Dog, why are you so forgiving with this bitch? I don't get it."

Tatum took another hit of the blunt. "Dog, she was there when I had nothing. I... I don't know. It's like she bet on my ass when it wasn't cool to bet on me, and she gave me my son. I hate her, but I can't hate her. You feel me?"

"Not in the least, my G. But what you need to do is—"

"Hey, boss." One of his guys came rushing into the house and headed straight for Stone.

"What's up?" The man looked at Tatum, who realized he felt uncomfortable because of his attire.

"Is that your lawyer?"

"Hoe, don't worry about who he is. Speak freely," Stone said.

"We didn't get the product."

Stone ashed out the blunt and walked over to grab his pistol, and turned around.

"Motherfucker, you got ten seconds to tell me where my product at. One...nine..."

"Okay, okay. I went to the spot like always. The Mexicans, they was there, but..."

Stone cocked his pistol. The man stammered through the rest of the statement.

"But what?"

"They told me to go to another spot."

"Okay. Did you go to the other spot?"

"Yeah, but when I got there, it was a few guys I didn't recognize, and they didn't give me the product. Told me to tell you they wanted to meet."

Stone put the pistol in his waist and picked back up the blunt, and lit it. He started to walk out the door but stopped a few steps later and turned to Tatum. "Come on."

"What?"

"You said you rolling with me tonight, so this what we doing. Come on."

All of the men in the house got up and went to their respective cars. Stone and Tatum and the man who informed them about the change in plans got in Stone's car. After twenty minutes, they reached their destination—a warehouse on the end of town. Stone parked his Lexus and walked outside. There were several Hispanic men but no Carlos. Tatum did recognize one face, though: Gustavo. As the men piled out the car, another Hispanic man with slicked-back black hair wearing a black silk shirt and cream colored slacks walked into the center of the mob.

"Which one of you is Stone?"

"That's me. And who the fuck are you?"

"I'm Enrique. I'm taking over the family business. My uncle Ernesto sends his regards."

"Okay...good to meet you. What's the hold up on our product?"

"My uncle...he is a sentimental man, and we've had to make some...shall we say, account audits, and the one thing that's glaring is we are getting paid handsomely everywhere but here in Houston. You guys are moving a hell of a lot of product, but you're paying fifteen-year-old prices. I love my uncle, but the only reason he's in this mess is because he wasn't good about business."

"So what does this mean? You trying to raise the price of the brick?" Stone barked in agitation.

"Si, Papi. Ten large."

"Bullshit. You don't have anyone paying you that."

"I'm making up for all the years you got over on us."

Tatum looked at his friend as he was getting agitated and stepped in before he did something stupid.

"My pops always told me a Mendoza man is an honorable man. I guess the Mendoza family ain't what it used to be."

Enrique turned his attention to Tatum, as did his bodyguards. He watched as Gustavo walked up to him.

"Hey, show some fucking respect, ése."

"Hold on, Gustavo. I want to hear this. You—just who the fuck are you, and who in the fuck is your pops?"

"I'm T.C. My pops is Johnny Clarke, and I know your uncle gave his word that our family would always get the family discount. Well, you're talking to my brother."

Enrique's eyes widened as he walked closer to inspect Tatum.

"Holy fucking shit! You're J.C. Money's mijo, little T.C. Man, your pops was a fuckin' legend, ése. He'd come down to Nuevo Laredo and fucking party. You probably have a brother there you don't know about, man," Enrique said as the men laughed. "He gave me my first pistol, my first nine drinks, paid for my first piece of panocha! You're like family, ése. He always said he wouldn't let his son get in the game. I knew he couldn't do it—the game's in your fucking blood, homes! My bad, ése, I didn't know. How's J.C. doing? I heard some bad shit happened to him."

"He's good. He hit a rough patch, but he's back on the mend. So are we good on the pricing?"

"We have no issue on the pricing, man. I'm taking five percent off this round as a sign of good faith."

"Then the word of a Mendoza man truly stands the test of time."

The two hugged in celebration. As they started to relax, Gustavo walked up behind Tatum and said, "Boss Tatum isn't in the life. He doesn't have the cajones his pops had. He's a fucking accountant or something."

Tatum scoffed at the wannabe tough guy. He looked at his new comrade.

"Enrique, is this guy supposed to be muscle? I know you're new, but do yourself a favor and stop fucking with this puta."

"I'm not the one out here skating by on my pop's name in the streets, homeboy. I'm putting in the fucking work."

"Stavo, I know you're interviewing for your job, but please don't get your ass beat pretending to be tough because this accountant will beat your ass." As Tatum walked away, Gustavo stepped in front of him.

"Prove it, ése," he said.

Tatum looked at Stone, who seemed entirely disinterested. He knew the tension between him and Stone had grown, but he didn't know it was to this point. After a spell, Stone stepped back and said, "The man called you out. That's your beef, homie."

Tatum's eyes widened. Gustavo stepped closer to him, getting eye to eye.

"Yeah, don't look to your friend for help. Our issue ain't got nothing to with this."

"I didn't know we had an issue."

"We do now, you puto. You think you're tough shit, prove it. This ain't high school, Tate."

"Gustavo, dog, I'm telling you, you gone fuck around and get what you're looking for, but it ain't gonna be none of what you want."

"Pinche cabron, you better show me some fucking respect." Gustavo shoved him. It was all the excuse Tatum needed.

He caught Gustavo with a left hook to the face, followed by two right hooks to the ribs. A strong left to the top of the head, and

Gustavo instantly crumbled. Tatum got on top of him and hit him repeatedly. One of the Hispanic men tried to interfere but was stopped by Enrique. Tatum pummeled the man until his fists were bloody.

"You better hope you don't fuck up this suit with your blood!" he said, standing up and kicking him in the ribs. He turned back, still aggressive. He wiped his hands and took off his suit jacket and his shirt while Gustavo was still lying on the ground as not to bloody them.

"I'm glad, Gustavo. I've been having a shitty week, and whooping your ass was just what I needed. You think I don't still know you're a bitch, Stavo? I will beat your ass every day for the rest of your life in front of your momma, and there'll never be a goddamn thing you can do about it. But If I'm wrong, get up off the ground so I can knock you back on your ass again."

Gustavo stood up, blood dripping from his nose and lips, and looked around over to Enrique for help.

"Like you said, it's between you and him."

As he turned the other direction to eye Stone, Tatum hit him with a solid right hand in the face.

"Don't look around at them, motherfucker! You wanted this shit! So look at the man in front of you telling you I'm gonna whoop your sorry ass and do something about it."

Wham! Tatum hit him in the face again, more blood trickling from his nose.

"Where's that tough shit, Stavo? See, that shit was good just talking, but now you realize you gotta move them hands, and you're in trouble."

Gustavo swung but missed Tatum, who hit him two more times until he heard a noise that sounded like ribs cracking. Gustavo winced over in pain.

"You need help now, don't you, little bitch? I bet you wish this was high school now, but ain't nobody coming to save you."

Wham! He hit him again. Tatum was releasing years' worth of frustration. He caught Stone jumping up and down, waving his hand

and cheering him on in his peripheral vision. He didn't care. He didn't even care about this fight with this guy in front of him. He was angry about Solomon and his powerlessness. He was angry about his job and what he was going to do with his life. And he was mad about what he said to Autumn. Gustavo Gonzales just so happened to be the fuse to light the powder keg, and he needed it. He couldn't control the variables in his life. It was all new to him. He was just trying his best to fit in. But in the hood, he knew how to handle the issues. And hitting this man until he couldn't stand anymore was perfectly fine for everyone here.

Gustavo rushed him, and Tatum caught him with a hard left to the face, knocking him to the ground. Gustavo laid there, crumpled in pain, but that didn't stop Tatum from climbing on top of him and grabbing him by the shirt.

"Act like the bitch you are and apologize for wasting these people's time." He could see the fear in Gustavo's eyes. He slapped him twice, further injuring his rival's nose. "I said apologize, motherfucker!"

"I'm sorry!" Gustavo screamed.

Wham! Tatum slapped him again.

"Say this is just like high school!"

"This is just like high school! Please, just...I'm sorry, Tatum."

Gustavo had tears in his eyes. Tatum knew he'd gone too far, but he didn't care. He stood up and dropped Gustavo's body to the ground. The beaten man scrambled away from him to rally back to his feet.

"Sucka-ass-punk motherfucker." Tatum barked as he realized Gustavo had enough. He'd been emasculated in front of his boss and his comrades. His days as an enforcer were over.

"Damn, Stavo, block next time," Stone said as everyone laughed hard, including Enrique.

Gustavo staggered over to his boss and said, "Let's get out of here."

Enrique said, "You're not coming with us, chica!" The men laughed again. "I mean, you're supposed to be the muscle, and you just got your ass kicked by a fucking accountant. I mean no offense." He directed the last statement to Tatum, who was busy still wiping the blood off of his knuckles and laughing along with the rest of the men in the warehouse. Gustavo turned towards Tatum and pointed.

"You're fucking dead, ése!" Gustavo screamed at Tatum, who put the towel down and walked in Gustavo's direction.

"Bitch, what you say?"

Tatum took off running toward Gustavo as if he were going to hit him again, causing the man to run off. He kicked him in his ass as he scrambled to escape the warehouse. The group of men continued to laugh.

Stone stood up on his car and yelled, "Now who else wanna fuck with Reverend Clarke?" referencing the moment he first got the nickname.

Tatum, normally introspective, knew it was good to let off a little steam, and if anyone deserved to be a punching bag, it was Gustavo Gonzales.

NEVER BE THE SAME AGAIN

*a*s the men were getting more comfortable, Tatum looked at the door that led to an empty office

"Gentlemen, we need to seal this bond with a shot of tequila!"

Enrique walked over to a table, and there sat a bottle of Patron. He poured three shots as the other two men walked over.

"To family," Enrique said.

"To family," Stone and Tatum said in unison. The trio drank their shots. When they were done, Tatum tapped Stone on the shoulder.

"Let me talk to you real quick." The two walked into the office Tatum had eyed before the shot. He closed the door and turned to face Stone.

"What the fuck was that?"

"That was a very entertaining ass-whooping."

"You know what I'm talking about. 'That's your beef, homie'?"

"Now you know Stavo been barking up that tree for a while. he got what he des-"

"Fuck all that! You're supposed to have my back, Stone." His friend cut his eye at him.

"You can accuse me of a lot of things, but not having your back will never be one of them."

"That shit escalated for no reason."

"See, that's the problem with you, Rev. You seem to forget how things work around here. When a man step to you, ain't no steppin' in. And if you didn't have your head deep in Art BAE's pussy, you'd know that."

"And just what in the fuck is that supposed to mean?"

"It means you're fucking up. You spend all this time trying to be a pharmacist to get a job to take care of your son, and eight months in Erykah Badu's pussy, and you're gonna be a songwriter? What in the fuck do you know about songwriting? Have you finished a song in that damn notebook of yours since I've known you?"

"Fuck you, Stone. What you want me to do? Sit around here with you and sell dope all day? Just because I have aspirations doesn't mean-"

"See, that's what I'm talking about right there. Aspirations? Motherfucker, just call them shits dreams. Remember who you are and get off that high horse. You needed this shit tonight to remind yourself of who you are. You're Reverend Motherfucking Clarke, and you've been fighting your whole god-damn life. See, you can say what you want, but I know you, and I know that if you were on your game, no way in hell would you have ever lost your son. This debacle is entirely on you."

His friend's tough love was hard to hear, but he respected him for it regardless of the methods. It wasn't long before that same dread head from earlier walked into the building.

"Hey, y'all good?"

The tension cleared; they were back to themselves.

"Yeah...always," Tatum said, looking at Stone, who nodded in agreement.

The dread head man turned to Stone and said, "Boss, that thing we were talking about...is Mike Tyson...I mean Reverend Clarke, coming with?"

Stone lit a blunt and took a long drag before responding.

"No doubt. He's the man of the hour."

"What thing?" Tatum asked.

Stone rolled his eyes and took a deep sigh. "Well, you keep claiming you want to be a songwriter. I know a dude who knows a dude who needs a few songs. I reached out to some people about getting a meeting with Preston Cole. He's gonna meet us at The Blue Lion to read them lyrics you been yapping about."

"Wait, what?" Tatum said with nervous excitement in his voice. His friend had just berated him about having *aspirations* but was helping him make one of them come true. True to his word, he always had his back.

"Stone, you don't know what this means to me."

"Alright, don't be a bitch about it. You just saved me some money on the dope and gave us ringside at a pay-per-view. Stay hard, bro."

Tatum laughed at his friend as the two exchanged a handshake, followed by an embrace.

"Well, come on. We can't keep Mr. Cole waiting. The only dude more sensitive than you is this diva."

The two men, along with the man with the dreads, walked out of the office to greet Enrique.

"My brother Enrique, you tell your uncle that J.C. Money's son sends his regards."

"Reverend...I gotta tell you; you did me a good service there. I don't need cowards working for me. Thank you for exposing that pinche pinocha."

The two men exchanged a handshake. Stone walked over with three shots of tequila.

"One for the road?"

The men grabbed their respective drinks out of his hands and took the shots. After a few pleasantries, they were all headed to the Blue Lion. Tatum was elated. He wanted to talk to Autumn and tell her he was about to show Preston Cole one of his songs. He missed her, and he realized he'd gone too far and didn't know how to say he was sorry. Yet, at the same time, he was just glad something was going his way. As they headed to the club, Tatum took the journal Autumn got him from his jacket pocket and looked at the song he'd written—the first one he actually completed.

He nodded.

"What, bro? You good?" Stone asked as he eyed Tatum's journal.

"Man, I'm good. I'm ready."

He was ready. A calm settled in that reinvigorated his confidence. Tatum was certain this song would be received well because he wrote it from the depths of his heart. In reality, it was the best thing he'd ever composed. As they pulled up to the club, Tatum took a puff of the blunt Stone had been puffing on the entire way. The two exited the vehicle. Before they reached the door, his phone buzzed. It was his dad again.

"Hold up. I'm gonna talk to Johnny real quick. Tell him about the—"

"Hit him up when we're done, bro. I wasn't playing when I told you this guy is a diva. I've gotten fifteen messages about this shit. He has to perform in a few."

"Oh...cool," Tatum said, putting his phone back in his pocket. It was then that he noticed the blood splatter from Gustavo's face and slipped off the jacket. He then checked the rest of his suit. It was good. Not even a drop of blood on his shoes.

"Smart move, Rev. Now come on, we got to get inside."

Tatum and Stone walked into the back of the club and went upstairs to one of the private rooms while a few of Stone's men went through the main entrance to make sure there was no trouble. Tatum opened the door and placed his suit jacket on an empty table. Preston Cole was sitting in the club listening to music.

"This shit is all wrong!" he screamed as he turned off the music they were listening to. He watched the two men entering the room and cooled his tantrum for the moment. Preston paused and looked at Tatum with familiarity.

"Didn't I meet you before?"

"Yeah, Austin," Tatum said, surprised he remembered the encounter.

"That's right. The guy with the journal and the art chick. And you know Stone?"

"He's my brother."

"Then this might be fated. Let's see what you got."

Stone leaned against the wall and took a deep drag on his blunt, letting Tatum know the floor was all his.

"Yeah, that's your beef over there, homie. Go handle that."

Tatum smirked and nodded. He went over to Preston and held his notepad for a second. Preston walked closer.

"Oh, I get it. You're an artist. You're sensitive about your shit. I respect that. Tell you what. We're gonna help this along. My man Stan over there is my engineer. Give him a beat, and I'll vibe to what you've written."

Tatum looked at Stan and said, "Give me something up-tempo."

Preston turned to Stan, who started playing several beats, each one met by Tatum's disapproval. After several selections, Tatum said.

"That's it! Right there!"

As the beat played on, he took a deep breath, opened his journal, and handed it to Preston, who, after reading the first few lines, started to sing the words in the cadence of the beat. Preston nodded in approval and took the journal.

"Yo, Stan, rewind that for me," Tatum said midway through the melody.

The beat started over and Preston, in true artist form, brought the song to life in a way Tatum never imagined. He marveled as people in this room, including his best friend, reacted to the words. After a spell, Preston motioned for Stan to stop the music. He turned to Tatum and said, "This is hot. You wrote this?"

"Yeah. I did."

"This is fire! What do you call it?"

"I...um...*Bedroom Details.*"

Preston continued to nod his head. He was highly animated but not as animated as a man in the corner singing the words from memory.

"Yo, Drinks, you like that song?"

The man stopped singing and stepped behind the bar.

"Is he in your band?" Tatum asked, unsure of the man's role.

"No, that's just Drinks. He's some buster that be around who wants to become a singer but ain't got it. He makes good-ass drinks, though, so I keep him around," Preston said as the people around him started to laugh.

"Yo, Drinks, you think I should do this?"

The man stammered. "I...I think it's—"

"Speak up! I can barely hear you," Preston said, clearly agitated.

"It's nice!" Drinks said more forcefully.

"Good, now make us some margaritas," Preston said in a cocky tone. Tatum now understood what Stone meant about the man being a diva, but he didn't care. An artist liked his song, and he was elated. *Damn, I wish Fatima was here.*

"I fucks with this song, Tatum. I fucks with you. Let's negotiate a price on what I can buy it from you for."

Tatum's eyes glazed over. He couldn't believe what he just heard.

"You want my song?"

"Hell, I want whatever you got if you're writing like this," Preston said.

Tatum looked at Stone, who had since come off the wall to stand side by side with his friend.

"We can make that happen, but the business end of it is gonna go through me."

Tatum looked at his friend and nodded in agreement. Stone was doing for him what he had done for Autumn

"Cool, let's celebrate. Yo, Drinks, are you done with those margaritas?"

"Almost. I just have to-"

"Yeah, cancel that and make us a few Crown and Cokes." Tatum looked at the man, who was frustrated and embarrassed and decided to come to his rescue.

"Actually...a margarita is fine for me," he interjected, nudging his friend in the arm. But Stone dismissed the opportunity to show compassion for the bartender.

"Yeah, make my Jack and Crown a double."

"And hurry that shit up, Drinks. I gotta get downstairs," Preston added. The bartender hurried over with the drinks, not even making eye contact as the men took them from his hands.

"To finding the missing piece to the puzzle," Preston said. The men toasted their success.

"Damn, Drinks, this is Crown and Coke?" Stone said, impressed by the beverage.

"Yeah, I... I put grenadine and a little splash of vanilla in it. I hope you don't mind."

"Shit, no! This the best damn drink I think I've ever had," Stone said.

"Now you see why I keep him around," Preston said, making sure the attention—and the credit—stayed on him. The men put their glasses on the bar and proceeded to the door.

"I'm gonna be in touch. Tatum, we're working together. And I'm excited."

"Me too. Thank you for this opportunity."

As the men walked downstairs, Tatum felt a lot better. He missed his son sorely. He thought about that turn of phrase 'the missing piece to the puzzle.' That was Solomon. He couldn't imagine life without his son. It was a non-starter of an idea. But as the drinks take their effect, he realized he couldn't imagine his life without Autumn either. He loved her unconditionally and unapologetically. She was the first thing he thought of in the morning and the last thing he thought about at night. He needed to apologize. He'd taken things too far. She wasn't the source of the problem. He took his anger about the custody hearing out on her, and while he wished she'd been more present for him, he knew he could at least make himself more available to her. Her life had left her scarred and hurting too. He took out his phone to text her.

He punched in the words *I'm sorry*. It wasn't much, but it was a start. He was about to hit send when Stone slapped him on the back.

"Reverend Clarke the songwriter. So that's what she got you over there singing, huh?"

The two men laughed. Tatum looked at his friend.

"Preston Cole liked my shit! Can you believe it?"

"Rev, you a bad motherfucker if you let yourself be. I never seen anyone trip themselves up more than you. I bet you thinking about that old girl right now."

Tatum's silence betrayed him.

"Yeah, I knew it, but you know what? None of that fuck shit tonight. Let's find that cat Drinks and get something whipped up. You gotta try that shit with the vanilla in it."

"I think he's over at the bar. I'll meet you over there. I'm going to the restroom," Tatum responded.

The two men started walking in their respective directions. Tatum pushed his way through the crowded club and pulled out his phone to finish his text.

I'm sorry.

He looked at it. He knew it wasn't enough and added *I fucked up.* He paused. *Man, I can't send this shit. I need to go over there.* Of course, Stone would never let him, and Preston would take his disappearance as an insult. He decided to just enjoy himself. He put his phone away, turned around, and excitedly jogged back onto the dance floor.

"Where in the fuck is Stone?" Tatum turned toward the bar and scanned the area but didn't see his friend. He turned back and looked toward the stage. Preston Cole was performing. He got excited at the idea that the man on stage right now would soon be performing his work. He bobbed his head to the beat, still searching for Stone. As he came around to face the stage again, he was surprised to realize Preston Cole was looking in his direction. He waved him on as he continued to sing. A second later, Preston Cole stopped mid-song, the club deathly silent.

"I told you you're dead, ése!" Tatum turned around. A man in a black hoodie with black sweatpants was stood in front of him, reaching in his pocket.

It was Gustavo.

"Rev, get down!" Stone raced forward screaming; his voice nearly drowned out as the rest of the audience shrieked in terror.

Gustavo held a .9mm Glock pistol.

Pop! Pop! Pop!

Tatum fell to the floor, blood pooling around him. He was disoriented as people scattered. Gustavo ran out of the club ahead of them amid more gunfire. Tatum pushed someone off him, who collapsed in the melee. He looked down to see that he was covered in blood, but he realized it wasn't his own. His best friend had shoved him to the floor and taken three bullets in the chest and ribs...He was bleeding profusely, faster than Tatum could stop it.

"Oh God, Stone!" he screamed as the first siren wailed in the distance.

26

CRY TOGETHER

"**M**r. Clarke?"

"Uh...yeah?"

"Your brother is out of surgery."

Tatum sat up, his eyes bloodshot. He was hungover, tired, and hungry. He'd been in the hospital all night. After taking a moment to gain his bearings, he asked, "How is he doing?"

"It's entirely too soon to say, but he told me I could share his information with you. We were able to remove all three bullets successfully, but one damaged his spine. We did everything we could but—" The doctor paused. Tatum was in no mood for a mystery.

"Just say it, Doc."

"There is a high probability your Kenley will never walk again."

The words cut like a knife. He couldn't believe it. He all but stopped listening to the doctor, and as the doctor continued, he stood up.

"Can I see him?"

"He just got to his room. He is conscious but weak. But please, understand, Mr. Clarke, that with physical therapy and human will, anything is possible. We just have to err on the side of caution."

"I understand. Thank you, Doc."

Tatum walked back into the room; he was wearing a pair of hospital scrubs as his shirt and suit now bloodstained from holding his friend as he bled across the nightclub floor, his lifelong friend disheveled and near dying. Now, Tatum wasn't sure what to say. All of his problems seemed small compared to what he imagined his friend was coming to grips with.

"Rev, I see you still got your journal."

The words brought Tatum relief as he sat next to the bed.

"Had it in my jacket pocket after."

"Yeah." The two were silent. Tatum knew his friend well enough to know his mind was racing.

"Damn, man, I just don't know what to say. I love you, bro. I…"

"There's my little dark-skinned Drake. Write me a song," Stone said jokingly. The words broke up the tension.

"Motherfucker! I guess they didn't operate on your brain."

"You never know at Ben Taub. It's a fifty-fifty shot," Stone said as the pair laughed.

Tatum smirked through the pain. Stone was doing the same, grimacing as he coughed. Tatum guessed he still had feeling above the waist. Maybe rehab could work. He could hope. But for now, his job was to keep Stone's spirit up. To make him believe he would get better.

"I want to tell you, Rev, I was jealous."

Tatum sat confused. "Wh—?"

"Remember the last year we played little league football? As a team, we were-"

"The South Park Snipers," Tatum said, laughing at the memory.

"Remember the last game of the season when we played Sterling?"

"Yeah…I remember."

"Last play of the game was a pitch to the outside. And I remember getting the ball. How cool the fall air was on my face. I had on these old Jordans I made into cleats. They were my lucky shoes, and I remember running, man. I got the ball and hit the outside pitch, and soon as I turned the corner, old bald headed Byron came running around the corner. That guy was a headhunter.

You tried to block him but got trampled, and it was him and me in a foot race to the end zone. I can hear him now. 'I'm gonna get you, Kenley.' That's what he was saying, and it was cold. We were both laughing. The whole thing couldn't have been more than eight seconds, but it was the best eight seconds of my life. I thought over the years, man, I'd get more moments like that but, I never had one even close. It was that one moment in my life where I was carefree and I was happy. Damn, man, what would I give to be back in that moment?"

Tatum watched as his friend drifted to their childhood. He could see, despite the devastating news he just received, what that moment meant to him. He put his hand on his friend's shoulder, wiping tears from his eyes.

"That motherfucker tackled me at the one-yard line, and we lost that year, and I remember you saying, 'We'll get them next year.' Hell, we all thought we'd just play them again next year. Except I didn't come back because I got kicked out of the foster home and started running the streets. When I started running the streets at twelve, I *knew* what I was gonna be at thirteen and every year after that. And I always knew that road would lead me to Huntsville Correctional, or the ground, or here, like everyone in my family before me. I knew when I started dealing in death, Rev, it was a matter of time before it caught me. So I was jealous when Autumn came around. I mean, she took your time away from me. It was like damn, man, not something else. I knew when I woke up, if you didn't get hit, you'd be right here. You're the only family I ever had. I already had to share you with everyone else and...I—"

"Stone, rest, man. Just rest."

"No, bruh, you deserve to hear this. I love you, brother. You had a choice in going into the life, and you didn't take it for granted. I admire you for that. When you stopped providing the pills, a part of me was real proud of you. I guess I feel like if you can make it however far you can make it, then maybe it's all not for nothing. Maybe it's a chance for the have-nots to finally have something, you know? Maybe we don't have to sell dope, go to jail, or take a bullet to the spine. And... if you can get out—truly out—it'll be proof, man. That if you could do it, then maybe I could've been that."

Tatum leaned in and hugged his brother—a brother not by blood but by choice. He felt his pain in their shared memories. The two shed tears as they released the embrace. Tatum sat back in the chair and started to smile.

"You know what I remember about that summer?"

"What?"

"The kool cup lady."

"Oh, hell yeah. Ms. Gray with them big-ass titties."

"Yep. I remember she would always wear those low-cut white T-shirts, and me and you would always make sure she handed those cups to us at the same time."

"Man, those perky nipples. She never wore a bra. I wanted to bite one of those motherfuckers so bad," Stone said, salivating at the idea.

"Hell yeah, man. I know we was kids, but as good as those snow cones were, I wanted to bite them titties too."

Stone chuckled at Tatum's statement.

"Yeah, man, she knew what she was doing bending over to give us snow cones. Had little boys beating off everywhere."

"Now, don't get it twisted, though. Man, Ms. Gray had an ass too now, looking like a thick-ass Beyoncé."

"Nah, Rev, you got it all wrong. She looked more like a '76 Pam Grier. No finer woman."

The two men paused and thought about the visuals. After a spell, they turned to each other and said, "Mrs. Parker!" the two laughed at the *Friday* reference.

"I gotta thank you, Rev. I know my dick works now. Just kinda got a half-chub thinking about them titties."

"You're crazy, Stone."

"No, I'm serious, Rev. All I heard when I heard I couldn't walk was, 'Damn, does my dick work?' Now I know."

Tatum sat back and chuckled at his friend's statement. He then followed up with a statement of his own.

"Stone, you know you were smarter than all of us growing up?

Yeah, I always liked to take things and put them in my journal, but you, man, you could've done and still can do anything. Even find love, man. You never had to be alone."

"I guess that's the difference between me and you, Rev. You grew up listening to Babyface and Jodeci, and I grew up listening to Dr. Dre and Too Short."

The two nodded in agreement.

"You ever think about that shit, Rev? Imagine messages like 'bitches ain't shit' being the soundtrack to your childhood. Then you get a bit older; all the songs was about looking for *a real one*. But a real what? A real bitch? These songs don't have any context to what a real one is. How the fuck are cats supposed to know what love looks like when all the music is about fucking?"

"Yeah, that, or I'm 'bout to take your girl."

"Exactly. But ain't nobody talking about love or this set of feelings when you find this real one. You just got this sex. That's it. But you, you always been allowed to be sensitive, and that's just not a space man, especially black men, can operate in freely. And that's how I knew you'd do good last night with Preston."

Tatum winced as he said the name. He turned to Stone.

"Yeah, about that. Wasn't long after you got here, Preston had one of his people call and say they were going to move in a different direction. Something about maintaining an image."

"Fuck that dude. He was kind of a hoe anyway. When I get out of here, I'm managing you. We're gonna do this together."

Tatum sat back and admired his friend's willpower. If anyone could beat the shitty hand he'd just been dealt, it was Stone.

He sat up in the chair and said, "Stone?"

"What's up?"

"You can never call me dark-skinned Drake again," Tatum said, completely dismantling a sensitive moment, laughing loudly and hysterically.

"Aw, go to hell, Tatum."

"All that sensitivity over there sounding like Ralph Tresvant."

"Man, fuck you, Rev. See, this is why men can't open up to each other. All that toxic masculinity. I was trying to have a real moment."

"You need a man with sens-a-tivity-" Tatum sang as Stone rolled his eyes and started to laugh.

"Alright, you got me. I'm Ralph Tresvant. Ha-ha, motherfucker."

As they chuckled a bit longer, Tatum put an arm on his friend, looked him in the eye, and became serious.

"And I'm Johnny Gill."

The two men nodded at the sentiment. A mutual understanding. They were brothers, and nothing was ever going to be able to change that. Not a woman, not a career, not even a bullet.

"I liked Autumn. I always have," Stone said out of the blue.

Tatum's eyes widened. "Hold on; I gotta call a nurse. Your legs can't be the only issue. You gotta have a brain injury!"

"Rev, I'm serious. I've never seen you happier, man."

"Then why all the slick comments?"

"I broke it down a long time ago. You're a black man in Texas. You go any further south, you in Mexico. The odds of you getting custody of your kid in the Deep South after Monique pulled her move—well, there are no fucking odds, you feel me? It wasn't going to happen. You would've left, and maybe you would've been happy for a year or two. But one day, maybe when you two had your own kid, you're gonna wake up, and you're gonna miss the shit out that boy, and when you do, you're gonna look at her and resent her. You may even get over it all. Call it the Lord's will or whatever, but you and I know that you're gonna resent her, and then none of this will be the same. And you're gonna hate yourself. I'd rather be the bad guy now than be the one to pick you up after that fall."

"Yeah, I feel that. I've been thinking about that myself. I miss that boy every day he's not here. I gotta make sure he gets off the ground, you know? I look at Autumn's upbringing—hell, even Monique's upbringing—and they didn't go through what we went through. They don't know the worst elements of this life. I know no matter what, I have to protect him from that."

"So what are you going to do?"

"For now, it's one problem at a time. The doctor said you can have ice chips. I'm going to go fill up this bowl and find a nurse."

"Get a fine one."

"I'll see what I can do."

Tatum headed down the hallway to get the ice chips. He turned the corner to ask the nurse where the ice machine was. The nurse was an attractive light-skinned woman with a fit, athletic frame. Perfect for his friend.

"Excuse me, nurse. My brother Kenley is in room 304, and he needs some ice chips."

"Tatum." The voice was familiar, so he turned around. It was Darlene, and she was in tears.

"Hey, Darlene, what are you doing here?"

"Your daddy has been trying to call you...Wait, are you okay?"

"It's a long story."

"So, you're not here about your father?"

"What...wait."

Darlene took a deep breath and held Tatum's hand, panic rushing over him.

"What's going on?"

"He was trying to call you."

"Darlene, tell me what is going on with my dad."

"Baby, there's no good way to say this to you. But Johnny died a couple of hours ago."

IN MY MIND

"*Y*ou don't have to give a eulogy if you don't want to."

"Mom, I want to," Tatum replied. He straightened his black tie and gave his mother a hug. It had been two weeks since Johnny Clarke passed. Two of the most difficult weeks of his life. Tatum had grown numb to the pain he'd endured and knew everyone in his life was concerned about him. But he had to present a strong front, particularly with his mother, who took the news of his father's passing harder than he expected. He watched her in deep thought as if she were searching for a memory.

She chuckled and said, "To think your father has been in shootouts, slept with all kinds of questionable tramps, been to prison, and used crack. None of that took him out."

"The man had Pancreatic cancer, stage 4. Never said a word. Why wouldn't he say something?" Tatum said, shaking his head.

His mother touched him on the shoulder. "Knowing Johnny, he probably took it as a challenge. Thought he was gonna beat it even till the end."

Tatum nodded, then chuckled himself.

"The last time I saw him, I... asked him if he was using because he was losing weight. He looked me in the eye and told me he was done with drugs, and I believed him. But I wish he would've told me he was done using because he was dying. That's what I don't understand. Why didn't he just say something?"

"Did you read his letter, son?"

Tatum went silent. He glanced over at the kitchen table.

"I... hadn't gotten around to it."

"Read his letter, baby. I'm gonna go downstairs for the car. I hate that I even have to ask this, but is Solomon going to be there?"

"I told Monique. She said she'd meet us there."

"What about Autumn?"

"We went bike riding the other day and talked about it. She understood with the way things have been with Monique it was best she just fall back."

"T.C.!"

"Ma, I *need* time with Solomon. It's...I can't let him miss this moment," Tatum said as the frustration saturated his expression.

"It's okay, baby. I understand." His mother rested her hand on his face. Finally, she gathered her belongings and reached the door. "You know, I'm not even going to get started. I'm just gonna let the Lord handle it because if I handle it, I'm gonna need bail money."

Tatum chuckled at his mother's honesty.

He was about to walk out when he decided to grab the letter from his dad and put it inside his journal. The moment he touched the letter, he broke into tears. He tried to be quiet because he didn't know how far his mother had gotten outside, but it was too late. He wept openly, the pain overtaking his being.

As he sobbed openly, he started to talk to himself.

"Man, if Stone saw you like this, he'd a call you a bitch," he said, chuckling through the tears. "If Johnny was here, he'd tell your ass to let them nuts drop." The words encouraged him. He calmed himself and stood up, still wiping his eyes. He looked at the letter again before closing the metallic flap on his journal. It was time to bury the dead. It was time to say his goodbyes to Johnny Clarke.

"Come on, T.C.; you can do this. This is what you do," he said, urging himself to be strong. He willed himself off the floor and went to the restroom to wash his face. He moisturized and put Visine in his eyes to hide the fact he'd been crying. It wasn't long before he got a text from his mother.

You OK, baby?

He responded with, *I'm fine just had to set the alarm and had an issue. Coming out now.*

The urge to cry came back, but he repressed it. He knew he had to be fine. He went to a cabinet and took a shot of whiskey to relax and find his courage.

He looked in the mirror and gave himself the once-over.

You can do this, he told himself. He then grabbed his keys and walked out of the house, locking the door behind him.

As he turned around, he heard, "Excuse me...Mr. Clarke?"

The voice was familiar, but he wasn't sure who it was. It was the enthusiastic bartender from the night Stone was shot.

"Drinks?" Tatum said, surprised at the man's presence. "What are you doing here?"

"I...um...I've been looking for you since the thing went down with Preston Cole."

The entire statement made Tatum confused and uncomfortable.

"Why were you looking for me?"

Drinks fidgeted at the question. He glanced over to the family limo as he paused

"Did I catch you at a bad time?"

"I'm gonna say that's an understatement, bro. But again, why were you looking for me? Why are you here?"

"That song the other day...I know you and Preston ain't doing it, but I think I could do it some justice."

"Drinks, I'm not even thinking about—"

"I know. I just...my whole life I've wanted to be a singer, and for whatever reason, it hasn't worked out. When I heard Preston sing those words, I knew—I just knew how it should sound. Look, I'm sorry about my timing, but I'm saving my money from serving drinks and getting studio time to work on an album, and if you're interested, maybe we could be partners. I'd like to bring your words to life."

Tatum didn't know how to respond. He honestly had too much on his plate to process what Drinks was saying.

"Man, I gotta go. I'll think about it, Drinks."

"My name Is Arthur, but I go by Autiztry."

"Alright, bro, I'll be in touch. I gotta bounce."

"How am I going to find you?"

"Hell, you tell me, detective. You know where I live," Tatum said as he walked toward the limo. As he got in, he looked over at his sister and his mother.

Savannah asked, "Are you okay?"

"Yeah, let's roll."

Tatum took one last look at Drinks and his house before pulling away to celebrate the life of Johnny Clarke.

When he got there, he saw his son standing in front of the church with his mother, who was, as always, dressed impeccably. For a moment, Tatum remembered why he was attracted to her. Of course, that was before he got to know her. Now, it was different. All they had in common was Solomon, and his heart was settled by his son's reaction.

"Daddy!" Solomon screamed as he ran to hug his father. Tatum picked him up and hugged him, and kissed him with no hesitation. He'd missed his son beyond measure. As he enjoyed the moment of holding, he realized Solly had a large bandage below his left eye.

"What happened to your face?" Tatum asked as he removed part of the bandage to see a visible chunk of flesh removed from his cheek. His temper flared as Monique walked over to defend what she clearly knew was making Tatum angry.

"He was playing with my momma's dog, and we told him to stop, but then the dog bit him. And before you ask, yes, I took him to the doctor. He needed seven stitches."

"Oh my God, I can't believe this shit," Tatum said.

"Really, Tate? Is this what you want to do at your father's funeral?"

"Don't give me that shit, Monique. I would've like to got into it *when* it happened, but I guess that was a non-starter because, you know and I know, it should've never fucking happened."

"I'm doing the best I can, Tatum. Shit, it's not like I got help."

"Are you fucking kidding me right now? You gotta be kidding me right now. Why are you so fucked up?" he said, pacing in front of the church before realizing his son was getting upset. He decided to calm down.

"Fucked up? Oh, I'm not fucked up, but I can show you fucked up. I don't need this shit. Come on, Solly, we're leaving."

"Daddy!" Solomon yelled as he hugged his father's leg with all of his might. Tatum looked at Monique. He was a landmine of confusion, unsure what to do. But as his son squeezed his leg, he decided to let cooler heads prevail.

"Monique, please. This...this is my dad's funeral. Look, I... might have...overreacted when I saw the bandage. This is a lot to take in. Let him stay. If not for me, then for Johnny. Him and my dad were getting close. He'd like him to be here."

Monique took a step into the church, then turned back and responded, "Well, I always liked J.C. He was funny and nice to me."

Tatum leaned down to pick up his son.

"It's okay, Solly. I got you. It's all going to be okay."

As he walked in carrying his son, he continued to eye the patch, something Solomon picked up on. "It didn't hurt, Daddy. I wish you were there, but Mommy told me you were asleep."

Tatum glanced at Monique, who looked away as they walked into church.

Can't afford to get mad, he told himself. He wanted no parts of this, but it felt good to hold his son today of all days. He looked at his son and kissed him on his forehead.

"Well, Solomon, I would have loved to have been there. I'm so sorry I wasn't."

"It's okay. Gran-Gran was there."

Tatum scowled at Monique, who was now greeting some of the family she was familiar with. Tatum sat in the pew and held his son while everyone took their place. Once the sermon began, Tatum watched as his father's old life and new life came together. A lot of the people Tatum knew growing up somehow found their way to the funeral. It was exactly what Johnny would've wanted. Tatum watched as his old Marine sergeant said a few words about his father, introducing a side to him he never knew. He also watched as Tabletop, a notorious drug kingpin, said a very touching thing. He laughed at the contrast. One thing was for sure: Each story from the men who got up and spoke eventually circled back around to how much Johnny loved his kids. It was surreal to hear, considering Tatum never quite felt that love.

"Baby, it's your time," Savannah said. Tatum wasn't sure he'd be able to do it without breaking into tears, but he stood up, took a breath, and went to the podium.

"Johnny Clarke is—well, was—a complicated man. He lived a lot of his life in the darkness, walking his way to the light. And he never gave up. I'll be honest; I thought I'd be burying this man a lot sooner than now. But he defied them all. He didn't raise me, but through his mistakes and his desire to correct those mistakes, he spent his days teaching me how to be the man he failed to be. And I thank him for that. I just wish it didn't take him leaving for me to understand what he was doing. He was teaching me grace, humility, and how to fix things when you're wrong. And while that doesn't balance the scale in my heart, it does make me realize he loved me very deeply. Thank you all for these stories. I've learned about my father in a light I could never see him in. Throughout all of his many lives, the one I'll always remember is today—the day I say goodbye to my mentor, my son's wonderful grandfather, and my very best friend. I'll never be the same without him. Thank you."

Tatum walked away as everyone stood to applaud his words. He picked up his son and held him tightly.

It wasn't long after the funeral ended and after the body was placed in the ground that the repast began. The liquor and stories flowed, and Tatum was enjoying the moment when he got an unexpected text.

Hey, I know today was tough, and I know you shut down from time to time. I also know things haven't been right since our argument a few weeks ago. I just wanted to let you know I was thinking about you. - Autumn

He looked at the text and knew he wanted her to be there. Things weren't where they needed to be after mediation, but he wanted to resolve it all. He was about to respond when he heard his son running up to him.

"Daddy."

Tatum hugged and kissed his son.

"Hey, big guy, how are you doing?"

"They have cotton candy here!" Solomon said as Monique walked up to him. It was time for them to go.

Solomon hugged his father as the tears rolled down his face. Tatum understood all the pain his son was going through. Not being with him pained him as equally as it did his son.

"I miss you, Daddy. Please, I want to come home."

The words crippled Tatum. The same words he spoke to the man he just buried so many years ago. The words he vowed to never let his own children say. His pain overloaded his senses. He had no other choice; there was nothing to consider. It was the one sin he could not commit.

"It's okay, Solly, I'm not going anywhere, I swear to you. Let me talk to your mother for a minute, okay?"

"I just want to go home, Daddy."

"I know, and I want you to come home too, Solly. Tell you what? Go get some more of that cotton candy, and I'll walk you out, okay?"

Solomon tilted his head downward and walked toward the candy.

Tatum looked at Monique and said, "Thanks for letting Solomon be at my dad's funeral."

"No problem. As you said, he needed to be here."

"Still, it means a lot."

Monique walked closer to Tatum and said, "Look, Tatum, Solomon needs his father, and as much as you might not want to admit it, I don't think right now is a time for you to be alone. So how about we do this? At least for the foreseeable future, we both come back to our home. We can figure out if we're going to work on our marriage or not, but I'll admit I need help with him. This is probably the best thing for everyone."

Tatum recalled the pain in his son's eyes. It was a deal with the devil—the same deal that got him into this mess in the first place.

"I don't know what you're trying to pull, Mo, but I'm gonna pass."

"Tatum, you're going to need to stop fighting me one day, no matter what. We're his parents. That's never going to change. Just think about it. If you want us to come over, we can be there tonight."

Tatum looked at his son and the bandage on his face. He knew he had to protect him.

"Always the puppet master. Let me walk you guys out," Tatum said as he took his son and Monique outside. He strapped his son into the car seat, kissed him, and closed the door. He barely waved to Monique as he looked at his phone and responded.

I'd like to come over.

2 8

HARD PLACE

atum waved goodbye to his son as Monique drove off. He
had several guests still celebrating his father's life, but the
one that mattered the most was gone, taking with him any joy he
brought to the occasion. Tatum, visibly isolated, stood in a corner
drinking whiskey, which made the congregants try to talk to him even
more. But he was in no mood to talk. The events of the last few weeks
had taken a toll beyond measure, and he just wanted to go to sleep, a
sentiment his mother recognized.

"Baby, why don't you go home? I'll stay."

"Ma, I can't ask you—"

"Johnny was my husband before he was ever your father. You're
not asking me to do anything. Go home."

He was in no mood to fight. He hugged his mother and caught a
ride back to his home with one of the guests who was leaving. When
he got home, he closed the door and walked to Solomon's room,
where he picked up his Black Panther stuffed animal. He couldn't
believe his son was bitten by a dog, and he knew nothing about it. He
crumpled on the floor, sobbing heavily.

"Lord, I can't take much more!" he screamed to the heavens. He
held the stuffed animal tightly, remembering how hard his son

squeezed his leg when he hugged him. He wiped his face and looked at his journal. He wanted to write but remembered his father's letter. He picked up the journal and opened it. He'd been avoiding this for far too long and decided now was as good a time as any to open it. He picked himself off of the floor and sat on Solomon's bed. He smiled when he saw Johnny's handwriting on the white envelope. He had several letters like this from when his dad was in prison. He brushed his hands across the letters that spelled his name. A wave of sadness hit him as he realized that whatever was on the other side of this envelope would be the last thing he'd ever hear from Johnny Clarke in this life. He wanted to savor the moment, yet he wasn't sure he was ready for it. Still, he needed his advice now more than ever, hoping that his father left some final words of wisdom for him on the page within.

He thought about the times his father called him on the day he died. *If I would've just answered the phone*, he thought to himself. He knew there was nothing he could do, but maybe had he been at the hospital to say goodbye, Stone wouldn't have been shot. Maybe he and Autumn would be in a better place.

He pushed those thoughts to the back of his mind. There were too many places to blame himself, and he could only deal with what was in front of him. He took a deep sigh, opened the letter, and gently removed the letter.

Hey Son,

> *This is a hard letter to write, but I'm glad God gave me time to write it. I knew I didn't have long for this world. I didn't want you to worry about me. I didn't deserve for you to worry about me. So I didn't tell you. Out of all my mistakes, the greatest joy I've had in this life was spending time with you. When I look back on my life, the only memories I think about are the ones with you. I knew that this day was coming, and I've been trying to right my wrongs. I was not being your father. Not being Savannah's husband was*

the biggest mistake of my life. I've written two other letters—one to your mother and one to your sister. Oh, and one to Solomon to read when he gets old enough. I owe all of you an apology for the way I lived my life.

T.C., nothing is more important than family. You inherited my generational curses, and as tough as this is for me to admit, I wasn't man enough to break them. But you are. You have what it takes to create stability with Solomon and Monique. S.C. needs his mother and father and if you don't take any advice from me, take this: Your reward for doing what's right will be one-hundredfold. The truth is you married this woman for better or worse. You've been through the worse. Maybe now is for the better. I don't want you to make the same mistakes I did chasing something that wasn't worth what it cost my kids. I can never forgive myself for what I've put you all through, and for that, I'm truly sorry. I can only hope that in time you'll forgive me. I also hope that you heed my advice because it comes from a place of love and experience. Marriage is about building. Right now, you've started building this child with Monique. Finish building what you started, and make sure you have all the resources you need because you love him. You may not want to admit this, but a valuable—no, invaluable—resource is his momma. Don't do anything that will put you in a position that you'll have to write one of these letters to your son one day. Take it from me. The cost is much too heavy. I hope you remember this. If you believe it or not, I still gotta tell you. I love you with all my heart, Tatum Lavelle Clarke. I'll be looking out for you on the other side.

Your Father,
Jonathan Maurice Clarke

TEARS FLOWED DOWN TATUM'S FACE. HE SPENT SO MUCH TIME BEING angry at his father that he never stopped to think he might not be there for him to be angry at. Their once complicated relationship became glaringly simple. He loved his dad and would never be able to talk to him again, and it hurt like hell. He sat and read the letter again, allowing the tears to fall from his face as he recalled the memories they had together. He looked at the curves of the letters and how his father arched the letter E the same way he did. He also realized now how foolish he sounded, accusing him of using drugs. He was just dying.

Tatum closed his eyes. He was in so much pain he didn't want to move. He didn't want to do anything. But he also didn't want to be alone.

He jumped up and forced himself to move. A minute later, Tatum was out the door and headed to Autumn's house. All the time he was recalling moments he didn't want to relive; Stone getting shot, his father dying and losing in mediation. He could barely remember the drive over before he was at his lover's home. The front door was open as always, but this time he welcomed it. He walked in and found her at her usual station painting. She turned around, startled by his presence.

"Hey...how are yo-"

"I'm fine."

They both knew he was lying; still, she said nothing. He went into the bedroom and noticed the tub was already waiting for him. He could smell the lavender in the air as he undressed without saying a word. He sat in the tub in silence. Autumn walked into the bathroom and disrobed, kneeling beside the tub.

He sat defenseless as she took the soap and washed away the pain of his invisible wounds. He had a warrior's pride, but his will was all but broken. Tears began to flow from his face as she scooped water to run across his face, masking the tears he did not want her to see. It was a futile effort, but they both understood his condition right now. Autumn stood up and sat in the tub. She tried to play music, but he stopped her. He needed the silence of the night, preferring the gentle ripples of the water. Holding her felt vital, a treat at any other moment, but today it wasn't enough.

"I just want to lay down right now."

Autumn put up no resistance. The pair got out of the tub and dried off, and laid in the bed. Tatum replayed the events of the day as Autumn sat next to him, quietly resting her head on his chest.

"I wish you would've gotten to meet him. He was a good guy."

"I know. He made you," Autumn said as he held her closer. She leaned into him and kissed him. He returned the kiss with one of his own. The kiss built in intensity as their pent-up passion unleashed itself, the air around them warmed by their bodies as the steam rose from their naked bodies. Autumn climbed on top of Tatum and descended on his emboldened member. As she leaned in, pressing her skin firmly against his, the two became as much one as two separate beings could ever be. They were one mind, body, and spirit, and this oneness manifested an ethereal love that radiated in concert with the steam leaving their bodies. He pushed with every bit of strength he had left. As she received him, her eyes rolled to the back of her head. They could not wait as elation flooded both their faces. This was a climax. It was what the eternal beings intended when they created man. This was making love made manifest. He looked into her eyes and whispered, "I love you." It was everything. She was everything. This moment was all that mattered.

He cherished making love to her. It was an intimate connection unlike any he'd experienced. Their eyes made contact as he slowly and repeatedly penetrated her with his manhood. He whispered, "I love you," again, affirming his feelings with each stroke as she opened more and more, welcoming the pleasure that his love brought into her life. At this moment, they lived as one, sharing the richness this bliss had to offer. This was no longer sex—this was making love, fear, and vulnerability replaced by certainty. An understanding that at this very moment, you were not alone. Another soul was experiencing the same set of emotions you were feeling. They were one, and it was all translated through their eyes.

Each stroke of his manhood brought the two closer to paradise, an eternity in the Garden of Eden without shame or sin. They could fall deeper into an endless sea of passion for one simple reason: she wanted him and he, her. Their climaxes occurred simultaneously, something neither of them believed possible, which only heightened their pleasure. The two lovers found irony in their intimacy and laughed at the realization that they were experiencing the thing neither thought could happen to them. Tatum kissed his lover, releasing her body from his hold.

He rolled over to regain his breath. He scanned the clock on the wall to check the time and noticed something missing from the living room wall.

"Hey, where is Fatima?"

"I sold it."

"You did what?"

"I sold it."

The words stunned him. Tatum was confused as to why she would sell her most beautiful portrait. Why would she sell a piece of her heart?

"You said you'd never sell that piece unless someone's life depended on it."

Autumn rolled closer and kissed him on his chest.

"Someone's did. Yours."

"Wait...you—"

"You spent all the money you had between mediation and burying your dad. I wanted you to know I was in this with you, so I paid your tuition."

Tatum sat up, flustered by the news he just heard.

"Autumn, you gotta get that painting back. Did you sell it to Montrice? Call him now. Tell him it was a mistake!"

"Blue, I-"

"Call him right now and tell them that you want to cancel the deal."

"Baby, what is wrong with you?"

"Nothing. You just call him now..." he barked. "Call him now...please."

He was trying to maintain his composure as Autumn sat up in bed and pulled the covers against her breasts.

"Blue, I didn't sell to Montrice. There was a bidder who came in much higher. I can't rescind the deal because I already spent the funds. Asking for something this big back would ruin my credibility as an artist."

Tatum shook his head in disbelief.

"You shouldn't have done that."

"I don't understand. You needed the money. If this is male pride, I thought we were past all of that."

"I didn't need it like this. I didn't want it like this."

Autumn turned on the nightstand light next to the bed, studying the concern on his face.

"Hey, where are you?" she asked.

He looked away. He couldn't answer her. She nudged him and pulled his face toward hers, trying to lock in on his eyes.

"Blue, where are you right now?"

He marveled at her curly hair, large light mochaasD cheekbones, and her full lips. This was a woman he had to talk to. Had to tell the truth.

"I understand what Adam saw in Eve. He'd been alone for only God knows how long, and then one day, this glorious black woman appears from out of the heavens, and she's the most fascinating thing he's ever seen. He falls madly in love with her. When God comes back after the serpent, of course, he's about to cast them out of the garden. He hesitates for one second before he said to Adam, 'I gave you paradise. Why betray me now?'

"And Adam looked at Eve, then back at God and said, 'You're right, you gave me paradise. Thank you.' I think the answer even surprised God because while he was referring to the Garden of Eden, Adam was referring to Eve."

Tatum turned away and released her hand, looking at the spot where the portrait of Fatima used to live.

"I know that's what he said because when I look at you, that's what I would've said."

Tatum let out a giant sigh and shook his head while Autumn embraced his words. He continued.

"I think the human experience is God trying to see what true love will do if faced with impossible situations."

"Tatum, why are you talking like this?"

He held her close for an extended period before letting her go.

"Because I mean it. When I look at you, when I look at us, I see tomorrow. I see every laugh we'll share. I see my best friend. I see...us. Not two individuals but one spirit inhabiting two different bodies. You get me in ways no one could ever get me, and there is clarity in that."

"Tatum...where are you?" she asked again, more insistent than the first time.

He closed his eyes and turned to get dressed. Autumn sat up in bed, confused. After he put on his shirt, he poured himself a glass of liquor from the bottle near the nightstand. Autumn leaned next to him as he finished the glass. He needed to be clear. As clear as that empty glass.

"I'm going to give it a try with Monique. She wants to go to counseling, and I need to get counseling at this point. I'm sorry."

"What are you doing? Where are you going? You think you can be anywhere else and be happy? Our souls are *bound*, you idiot! You just said so yourself."

"She has my son, Autumn! I... I'm a parent before I'm anything else, and I can't live like this. This is killing me..."

Autumn put on a tank top as Tatum finished getting dressed.

"You come to my bed to be restored, and I made love to you because I know what we share. And then you drop this? You have an obligation to your son, but what about your obligation to me? You told me you wouldn't hurt me like Kaleb, but here we fucking are. I don't know if you care about Monique or if you really can't see you can be a father outside of being at home with your son, but I want to be with the man I *love*. How can you do this to us? How can you sit there and build a world just for the two of us, say all the wonderful things you just said, and walk away? I love you. We made love. We looked in each other's eyes, and we kissed as the heavens watched, and now you're just gonna go?"

"I can't fight anymore. I don't even have a damn job. How am I supposed to feel like a man? I'm hurting so bad right now. I've lost everything."

"But you haven't lost me! You haven't lost us. I sold a piece of my heart for you. My *heart*, Blue! Do you have any idea what you have taken from me as an artist? Not some amateur who's afraid to release his work, but an actual artist?"

"I didn't ask you to do that."

"Of course not. I did it because I love you. I did it because you needed me to. But you don't know a damn thing about it because you wouldn't do that for the woman you love. You don't understand the sacrifice. And don't understand the sacrifice because you're not an artist! You've never had the confidence to put one creative thing out in your life. Never took any real risk. You've never made a song—an actual song! You just have a bunch of theories in your head of how things could sound or would look, and that's not art!"

"Damn it, Autumn, I'm doing what a man is supposed to do— take care of his kids. No one asks a woman to walk away from her ki-"

"I don't want to hear that shit, Tatum! This was supposed to be *us*. Do you know what that means? We were supposed to make this decision together. We were supposed to bury one another. I put together all the songs on your stupid funeral playlist for when you pass on. You're walking away from your *life*! The one we built, and don't tell me you don't want it because I see it in your eyes."

There was nothing he could say. Anything contrary to this would be a lie.

He stood up, and without looking back, responded, "It's not about love. I'm raising my child. If you can't relate to that, I can't relate to you."

"Get out."

Tatum said nothing as he walked toward the door, her footsteps echoing behind him. At the door, he turned around and said, "I'll pay you back for the paint-"

"Just get the fuck out!" she screamed as she slammed the door in his face. Tatum stood there. He desperately wanted to apologize. He wanted to say this was a terrible mistake, but right now, he just wanted to hold one person. He walked to the car, turned it on, and pulled out his phone to place a call.

"Hello."

"Yeah, Mo. Is Solomon up?"

"I was about to lay him down. Did you want to talk to him?"

"No, I want you guys to come home. Meet me at the house tonight."

29

SWEETEST THING

"As you know, my husband, Tatum Lavelle Clarke, is graduating today at noon, and we're having a get-together later tonight. Come by the house, and we're going to turn up. If you know, then you know. Deuces!" Monique said as she posted a story on her Instagram Live. Tatum ignored the story as he held Solomon. He was in no mood to celebrate. He didn't even want to be here, considering the cost of what it took to get here.

"Daddy, are you happy?"

"What? Um...yeah, it's just a big day. Daddy is happy you're here to see this." He leaned in. "Daddy worked really hard."

"Attention, all graduates! Dr. Peterson, the master of ceremonies, has called for all graduates to enter the south lawn. Your family can meet you on the opposite side." As the families were going to take their seats, the coordinator walked up to Tatum. "Mr. Clarke, Solomon can't cross the stage with you, but if you'd like, he can walk down the aisle with you, and I will take him personally to the other side."

The news startled Tatum. "Wait...you?

"Everyone here knows Solomon. He has spent enough time on this campus to earn his associate's."

Tatum smiled. "Okay, I'm gonna take him." He looked at Monique, who nodded. "I'll meet you on the other side.

Tatum took his son down the south lawn. As the graduates stood in the line, he stared at the back of the audience. He was hoping she'd be there, but he understood why she wasn't. After a few minutes, the ceremony finally began. Dr. Peterson delivered an inspiring speech. He wished it all ended differently, but he could only look forward. At the end of the speech, he finally heard the words he'd been waiting to hear for the last four years: "All rise."

He stood up and held his son's hand as they walked to the edge of the stage looking back one last time to see if she came. It saddened him that she stayed away, but having his son see him cross the stage cheered him a little. "Okay, Solly, Daddy will be right back. Go with the lady over here, okay?"

His son hugged him and said, "Good job, Dad."

Tatum smiled. It was worth it all as he gave the coordinator Solomon's hand. He took the stairs to the top of the platform where Dr. Peterson seemed prepared for his presence. He wasn't sure how he felt about him, but it didn't matter. If nothing else, he'd earned his diploma by paying a price higher than he could ever express to anyone. He lifted his head proudly as he walked with hands outstretched, never hesitating to make eye contact with Dr. Peterson, unapologetically proud of his achievement.

"Tatum mouthed the words "Thank you" as he received the diploma from Dr. Peterson, who barely acknowledged him. Tatum thought it best to move on quickly, but his mentor suddenly hugged Tatum for an extended period of time.

"Congratulations, Mr. Clarke. I'm very proud of you," he whispered in his ear. He released him and continued his duties as master of ceremonies. It felt good to hear that, and Tatum was determined not to let him down again. He planned to never let anyone down again.

From the high point of the stage, he glanced once more to the back of the crowd. She hadn't come. Deflated, he came off the stage and hugged his son.

"Congratulations, Daddy!"

"Never ever ever give up on your goals, son," he said, giving him a giant bear hug. As he started to embrace his mother and then his wife, he looked toward the back of the crowd over Monique's shoulder. His heart skipped a beat. Autumn was there, but she was leaving.

"Mom, where's that bag I gave you?"

His mother handed him a blue gift bag.

"I'll be back."

Tatum jogged toward the exit, then picked up the pace as he neared the door, hoping she wouldn't get away. He was twenty yards from the field when he yelled out.

"Autumn!"

She turned around, and to his surprise, smiled.

"Hey, Blue."

"Coming to check on your investment?" he said, catching his breath.

"Something like that. I know how hard you worked to get here. I just wanted to say congratulations."

"Thank you. And about the money. As soon as—"

"I know you're going to do the right thing. It's who you are. But you're gonna have to send the cash to Austin."

Tatum stopped. "Wait, what?"

"Yeah...I took Montrice's offer. I'm going to open up a physical gallery."

"What are you going to call it?"

"Autumn's Song, of course. That's what it's called online, so—"

"Branding. I get it."

"Yeah, someone convinced me I need to take a shot on myself."

Tatum smiled. He was happy for her yet wanted to tell her he was sorry for the abrupt way their relationship ended, something neither of them wanted. He also felt terrible about her selling one of her most valuable portraits. He looked at her and wanted to apologize but knew it would only open a floodgate of emotions and conflicts unable to be resolved. He had nothing at this moment: nothing but the words in his heart.

"I want you to have this."

Autumn shook her head, "I don't want anything from—"

"Please open it."

He handed her a wrapped book. She opened it. Inside was his journal. Her eyes widened at the sight.

"I'm working on the fifteen thousand dollars, but right now, I leave you the last journal I'll ever write in. There's a total of seven songs. They might suck, but they come from my heart. I know it's not your Fatima portrait, but it is truly a piece of my heart. Hell, it's all of my heart—and it's yours."

They had been through so much together. He wanted to be with her, but he couldn't, and she wasn't going to wait. There would be no rescue. She may not have wanted his journal, but she knew what it meant to him. The last song in his heart was written.

"Thank you, but we both know this is a consolation prize," she said, accepting his peace offering. After a pause, a tear rolled from her eyes.

"Damn it! Why can't we be together, Blue?"

Tatum sighed and said, "It wasn't supposed to go this far. It was *never* supposed to go this far. We were friends, Autumn. Do you remember that? Do you remember what that felt like? We could just talk about anything all day. You'd call me, and I'd listen to your whole day. And then I became the long-winded one. We'd both just be there for each other the way friends do. We started a book club together, drank coffee and tea, and we'd try the most random restaurants just to judge the food. We were our own inside joke, and when we took it across the line, you said we'd just play it by ear. It wasn't supposed to be serious."

"But it got serious! The night you called me your Fatima, made it serious. Who are you kidding? You think after we fell in love and you say and show me all of the wonderful things any woman would cherish in a man that we can just go back to being friends? Well, let me not equivocate, Tatum—I don't want to be your friend. I want to be your wife! Why do you think anyone does all this? To find what we already know we have. We made love."

275

"Autumn, I-"

"We made *love*, Blue. The moment that happened, all that friendship shit—everything you just said—went out the window. This is you and me: Blue and Fatima. This is us. Soulmates."

She wiped a tear from her eye as she looked at him again with a sincerity strong enough to make him shed tears of his own.

"You sit here and try to pervert the truth by saying we were friends. Don't get me wrong. You were an amazing friend. And you are—were—an amazing boyfriend. Why wouldn't I want you to be my amazing husband? Why wouldn't I want someone who thinks about me the way you do, the thoughtfulness you've shown me? Why wouldn't I want someone like that around for the rest of my life? The reality is we both know we were never meant to be friends. That was just the gateway to love."

Tatum looked away as she held on to the journal. He knew that she spoke the truth. Still, he didn't know how to respond.

"When you came into my life, I wasn't looking for a lover. I wasn't looking for anything. You had just gotten divorced. You wanted to talk, so I listened. We became good friends and ultimately the best of friends. We saw each other for who we are in this world."

"That's true."

"I need you to see me now. I have never loved someone more, and I will spend the rest of my life making sure you know that. Somewhere between all the layers of love/hurt/desire/frustration are just two people who want to be together. Two spirits who don't want to hurt anyone and enjoy each other's company. Two people who are better together than they are apart. I love you, Autumn, with all my heart. I'm just not sure how to love you and go against everything I've ever tried to be, what I'm supposed to be."

Tears flowed from his face. She walked closer and held his hand.

"Make no mistake about it, Tatum Lavelle Clarke. I am in love with you too. But loving you does nothing for me when you're in someone else's bed every night."

Her words—ones he hadn't considered—cut heavy into his spirit. She was the missing page in his book. His North Star. He'd never truly felt oneness with anyone until he met her. Even before they fell in love, they had a connection he could not describe. He wondered why it happened this way. He wondered why he couldn't just have it all. But leaving Solomon meant abandoning his child to a wolf who, in reality, would make their lives a living hell. He knew it, and although Autumn wouldn't admit it, she knew it too. He wanted to lie—say anything, beg her to stay while he figured it out. But he couldn't.

"I had this finish line in mind. I used to daydream about waking up next to you and looking in your eyes the way I do when we're in our sanctuary, knowing that you belong to me and me to you. I thought, damn, I have someone who is committed to me the way I want to commit to her. I used to imagine how it would grow. What it felt like to get to know your parents. To talk to your father about *our* wedding and get his blessing after earning it. But the entire time I've been with you, I've had one hand tied behind my back. I used to hope that in this space, with nothing in my way, I could love you like the stuff of legend. Holy shit, Autumn, I would really be able to cut loose. Then I realized that this was a fantasy. I thought to myself, this was meant to be. That life doesn't work out the way it should but the way it wants to. Still, I had hope. Fuck that! I had faith. I mean, life gave me so many lemons that maybe I was owed this one. Maybe now I don't have to worry about the bittersweetness of life. Maybe just this one time life would just give me the happiness I dreamed of. Wondering what our children would look like if we had any. All I had was faith." A tear rolled from his eyes as he came to the bitter grips of his reality. He took a deep breath and pressed on.

"I always dreamed of marrying you, Autumn. Maybe those were fairy tales I told myself. Maybe that was the lie we both couldn't see because we were in so deep, but in my heart, I knew you were the one. People tried to convince me I was wrong. People tried to tell me this wasn't real. But the only person in the world I would listen to when it comes to any of this is you because you're the only one who under-stands. You feel it too. I don't know, maybe I thought I was gonna get a clean getaway with my kid, and life would be this brand-new fairy tale we could make together. But when I found out that no matter what I did, I wouldn't get custody of Solomon...what choice did I have?"

"I can't answer that, Tatum, but I can say that I believed in us too. I thought that this was it. I finally found love. You'll never know how much this hurts because I couldn't see anything but us. But if I can say anything for you to think about, it's this: you're not your dad. I know you believe that fathers have to live in the home with their kids, and I know that you feel that way because your dad abandoned you, but is finding happiness abandonment?"

"The fact you're even asking me that tells me you truly don't understand how torn I am. I do *everything* for Solomon. I've been everything for Solomon."

"And now he has a mother."

"And he has a fucking dog bite on his cheek. I don't know anything about where it came from or what kind of dog it was. Do you know how helpless that makes me feel? Since you've known me, has Monique ever seemed like the loving parent? I can't go anywhere without him because he's my son. I brought him into this world, and I'm on board to see him through this world or die trying. We don't have the typical parent-child relationship."

They stood next to each other in silence, neither one willing to admit or accept the idea that their love had to come to an end. Despite knowing better, the man could not move beyond the childhood trauma of abandonment. He couldn't even admit it to himself. He wanted to cry but knew this was far more painful for Autumn. She wasn't just angry—she was hurt—the kind of hurt she wanted to run from, even if it were from her best friend.

They were standing on hallowed ground, the place they first met. The place where they both found love, was the place it was going to die.

Tatum wanted to say something—anything—to break the silence, but it was Autumn who spoke.

"Although I'm hurt and angry at you for this shit, I understand what you're trying to do. I understand you feel you have to do it the way you're doing it. Now I want you to listen to me. I'm going to have to disconnect from you. If you choose to stay with your child, and as a result, his mother, then I can't control that. Maybe in time, we can find our way back to friendship, but this is tearing me apart. Knowing that the man I love has chosen someone other than me hurts."

"I wish I was more, but I love my son." It was all he could say. He had nothing left to give.

Tatum watched her as she walked closer to him and kissed him on the cheek one final time. He closed his eyes, trying to capture the exact pressure her lips left on him. She looked back at him with a smile on her face and tears in her eyes. Both spirits understood their honesty.

"You were an amazing boyfriend, Tatum Clarke, and an even better father. Solomon is a lucky kid."

She turned around and walked away. He wanted to go after her, truly tormented. She was taking a piece of him—the most important pieces of him—with her with each step. True love, the kind of love so profound you only have it with one person because you'll never allow yourself to be that open again. She wouldn't be the one that got away —she would be the only one to ever matter. She was all that he'd ever desire. She was paradise, but paradise would have to wait. His desires, his purpose, his happiness—all were secondary to his love and obligation as a father. He'd never be able to live with himself, and they both knew it. Yet with all that had happened, from losing his job, his friend, his father, and the ability to parent in peace, losing Autumn was like losing hope and the core of joy itself. He thought about all the wonderful moments they had and the moments they wouldn't have. Looking at her, he realized he wanted her face to be the last thing he'd ever see when he left this earth. When they were both old and gray, he wanted to look at her and know love was the last thing he saw. With each step away, his heart grew colder. Their season was over.

Winter had set in.

30

LOVE IS STRONGER THAN PRIDE

ew Journal Day 20

I loved an angel once. She loved me back. I don't know why.

*It's been about three weeks since I last saw her. I've tried to keep
myself busy. I haven't been motivated to look for a job, which
doesn't seem to bother Mo for some reason. I guess it will once
unemployment runs out. Hell, I don't even think I want to be a
pharmacist. Lately, I've just wanted to create music. Ever since I
wrote those songs in the journal I gave her, I've felt like there's a
flood of emotions I could bring to life. I should take Drinks up on
his offer. Maybe write some songs and see what happens. No
matter what, things just aren't the same without her. I keep trying
to tell myself I'm doing the right thing, but I don't know what that
is anymore. There is a sadness that comes with ending a
relationship, and it's nothing short of grief. I've had more than my
share of it, so I understand I'm in mourning for us as well as my*

dad. I miss her every day. I miss us. She has the most annoying cackle I've ever heard, but I'd love to hear it right now.

Missing Fatima is like missing a piece of my soul. It is a place inside me that I can't replicate, no matter how hard I try. I'm different without her. Distant. The grass lost its color, the sky's a bit duller. They say you shouldn't define your happiness by another person, but if you ask me, that's the silliest shit I've ever heard. Most of us, if we're honest with ourselves, are only happy—truly happy— when we are with another person. And I don't mean that without them you can't be happy, but life isn't meant to be lived alone. Who wants to go on that adventure? Give me love any day of the week. Like the old song goes, love and happiness, I lost both of those things the moment we were no longer together.

Solomon is as happy as I've ever seen him, and that's important to me. As for me? Well, I'm content.

We went to Hermann Park today, not far from the museum. I'd be lying to myself if I said I wasn't secretly hoping she'd be there waiting like the woman at the well. That maybe one fine day, I'll have the conviction to follow my heart for one brief moment in this life and allow it to guide me to the place I know destiny has been leading me to. But, when I go to Hermann Park, I never go by the hill. I never walk through the wooded area into the vineyard where the wedding—my wedding—should take place. Instead, I go to the playground and watch my son smile as I try to recall that I did find love. True love. In Solomon, I love him so much that I was willing to sacrifice something greater than my life. I was willing to sacrifice my happiness, and that, in and of itself, takes courage. I won't apologize for that. Still, when the leaves blow, when the wind changes directions, and when the temperature drops, I can't help but look back toward the museum district, toward Egypt, and wonder if chasing the pyramids was worth it.

TATUM CLOSED HIS NEW JOURNAL AND LOOKED AROUND HIS HOME. His son's Black Panther and Killmonger toys were on the floor exactly where they belonged. Solomon was coloring on the floor the way he should be. Still, the more content he was with Solomon being in his life. The more he knew, something was missing. *She* was missing.

Living without her was the single hardest thing he'd ever done. He was in love—the kind of love men just don't fall in. The kind of love kings waged war for. Yet, he was a prisoner of his own choosing. He chose the inmates, the cell block, and above all, the warden. But he had to be in his son's life at all costs, even if it was as a detriment to himself. That's what parents do, and he was no ordinary parent. He was *the* parent. The only one that mattered, and everyone knew it, including Monique. He got out his phone and opened the Instagram app, and found his online friend autumn.elders.

He looked at her profile. She was working on a new painting, and as always, it was beautiful. Yet the sadness in it twinged his spirit a little. He wanted to like it. In truth, he wanted to send her a message. But anything he could say wouldn't change his outcome.

He closed the app and continued to watch his son work on his drawing.

He grabbed his cup of lemon-ginger tea and Solomon's picture: him, his dad, and Johnny. He smiled at his son's impression of each man. The size of the fish they caught was overstated. It was as big as a whale, and so was the kiss Tatum gave him on his forehead.

"That's me, you, and Pop-Pop?"

Solomon looked at his dad and continued to color.

"Yeah. I miss him."

Tatum sat down next to his son and put a hand on top of his head. "Yeah, I miss him too. I miss him every day."

Solomon looked at his dad as if to speak but then stopped himself.

"Something on your mind, S.C.?"

"No, sir."

"Are you sure?" Tatum moved in as he rubbed the boy's belly. As Solly giggled, Tatum decided he wouldn't press the issue.

"Okay, well, since you're not talking, I'm gonna go lay down for a little while. When you're ready, just come get me for story time." As Tatum got up to go lay on the couch. He heard his son's voice.

"Dad?"

"Yeah?"

"How do you spell happy?"

"H-A-P-P-Y," Tatum responded as Solomon wrote the letters on top of the drawing of the three men. Tatum resumed his course to the couch when he heard his son call him again.

"Dad?"

"Yes, son?"

"Are you happy?"

The words jolted him. For a moment, it felt like divinity was speaking through his son. Maybe he underestimated how much people could see through his brave face. Or maybe his son saw through the cracks in his armor.

"I'm very happy, Solly," he said, assuring his son. Even though it was untrue, he didn't want his son to worry about him.

"Why do you ask that?"

"I don't know. Because we don't play action spies, and you don't spin me around anymore. And I don't think you like Mommy very much."

"Solly, I... I love your mother very much. After all, she gave me you!" he said, nibbling on his son's neck playfully. It was a lie he forced himself to tell. One he had been trying to convince himself of since the funeral. It was a lie he'd been living.

"Well, why don't you laugh with Mommy the way you did with your art lady?"

"What do you mean?" he said as he again tickled his son before putting him on the black couch in the living room.

The distraction didn't work.

"When you talked to the art lady, you used to laugh so loud I couldn't even go to sleep."

Startled, Tatum rubbed his son's head aggressively.

"You heard me at night?"

"Uh, yeah. You were loud. It was always. 'Oh, baby, I wanna feel your butt.'" Tatum's eyes widened. It made him chuckle, though he was a bit embarrassed. He knew his son probably heard a lot more but was being polite.

"I was loud, huh?"

"Really loud. It was so annoying," Solomon said, scrunching his face to express his displeasure.

Tatum jumped off of the couch to dive tackle his son. The pair laughed until Tatum, at last, responded to his son's statement.

"I'm really sorry. We're gonna start playing action spies again tomorrow, okay?"

"OK."

"And to answer your other question—yes, I'm very happy because I have you."

"It's okay, Daddy. You can leave me with Mommy, and I can come to visit you."

"Solly, look at me. I don't care where I am or what is going on—you will always be at home with me. Do you hear me?"

Solomon nodded.

"I need you to understand this. It's me and you. I love you more than Spider-Man, Wolverine, and Superman all in one."

He hugged his son. It was the hug he remembered his dad giving him when their relationship was restored.

"Alright, it's time to go to bed," his mother said, entering the room. Solomon looked at his dad for confirmation, who nodded. The child kissed him on the cheek and ran into the bedroom to lay down.

Tatum got back up on the couch and resumed looking at his phone. He could feel Monique looking at him. Still, he ignored her. After a spell, she finally said something.

"I'm throwing a little kickback. Raylene is going to come through if that works for you."

"It's your world, Mo. I'm taking Solly to my mom's tomorrow to help her with the rest of the graduation thank you's after we go to see Stone."

"How's he doing?"

"He's getting better. Still not walking, but we know it's going to be a long road."

"Okay, that will work. I'll pack him a bag."

Tatum nodded and resumed scrolling through his phone. The awkward tension lingered in the air until finally, Monique said, "Are you going to lay in the bed with me tonight?"

"Nah, I'm good," Tatum said.

Monique joined him on the couch.

"Look, if we're going to give this a shot, we need to do what couples do and-"

"I'm fine on the couch. Sleep wherever you want."

"Fine. But at some point, we need to figure out how we move forward as a family." Monique got up and walked into the bedroom.

Tatum just didn't see how that could happen.

HOW COME YOU DON'T CALL ME ANYMORE?

"*I* think that's all of them," Savannah said to her son.

"Well, if it isn't, let's pretend it is. I'm beat," Tatum said, stuffing the last envelope at his mother's kitchen table. He put the envelope on the pile and looked in the living room to see Solomon playing with his toys. The day had been long, and he still had to pick up several items for Monique's kickback at the house. It was all a preoccupation to keep him from thinking about the woman on his mind.

"How's Stone doing?"

"Huh? Oh...he's good. He was excited to see Solly, so that was fun."

"Oh yeah? Is he making any progress?"

"I'll be honest—it's slow, but he's determined. And get this: he's thinking about getting out of the game."

His mother stood up and packed the envelopes.

"That one right there, you can never count him out. When he's focused, he's like a dog with a bone. He'll walk again, you watch. What is he planning on doing?"

"Well...he's trying to convince me to maybe...go into songwriting."

His mother paused in her tracks.

"Now, this brings my heart joy. So you finally showed someone what you've been toting around in that journal of yours."

Tatum was shocked by the statement.

"How did you—"

"Child, please. You've been carrying around a journal since you were twelve years old. Don't think a mother isn't gonna take a peek. You had some good stuff too. I remember this one poem you wrote you called *Ebony*. Would've made a real good song."

"Ma! That is such a violation."

"Boy, please. You were ten pounds and eleven ounces of natural childbirth. *That* is a violation. I was doing my job as a mother. Besides, it will do you some good to get what's going on off your chest. I'm tired of you sitting right here moping around feeling sorry for yourself."

Tatum took a deep sigh while his mother began to mash up the meal to make a West Indian curry chicken dish served with rice and peas. As she was mashing, she asked her son.

"Have you seen Autumn?"

Tatum pressed his lips together to repress the pain he was feeling. After a moment, he responded, "She moved to Austin and doesn't want to see me. I... I messed up, Ma."

His mother stopped mixing the food and turned to Tatum.

"Now I want you to listen to me, son. Quit beating yourself up for the way you've responded to stress. You went through the hardest thing most men could ever go through. You lost your job, you lost your father, and you almost lost your best friend. And above all else, you lost custody of your child. You lost everything you built a foundation on. How you're still standing is beyond me, and that's something you need to pay attention to because when hard times come, you need strong people in your corner. You were drowning, and like your daddy, you don't know how to ask for help. But make no mistake about it—you're human. You earned a minute to get yourself together and figure out what was going on with your life, and that's what you did. You started with the foundation. You got your son back in your life by any means because that's what a good parent would do. Now, this won't be your last hard time in life, and the last thing you need is somebody who is gonna cut and run. You already got that in Monique."

His mother went back to mixing the peas. She gave him a bite of the meal for good measure.

"Perfect," he said as he savored the taste of the meal, though he could have just as easily been talking about her advice.

His mother resumed her thoughts.

"Let me tell you something else. You should have never fallen in love while you were married, but you did, and you're both dealing with the fallout from that. As far as Autumn goes, that girl is either prideful, stupid, or she never loved you, and if I had to guess, I'd say she's part prideful, part stupid because if that girl really loved you, she should've come to you and asked how can we make this work. That part is pride. The stupid part is, and maybe it's just ignorance, is thinking she's gonna just waltz out there and find another connection like the one you two have because they just don't go growing that shit on trees, and whenever she gets to the end of that pride, she gonna kick herself in the ass. Because, honey, let me tell you, they just don't make men like you any more. And I'm not saying that because I'm ya momma—I'm saying it because it's true. And don't think for one second Autumn doesn't know that. Your problem is, so does Monique." Tatum sighed, listening to his mother's diagnosis. It was good to finally talk to someone unfiltered about everything that had been troubling him.

"Ma, I just want things to go back to the way they were. Before all of this."

"Well, you kicked a hornets' nest, and now you have to deal with the hornets. There is a reason why God only gave us one heart instead of two. It can only be in one place at a time. Your heart is with Autumn. You'll never love Monique again."

"I know that, but you know how Monique is. Truth is, I don't know how to do this right now, and I'm afraid when I do figure it out, Autumn may never forgive me."

"Then maybe you're the stupid one, T.C. That woman loves you.

She's just upset because she's not getting her way at the moment. If she's as smart as you say she is, she fully understands why you're doing what you're doing. She doesn't like it, but she understands it. She doesn't hate you, baby—she's hurt by you, and there's a difference."

Tatum stood up and walked to the stainless-steel refrigerator.

"You know I'm not trying to hurt anyone." Tatum opened the refrigerator, looking for something to drink. "Man, how did I get in this mess?"

"By being an asshole."

"Ma!" Tatum said, surprised.

"I'm serious. All of you men are assholes. See, all you and your little man friends want to do is run around and put your dicks in our faces hoping someone will touch them, all while we're minding our own goddamn business. Then, once we give you some loving, you leave us to raise your seed. And when you no longer see fit to participate, you run over to those same friends you conspired with to say, 'duh she's damaged goods.' And they tell their friends stupid shit like, 'She's got baggage,' when the only baggage most of us ever carry is fallout from the damage you left. That makes you and your gender assholes."

Tatum sat back at the table, shaking his head at his mother's statement. He looked in the living room at his son, who was still playing with his toys. Finding nothing to drink for himself, he pulled out milk for Solly.

"But I'm not an asshole, Mom. I'm trying to do right by Solly."

"Son, through the eyes of a woman, all men are assholes, 'cause no matter who you're with, you're gonna put up with a certain amount of shit."

Tatum appreciated his mother's bluntness. His father always called his mother his West Indian firecracker. He now understood why. As she finished making the dumplings, she took a sliver and fed Tatum a piece. He nodded his approval as she wiped her hands on a napkin and took a drink of water from a glass next to the stove.

"Look, son, life is one beautiful river, but people don't realize part of the river is the rocks. And you never know when you're gonna hit a rock until you hit one. The thing about the rocks is they hurt like hell. Hell, a rock can kill you or leave you out there stuck in the water with no way around it. But if you can get past the rocks, you're on a beautiful journey."

His mom went back to mixing the rice and peas, but she wasn't done speaking.

"You think I woke up when I was twenty-five and said let me marry one of the biggest drug dealers in Houston? Hell no, I married a confident, handsome young man fresh out of the military who treated me better than anyone I'd ever met. He had a good head on his shoulders, but he idolized his older brother."

She paused as she started to relive the moments of her life that Tatum had never been privy to. It was the first time he remembered her talking about this father with such regard.

"See, ya Uncle Jackie was everything to your father even though Jackie was rotten to the core. Didn't matter. Your father would follow that man to the gates of hell, and he did because he had the same issue with loyalty that you got. What makes you an asshole, in this case, is you don't understand that history with a person don't oblige you to loyalty."

She stopped again and grabbed the pepper to season the peas, shaking the bottle. A rush of emotions came over her as Tatum took the milk to Solly. When he returned to the kitchen, his mother started right up again.

"Johnny never wanted to be J.C. Money. When I met him, all he wanted to do was be an electrical lineman. You know, one of those people who climb and fix the poles. He would talk all the time about how much money they make. He even signed up for a class, promised we'd get a house in San Diego, and live the rest of our lives by the beach. One day your Uncle Jackie, drunk and high as usual, said to him, 'Why you want to go busting your ass climbing poles all year when you can sell what I sell and get them so high they'll pass those sons of bitches on their way to the moon?' And from that day forward, Johnny Clarke became J.C. Money."

Tatum marveled at the revelation. He finally understood why his dad looked at the power lines the way he did.

"So that's why he used to do that," Tatum said, thinking about his father's obsession.

"What's that, son?"

"Nothing, Ma. You were saying?"

She chopped up the baked chicken breast with the speed of a professional chef. It wasn't long before she picked up where she left off.

"Now we weren't hurting for money, so why he decided to do the dumbest of all shits, I'll never know. But I do know Jackie Clarke ruined Johnny all the way around. His brother had the absolute worst influence on him. You know he didn't even start using until Jackie died."

The statement heightened Tatum's interest. He wanted to know more without asking.

"I knew something happened, but I never really knew what," Tatum said, processing this new perspective about his dad. It was a treasure trove of information he never knew. He watched as his mother wiped her hands with the towel again. She took a deep breath and continued.

"You was young, worried about kid stuff. But one day—and I'm not sure about many of the details because your father never wanted to talk about it—Jackie and your daddy were working with the Mendoza brothers. They were on the rise out there in Mexico."

"He always talked about New Laredo."

"Oh, he loved it down there. Probably where he did all his fucking around. Well, he took me down there a couple of times, and I met Esteban and Ernesto, and those two were like Jackie and Johnny. The same way Johnny looked up to his big brother, Ernesto looked up to Esteban, and Esteban and Jackie were peas in a pod. Both partied harder than they worked."

"So you saying he was a ho."

"Let's just say if you threw a donut in the air, he'd fuck it before it hit the ground."

His mother's response made Tatum chuckle. She continued.

"So Esteban was always sleeping with someone's wife or someone he had no business sleeping with, and you can only do that kind of stuff for so long before you run across someone just as crazy as you. So this guy came into this nightclub one night to kill Esteban, shoots him dead, but in the process, he killed Jackie too. Your dad and Ernesto were good ever since."

Tatum tilted his head, listening to his mother's story.

"So by good, you mean they avenged their brothers?"

"I don't know this to be a fact, but I'm sure your father went after the men who killed his brother and... I don't know. It broke him. He was able to keep it together for a while, but it wasn't long before he started using it to take the edge off. When Ernesto found out, he wouldn't hurt your father, too much damage had been done, but he couldn't work with him anymore either. He was out of the game. I don't know if it was losing Jackie or maybe being involved in killing the man who killed his brother, but he never forgave himself. He hit one rock and was never right again. How many have you hit in the last year?"

Tatum realized his mother had a way of bringing things into focus, but he was still unsure of what to do. He closed his eyes and tried to fight the pain that came with missing Autumn. His mother walked over to him and put her hand on his cheek.

"I don't know what to do, Ma."

"Then figure out what to do. It doesn't have to be right now, but you have to figure it out. You're the only one who can."

"I'm just doing the best I can. I don't know what everyone wants from me."

"Listen to me, Tatum Lavelle—the question is not what does everyone else want. The question is, what do *you* want? Do you want happiness? Because as a parent, that's what I want for you. I want you and Solly to be happy. If you guys are happy, then I'm happy. So do whatever you have to do to get there. If you're happy with Monique, fine, I'm happy for you. But if this other woman makes you truly happy, like the way I've seen you walking around here before all this nonsense started, then there's no way that it can't rub off on Solomon and me and everyone and everything else. You found the kind of joy people spend a lifetime looking for. It'd be a shame if you threw that away."

Tatum looked at his son, who was playing in the living room, and looked back at his mother. He hesitated before finally asking.

"How do I know if it's love? What if it's just grass that looks green from here?"

"Well, you would be the expert on that between the two of us because that love shit has never paid me any dividends. But if I had to guess, I would say it would have to be if you can't stop thinking about a person, and they're part of everything you do and everything you see and everything you feel. If the world just feels a little bit less enjoyable without their presence, I would think that that would qualify as true love."

Tatum understood where she was coming from, and for a woman who said she never understood true love, she had a great way of explaining it.

"Did I love Johnny? Yes. Did he love me? I'm sure of it. But even on our best day, we didn't have what the two of you have. It would be a shame if that went away. And I know what your daddy told you about being a good father and husband, and in a lot of ways, it's sound advice."

Tatum cocked an eyebrow, wondering how she knew about that too.

"Yeah, I read all the letters first. Again, I'm your momma. I needs to know."

Tatum smirked at the notion his mother took a peek at his letter. He didn't know when she did it, but she always knew everything that went on.

"Johnny tried to give you the best information he could because he loves you, and he was guilt-ridden. He didn't want you to repeat his sins, but those are *his* sins, not yours. What you have to ask yourself is can you see yourself spending your life with this woman?"

Tatum looked out the kitchen window into his mother's flourishing garden, her tomatoes as big as baseballs.

"I don't know if it was better to have loved and lost because the losing hurts like a son of a bi...gun," Tatum said, realizing he was still talking to his mother, who was handling heavy objects.

"But I tell you what—there are moments in my life with that woman I wished would never end. I've never felt more...filled with purpose. I felt like, as a man, I understood who I was, and I was just a piece of a larger, more beautiful thing like we were a force together. A force that could not be stopped. Being without her is like being without oxygen. Yeah, I could move on and work on things with Monique, but why should I? I can say with confidence I love Autumn with all my heart. There are days I wake up, and I remember what holding her feels like. The exact temperature of her body under a cool blanket. How she always smells like pears and lavender. It's like she has this master key to my heart, and no matter how many doors I lock trying to heal myself, I see something or smell something, and she is right back in my heart because she never truly left; it's hers. Sometimes, when I close my eyes and recall every freckle, every blemish on her body. And I know we probably shouldn't be talking about this, but yeah, I remember her like my own skin. I am in love with her."

Savannah paused, washing the dishes, and walked over to her son.

"You notice all this time you haven't said one word about Monique?"

"Yeah. I mean, what's there to say? We're trying to like each other for Solly's sake."

"Hard to try to like someone once you've been loved."

"Man, don't I know it."

"Then baby, if you know it, why are you anywhere else?" Tatum took a deep breath and finally leveled with his mother.

"Hell, I don't know, Ma, I don't know why I'm doing anything at this point. I just feel, I just feel like I'm trying to do the right thing with the wrong person."

Tatum threw his hands up in frustration. "If I'm with Autumn, I lose Solly. If I'm with Solly, I lose Autumn. I feel like anything I do, someone loses, and for me, that person can't be Solomon."

"Tatum, you sweet, stupid, little boy. You're not a martyr. This is your life we're talking about. You think when Solomon gets old, he's gonna give a damn about you being here for him? No, he's going to be out here living his life, hopefully not dealing with the same shit you're dealing with. If you love that woman, sit her down and figure out how to be together no matter how long it takes. Now hand me that water."

Savannah walked to the edge of the kitchen and started putting their food in bowls as suppertime crept closer. She gave Tatum his bowl at the table and handed Solly's his in the living room, figuring she'd let him eat there so she could keep talking to her son. Solomon kissed his grandmother on the cheek, then she returned to the kitchen and picked up her water bottle, sipping some before she spoke.

"This is probably my fault. There's no question your childhood was less than ideal. I know I asked you to help me with your sister; you were always responsible, even at a young age. Maybe it was too much for a child because now all you know how to do is sacrifice. I guess I need to be apologizing for that."

"You never need to apologize, Momma; you gave me life. This isn't on you; it's my doing. I just feel like when things started going bad— like really bad—she just became another thing, another expectation, another reminder of my shortcomings. I was trying so hard just to hold it together, and she wanted to know about when we were moving on with our relationship. It felt selfish. It felt..."

"Child, hush."

Savannah opened the refrigerator and pulled out a fruit medley with sliced pineapples, strawberries, kiwi, and mangoes to share. As she took a bite of the kiwi, she said, "You ever see that show *The Real Housewives*?"

"Yeah."

"I hate that shit. All these women and not one husband on the show, and all these young girls want to be like one of them. If you ask me, *The Real Housewives* are ruining real housewives. Someone needs to sit this whole generation down and tell them memes don't keep you warm at night, and they don't buy you flowers or pay bills. What you both have to do is mature. Life don't work out the way you imagine it to—it works out the way you fight for it to. I wish I could tell you that you had an easy road in front of you. You're such a sweet person. I wish I could tell you that it was all going to work out. But I ain't never lied to you, and I ain't gonna start now. Your road is a hard one like anything else in life worth having. And no matter what you do, you're going to let someone down. Just make sure you're able to live with that. Anything you truly love is going to be painful, son. There are times in our lives when love, or the absence of it, will keep you awake at night not eating, sick, lonely, crying, and you realize that love in and of itself has brought you here. Because love is only love because of the bitterness that is pain. It is only in that pain that you reflect on things you perceive are beyond your control. And then you realize if it wasn't for love, you would have never gotten here. You can only truly appreciate a peak if you've been through a valley. See, you needed help to sort through your mind, and when she pushed, it was just easier to walk away. You couldn't walk away from Solomon, and Monique is the devil, you know, so you did what you needed to do to protect yourself."

Tatum took a kiwi for himself.

"You're pretty good at this," he said, laughing. "Yeah, that's exactly how I feel. How did you know?"

"Because you're not the first man that has been torn over a woman son. You have a strong sense of family and duty and an even stronger sense of loyalty. You've always been like that. What's worse is people know this about you and want to have that in their lives, which is why Monique can play this game. She knows you don't care about her. She just knows that you'd do anything for Solomon, and in some ways, she wants you to stay around until she figures herself out. She hopes it's you, but she doesn't know, so she's willing to waste your time until she figures it out."

"But why is that? I mean, I know she doesn't really care for me. Hell, she doesn't even really want to be a mother. Why is sh-"

"Because everyone wants the best thing they can find, whether or not it's the best thing for them. Monique and Autumn are no different in that sense. See, Monique knows you're a good man, so she doesn't want anyone else to have you, while Autumn's a woman in love, and there is no more selfish creature on earth, believe me. I've been one for a long time, and rightfully so. When she met you, she knew you were married, and every woman who goes down this hole in the back of their mind knows that this is always a possibility. But when she fell in love, nothing else mattered to her. Not Monique, not Solomon, only you. She only sees *her* man."

Tatum processed her words. They were truly insightful. His mother took a piece of pineapple and gave it to him to eat to indicate its sweetness. Like him. Like her.

"I want you to be happy, Tatum. You're my son, and I love you. It's that simple. I'll never say anything bad about Monique. She gave me my grandchild, and for that, I'll always be thankful. But we both know she doesn't make you feel alive the way Autumn does, and why would you live a life with someone who doesn't ever make you feel alive?"

That was the one question Tatum couldn't answer.

WHO IS HE AND WHAT IS HE
TO YOU?

eing with her is paradise, but it seems I'm not ready for paradise. Tatum recalled the words he wrote in his journal. His mother had made the most compelling argument he'd heard, and while it was everything he needed to hear, he also knew how much she sacrificed for them. For the time being, he was doing the right thing. Still, the more he thought about his mother's words, the more restless he became. It was true; a child needed his mother and father, and Solomon was happier than he had been in a while. But Tatum knew his mother wasn't raised in a single-parent home and never truly understood what it was like growing up without a father. He was ready to finally admit the most damning thing, something he realized the night of his father's funeral. The pain was all-encompassing. It was the only emotion he felt since it overwhelmed the others. He didn't have the strength to fight for custody, and he couldn't spend another moment without him. It was best to forget the idea altogether.

He checked the time as he left his mother's house. He still had a few hours to run to the store to pick up some things for Monique's get-together, but he was in no mood to get together. He left Solomon at his mother's house and decided to go straight home, have a drink, and go to sleep. Whatever Monique's plans for her kickback, he no longer wanted to pretend his way through. As he pulled up to his home, he decided to park in front of his house in case his not going to the store became an argument. He got out of his car and walked to the front door. The closer he got, the more he heard what sounded like indistinct chatter evolving into a shouting match. He opened the door and saw Monique and Raylene standing in the middle of the living room arguing.

Shit, he thought to himself. He didn't want any part of whatever they had going on. But it was too late—Raylene was storming his way as Monique dashed in front of her to cut her off.

"Tate, you're back early! Can you go back to the store? I need a few things. Raylene, go ahead and leave, and we'll talk about it later."

Raylene stopped and looked Monique up and down.

"Bitch, I ain't going nowhere," she said in a tone that sent shivers through Tatum's skin.

"Okay, whatever you two have going on, I don't want to-"

"Oh, you're gonna want to hear this."

"Tatum, come on, let's go inside. I'm done with this crazy bitch."

"I'm the crazy bitch? Oh, I got your crazy bitch" Raylene fired back.

Tatum, confused by the entire thing, decided to consider the silver lining.

No way she'd going to have a party tonight if she's fighting her best friend, he chuckled inwardly.

"I don't need this shit. I don't need a snake-ass friend like you, Mo," Raylene screamed.

As the two women exchanged curse words and slurs toward each other, Tatum did the one thing he didn't want to do: step in.

"Look, y'all can argue all you want somewhere else, but I got neighbors, and it's not gonna be long before they call the cops if they haven't already. So figure it out."

Tatum took a step toward the bedroom, but Raylene's next words made him come back.

"Oh, it's already figured out, Tatum. See, Monique fucked Darren."

Tatum turned around and looked at Monique, who looked like a deer frozen by the headlights. Raylene continued.

"Been fucking him. I guess since she got back with you, she stopped sleeping with *my* man because, heaven forbid, Monique Clarke the princess can't have every whim of hers fancied."

"Raylene, y'all wasn't together. It was an accident."

"Bitch, don't lie to me. I got the receipts! I can't believe you would do this to me, Mo, after all the years we've been down. How hard I've been in your corner, and this is the shit you do to me?"

Raylene said in frustration; it was clear she was angry and had been crying. She tried to take a swing at Monique, but Tatum stood in between the two to stop her. Raylene backed off and looked at Tatum, then back at Monique.

"You know I was gonna fuck him," she said, pointing at Tatum.

"I saw him in Austin looking hella good, but I didn't because that was your ex. Instead, I called you and give you the 411 on what's going on. Little did I know the night I'm telling you I see Tatum, you're in my house, in my bed, fucking my man!"

Tatum's eyes widened as he looked at Monique, but he couldn't help but chuckle. "Wow, so you weren't even with Solly the first weekend you asked to watch him?"

"No, that bitch was at my house from Friday night till Sunday morning."

"That's not true! I'd never do that to you, Raylene."

Raylene took out her phone and opened up her picture gallery. She showed both of them a picture of Monique's blue Avalon, license plate COCOGRL, sitting in the driveway.

"Bitch, I got the receipts!" she screamed. Tatum watched as Monique's mouth flew wide open. "See, I thought something was off 'cause the security cameras never seem to work when I was gone, but my neighbor, Ms. Martha nosey-ass, who I always try to avoid, comes up to me and asks me if I had company, and she shows me this picture. It all fell into place. You're a motherfucking snake, Monique, and I'd spit in your face, but my spit deserves better than that."

"Raylene, I'm-"

"Bitch, I'm talking," Raylene said, cutting her off. Tatum sat and listened quietly, intrigued by the revelation. Raylene continued her tirade against her former best friend.

"See, I did come over here to whoop your ass, but I ain't catching no charge for you. 'Cause, you are a low-level bitch who ain't worth the pussy you sit on. But since you want to play games with people's lives, watch and learn, bitch. I'm about to become a motherfucking PlayStation."

Panic spread across Monique's eyes as she scrambled to get out of this situation.

"Tatum, come on, put her out. We don't have to listen to this crazy hoe. She's sloppy drunk."

Tatum looked at Raylene and back at Monique

"That's your beef, homie," he said as he leaned against the wall of his home and folded his arms to watch the fireworks. Raylene, offended by Monique's last statement, retaliated.

"Crazy? Oh, I got your crazy! And since you proved to me that these hoes ain't loyal, let me join the game." She looked at Tatum and continued. "Yeah, I called Monique after I saw you in Austin. When she found out you were on a date, she was furious, talking some shit like 'I'm babysitting, and he's out here going on dates?' She started plotting to get Solomon from you that night—from my bed." Raylene tried to swing at Monique, but Tatum jumped up and intervened. His neighbors might call the cops if they heard shouting. They would definitely call the cops if they heard assault.

As Raylene composed herself, Tatum responded, "I kinda figured as much, Raylene. I didn't know about Darren, but the timing of everything else was too spot-on. Now come on, she's right. You're drunk, and my neighbors are coming outside. I don't-"

"She got you fired."

The words stopped Tatum dead in his tracks. He looked at Monique, who was speechless. He spun around to Raylene, who now had his undivided attention.

"Yeah, bitch, that's right. All the dirty laundry is coming out tonight. You want to fuck my man; I'll fuck up your whole world."

Monique moved in front of her friend.

"Raylene, I'm sorry. Tatum is right. Let's just leave so we can talk about it all. Just don't—"

"It's too late for that shit, Mo."

"Wait, how did she get me fired?" Tatum interjected.

"Please don't do this," Monique said, looking at her friend. There was no use, though. Raylene persisted.

"She didn't want to take the chance you'd get custody of Solomon, so she called your job and told them about some pills or something you use to steal back in the day. They told her they'd tell you it was an internal audit, but there was no damn internal audit. That's just some bullshit they made up to tell you. She even got a whistleblower payment or some shit behind snitching. Seven thousand dollars? She laughed about it to me over the phone."

The words hit him like a fiery boulder falling from the sky. He looked at Monique, who was now looking away.

"You did what?"

"This bitch is lying!"

"No, this bitch is *done* lying for your sorry ass. But that ain't even the worst thing she did to you. Tell him, Mo."

Monique froze and looked her friend in the eyes with a compassionate plea.

"You can't do that, Raylene. Please, you proved your point."

"I remember the call like yesterday. You and Tatum were about to break up, and you knew it. You went over to have one last goodbye fuck session, remember?"

"This bitch is lying. Get the fuck out of my house!"

"You called me asking me what perfume to wear and-"

"Get out now!"

"If you should wear a trench coat or a wig...oh, and yeah, I almost forgot—"

"Raylene, do not do this!"

"How many holes should she poke in the condoms?"

With all of his immunity to Raylene's antics, those words caught him off guard. He looked at Monique, who lunged at Raylene.

"You're lying!"

"Bitch, you knew if you got pregnant, he would marry you even though he didn't want to be with your sorry ass because that's the kind of guy he is. And sure enough, your evil little plan worked. But you fucked with the wrong one this time." Raylene shifted her attention to Tatum. "I should've told you all this shit years ago, but I didn't. The one thing I realize now is that all men aren't dogs. Women like this bitch creates them."

Tatum stayed silent until he reached the front door and swung it wide open.

"Get the fuck out, Raylene."

"Yeah, I'm leaving. I've spilled enough of this hot tea all over your living room. I'll leave you to clean up the mess."

Raylene walked in front of her friend as if stepping up for another fight. When Monique didn't take the bait, she walked out.

Tatum closed the door and locked it. He looked at Monique, who stood there stunned and speechless and embarrassed. He shrugged his shoulders and as if nothing had happened.

"Yep, no party tonight."

He walked toward the patio, closing the door behind him.

33

HOLD ON

*T*atum sat on the patio and found a cigar he'd been saving for graduation. He then opened up a bottle of Crown Royal Special Reserved; he also saved for the same occasion. He normally would have poured a single glass, but today deserved an entire bottle.

"Alexa, play J.C. Money playlist."

He lit his cigar and took a puff, smiling at the football in the yard that he and Solomon played with. *That's the Way I Feel About You* by Bobby Womack drifted over the speakers, and he just relaxed. He played the song several times before moving on to the rest of his father's list.

Monique walked out onto the patio as he enjoyed D'Angelo's *Lady*. She was silent but appeared as if she wanted to speak. He said nothing as he took another puff of the cigar. She walked into his peripheral vision and stood quietly. Tatum let her sweat for a minute before breaking the spell.

"Man, you remember this song?" he said before sipping his Crown Royal. He tapped his hand to the rhythm of the baseline as she sat next to him. He bobbed his head as she looked at him with uncertainty, unsure what to say next. He decided to help her out.

"Where were we the first time we heard this? I think it was Club Indigo."

"Yeah. That little retro teenybopper club that tried to be a lounge."

"Yeah, that was the corniest shit ever," Tatum said, laughing. Monique chuckled nervously in agreement.

"They had that whole bad '90s movie vibe to the place," she said, "and we were both in a classics feel at the time."

"I'd never heard D'Angelo before that day."

"I know. That was what made it so crazy. He had mad hits. And you being the music guy, I figured you'd heard him before."

"True, but you know I was in a super gangster rap phase at that time. I wasn't really listening to R&B like that. Not until I met you."

"Really? Because I know you and J.C. would bond over music. That was your thing."

"Yeah, but remember how distant we were then. Took a while to come back to the classics. Most of my music around then, people ended up high or in the morgue in four minutes or less.

The two laughed

"True. You had a T.I., Jeezy, and Rick Ross vibe going."

"Can't forget Gucci Mane."

"Gucci!" the two yelled in unison. And laughed again. Monique poured a glass of the liquor and drank a little of it herself.

"Oh man, how could I forget Gucci Mane? And what was that other group you liked?"

"The Lox."

"Yeah. You're the only person I know who was into them so heavy."

"Yes, man, they will kill you, your grandmother, her cousin, and the pet goldfish all in three minutes or less."

The two started laughing harder as Tatum sipped more of his liquor. As the anticipated awkwardness refilled the air, Tatum asked Monique what she came out here to talk about.

"So is what Raylene said true?"

"Which part?" She responded

"Which part isn't?"

She squirmed. She didn't want to answer the question.

"Look, Tatum, I-"

"We both know it's true. This is more rhetorical than me actually expecting an honest answer from you."

Her eyes validated his statement. He took another puff of the cigar and said, "You know, one of the last nights I saw Autumn, we had this perfect night. She asked me if I wanted anything to eat, and she made this sausage and pasta joint with bell peppers, onions, and some other shit. It was amazing. I walked in, and from the moment I saw her, I couldn't keep my hands off her. Wasn't long before we were making love while she cooked. We listened to Marsha, and Chrisette, and Prince, and it was amazing. We took a shower and washed each other, and when we were done, we slow danced to Tamia; ironically, that song, *I'm Officially Missing You*. And when we laid back down, I whispered in her ear a song I made up in my head. It was called *Everythang*, I think. And as I sang that song and she struggled to enjoy my awful voice, I thought, 'Why can't every day of my life be just like this?' It was perfect. I felt like...like I was a mile away from heaven because she was my version of paradise. And yet armed with all that information, all that knowledge, I'm here. What's funny is, every morning, I ask myself why? To break some generational curse I had no part in making? Was my childhood that fucked up that I can't imagine leaving my son or even spending time apart with my son until I let the courts figure it out? Am I tied to so much trauma that I can't see myself being happy without making sure my son is guided as best as I can? And I learned the answer is yes. I'm fucked up. I'm a goddamn head case! My dad was a drug dealer, a drug addict who taught my best friend how to sell dope. That's before you even get into what was going on in the house of Savannah or before I met you."

"Tatum, I know what you heard was fucked up, but I swear—"

"Let me finish," he said as he took a long drag of the cigar and holding it before releasing the smoke into the clear night sky. He took a sip of Crown Royal and finished his thought.

"The truth of the matter is not that I can't leave my son—my son with you, his egg donor—it's that somewhere inside of me, really rooted, even deeper than this love I so desperately desire, I am not built to take another parent away from their child. And that's where you win, Monique. Because if your goal was to make sure I was unhappy, you won. There's nothing satisfying about being here with you."

He sipped his Crown as she struggled to process his words.

"Are you're telling me this to hurt me back? I was sorry for what I did, T. I—we—can talk about all this in counseling."

"I'm telling you because I just don't care no more. What else can I lose? My freedom? You already have that."

He took another sip of the drink he'd been nursing as Eddie Kendrick's *Intimate Friends* came on. He started nodding his head to the beat and singing the chorus. He could sense Monique trying to figure out what to do next. It wasn't long before she had something to say.

"Tate, listen, I... I know I made mistakes, but I meant it... about giving ourselves a second chance. The first thing we gotta do is forge-"

"I thought about killing you today."

He heard her gasp as he said it. He took another sip of his Crown and puffed the cigar.

"When Raylene walked out that door, and I locked it, I looked at you, and for a split second, I really thought about it. It would've been all too easy, too 'cause I wouldn't have done no violent shit. Do you see how quickly you just picked up that glass? I thought, imagine if I laced her drink with...well, there are so many untraceable drugs and interactants, the possibilities are endless. You could've dropped dead at work tomorrow. You could have just died, and I would've gotten whatever benefits you have. Got it all and put it to good use, and no one would've known but me and well...now you, but as tempting as that sounds, I couldn't do that to Solly because I love him. Everything I've ever done since he's been born has been for him, including being here, and you know that. It's what makes you feel so safe around me. Everyone else treats me like a goddamn lion that just got out of his cage, but you, you're the ringmaster. You just crack your whip, and here I am, the top of the food chain sitting on a stool with a birthday hat on. You're good at it, you know, and I'm not even sure why I fell for it. I know it can't be love because we, even at our best, never truly had that. So it must be out of obligation. You gave me my son, and by proxy gave me purpose and the chance to deal with all my own fucked-up trauma via Solly, which is probably also fucked up, but one issue at a time. Point is, it's safe to say I'll probably never be able to kill you outright. The problem is that the option of killing you, which was never there before, is now on the table. I can't repack that. I mean, since we've been out here, I've probably thought about a dozen ways to do it."

Monique looked at the glass she had been drinking from.

"I didn't poison your drink, Mo. I probably would've used an aerosol. Maybe your deodorant. Or, man, something with latex. Wouldn't that be ironic?" he said, taking took another puff of his cigar.

He could sense Monique's uneasiness as she put her glass down and said, "Tatum, look if you want to talk about what I've done, we can do that. I know it's bad, but this isn't you."

He took a sip of his drink and continued ignoring her statement.

"We were a beautiful-looking couple, weren't we? Like Black Barbie and Ken. Hell, we even had the black kid that comes with the Christmas bundle that they never give a name 'cause they don't know what to call him. Don't get me wrong—we had our challenges, but it was a good life. I was content with you, and you knew that. Then one day you weren't home. Of course, my first call is to your mom even though that bitch will lie four ways in the same breath, and she swore she didn't know where you were. It's funny when I think about it now. I don't know if she was that believable or if I was that dumb because you'd think your momma would be the first to file a missing person report, but nobody even mentioned it."

"Tatum, I'm sorry. I know you don't believe me, but I am sorry. You have to believe that I've ch-"

"You know I use to wonder all the time how you could just leave that boy like that. My mom told me even back then that maybe it was postpartum depression, and maybe it was. I don't know what's true with you, Mo. Whatever it was, it doesn't matter—you weren't there, and in a way, I thank you for that. Because if you wouldn't have left, I don't think this protective instinct would've developed the way it did. The question of if I'm a good father would probably still irk me if you would've stayed. Now I know. We both know. I'm the best option he's got, so I can't kill you because I can't go to jail. Not behind you or anyone else."

Monique eyed the patio door as if looking for an escape route. Her fear was evident.

"I didn't want to leave, Tate. I did this thing. This terrible thing. I didn't know how to look at you. That morning you were so focused, so driven. You were changing then. Stopped hanging out as much with Stone. All I wanted was time. When I had Solomon, you were at every appointment. I could tell you weren't the same, but once he got here, he had your eyes. It was like he kept looking at me. He wouldn't stop looking at me as if he knew what I'd done. When I left, I thought maybe I'd take some time to come back and make it work, but I remember the way those eyes felt every day. I couldn't have two sets of eyes look at me that way. I couldn't look at you anymore."

"I don't care, Mo. I don't care what that means for you. It doesn't even matter that this was four years ago. It don't even matter that we're in a better place. I just don't want to be here. Not with you."

"I know it's a lot to ask, but if you could try to for-"

"You don't get it, do you?" Tatum said, taking a big swig from the bottle. "Why do you think I'm here? Do you think I have any interest in working anything out with you? You're not this delusional. All that matters is my son."

"You won't get Solomon. You can't take him." Tatum put the glass down and turned to look Monique squarely in the eyes.

"You're right, and I won't take Solomon. You're going to let me raise my son in peace because that's what I was doing for the last four years. And at this point, Mo, if it's not peace, it's war. And if it's war, it's all-out. It won't be today, it won't be tomorrow, but one day this thought is gonna pop back up in my head. It will be so far from now you'll ask yourself, 'Was he serious? Maybe he was drunk.' I'll go to every game, every play, every science fair. I'll never miss a day of my son's life, but I don't know if I could put the feeling I felt when Raylene told me what she said back in a box. If you make my life any harder than it's been, I will kill you, Monique."

"You need to quit saying shit you don't mean! This is starting to—"

"I'm tired, Mo. We had our shot, and it didn't work. I ended up with a bunch of excuses—so many that's all I know how to give other people. I am tired. No back and forth this time. This is the only deal on the table. If you decide you're going to leave because of what you just heard and try to get anything more than supervised joint custody with me as the custodial parent, I will never stop coming for him. Through the courts, through every legal action, I'll pay whatever just to get rid of you. And when have you known me to fail at anything I truly put my mind to, Mo? What are the odds your friend doesn't say what she just said to the judge? I'll get four jobs just to keep you in court until you finally realize that what you're doing out of spite, I'm doing out of love. Do you want the money? Fine, take it. You want this house? Then take this motherfucker. I'll trade it all in for you to leave me and my son alone. From now until Judgment Day, I will never ever, in this life or the next, stop fighting for my son. So just let us go. Don't spend the next twelve years at war with me when all I want is to give our kid love."

Monique put her glass of Crown down and yelled, "Why can't you apply that passion to us? Why can't you stop fighting for our lives? Our marriage? I am Solomon's mother, and I have a say in who he's around, and I don't want him around that woman."

"And here I thought it was all about Solly..." Tatum said sarcastically. He took another sip of his whiskey and continued.

"All this time, you weren't getting back with me not because you wanted Solly to be happy but because you wanted me to be unhappy. Well, you win Monique, I'm unhappy as fuck right now with you, with this whole arrangement. Every morning I wake up and realize you're still here, and that's a reminder that I don't want to be. But I'll be here if that means it's the only way I can be with Solomon."

"You think somewhere in that poisonous mind of yours I'll have some emotional recompense? I'd say it's overdue."

"Bitch, please. I will never feel anything for you but pity because you're going to spend a lifetime wrestling with the fact that no one but me has ever loved you. And now that's gone. But as far as Autumn goes, let me put your mind at ease. I'm gonna have my son around whoever the fuck I want because *I'm* his parent."

Tatum had reached the point where fighting cost him nothing. He was genuinely indifferent about Monique Harrison. He saw her in a light he'd never seen her in before. There could never be love here, and in so many words, he had just told her as much. This wasn't some cat-and-mouse game of power. No matter what happened next, this was the end.

"It's not an ultimatum, Mo. I don't need an answer at all. If you leave, it's because you decided that enough is enough, and it's time for us to both move on to the next stage of our lives and not hurt each other. But if you're here tomorrow or any day after that, just know I am only here for my son, and the minute I know he's going to be okay, I'm leaving, and we'll never talk again. You can't hurt me anymore."

Monique started to cry. He thought maybe she was genuinely hurt by his words, but he didn't care.

"You don't know what love is, Monique. I'm not sure you could recognize it unless it's in the form of attention, good or bad, and to be honest, that's just not my problem."

Monique nodded as her eyes scrambled for a response. Tatum watched her become as sincere as he'd ever seen her be.

"I'm not sure why I'm like this, Tatum. I'm not sure. I...do love you. It's just that...you know, when we were in high school, you and I had everything. You would tell me I want a family like that, or man, that car is nice. I want to get a car like that. All because my parents would buy me things. So yeah, I had the latest car and latest clothes because my dad was around. But that's as far as it went. I had things. There was no love. You were the first person who showed me any love. And when you married me, you did right by people, and it took a while for me to realize that attention and love aren't the same things. So you're right—I didn't know the difference between love and attention, but I do now, and I'm begging you, please, let's try this one more time."

Tatum took a sip of the liquor and turned to the mother of his son. The woman he first fell for. Her eyes were sincere and filled with pain. Her words were a remnant to something he wanted to hear years ago for, a paling truth. For the first time, she was vulnerable, and he marveled at the irony. He put the bottle down and leaned over, looking deeply into her eyes.

"Yeah, I don't give a fuck. Never will. You know where I stand. Have a good night, Mo."

Monique knew there was nothing else to say. She got up and walked off the patio, closing the door behind her as he continued to listen to his music, a bottle of Crown Royal in hand.

EPILOGUE: IF THE WORLD WAS OVER

"*A*utumn, you're gonna be late," Charlie said as she put on her silver hoop earrings. She was nervous as she clasped the back of her left earring and looked at the diamond and sapphire encrusted paintbrush and silver necklace, one of the gifts Tatum gave her for their six-month anniversary. She hesitated to put it on. Why hold on to this most bittersweet item? Simple. Because of the man it reminded her of.

She picked it up and placed it around her neck.

"Wow, you look stunning," Charlie said as she made an entrance in a teal-colored dress. She had been ready to stand out. This was her moment, after all. Autumn's Song would officially open tonight. It was an accomplishment that she didn't think would become a reality, and although she put in the work to make it happen, she knew it was in large part due to him...

Focus Autumn, she told herself. Any long spells thinking about him would bring on a wave of emotions ranging from joy to utter tears, and today she didn't want to go there. Today she wanted to be all about the fact that she was finally the owner of her own art studio. Her dream had finally come true.

"I still can't believe you took those paintings off the wall and put them in your studio," Charlie said as he glanced her over once more, straightening her dress for good measure.

"It's art; it's beauty; it's truly my heart. It's for all to see. I don't want to hide anymore."

"Well, hurry up because you're already in hiding. We're beyond fashionably late."

"I know, I know. I'm hustling." Autumn checked herself in the mirror once more to make sure she looked the moment. Charlie walked up to her and redirected her to the door.

"So how does it feel, Ms. Art Studio Owner?"

"It... feels surreal, but I've been so busy the days have flown by."

"I know, and so are the hours. So hurry up. We're going to celebrate and paint the town tonight—literally!"

Autumn smiled. Charlie was a good friend and was one of the things she missed most about Houston. It had been her home, but her future was being born in the city of Austin.

Focus Autumn. Don't drift down that rabbit hole.

"How do I look?" she asked.

"Like a Basquiat in motion," Charlie said as she turned around to dazzle him.

"Well, thank you."

"I'm serious. If I didn't play for the other team, I'd—"

"Charlie, you're a nut. You know that?"

Charlie walked closer to her and looked into her eyes.

"I know you wish he was here, but today is *your* day. Go and slay them, girl."

Autumn hugged him and decided to take his advice, however hard it might be.

She walked down the stairs into the studio from the back entrance, where she was overwhelmed by an ensemble of her closest friends and family. Since the last time she was in Austin, her father had done a lot of work to strengthen their relationship. She was glad he was here. More importantly, she was glad he came out of retirement to paint the centerpiece of her studio. It was all she could ask for. Almost.

"There she is!" Keith Elders said. As the crowd clapped for

Autumn, she waved at everyone and stood next to her father, the master of ceremonies for the night. It was time to unveil her father's masterpiece and officially christen her studio. Her father, in an all-black suit, took the microphone and addressed the audience.

"We all know why we're here. Many of you went to school with Autumn before she got kicked out, and some of you worked with her down at the Paint & Sip, but I had the pleasure of raising her, and let me say, my daughter, is a handful. She's stubborn and a bit misguided. But the one thing I've always known is, she's gifted, and I'm proud of her." Autumn smiled as the audience clapped for her. Her father continued, preparing to unveil his work. "Now, I haven't painted in a long time, and I'm a bit rusty, so forgive me."

"I'm sure it's fine, Dad," Autumn said, chuckling along with the audience.

"Well, if not, you're stuck with it; I want my check," he said as the audience laughed louder. She hugged him, and he continued. "Care to do the honors?"

Autumn smiled as she walked over to pull the curtain off the painting.

"Dad, you're so silly."

Smiling at the audience, Autumn pulled the curtain away. As the audience applauded, she turned to look at it and gasped. Her stomach tightened, and she became so lightheaded she hyperventilated.

"No..."

Tears fell from her eyes. She was looking at a miracle. Not a replica, but the work she'd been looking for, for so long was in front of her. Her heart was home.

She was looking at Fatima.

All the memories that came with it flooded her mind. The morning she painted it. The man she painted it for. The bliss that came with it. She had desperately wanted the painting back and had twice contacted the owner to refund his money. She even talked to her father in hopes he could loan her the funds to acquire it. She tried to get herself together as not to make a scene in front of the crowd, but it was too late.

"Oh, that's beautiful, girl," Charlie said. "Did you paint this?"

"Yeah...a lifetime ago."

Even after all this time and the horrible way things ended, the painting, and by proxy Tatum, was able to make her smile like no other man before. And that made her sad. It was the battle she wanted to avoid.

"You guys have to excuse me from crying. I thought I'd never see this portrait again, but my dad found it. I know we've had our differences but thank you. You don't know what this means," she said, giving in to the tears. "How did you ever find it?"

"Well, that's the craziest story. It found me."

Autumn looked stunned.

"Dad, what are you talking about?"

"Hello, Fatima."

Autumn froze as if she'd heard a ghost. More tears fell from her eyes as she was hit by the voice she'd grown accustomed to loving. She turned around to find him. *He* was standing there.

"Blue?" she asked as if to confirm her disbelief. Her emotions were raw as she sobbed.

The man that would be king. The one who fought her dragons, his demons, and hell itself was worse for the wear in a navy-blue suit and face that spoke of months without sleep as if he had not had a good night since their last night together. She hated him, and she loved him, but there was no denying he was the love of her life. The man who hurt her the most was her soulmate. Her everything. The only man she ever truly trusted with her heart. She looked into this battle-worn face and smiled. He was not the same lighthearted spirit he was when they met, but he fought like hell, and that made him king. This wasn't a fairy tale, but it was as close as a living person could get.

"I thought I'd never see it again."

"I told you I won't let you hit the ground even if I'm falling myself." He walked closer to her, looking deep into her eyes.

"Why are you here?"

"Because I'm finally ready for paradise."

She put her hand up to her face and pressed her lips against her knuckles, a dam to hold back the flood of emotions washing over her at the moment. She watched as a tear fell from his eyes.

"I don't know where to begin. I don't even know if we can begin, but before I say anything else, I'd like you to meet someone."

She looked behind him, and a little miniature Tatum in an equally dashing blue suit stood there. Her eyes filled with tears. She watched as the child spoke.

"Hi. My name is Solomon Clarke. It's nice to meet you. My dad has told me all about you."

Autumn leaned in, wiping tears from her eyes.

"Oh really? What did he tell you about me?"

"He says you have a pretty smile, a big heart, and he can't wait to take you dancing."

The End

AFTERWORD

~

Thank you for reading *Autumn: A Love Story*. It means a lot to me that you have stayed with me along this journey. While I did the best I could to loop every loose end, the ending does leave plenty of unanswered questions. A few of which are: Does Tatum sell his song to Drinks? Does he write more? Does he land a job, and if so, doing what?

I hint at some of the answers, but I want you to know more concretely. The songs from Autumn: A Love Story, the Soundtrack are all written by Tatum Clarke and performed by Autiztry (Drinks stage name). The songs are written from Tatum's perspective. I thought that it would be a fun, interesting wrinkle to bring this story to life. The songs are free on my website or any streaming platform; just look for Autumn: A Love Story: The Soundtrack to the Novel, and you'll find what I hope to be seven enjoyable songs themed around this novel.

How did Autumn's studio work out? Our team created an actual Instagram profile so that you can follow Autumn. If you enjoyed the book, log on to Instagram and follow @autumn.elders and check out some of the visuals from the story. This, along with the playlist and soundtrack, adds another enhancement to Autumn's world. It's my desire to give you an experience no other writer has given you. If you like the story, show some love and support by:

1. Leaving a review. It's a great way to help me out I love reading them but truth is I can't do this without quality people like you spreading the word about my work. You can leave a review on Amazon by finding the book's title and right underneath the ad copy, type in the leave a review box, or if you're on a tablet/ phone, clicking the link here.

2. Follow Autumn on Instagram @autumn.elders (the same profile from the story). There, you can see all the artwork from the "Autumn's Song" Gallery, along with her personal thoughts throughout her journey.

3. Join our mailing list. I won't spam you to death, but this is the only way to get the Norian Love Experience Box. If you haven't heard about it or seen it, I highly advise you to visit my website www. norianlove.com and take a look as there will only ever be a limited quantity ever made.

4. Shoot me an email or hit me up on social media. It would be nice to talk to a living person instead of the characters in my head. :-)

Thank you for taking the time to read this story. I genuinely hope you enjoyed this as much as I enjoyed writing it.

Norian

ALSO BY NORIAN LOVE

Novels

Money, Power & Sex: A Love Story

Seduction: A Money, Power & Sex Story

Ronnie: A Money Power & Sex Story

Donovan: A Money Power & Sex Novella

Poetry

Theater of Pain

Games of the Heart

The Dawn or the Dusk

Music

Autumn: The Soundtrack to the Novel

CPSIA information can be obtained
at www.ICGtesting.com
Printed in the USA
LVHW011309230821
695886LV00004B/534